DEEP NIGHTS

DEEP NIGHTS

Charles J. Starr

Copyright © 2005 by Charles J. Starr.

ISBN :	Softcover	1-4134-7520-5

All rights reserved. No part of this book may be reproduced or transmitted in any form or by any means, electronic or mechanical, including photocopying, recording, or by any information storage and retrieval system, without permission in writing from the copyright owner.

This is a work of fiction. Names, characters, places and incidents either are the product of the author's imagination or are used fictitiously, and any resemblance to any actual persons, living or dead, events, or locales is entirely coincidental.

This book was printed in the United States of America.

To order additional copies of this book, contact:
Xlibris Corporation
1-888-795-4274
www.Xlibris.com
Orders@Xlibris.com
26897

For the men and women of the Dallas,
Texas Police and Fire Departments.
And especially for their dispatchers.

Prologue

"I shot the black guy in the alley," the man in the middle said. "You know, the one that didn't have a weapon."

David understood him. Anyone living in New York City or watching television or reading newspapers anywhere in the world would understand him. About two weeks ago, two plainclothes police officers from the New York City Police Department's elite Anti-Crime Unit were following a young black man. They thought he might have been connected to a shooting that had occurred earlier in the evening. The black man, who in the end would turn out to be a recent immigrant from Zimbabwe, walked into an alley. The officers followed him. What happened next was up in the air as the officers in question had exercised their right to remain silent and Thalabo Malobeki wasn't talking either.

Every press outlet imaginable had reported that the two officers fired twenty one rounds between them. They hit Mr. Malobeki, the father of three, seven times, killing him. The resulting public clamor deafened any voice of reason. Everyone had an opinion and the loudest ranged from uninformed to ignorant. The special interest activists were in their element. Everyone with an axe to grind tried to get in the game. David wanted nothing to do with it, in any way, shape or form. He sat silent and still, considering the three men in front of him.

Mr. Donovan, the real estate developer that made up 80 percent of the firm's business, sat across from David at the large polished wooden conference table. David knew Mr. Donovan to be comfortably over six feet tall and a little stooped. His hair had thinned and grayed, but he had remained lean. Thick lenses in black horn-rimmed frames were a reluctant acknowledgment to age, grotesque on his thin face.

Next to the patriarch were two men in their late twenties. One, to Mr. Donovan's immediate right, shared something of a family resemblance, tall, thin-faced and similarly featured. He looked tired in his rumpled sport jacket. He had just spoken. Next to him was a swarthy, stocky individual who had not shaved or changed out of dirty work clothes for the meeting.

"David," Lawrence Kingsley, a name partner at the law firm that paid David very well, said, "The Donovan family would like us to defend Brian."

"We're a real estate firm," David replied.

"We provide quality legal services to our clients. Mr. Donovan has specifically asked for you."

David looked across the table at the rich old man. "I'm a construction litigator, Mr. Donovan. You know that. I've represented you successfully in contract matters. You know I don't practice criminal law."

Donovan waved off Lawrence, who was about to speak. "I've been in your office, young man. I've seen it hanging on the wall. What was it again? Houston?"

"Dallas."

David knew the old man referred to the display of police and Army decorations hanging in his office among the diplomas and bar certificates.

"I don't care about your specialty," the old man said. "I think in this case a police officer should defend a police officer. You handle yourself well in court. I am not persuaded that your skills are limited to one area of the law. I am a client of this firm where, coincidentally, a former police officer is on staff. That is something I both desire and require."

"The Police Benevolent Association has more than qualified lawyers for Brian, and he wouldn't have to pay for them."

A startled Lawrence sucked air through his teeth.

"Don't care about the money, young man. I know what Brian needs."

David wanted to buy time. He stood up and walked over to a silver coffee service. He reached for a cup and saucer, enjoying the feel of the heavy china. He filled the cup with steaming liquid out of the urn, adding milk and sugar and stirring slowly. He liked drinking coffee out of real cups, and he liked working at a law firm that had a conference room like this one: cream carpeting and wall coverings were highlighted by deeply polished hardwood furnishings and molding. David found the working conditions here more pleasant than the infantryman's life of dirt, combat rations and fear or the police officer's life of frustration, fast food and fear.

David caught his refection in the glass of a painting hanging nearby. He wore a gray wool, athletically cut Brooks Brothers, one of his trial suits. He had in fact only just returned from court, where he had settled a case before the jury could rule, saving his client a million of dollars in damages. He stood 5'11" tall. His regular features were somewhat closely set in the middle of a round face. Gray had just begun to show up in his straight, conservatively cut brown hair, but at 38 he still had his hairline. After another sip, David's calm brown eyes found the prospective clients he wanted to turn away.

"About that, perhaps Brian has other ideas. What do you have to say about it?" David asked, looking over at the young officer.

Their eyes met. Brian's haggard face spoke to David about sleepless nights spent in self recrimination. He had the air of condemnation commonly found in recent arrestees. Brian picked at his cuticles insistently without looking down. His hands shook.

"Can you do it?" Brian asked in return.

David shrugged and looked non-committal. "Who are you?" he asked the third man.

"Friend of his," the man snarled. "Yo, Brian, the PBA guy got it all over this skell. Let's go." He moved to get up.

David sipped his coffee, replacing the cup in the saucer. Brian maintained a steady gaze aimed at David's face, his troubled unblinking stare reminding David of the forgotten stresses of his own police experience. That stare, and not the challenge of Brian's friend, motivated David to speak.

"In People vee Goetz, the New York Court of Appeals presented the elements of the justification defense. To successfully assert the use of deadly force in self defense, the accused, and like it or not, that is what you are now, Brian, has to prove four elements.

"Before we go any further," David continued, "you need to think about your right to the attorney-client privilege. If you act in a manner that fails to protect the information you share with an attorney, the privilege is waived."

"How's about that in English," Brian suggested.

David bobbed his head in the direction of the third man sitting across from him. "We talk in front of him, you have no attorney-client protection."

"Fuck you, shyster," the third man said.

"Alan is my best friend," Brian said. "He stays."

"Yeah," Alan said.

"As you wish. The four elements of the justification defense are, one, that the person using deadly force in self defense must be faced with a threat of force that could cause death or serious bodily injury. Two, the threat of that force must be imminent in nature. Three, there is a general duty to retreat, although law enforcement officers are usually exempted from this element. Lastly, the actions of the person asserting the defense must be judged objectively reasonable."

David picked up his coffee cup again, scraping the bottom against the saucer before he lifted it to his lips. The men around the table digested David's remarks in silence, until Alan spoke up.

"We got this licked," Alan said intently. He held up four fat fingers and began ticking off his points. "One, the skell coulda had a gun. Two, he coulda shot you. Three, we don't retreat and four, you're damn right it was reasonable!"

"Will it be that easy?" old man Donovan asked.

"No sir. I predict this case will go to trial, because of the public interest. So you are going to have to present the facts to a jury. Juries hate the shooting of people who are unarmed. You need a good litigator."

"How are you going to do it?" Mr. Donovan asked.

"I'm not going to. It's not my case," David responded.

"Okay Mr. Lane, how would you do it if you had to?"

David looked at Alan. "Are you carrying?"

"Yeah," Alan said warily.

"Stand up, please," David said.

Alan squinted at David and did not comply.

"Alan, stand up," Old Mr. Donovan ordered.

Alan stood. David suspected Alan was one of Brian's colleagues from Anti-Crime. His hair hung in long, tangled mats and he had not shaved in about three days. A dark blue sweatshirt hung over large pectoral muscles and a larger belly. Weightlifter's biceps stretched the arms of the sweatshirt taunt, and his blue jeans were stained and faded. Overdeveloped latisimus muscles propped his arms up out from his sides. Coming to his feet, Alan glared at David.

"You carry a Glock?" David asked.

"Yeah."

"Pull out your wallet."

"Why don't you kiss—"

"Alan, your wallet," Old Mr. Donovan said.

Alan reached around to his right rear pocket with his right hand. He pulled out a thick black leather wallet and held it loosely at his side.

"Switch hands," David said. "Okay, hold it so that the fold is between your thumb and forefinger. Good. Now draw your weapon."

"Here?"

"Yes. Clear leather and hold it parallel to your wallet."

Alan reached under his belly and pulled the Glock out from the front of his jeans. David noted he carried a smaller version of his duty weapon, probably a Model 26. Alan did what he was told, having to stretch across his ample belly to line up the wallet and pistol. Soon everyone was looking at two thick, black rectangles of the same width and length, one in each hand.

David turned off half the lights in the conference room. Everyone looked at the two accessories, the wallet as viewed from the fold and the pistol viewed from the top, in the half light. Neither was distinguishable from the other.

"If I had to do it, Mr. Donovan," David said, "I would start with the reason Mr. Malobeki—"

"Who?" Alan asked.

"—was followed into the alley," David continued. "News reports indicate he matched the description of a shooter wanted regarding an earlier incident. I would build the case that in general and in this incident in particular, anti-crime work is dangerous. That no law requires police officers to die before they are justified in using force in self defense. That in this case, it was reasonable for the officers in question to assume Mr. Malobeki was a threat until proven otherwise."

"Go on," Lawrence urged.

"Well Lawrence, the rest of the situation depends on the facts of the case. We know Malobeki went into the half-lit alley and here we see the ramifications of that decision. Let's say he was asked to produce identification, a routine request made by officers on the street. In here we can't tell the difference between a pistol and wallet, in our comfortable, stress-free conference room. The jury won't be able to either. Retreat is out of the question. So is waiting to get shot. One has only to prove to the jury that it was reasonable to act in self defense in this situation to get the officers off." David turned the lights back on and nodded at Alan, who holstered up.

"How soon can you start work on the case?" Mr. Donovan asked David.

"I told you, I'm not interested. Sorry." The light switches were next to the open door. David pivoted sharply and spun out of the room, into the corridor. He headed for his office.

David occupied a small chamber far from either corner. His office boasted a breathtaking view of the bricks that made up a part of the next building. David did not sit down right away. Instead, he looked up. Over the bookcases, in glass covered black metal frames, were his diplomas and bar certificates. They had been arranged around a darkly stained wooden display case. David slipped out of his jacket before taking the display case off of the wall. He sat down behind his desk and leaned back in the leather chair.

Military decorations dominated the left side. A Special Forces pin and two staff sergeant chevrons made up the top row. The Combat Infantryman's Badge, a depiction of a musket on a blue field, over wreaths, constituted the second row. Below that were decorations, a Bronze Star with Combat "V" and a host of others, followed, lastly, by jump and air assault wings. David brushed some dust off the top of the box with his fingertips. On the right sat his silver police badge, under a Dallas Police Department patch, over two hero bars and one marksmanship bar. He thought it had been a good idea at the time, to put this stuff up, but then again, that was how he ended up telling his firm's best client, "no." Not a good career move.

The Army. The Army and the police and Brian Donovan. He took a moment to remember the late spring of 1992, when he had come home after the first war in the Persian Gulf.

Chapter 1

As they descended over the mid-cities, David craned his neck to look past his seat mate and out the window at downtown Dallas. The lights of Reunion Tower and the great green outline of 901 Main Street punched through the darkness. David wondered how many calls were holding for first watch. The guys assigned to the even-numbered units were surely on their way in. They would need enough time to get into uniforms before shift change at 11:30 PM.

The wheels went down with an uninspired clunk and the pilots started their rapid, jolting course corrections. The minor changes made David nervous; even after the 37 jumps and countless helicopter rides he'd made in the ten years he'd been airborne, he did not feel comfortable in the air. The engines screamed, cut out and screamed again. David sweated bullets as the rubber gently kissed the runway. Only the vigorous breaking settled his stomach.

At the gate he retrieved his dress green tunic from the overhead bin. On the sleeves were the gold chevrons of a Staff Sergeant of the United States Army, three gold stripes pointing up, one gold rocker hanging from the bottom. The dagger and lightning bolts insignia of the Special Forces was high on the left sleeve. He would need to get it moved to the right, now that he had seen combat. Three gold service marks anchored the lower left forearm. The Combat Infantryman's Badge, a moderate amount of ribbons and jump and air assault wings decorated the area over his left breast pocket. He slipped his tunic on over the proscribed light green shirt and dark green tie. After buttoning it, he smoothed it, hands flat against his torso, down to the matching trousers with their razor creases, which terminated in a pair of shined black combat boots. He put on his green beret, flash upright and over his left eye. Then he grabbed his black nylon carry-on and trooped off the aircraft with the rest of the passengers, happy to be on the ground and back home.

At the end of the jetway, David walked into a carnival. Several trumpeters and trombone players, in the purple and gold of the Richardson Eagles marching band, were off to the left. Civilians holding small American flags grouped in the center. Others walked toward the gate area to see what was up. A man with a television camera balanced on his shoulder stood off to the right, and only then did he recognize the small, painfully thin blond reporter standing next to Charlene.

"There he is!" someone shouted.

The band started playing a sloppy version of the United States Marine Corps hymn. David sighed. Two blond cheerleaders, up from central casting, also wearing Richardson High School colors, shouldered their way through the crowd and started jumping around.

Charlene remained standing next to the reporter. She did look like a dream in a forest green, button down blouse, neatly pressed khakis and cordovan loafers. From across the room he noted the familiar blond bangs covering her forehead and the curls flowing down to her shoulders. He knew her hair to be naturally medium brown and straight but what the hell, he liked it none the less. Her blue eyes, over a regular, flawless nose, focused on him and her heart shaped red lips spread into a smile. David became swept up in the moment and was about to drop his bag and run toward her when she responded to something the reporter said by turning her head slightly, nodding and then running toward him. The thought that a reporter was choreographing this homecoming stopped him in his tracks.

Charlene ran toward him and just in time, he decided to play his part. He scooped her up and spun her around and then planted a kiss on her that the television audience would appreciate. His confused feelings over this public display faded at the feel of Charlene in his arms. He luxuriated in the sweet smell of her and lost his mind in their embrace.

"Staff Sergeant Lane . . . Staff Sergeant Lane?"

Someone pulled at the bottom of his tunic.

"Staff Sergeant Lane? How does it feel to be home? How does it feel? Did you miss your fiancee?"

That wholly unexpected word shattered his moment and brought him back to reality.

The reporter had held up her hand, silencing the musicians and spectators. They waited expectantly for his answer. David, ever the good soldier, knew what he had to do.

"It feels great to be home and boy, I sure did miss Charlene." David looked down at her and smiled. "Now if you all will excuse us, we've got some re-acquainting to do." David scooped up his bag, took Charlene by the hand and made for the exit. "Thank you all for coming! I really appreciate it!" he shouted, as he started to run, pulling a reluctant Charlene behind him.

"David! We could have stayed a little longer," Charlene said, in her mostly neutral accent that could signify Scarsdale, New York just as soon as North Dallas, Texas.

"Sweetheart, lets get lost. We don't need all those people for a homecoming. That's something we can do all by ourselves." David gripped Charlene by the shoulders and kissed her again. Their tongues dueled until Charlene pulled away.

"I worked really hard to arrange this for you. The least you could have done was let me speak with Janice."

"Janice who?"

"The reporter. Why did we have to run out like that?"

"Because I couldn't wait to get my hands on you. Let's go off somewhere, Okay?" David was quickly approaching the end of his rope.

"It's good to see you," she said, rubbing his shoulders.

"Sweetheart, did you tell them we were engaged?"

"Well . . . it was the best way to get all those people there. Let's go find a TV and see what it all looked like."

"I've got a better idea. Let's go find a bed and—"

"Oh, you. Tonight's a school night."

"What, are you kidding?" he asked.

"You know the rules. Nothing like that on a school night."

"But I'm home from the war! Alive!"

"David, let's not fight. It's late. Where would you like me to take you?"

Well, how was that for a stick in the eye, he thought. He retreated inward, not wanting to start something, but intensely disappointed at the evening's outcome.

"Run me down to Metro Division. My truck is in the parking lot."

"Well that's all the way downtown!"

"My apartment is about as far. Where did you think you were taking me?"

"Long term parking?"

"Okay. Why don't I take a cab. Just drop me at the arrival level."

"No. I'll take you," she said, a sour expression appearing on her face.

They found her Mustang and sped out of the airport, picking up Interstate 183, eastbound. They rode in silence until they reached I-35, when Charlene tried to strike up a conversation. David answered as required, but did not go out of his way to carry his end. The tension between them built until Charlene started sharing the day's gossip with David as if he had not been away for seven months.

David had expected to feel all sorts of things, emotional and otherwise, when he reunited with Charlene, but annoyance wasn't one of them. Annoyed was how he would describe himself, however, when they finally pulled into the rear parking lot of the Metro Division complex. He directed her to where he had parked his truck in a corner spot at the rear.

"It's good to see you, David," she said, smiling at him as he moved to get out.

David leaned in and kissed her again, as deeply as before. "Good to see you, too."

"I'm sorry David, it's just that it's a school night and you know how I am when I don't get my sleep."

"I do sweetheart. Why don't you get going?"

"Will you need help starting it up?"

"I don't think so. She'll start right up, I'm sure," he lied. He would at least need a boost for the battery.

"Well, okay then. Hey, Mama wants to have a little coming home thing for you on Saturday. Do you think that will be all right?"

"That would be fine, Charlene. Go on now."

"Okay, 'bye." Charlene put her car in drive and rolled away without a backwards glance.

David balled his fists, rested them on his hips and watched her drive out of the parking lot. He shook his head slightly from side to side, until he remembered about his truck. He turned around to face it and then began a slow inspection, circling the perimeter. In a fit of Texas spirit, he had bought the blue Ford F-150 new when he had first moved to town. It had been his only vehicle for the last five years. He drove it everywhere. It had even been back and forth to New York several times. It was a good truck, and he was glad to see that it looked fine.

David's attention turned to the Metro Division compound. There were two parking lots between two low, tan brick buildings. The larger building, furthest from the freeway, was Metro Division itself. In addition to housing the patrol officers and detectives that made up Metro Division, the offices for the Tactical Division and Traffic Divisions were there as well. The department's Quartermaster's warehouse stood at the opposite end of the parking lot. To David's right, as he faced the Metro Division building, were the garages and the automated car wash, famous for ripping the light bars off the tops of the squad cars.

Other City of Dallas buildings were in the compound, but they had nothing to do with the police department. He checked the time. Even though it was still early for the first watch officers, the overnight guys, his friends and colleagues, to start arriving, he expected the sergeants would be in. He felt like saying hello. He circled the building and made for the public entrance.

He found himself in a foyer, painted a mixture of tan and yellow, the floor waxed to perfection. It smelled of disinfectant. A large expanse of tempered glass shielded a work area with several desks, a floor safe and rows of charging hand-held radios. He could hear the division's communications traffic over a loudspeaker set high on a wall.

A thirty-five year old African American woman sat behind one of the desks, talking on the telephone. Her straight black hair fell around a pleasant, narrow face. She wore the blue uniform of the Dallas Police Department, but without a badge or sidearm.

"Excuse me, miss, but can you help me," David said, wrapping the safety glass with his knuckles.

"One moment please—oh my God! David Lane, how you been?" she said. Then into the telephone, "Yes sir, you need to call City Hall in the morning. Yes sir. Sir, one of our officers just got back from the war. Please call City Hall in the morning, and now, if you will excuse me," and after listening for a moment longer, she hung up the telephone. "David Lane, you just come right around here this minute!"

Shonda Toogadoo, a security specialist, buzzed him through a door, into an administrative area adjacent to where she had been working. Essentially a hallway, doorways led to the front office, the supervisor's offices and the lobby. In the middle of the hall stood a waist high blond wood conference table.

"Senior Corporal David Lane, how do you do!" Shonda squealed, approaching him for a sisterly squeeze.

"I'm okay," David said, enjoying the genuine welcome.

"Now, you didn't get into no trouble over there, did you?"

"No ma'am."

Shonda stepped back and surveyed his appendages. "Nothing got blowed off, did it?" she asked, running her hands up and down his arms, making sure his sleeves were filled.

"No ma'am."

"That is just real good. Sergeant Karangekis is in. Would you like to see him?"

"I sure would."

"You just wait right here." Shonda disappeared into the supervisor's office suite.

Costas Karangekis soon stepped out of the suite, hand extended in greeting. David felt warm affection when he saw the broad face with its full cheeks and slight double chin, lined by administrative concerns, smiling at him. Costas, now in his late forties, had gained a few pounds over the years and his Sam Browne belt bisected the sergeant's spread, creating a small bulge over and under. He still parted his thick dark brown hair neatly on the right.

"David Lane, good to see you back. Healthy, I hope?"

"Sure Sarge, still in one piece. Good to see you, too," the two men shook hands with enthusiasm.

"Not too rough over there, I hope?"

"Nothing I couldn't handle. How have things been here?"

Costas's eyes turned melancholy. "Some changes and as they affect you, well, I'll be up front with you, Dave. I need senior corporals. We're way down on field training officers. I've got a class of rookies coming tomorrow night, and another in two weeks. I hope you're coming back to deep nights?"

"Wouldn't go anywhere else, Sarge. But we had tons of senior corporals. What happened?" Dave asked.

"Most rotated off. To days or elsewhere."

"Who is gone?"

"Out of our sector? Let's see. Tim went to Traffic and Bruce took a detective slot in auto theft. Some others quit, too. There have been some changes in the department, Dave. Hey, hang around while I make this call, you'll like it."

Costas walked behind one of the desks in the front room and slipped on a pair of metal framed bifocals. He looked down at a small sheet of note paper. Then he picked up the telephone, cradled the receiver between his shoulder and ear and dialed.

"Good evening, this is Sergeant Karangekis of the Dallas Police Department. May I speak with Mr. Scott, please?"

Costas covered the mouthpiece with his hand and started to speak to David, when he suddenly reversed himself and spoke into the telephone once again.

"Mr. Scott? How are you this evening? . . . It sure was. I thought for sure we'd get some rain. Anyway, sir, are you the Mr. Scott that called the mayor earlier this evening? . . . Yes sir, about the two speeding police cars."

Costas looked up and smiled at David. After covering the receiver again, he told David that Mr. Scott was recounting the story he told the mayor earlier. "He saw two marked cars speed up to a red traffic light, stop, and then run the light while accelerating 'aggressively.' All without lights and sirens." The Sergeant spoke into the telephone again.

"Yes sir, that's right. Well, the mayor called the chief, who called the division commander, who called the lieutenant who called me . . . yes sir, it does.

"Anyway, I would like to tell you that from the unit numbers you gave the mayor, I was able to identify the officers and the call they were on. I have severely chastised them for driving fast without lights and sirens. They have assured me they will not drive quickly to answer a call in your neighborhood again and we are sorry you were dissatisfied with your police service tonight. Please have a good night and stay safe."

Costas paused again. Then he said, "are you asking about the nature of the call?" Costas winked at David. "I see. Well, it doesn't really matter, does it? I mean, the young officers were driving in a manner you did not like and . . . I understand, sir . . . Well, they were dispatched on a call to a home in your neighborhood where a young girl was babysitting. She heard a loud noise in the back yard, but I told them never to speed to a call again unless they knew for sure what the problem is."

"I don't know. Now that officers can't sneak up on a situation like that, they ought to take their time. After all, lights and sirens cause their own problems. Maybe the police telephone operator should have sent the young girl out into the back yard to take a look. Of course, she was supervising two boys, an infant and a toddler, so maybe that is not the best idea, but you can be sure the police will never rush to assist a babysitter in your neighborhood again."

Costas looked up at David, nodding slightly, listening to the other man on the telephone.

"I'm glad you can see why they would not use sirens under the circumstances, but I assure you it won't happen again. You know, in this matter I find it interesting that a fourteen-year-old was sitting for an infant. How many girls that age are comfortable with infants today? . . . Your daughter? Why, what a coincidence. What was your daughter doing tonight, Mr. Scott?"

Costas covered up the mouthpiece again. The fingers of his left hand were extended straight, held tightly next to one another. The gesture looked strangely delicate to David.

Costas spoke to David: "I heard from the officers that his daughter was the babysitter. This is going to be great. It's always different when it's about them, isn't it?"

Then, back into the telephone, Costas said, "well, yes it was. She's fine. They couldn't find anything, and the parents arrived not long after. Where is she now? I see, upstairs asleep. Didn't you talk to her when she got home? I see . . . working late. Anyway, all's well that ends well."

Covering the receiver again, Costas said to David, "now he's concerned about the officers."

Costas resumed talking into the telephone. "That's all right sir. I've already explained the situation to the lieutenant. I expect the division commander will want to hear about it in the morning, and so on up to the mayor. I'm sure they will be disciplined . . . . That's the way it is, sir. After all, your the one who called.

"More importantly, you can see why the officers chose to get there quick and not use sirens . . . no, sirens can turn a burglary in progress into a hostage situation in a second. Calls with children always get attention. These officers know what they are doing, sir. I'm sorry, what did you say? A break? I'll relate that to the Lieutenant, that you want to give them a break. Yes sir. Goodnight . . . Okay, goodnight, sir . . . good night." Costas hung up the telephone with a sigh.

"Seventeen years and that is the first time that's happened. I'll cherish the memory forever. David, can you make detail? Great. Let me get ready and I'll see you in there." Costas stood up and the two men shook hands. "It's good to see you again."

"Same here, Sarge."

David left the office and walked back to the administrative area. He quickly located his mailbox on the wall, one of many narrow slots arranged alphabetically. Each of the boxes contained varying amounts of paper, and in some boxes the piles were neat and symmetrical, while others bulged with refuse. David pulled a small irregular pile out of his own box. Someone had been cleaning it out regularly, as he did not find any routine departmental communications in it. There were notes and pertinent memos, however. He put the pile back in for later. David turned around and saw a familiar face.

"Calbert! How the hell are you," David said, stepping around the tall conference table to meet Calbert Mobley as he walked into the administrative area. The two men warmly shook hands.

Calbert was a tall black man with a droopy, frequent good natured grin. He had the build of a professional basketball player, useful muscle stretched over a ceiling-scraping frame. David had ridden with Calbert often over the years, and knew his loose, lanky walk to be deceptive. Strong, decisive and an all around good police officer, Calbert's easygoing nature had defused more than one potentially dangerous situation. David thought it was too bad that Calbert had such trouble making the senior corporal test. He really should be training rookies.

"Cal! Congratulations!" David's eyes had traveled down to Calbert's sleeves as he had thought about the man's rank. Two silver stripes appeared where none had been seven months before.

Calbert smiled shyly, looking uncomfortable. "Davy, how you been? They treat you right over there?" the big man said gently, changing the subject.

At that moment, a crowd of third watch officers streamed in from the parking lot, carrying duffle bags full of equipment and clipboards. They gathered around the tall conference table to finish up their final paperwork and gossip as the shift ran down. David knew many of them by sight, some by name and was friends with a few. They noticed him right away. Most of the group clustered around, voicing their relief at seeing him back from overseas.

As the minutes to the end of the watch ticked off, the group around David changed. Uniformed third watch guys slipped away, to be replaced by David's first watch colleagues. When the third watch officers rejoined the group, they wore the accepted commuting attire: worn t-shirts and jeans. David appreciated the easygoing tone of the group and he felt relaxed and comfortable in the hallway, speaking with friends and acquaintances, laughing at their jokes.

Then the sergeants turned the corner, walking purposefully, clipboards swinging in their hands, moving down the hallway in a small pack.

"Detail," someone shouted.

The small group around David broke up. Uniformed first watch officers and David, his Army greens contrasting with their Dallas police blue, followed the sergeants, while most of the off-duty guys broke away for the door to the parking lot, personal cars, and home.

On the way to the detail room, the hallway grew wider. Small blue tables were placed in a row, each surrounded by blue chairs. Vending machines anchored each end open area and over the soda machines, on brackets, were two television sets. David was glad the broadcast television schedule had not changed. They walked into detail to the opening bars of the theme music from reruns of HILL STREET BLUES.

David filed in with the rest of the watch, talking and laughing with the men he would be riding with soon. The group sorted itself out by sector assignments. Adam sector sat at tables facing the supervisors, Charlie sector had the left wall, Boy sector on the right and the bad boys of Dog sector lined the rear wall. The respective sergeants for each sector sat together, shoulder to shoulder, behind a table at the front. David nodded to Costas as he was about to sit down. The officers had freed up David's customary seat, second from right, his back to the rear wall.

The room itself had not changed. The white tile floor, tan-yellow walls, no frills office furniture and disinfectant smell were there, as was the plastic accordion partition that made up the left wall. But at the front, on the wall over the sergeant's heads, were two columns of names. The names had been written neatly, in a feminine hand, with a black magic marker on yellow placards. A large bow tied out of a broad red, white and blue ribbon split the columns in the center. The placard positioned second from the top on the right side had David's name on it. This small gesture of remembrance touched David, and he had to swallow down a lump in his throat. He scanned the room and realized everyone was looking at him and smiling. He doffed his beret and ran his fingers through his hair.

"Let's get started," Costas said. "As you can see, Dave Lane is back in town. All hail the conquering hero. So what brings you back, Dave, got tired of working for a living?"

"No Sarge, the working was okay. It was working with competent leadership got a little boring. I thought I might come on back here for a change."

All the officers in the room started shouting and applauding. Several stamped their feet, as well. Costas raised his right hand.

"All right people, settle down," he said. The noise ran its course and Costas continued. "Dave, good to see you safe and sound. When do you think you'll be coming back to work?"

"I thought, maybe tomorrow night? I'll start then, if it's all right with you?"

"That sounds good, I appreciate it. The Lieutenant asked me to remind everyone to write their reports on the mobile display terminals. If you get your reports in over the MDTs that same shift you work, there won't be any open numbers on your badge. The Lieutenant would like to see a higher clearance rate at shift change."

Detail went on that way, discussing administrative issues, point after point, until, almost as an afterthought, the sergeants brought up crime.

"Lastly, Intelligence believes a large shipment of heroin is coming into Dallas, up from down south. Word is an independent is bringing it in. Let us know if you start to see heroin on the street. That's all. Stay safe out there."

Detail broke and David was once again the center of attention. The officers from his sector surrounded him and showered him with greetings and were obviously happy to see him. Officers collected their gear and the group moved out to the parking lot. David walked out back with several third watch guys who were off-duty and on their way home. He spoke generally about the war, and with a few careful questions was soon able to listen more than speak.

At his truck, his first watch colleagues roared up in their squad cars, white Ford Crown Victorias and Chevrolet Caprices with blue writing and City of Dallas emblems, replacing the third watch guys as they left for home.

"This thing been here all the time you been gone?" Jimmy John McElroy asked about David's truck.

Jimmy John had over twenty years in the department, and except for a four year stint as a general assignments detective, all those years were in the patrol bureau. Native to Northwest Texas, he was a genuine, real life cowboy, having worked with cattle for real both before and after getting his Texas peace officer commission. He had a narrow, lined face, perpetual tan and blue eyes. In his late forties, his almost six foot tall, wiry body carried no extra weight at all and the only thing holding up his Sam Browne belt was his pelvis. David knew he had experienced much that urban police work could throw at a cop, and it had caused him to become thoughtful rather than bitter or cynical.

"Sure has. Think it will start?" David replied.

"Let's get a car up here. Good thing you backed it in," Jimmy John said.

"I'll bring ours!" yelled out Mike Michaelson, a much younger version of Jimmy John.

Just as tall and thin as the older officer, with jet black hair and pale white skin, Mike, with two years on, had yet to really get to know police work. Veteran officers could easily tell. Mike was still motivated.

David walked to the back of the truck. It looked as good now as it did when he pulled it into the lot in the early autumn, except for all the dust. He unsnapped the soft bed cover and flipped the gate down, displaying some automotive equipment.

"What's that stuff for?" Randy Coffman asked.

Randy, a short white officer who favored a buzz cut for his brown hair, was as short and barrel chested as Mike and Jimmy John were tall and thin. Randy and Mike had similar temperaments and liked to partner together.

"Jumper cables, starter fluid and a jack," David said.

"Cool." Randy reached for the jumper cables and met up with his partner at the front of the pick-up.

David opened up the cab and opened the hood. Randy propped it open. David undid the air filter and sprayed some starter fluid into the intake. Mike and Randy hooked up the jumper cables, arguing the entire time.

David slid in behind the wheel. "Here goes nothing!" he shouted, and turned the key. It barely cranked, turning over slowly. Jimmy John snatched the starter fluid off of the fender and sprayed more of it into the intake.

"If some is good, more's better," he said.

The faithful truck turned over, coughed and then caught, roughly at first, before smoothing out. All the officers standing around were men, and the robust sound of the running v-eight, silent for so long, had them smiling like boys.

"First On Race Day," David said, sliding out of the cab.

"Found On Road Dead is more like it," Randy muttered. "Why don't you drive it? Let's see if it'll go," he said, louder.

"Won't go anywhere while it's up on those jack stands," Jimmy John said.

"Jack stands?" Mike asked, before bending at the waist and looking under the truck. "Cool. I'll go get a jack."

"Let's go get a jack," Randy said, and he and Mike unhooked the jumper cables and sped off to the garage in their marked car.

"I've got a jack in the back. Randy saw it," David said to Jimmy John.

Jimmy John smiled and shrugged.

"How's Leslie?" David asked.

"He's doing good. Off tonight. I think he's getting a rookie tomorrow, so I think he wanted to take it easy," Jimmy John answered. "Him and Hermondo, anyway."

"And Roy?"

"Same thing, getting a rookie tomorrow, so he took tonight off."

"How many we getting tomorrow?"

"Three. Leslie, Roy and Tom. Come to think of it, he's off tonight, too."

"How did you escape a new rookie?"

"Got one." Jimmy John extended a thumb and pointed over his shoulder at his cruiser. David saw a young, male African American head, looking down, behind the driver's seat.

"You don't let him out of the car?" David asked.

"Re-doing an accident report."

"How is he?"

"Pretty good. He'll make it. I've got to break him of his ticket writing habit, though. Tried to write a nurse last night."

Mike and Randy drove up fast and screeched to a halt. The trunk lid opened and three people stepped out of the car. They had brought Lisa, a short, broad-shouldered City of Dallas mechanic from the garage. She had a round nose, stringy bond hair and a handshake that could crack walnuts.

"Hi David," she said, smiling shyly.

"Hey Lisa, how you doin'?" he said, knowing that she especially liked his New York accent.

"Good," she said, giggling.

Mike and Randy had gotten Lisa to lend them a floor jack. While David and Lisa talked, they had pulled it out of the trunk of their patrol car and started on David's pick up. Lisa drifted over to where Mike and Randy were working to supervise. David turned his attention back to Jimmy John.

"Jimmy John, Jane still around?" David asked.

"Nope. She took a detective's badge at CAPERS."

"CAPERS! She didn't have any experience. How did she get that?"

"Lots of changes lately, David."

"So I've been hearing. Only nobody is saying exactly what those changes are." David pointedly looked at Jimmy John, thrusting out his chin and tilting his head just a little. He even leaned in slightly, for emphasis.

"Okay, okay. While you were gone, the City enacted a plan where all City departments have to mirror the racial makeup by percentage of the City. Nobody's really worried about the Mexicans, but everything needs to be thirty percent black by July first."

"You're kidding."

"Oh, that ain't the half of it. Not just every department, but every part of that department, like CAPERS and Traffic and Tactical, all need thirty percent black officers."

"Cool! Okay, David, you're good to go!" Randy shouted.

"Thanks guys," David said. Then to Jimmy John, "I'll let you go. See you tomorrow night?"

"We'll be here. Me and the rookie."

David shook hands all around and drove Lisa back to the garage. She topped off his tires for him and mumbled something about being glad to see him again. Soon he headed north on Central Expressway. It wasn't until he had exited onto Mockingbird that he figured out the major implication of what Jimmy John had told him.

"The Department as a whole isn't thirty percent black," he said aloud.

The red light stopping David had turned green. He sat at the light working through the ramifications of the new policy. After a polite interval, the driver behind David pulled around, without honking, knocking David out of his reverie. David drove on.

With the unavailability of enough blacks to implement the plan, movement in the Department for whites would simply cease. White officers were going to be held in place as supervisors scrambled to do the best they could with what numbers were available. As he pulled into the parking area of the apartment complex where he lived, he realized why Jane was able to get a spot in the Crimes Against Persons unit. No supervisor could be criticized for having a female in a slot. That would be one slot less for the supervision to be held accountable for. David parked conveniently close to his apartment.

"Wonderful," he said to himself, as he got out of his truck. David loved his apartment complex. The trim lawns and neatly tended garden beds appeared to have been transplanted from a golf course. Three tan brick buildings made up the complex, and David had a spacious one bedroom on the third floor of the middle building. He trudged up the outdoor staircase with his two bags and unlocked his front door.

He stepped inside and turned on a light. The apartment was painted flat beige throughout. It had been decorated in the style of single man neat. Over the years, David had acquired some furniture. A black leather livingroom set, couch, love seat and armchair, were nearest. He had assembled the coffee table and entertainment center himself, from kits. In the dining area, he had positioned a chrome and glass table, surrounded by four chairs, in front of the sliding glass doors that lead to the balcony. David had never mounted anything decorative on the walls and inexpensive blinds covered his windows.

He took his bags into the bedroom. The large room easily held a desk, queen-size bed and dresser. David slipped out of his tunic and hung it on the uniform side of his walk-in closet. There were several uniforms there; Dallas Police blue, Army dress green and woodland camouflage. In the corner of the closet, half hidden, his narrow, green firearms safe sat, still locked and secure.

David began to strip. He felt pretty impressed with himself on account of how organized he had left things. Other than a dusting and a shopping trip to fill the refrigerator, everything seemed to be okay. He put on a dark blue t-shirt, worn blue jeans and a pair of brown ropers.

He walked out to the kitchen and slid the refrigerator away from the wall and plugged it in. The compressor started right up. David yawned, suddenly tired. On account of his switch back to deep nights, he wanted to stay up late. He decided to go to the nearby Albertson's and buy some food.

Back in his bedroom, he unlocked the metal firearms safe and reviewed the contents. In the long gun section, both his double barrel, over and under twelve gauge and a Remington bolt action in .30-06 were present and accounted for. On the top, in the pistol section, his two Berettas and a five shot Chief were right where he had left them.

David took a box of .380 ammunition, the smaller Beretta automatic and two magazines and sat down on his bed. After a safety check, he loaded the two magazines. With the snick of each bullet going home, the apartment became larger and quieter. He found himself thinking about Charlene and getting seriously annoyed at her absence.

He finished loading the magazines. At the safe, he slid a magazine into the handle, pointed the pistol at a telephone book on the floor and snapped the slide back, letting go of it immediately, so that the slide slammed forward, placing a bullet in the chamber. David topped off before slipping the pistol into an inside-the-pants holster. He clipped the holster on his right side, inside the waistband of his jeans and put the extra magazine in his front left pocket.

Then he reached inside the safe and pulled out a black leather wallet. Opening it up, he examined his Dallas Police badge and the photograph on the identification card. He huffed a breath on the silver badge and rubbed it on his thigh. He would need to buff it up before tomorrow. He closed the wallet, slipped it into his right rear pocket and locked the safe.

At the hall closet, he put on a denim jacket that had been with him for years, and started to leave for the supermarket. He stopped at the door to lock it, and looked into the dimly lit apartment. It, like the 'fridge, was empty. Empty and quiet. David cursed Charlene for the first time that night, and pulled the door shut with a satisfying smash that rattled his windows.

Chapter 2

"That wetback mother fucker din' know shit," Juwan said, half to himself, as they drove the ten kilos of heroin down I-20. Juwan adjusted his grip on the wheel as the skyscrapers of downtown came into view, against a clear blue sky, the morning after David Lane had come back to town.

"He wasn't no wetback, Juwan," Andree said, eyes closed, head leaning against the passenger door. "He was one of them white boys with wetback names. Got some wetback in him from way back, but ain't no thing."

Andree Jamison, a diminutive, slender black man, about twenty-four, with delicate features and tightly curled hair that fell to his collar, had put the entire operation together, and he was tired. Put it together, executed it and planned to be its chief beneficiary. His hazel eyes remained closed as they drove on in the swaying panel truck. His skin, normally smooth and the color of milk chocolate, currently played host to a rash of pimples on both cheeks, as well as plenty of Mexican dirt. They had been driving, switching off for rest, for most of three days now.

Even if Andree was not thinking of his business concerns, sleep would have been difficult, as the rented yellow truck lurched and yawed its way down the interstate. Every time he moved either of his feet, layers of junk food wrappers on the floorboards crackled away. Lastly, truth be told, he, Juwan and the inside of the cab stank like the county jail in-take on the Monday morning after a rough weekend. Maybe they ought to stop and eat a real breakfast, and perhaps doze in a parking lot. Then again, they were so close to home.

He and Juwan had crossed into the United States at Boquillas, their truck full of washing machines. Inside one of the machines were the ten bags of barely cut heroin. The white boy wetback passed them through because it was already hot in Boquillas. Too damn hot to unload and search a panel truck full of washing machines.

Andree was not a gambling man. He was a businessman, and he knew better than a Wharton MBA that risk meant money. Like any good business executive, he minimized his risk. For instance, the customs inspector that had let them back in had not caught the excellent forgeries regarding the washing machines. He had no idea that Andree and Juwan had driven them into Mexico at Nuevo Laredo, with equally well forged documents, now nothing but ash blowing around in the winds of the northern Mexico badlands. The customs inspector had no idea the machines had not been manufactured in Torreon and that Andree and Juwan were on a drug run.

Of course, under normal circumstances, the risk minimization policy would preclude Andree from driving his own dope, but this was a first run. Andree usually never touched product, guns or the stolen stuff the junkies would bring in to pay for their hits. Even though he was twenty-four, it had been a long time since he had touched product. Now guns, that was another story, you understand. Some things can't be avoided. But overall, Andree, the man who was so smart he still did not have a record, was pretty smart. He knew things.

He knew the Dallas narcs and the DEA had broken the ring bringing in Black Tar heroin, but that was two years ago. Black Tar had dominated their thoughts and sucked up their resources. In that time, Andree went independent in the crack cocaine business. That would be the crack cocaine trade that had grown unchecked and was now tearing up South Dallas, East Dallas and Oak Cliff. As the law scrambled to get on top of crack, Andree felt the time was ripe to reintroduce heroin to the marketplace and that he was the man to do it.

Andree was the man with the plan. Even though his organization was young, he controlled the crack trade in several neighborhoods. He liked the area around Fair Park and had recently branched out to the North, up Central Expressway. That was solid. Bread and butter. But this heroin thing was going to take Andree to a whole new level. All he had to do was lick the small cash shortage problem he had recently discovered. Then, it would be off to that whole new level.

Andree, who had left high school in the middle of his junior year, had never learned accounting. If asked, he would have said double entry was something two brothers did with a girl. But he did know how much each corner should yield and he knew how much his gross was off. He had set a simple trap before he devoted his full time to the heroin run, and when he returned to Dallas, he would be able to work it out.

Andree had not noticed that the panel truck had drifted part way into the center lane. Neither had Juwan, until the loud horn blast from a passing big rig, designed more to wake Juwan rather then voice displeasure, caused Juwan to swerve back into the right lane.

"Sorry Andree, sorry," Juwan said, eyebrows high in panic. He turned his head from the road to Andree, back and forth, back and forth, shaking his head in an attempt to banish his fatigue.

"Ain't no thing, man. Just pull off and we'll get something to eat. Then we switch out."

"Okay, Andree, okay. Thank you, man," Juwan said, shaking his massive head from side to side in a show of self recrimination.

"Ain't no thing, brother."

Chapter 3

At about ten thirty that night, some twelve hours after Andree and Juwan and their heroin passed over the Dallas city limits, Bill Cobb sat at one of the small tables outside the detail room in the Metro Division building. Bill, with his medium brown hair and fair white skin, sat fairly still, watching everything. At five foot ten and a fit one hundred and eighty pounds, he was a standard issue DPD rookie, freshly scrubbed and earnest.

He and Theodore Guffy and Robert Richardson sat together at the small table. Classmates at the Dallas Police Academy, they were the only three from their class posted to Metro Division. That very day they had completed their first phase of field training. The change from first to second phase also meant a change from days to deep nights. They had gotten off at four that afternoon. Bill yawned.

They had spent so much of the last eight months together that the three of them had very little to say, as they waited for detail and to pick up with their new field training officers. It wasn't like the three of them had been especially close. Bill lamented the fact that all of his friends from the academy were split between Pleasant Grove Division and Oak Cliff Division. And while Robert and Theodore weren't bad guys, well, they weren't the guys he saw off duty.

Robert was a slender, five foot six inch bundle of nervous, compulsive energy. His dark eyes darted around the lounge area without rest. His dark brown hair and pencil thin mustache were neatly trimmed. Like Bill, he had worn a freshly pressed uniform for their first night, but unlike Bill, his uniform showed no wear at all from the previous six weeks. While they had been working days and they had not seen much action at all, there should have been some breaking in of his gear. The metal devices on his shirt gleamed and his patent leather dress shoes looked out-of-the-box new, not even marked from normal use. Robert sat with his legs crossed. With pursed lips, he flicked an unseen piece of lint off of his knee.

Theodore could not have been more different than Robert. Tall and thin, with greasy brown hair and that day's worth of whiskers on his receding chin, Bill thought of Robert and Theo as a before and after set of pictures. He had no explanation as to how Theo's stoop-shouldered body could shrink into Robert's ramrod straight miniature monument to tension, but such are the thoughts of a bored young man.

"I don't know what they been saying about deep nights. In the MP's, back when I was in the Army, them overnights was pretty quiet," Theo said, breaking the silence around the table.

"Theo, you aren't in the Army anymore," Bill said. "And this isn't Kentucky, either."

"Why William," Robert said, using Bill's full name. Robert preferred the formal version of his own name, and assumed everyone else thought the same. "You wouldn't be buying into that hype about deep nights being more dangerous and more difficult than days or evenings, would you?"

"I'm not thinkin' of it exactly that way, Robert. But we've been on days for six weeks. I drew my pistol twice. Both times were at burglary alarm calls. Both times, residents had left their porch doors open on their way to work. Now them deep nights guys, well, every morning they show up here exhausted. Something must be going on out there."

"That something is sleeping, I assure you. Of course, that rhetoric you just spouted would make good copy when I run for office," Robert said.

"What you running for? My Daddy's friend is on county council back home," Theo said. "He says county council is the seat of democracy. You gonna be in the seat of—"

"Good morning, I mean evening, boys. I'm Sergeant Karangekis, Costas will do, and I've got your field training officer assignments," Costas had walked over, holding a clipboard.

"Bill?" Costas asked and he and Bill shook hands, and then did the same with Theo. "Do you prefer Rob or Bob?" Costas asked their classmate, sticking out his hand.

"Neither. I prefer Robert," he said, taking Costas's hand briefly.

"Okay. Robert, you are assigned to Tom Pointer, he's about six foot tall, a senior corporal—"

"I thought all FTOs were senior corporals?" Robert interrupted.

Costas smiled and nodded. "White, with brown hair. Early thirties. Bill, you find Roy Adams, about ten years older, stocky if you know what I mean."

"Yes Sergeant," Bill said.

"Theo, you need to find Hermondo Acevedo. He's just like Roy, only Mexican. Y'all have a good night and we'll talk again soon."

"Sergeant?" Robert asked, "before you go, am I right to assume we will be let go early, to get some sleep? I mean, we did put in a full day today on days."

Costas nodded and smiled again. Then he walked away without a backwards glance.

"You think he could have answered me," Robert said.

Bill cringed. He believed there was no value in drawing attention to himself until long after his probationary period was over. Bill and Theo remained silent, letting Robert's last comment hang uncomfortably in the air.

Officers began to crowd into the building as both shifts arrived, the third watch officers to get off and go home and the first watch officers to attend detail, draw their equipment and hit the street. A group quickly grew around an athletic looking senior corporal who appeared to be in his late twenties or just thirty. The others were congratulating him and welcoming him back. Bill wondered if he had been in the gulf war.

"Here come the sergeants," Theo said.

Bill saw a small group of officers with gold sergeant's stripes on their sleeves walking down the hallway. Other officers started meandering toward the detail room and the group Bill had been watching broke up. Bill stood up and started toward the detail room himself, just as the theme music from HILL STREET BLUES started coming out of the television sets in the corners.

Unlike days, most of the officers took the seats along the walls of the room. The new rookies had no choice but to sit at the farthest front table, three new faces in a room lined with blue. Bill looked around and met the eyes of the officer that had been the center of attention out in the hall. He received a sociable wink and subtle nod in greeting. Bill was close enough to notice a small pin made up of crossed arrows and a wreath over the officer's nameplate, which said "Lane."

"Good morning," Sergeant Karangekis said, getting everyone's attention. "I'm sure most of you have noticed, but Dave Lane is back from his desert expedition," he motioned over at David, who waved genially. "Dave chose to come back to Metro's deep nights even though department policy has been to let the officers pick an assignment anywhere—"

"Wait a minute, Sarge, you never mentioned that," David interrupted.

"Did I have to? Where else would you go?"

Tired laughter came from around the room. Once the Sergeant had his shot, several others took their own:

"Done sifting sand, Dave?"

"It took the Army this long to figure out your productivity level?"

"Hey Dave, Iraq is that way."

Mixed in with the good natured ribbing were many quieter waves and welcome backs. Bill was impressed with the obvious respect and affection the others had for David, and he wondered if they would ever look at him in the same way. The room quickly quieted down and the sergeant continued.

"Of course, David, we all extend our congratulations on the news of your engagement, announced last night on the ten o'clock news," Costas said.

"Now Sarge," David said, jumping to his feet and standing ramrod straight, "that was a misunderstanding on the part of the reporter. Charlene and I are not engaged. She was good enough to pick me up at the airport. That was it." His good natured, easygoing demeanor had disappeared and a New York accent, barely noticeable before, came through loud and clear.

The room went silent.

"Okay David. Sorry about that, I should have asked. Good to have you back," Costas said as David sat back down. "Moving on, the new lieutenant needs everyone to update their form 19a's. Shonda's got them waiting for you. If there are no changes, just initial it. The sexual assault addendum page is up on the mobile display terminal, so now all reports except wrecks can be done on the MDT. Dave, get with someone for the details."

"He won't need to, Sarge. No arrests means no reports," Tom Pointer shouted from the back wall.

Tom wore a brown buzz cut on his large head. His prominent chin, large forehead and awkward build, a long barrel shaped torso on top of thick, short legs, worked together to create the impression he drove in right off the farm.

"Don't mind him, Sarge. Tom's confusing his activity sheet with mine," David said.

"All right, boys. Last item: Intelligence is still pushing the heroin thing, so let us know when you start to see any on the street. Got some rookies here. Tom, could you wave? Thanks. You have Rob Richardson—"

"*Robert* Richardson," Robert said.

Costas, who had been writing on his clipboard, put down his pen. He and the other sergeants stopped what they had been doing and the line of supervisors looked out over the assembled officers. The officers themselves had ceased their few whispered side conversations. Costas drummed his fingers on the tabletop one time.

Bill felt acutely embarrassed. Not only for Robert, but for himself as well. Robert was messing up their first day on nights.

"Roy, You've got Bill Cobb, Bill, if you would?" Costas continued.

Bill stood up and looked around the room. A large, round man, in his middle forties, with a disgusted look on his face, stringy brown hair parted in the middle, and a busy mustache, wearing a rumpled uniform, waved curtly with his right hand from the back of the room. Bill sat down again in a hurry.

"Hermondo? You've got Theo Guffy. Theo? That's Hermondo Acevedo."

Theo stood up. "I'm real glad to be here. I used to be with the MPs and—"

"Have a seat," Hermondo said. Hermondo was a shorter man than Roy, but equally as round. His black hair, sprinkled liberally with gray, was neatly cut and his mustache trimmed. Large eyes were set forward, and his lids traveled slowly over the course of his blinks, slowly closing and slowly opening. His large, muscular shoulders rested in forward position.

Theo dropped like a stone.

"Rookies, get with your FTOs. And all of you, stay safe out there. That's all."

Some officers slowly rose to their feet. Others were quicker. They clustered around David. Bill struggled with indecision as he stood by his chair, unable to find Roy, not knowing what to do. He looked around and saw that Theo stood babbling next to Hermondo. Bill looked for Robert, and found him still sitting in his chair, waiting for something. Tom was one of the officers standing around David.

If Robert is sitting around waiting, Bill thought, then sitting around waiting must not be the thing to be doing.

Bill stepped out of the detail room and went to get his gear. There were little piles of equipment up and down the halls, stored in different containers, from catalogue cases to ratty, stained gym bags. Like the others, he had left his black nylon gear bag, with his PR-24 baton, four cell flashlight and police hat in the hall, against a wall.

Bill had received his bag as a gift. It was specially made for police work and came with the loops for a baton and flashlight. In addition to a cavernous main pocket, it had lots of little zippered pockets around the outside. After six weeks of patrol work, Bill had filled them to capacity. Bill was pretty happy with his bag. At least it did not say POLICE in big white letters on the outside, as Theo's did.

Having learned the hard way, he checked the metal emblem on his police hat. As had happened on days, someone had turned it upside down. He righted it and started looking for Roy. With a little help, Bill found him in the sergeant's offices. Roy gave him the beat car number and sent him out into the parking lot to set it up.

"You're driving, I feel like shit," Roy said, flipping him the keys.

Bill carried his gear out the back door to where a line of marked police cars were parked in diagonal slots. Around most of the cars, uniformed officers were arranging equipment and adjusting seats to their preference. The metal on metal sounds of the opening and loading of shotguns cut through the hum of idling engines and shouted conversation.

Bill found their car parked in just about the middle of the commotion. When he opened the door, the odor of tobacco mixed with saliva committed a felony on his nose. Burger wrappers and empty cups littered the floorboards on the passenger side.

Bill sighed and got to work. He slipped in behind the driver's seat and moved it up; obviously a professional wrestler had last driven the unit. He started it and boosted the air conditioner while lowering the windows. Bill picked up the trash and walked it to a nearby refuse can. He loaded the shotgun and slid it between the seat and the door, along with his baton and flashlight.

His aluminum clipboard went to the middle of the back seat. He slid his MDT guide between the seat and the metal tower that supported the controls for the lights, sirens and radio. Bill still liked to have the thick, photocopied manual handy. He slid a bound, comprehensive Dallas area map next to it. After he logged onto the MDT and got it going, he had nothing left to do. By that time he was alone in the staging area. At least it was a clear, starry night; not a cloud in the sky and still cool. He wondered how Roy would take it if he drove over by himself to get the car washed.

Not fifteen minutes into the shift, and Robert had already developed a profound dislike for his training officer. First off, Tom Pointer looked like a rube. Robert had thought he looked like he had just driven in off of the farm, when in fact, Tom had just driven in off of his farm. Second, Tom would not let Robert drive.

"Gonna take about a week to get used to you. We'll see how you do," Tom had told Robert as they pulled out of the Metro Division parking area, and just before he launched into an interminable lecture regarding the spiritual benefits of running fifty head as a part-time proposition.

"Keeps me in touch with my Texas heritage. You native to Dallas?" Tom asked.

"Yes."

"Well that's just fine. I need a break from training rookies from Michigan. So Bobby, how do you like police work so far?"

"I prefer Robert and I like police work just fine, thank you."

"How was first phase? Days, wasn't it?"

"Yes, it was days. And it went fine. I have no idea why we need to go through three phases and a final evaluation period. That's like four phases. I know how to do this job already," Robert replied before yawning broadly.

"Why don't we swing by Joker's and get you some coffee, before you fall asleep at the wheel here."

"You're the one at the wheel," Robert said, "and I don't drink coffee."

"Do you have a problem with that?" Tom asked, followed immediately by "and you will."

"Yes I do. I just spent six weeks on days learning this job. I should be shown the respect due and be permitted to drive."

"Know the job real well, do you, Robert?"

"Well enough."

"Then why doesn't the dispatcher know we are clear yet?"

Robert blushed furiously and grabbed at the unit's microphone. He keyed the mike, stepping on the end of another unit's transmission. "One-Dog," he said, before releasing the key. "What unit are we?"

"Six car," Tom said.

Robert keyed the mike again. Holding it close to his mouth, he said, "One-Dog-Six, clear two."

"One-Dog-Six," the male dispatcher replied in detached confirmation.

Hermondo, like Roy, had given his rookie the keys. Theo felt odd with Hermondo standing over him, watching him prep the unit, arranging his equipment and turning on the electronics. Hermondo's large eyelids slowly, regularly blinked over his protruding eyes as Theo told him all about his MP work in the Army. When Theo was done with the unit, he still had a little more to say about the Army. He liked the way Hermondo listened. After a while, the odd feeling fell away. Eventually, Theo noticed the only two cars on the ramp at Metro Division were Theo's and Bill's.

"Ain't we going to go out?" Theo, who stood by the open driver's door as the unit idled, asked.

"Just as soon as you put the car in drive and point it at an exit," Hermondo said, with one long, slow blink.

"Okay!" Theo said, jumping in behind the wheel, beginning a new discourse on driving in Kentucky.

Theo put the unit in gear after Hermondo buckled himself into the passenger's seat. He kept talking while Hermondo looked straight ahead and blinked once, long and slow.

Roy eventually made it out to the car and buckled in. Even though Bill had never seen Roy before, he thought Roy's color was bad. The larger, older man wheezed and groaned as he adjusted himself in the passenger seat.

"Bill, I'm sorry, but I think I'm coming down with something here. We may have to knock off early tonight. You don't mind if we save the pep talk for tomorrow, do you? Good. Let's go to Joker's. I need something for heartburn," Roy said.

Bill backed out of the spot and exited the parking area. Once in the flow of traffic he asked Roy about clearing.

"Oh, hell, yeah," Roy said, massaging the upper part of his left arm.

"One-Dog-Four, clear two," Bill said into the microphone, feeling like a competent officer as he drove and spoke on the radio at the same time.

"One-Dog-Four," the dispatcher replied.

Roy directed Bill to a Seven-Eleven where Baker Sector rubbed up against White Rock Division. By the time he and Roy pulled into the parking lot, there was a line of white Dallas police cruisers taking up the available spots. Roy was up and out of the car in a flash, while Bill turned it off and stumbled out over the shotgun, baton and flashlight. He finally caught up with Roy near some counter space at the rear of the store, convenient to the coffee pots and fountain drinks.

"Use these for drinks," Roy said, handing him a white courtesy cup with the Seven-Eleven logo printed on it. "Coffee and cokes are free, the rest of the stuff we pay for." Roy stepped away and poured himself a cup of coffee.

Bill stood there for a moment, plagued by indecision. After he saw most of the officers drinking out of the white cups, he overcame his discomfort and poured himself half a cup of Diet Coke from the fountain. He moved as nonchalantly as possible and worked himself into the group. He remained far enough away so that he did not annoy any of the officers, but edged in close enough to hear the conversation. When Bill finally looked around, he noticed he stood near David, the officer that was just back from the gulf.

"The Joker's dead?" David asked the others.

"Yup," Tom Pointer said, "his daughter got a job at an Aco's Tacos in Mesquite. She worked the late shift and he went to pick her up. Two jicks from Oak Cliff Division had driven out there to rob it. They walked everybody into the freezer and shot them: an assistant manager, the two employees and the Joker, who had been sitting in the restaurant reading the paper."

The story shocked Bill, who looked over at David. He watched David drift into a thousand yard stare. With Tom in here, Bill thought, then Robert had to be in here as well. Bill looked around and found Robert standing alone by the magazine rack, surveying the covers.

"Which daughter was it, the one at TWU?" David asked Tom.

"The one in high school, the 16 year old."

Before David could answer, the dispatcher started what would be a series of 911 calls that would empty the store in short order. "One-Dog-Four, see the man, disturbance in alley, loud noises."

"One-Dog-Four," Bill heard Roy say into his radio. "Rookie," Roy said to Bill, "let's go." Roy slapped some dollar bills on the counter by the register, finished drinking the contents of a small bottle of Pepto Bismol and headed for the door without waiting for his change.

"One-Dog-Six, it's the major 7 on I-30, westbound at Fitzhugh. Cover the AI," the dispatcher's measured, calm male voice said.

Robert did not look up from the magazines. Across the room, Tom made no move for the radio on his belt, but kept his eyes on Robert. When an officer started to say something, Tom waved him quiet.

"One-Dog-Six?" the dispatcher asked.

Bill wanted to alert Robert to his call, but at the same time, he would not mind Robert failing a little. Then his sense of comradeship overcame his fascination with the coming train wreck of Robert's night. Bill took a deep breath in preparation for shouting to Robert when he felt a hand on his shoulder.

"If I were you, I'd worry about catching up to Roy," David said, nodding at the front door.

Bill smiled to cover his embarrassment and nodded in silent thanks to David before hurrying out of the Seven-Eleven. Tom swore loudly in disgust before marking en-route to the dispatcher. Bill passed through the door just as Tom scornfully called for Robert to get his act together. The last thing Bill heard was David add himself to Tom and Robert's motor vehicle accident.

"Let's go," Roy said, as Bill took his place in the driver's seat.

Robert smarted sharply from his treatment in the Seven-Eleven, working his animosity and hurt like a sore tooth as he drove around, looking for Fitzhugh Avenue.

"Partner, did you hear that? DFD is en-route. They can't work a car fire if traffic is bearing down on them. We need to get there, so let's get to it, partner," Tom said. He did not yell, but Robert could tell that his perception of a delay did not please him. Not that Robert thought they were late.

"Okay," Tom continued, "do you know where you are going?"

"Fitzhugh at RL Thornton Freeway," Robert said testily.

"Don't talk to me that way, Bobby. Can you get on the freeway east of the wreck if you pick up Fitzhugh?"

"I don't know!"

"You don't know!" Now Tom was yelling. "It's your job to know! There are victims out there, not to mention that your fellow officers and the fire department are in traffic needing to work this wreck! They need you to protect them from traffic! Traffic kills!"

Tom calmed down a bit and started giving Robert directions. "You've got to come up on the wreck from the east, so's you can get between the drunks and the folks working the wreck," he said conversationally.

Tom directed Robert through side streets east of Munger Boulevard until they were up on the freeway, heading west.

"So you see," Theo droned on, as he drove north on Preston Road, "that's how them back roads can get covered with snow in the wintertime."

Hermondo blinked slowly, looked straight ahead and remained silent. His hands were clasped loosely in his lap.

"One-Dog-Three," the dispatcher called, "man refusing to leave, 900 Elm."

"I wonder why they don't hook up some big drums to trucks and roll that snow flat. Then there'd be some kind of surface back there," Theo said, as he passed through the intersection of Preston and University Boulevard at 23 miles an hour. Theo had unwittingly left Dallas and entered Highland Park.

Hermondo blinked his slow blink.

"One-Dog-Three?" the dispatcher asked.

Theo began to feel that something was wrong, but he could not think of what it was. The effort of trying to work it out taxed him to the point where he was not able to drive, talk and figure things out at the same time. As much as it pained him, he stopped talking.

"One-Dog-Three?"

"What unit are we?" Hermondo asked, without looking at Theo.

"Dog-Three," Theo replied.

"Dispatcher trying to reach you?" Hermondo asked.

"I don't know, is he?" Theo replied.

Hermondo shrugged.

"One-Dog-Three, did you get your call?" came over the radio.

Theo fumbled for the microphone. "One-Dog-Three, no, could you give it to us again?"

Hermondo blinked, slower than usual, and at the apex of the blink, kept his eyes closed a little longer than normal.

"Man refusing to leave, 900 Elm."

"Ten four. Three en-route," Theo said. He slammed the microphone into its clip, put both hands on the wheel and stomped on the accelerator. The large car leapt forward, north on Preston, heading deeper into Highland Park, away from downtown Dallas.

Clouds had rolled in by the time Bill found the alley, just south of the central business district and north of Splendid Avenue.

"Code six," Bill radioed the dispatcher, giving him the signal to indicate they had arrived.

"See anything?" Roy asked.

"No."

"Let's drive down and look for a body," Roy said, rubbing the biceps of his left arm.

Bill turned the front of the car into the alley, crunching gravel as they drove slowly behind the apartment buildings.

Tom stopped the car in a trough between the crests of two asphalt waves on I-30. Robert marked out and planned to wait for Tom to tell him what to do. Before Robert could ask for direction, Tom had gotten out of the car and into the trunk. Robert stepped onto the shoulder and watched Tom begin the flare line, blocking the left lane of traffic. Robert did not think to help, as curiosity regarding the accident itself took hold.

Robert walked up the hill, away from Tom. Cars in the left lane had come to a stop. Traffic moved slowly in the middle lane and flew past in a blur on the right. At the crest, he looked down into another trough and saw the aftermath of disaster. In spite of himself, he kept walking toward two burned out vehicles, one destroyed from the passenger section back, and the other from the cockpit forward. In the dark punctuated by flashing emergency lights, Robert could barely make out colors. The car that had been hit in the rear sat in the middle of a rough circle of white foam. Robert had never seen anything like this. Not on days. Not before becoming a police officer. Never.

That was when he noticed the body. What was left of an Asian male lay spread eagle on the ground. Except for his belt, his red bikini briefs and scraps of a brown shirt left around his shoulders, he had been burned naked. When Robert noticed that the width of the victim's trunk was off, he moved in closer. Between the neck and the pelvis, the trunk appeared half the normal width. It looked fine, other than the charring, from the front. From the side, it appeared little more than smashed flat. That condition gave his head and hips a weird angle relative to his middle.

All at once, Robert's mouth went dry. The scene receded in his field of vision rapidly, so that he appeared to be looking at the dead man through the wrong end of a telescope. He felt light-headed and could not seem to catch his breath. The world shifted. Robert took a step, trying to regain his balance. His knees buckled instead. As he started to go down, something grabbed his right arm hard enough to hurt.

"Hey, look at me," someone said.

Robert tried to turn around, but his legs felt like rubber bands. It took all his concentration to stay upright.

"Rookie!"

Robert was spun around and given a good shake. His vision cleared and he came back to the present. The senior corporal that had just come back from the gulf had him by both arms. Robert was surprised to see him wearing his blue uniform cap.

"I think I'm okay," Robert said.

David let go of him. "All right. Why don't we go help Tom with the flare line?"

"Don't I have to get some information?" Robert asked, not relishing the thought of having to face the accident scene again.

"Turn this way," David prodded him to face left.

Robert saw a tall Dallas officer interviewing another Asian man, who was untouched. As the two men spoke, the Asian man started to cry, and buried his face in his hands.

"The accident investigator will handle it. You lucked out," David said. "Don't get too used to it though. Rookies do all the work out here."

Robert looked at David to see if he was taunting him, but David smiled.

"Best training is by doing," David said.

As the two men started walking away from the wreck, Robert observed David's long blue raincoat with a bright orange lining and his police hat with the issue blue nylon cover. Robert had never worn his on days. He was about to ask David why he chose to wear those items when the thick, large drops started pelting him.

Theo was lost and he knew it. As he drove slowly north on Preston, in the right lane, he gripped the wheel so hard his knuckles were white. Sweat poured down his back, underneath his ballistic vest. He looked frantically from side to side. He prayed for a familiar sight in the neon-lit night.

"Partner, if you don't speed up, you're going to mess up the traffic patterns all over the city," Hermondo said.

"Huh?"

"Speed up or pull over. None of the other drivers want to pass you and you can't drive 20 miles an hour on Preston all night."

Theo pushed down on the accelerator.

Bill had not driven far when they found a body lying perpendicular to the alley. Bill brought the car to a slow stop, but beyond that, he could not act. He had never seen a dead body before. The thought that moments ago this person had been alive filled him with indecision. He began to think on the vagaries of life.

Roy lowered his window. The unusually loud hum of the engine sounded out of place to Bill. He thought a moment of silence might be more appropriate. Bill turned his head and caught a whiff of rain in the humid night air.

"Come up on over here, baby!" Roy shouted.

Roy shocked Bill in that he would show such disrespect for the dead. Bill received a second shock when the body sat up. It turned out to be a black woman, about Bill's age or younger, wearing a dress with a print pattern in blues and greens. She stood up and walked toward the car.

As soon as Roy opened his door and started to get out, Bill followed his lead. The woman, who was almost six feet tall and very thin, wobbled over to Roy's side of the car. Roy burped loudly. In the glare of the headlights, Bill saw that she had taken some hits in the face recently. She moved around the front of the car to stand by Roy. He arranged the spotlight so they were illuminated, but not blinded. Dead leaves and dirt matted the back of her hair.

"Want to tell us what happened, baby?" Roy asked tenderly.

"See here, Lyzel done slap me upside my head," she said, looking down.

"Partner, why don't you get all the information from the lady and I'll call for an ambulance," Roy said.

"I don't need no amb-lance," she said.

"I know it baby," Roy answered, "but it's something they make us do now. I got no choice." Roy nodded at a hesitant Bill.

Bill nodded back and walked around the front of the car to conduct the interview, while reaching for the notebook he kept in his shirt pocket. He adopted the correct interview stance, right foot back, weapon positioned away from the interview subject, notebook in his left hand and that hand positioned between himself and the young woman.

"Good evening. I am Officer William Cobb of the Dallas Police Department. What happened tonight ma'am?" Bill said.

The woman looked at him as if he were an emotionally disturbed person that was capable of anything, especially hurting her some more. Then she looked over at Roy.

Roy stood behind the passenger door with the microphone in his left hand. He held it to his mouth and keyed the microphone. "One-Dog-Six, start an amb-lance out to our location, please," Roy said.

"One-Dog-Six," the dispatcher responded.

Then to the woman, Roy said, "just tell him what happened, baby."

The woman turned back to Bill and said, "Lyzel done beat me up."

Bill was taken aback. This was the first assault report he had ever taken and for a moment, the circumstances stunned him. Bill himself would never think of beating a woman up, not unless she was a realistic, direct threat to him. Here this woman stood in front of him, broken of spirit, bleeding and with a swollen face, and he can't have imagined she'd been much of a threat to anybody. That, and her matter-of-fact attitude toward the situation flat out shocked him.

"You might want to start with her name," Roy said, rubbing his left arm.

After questioning, Bill managed to write down her name, date of birth and address. There was no telephone number. Bill added her complete statement ("He done beat me up") before the ambulance arrived. Her condition deteriorated throughout the quick interview. Bill began to worry that she would get really sick while he was in charge, before the Dallas Fire Department showed up.

Bill felt immense relief when the Mobile Intensive Care Unit turned into the alley. The red and white vehicle displayed the emblems of the fire department and the emergency medical division. The cab was that of a full-size pickup truck. Instead of a bed, there was a large box at the rear.

Bill followed as the DFD emergency medical personnel led the woman into the back of their vehicle. Inside, there was room for two people on stretchers and the paramedics. All the emergency medical equipment and supplies had been neatly arranged on shelves. Bill watched for a while, and then walked over to Roy. He gave Roy the long version of her statement.

"I guess we can go look for Lyzel now," Roy said, without making a move to get into the police car.

"I guess so," Bill said, with a growing awareness that he had screwed up somehow.

"Known him long?" Roy asked.

"I don't know him at all!"

"Then how you going to know you got him when you get him?"

Bill considered for a moment. "I guess I need to get a description, huh?"

"Might be a good idea. Might also be a good idea to get it right now, before the amb-lance leaves and we got to drive on down to Parkland to get it."

"Hey guys," one of the paramedics yelled out the side hatch of the ambulance, "concussion, definitely. We're transporting to Parkland."

"One second," Bill yelled, reaching for his notebook as he ran over to the open hatch.

Then it started to rain.

A drenched Robert sat in the passenger seat of the One-Dog-Six car as they exited the freeway. The rain had come, dumped gallons on him, and left in moments. His overall bad mood, originally due to his discomfort with his training officer, became worse. Wet feet, the taste of bile in the back of his throat and a case of the shakes he couldn't get under control contributed to his sour feeling. He hoped Tom didn't notice his hands trembling in his lap.

It made him shiver to recall how the accident investigator described the wreck. The second Asian man had been standing right behind the decedent, so close they were touching, as they changed a flat tire in the left lane of Interstate 30. The accident and fire had left the second man unscathed. When Robert and Tom cleared the scene, the survivor was in the middle of a mental breakdown, unable to reconcile his survival with the burned dead body of his companion.

"Rookie?" Tom fairly shouted.

"Huh?"

"I asked you if we were clear."

"Clear, oh yeah." Robert picked up the radio. "One-Dog-Six, clear two."

"You don't have to clear two every time, just the first time. 'Clear' would have been fine."

"Oh yeah."

A frantic radio call rudely interrupted Robert's retreat back into his thoughts.

"Shots fired! Shots from a white over blue Ford Bronco, late eighties by a white male, brown mustache, firing an Uzi. South on Haskell." The call had been put out by a voice that Robert had not heard before. "For information, he's shootin' at me."

Time suddenly shifted into slow gear for Robert. Fear stirred up the discomfort he already felt from working the wreck. The idea of someone driving around, shooting at police officers unsettled him. The bile taste became more pronounced.

"10/4," the calm male dispatcher said. "All units, shots fired at an officer. Suspect vehicle is a white over blue Ford Bronco, 1988 or 9, no plate. Suspect is a white male, mustache, brown/brown, firing an Uzi. Last seen southbound on Haskell. Units mark out."

Tom punched the accelerator and the car lurched forward, slipping on the wet pavement. The radio exploded with chatter. Tom hit the air horn to part traffic. The order in Robert's head fell apart and he could not gather his thoughts in any coherent manner. Flashing red lights illuminated the neighborhood from somewhere, adding to Robert's confusion. It was loud. Tom's shouting did not help the situation.

Then the following thought broke through the clutter in Robert's brain: your training officer is shouting at you!

"Yeah?" Robert managed to croak.

"Mark out! We're right on top of it!"

Robert had no idea what Tom was telling him, having forgotten everything he had ever learned about anything in general and police work in particular.

Tom cursed and reached for the microphone. He waited for a break in the traffic and added them to the call, while driving one-handed incredibly fast through side streets. Robert wondered why they didn't hit anything.

"You still here, rookie?" Tom asked.

Robert heard the question and even realized he needed to answer it. Instead, he sat in the rocketing car unable to move at all.

Theo and Hermondo sat in their unit on the deserted concrete apron of a closed gas station. Theo felt so out of sorts he had nothing to say, for a change, as he gazed out over the intersection of a major road and a large wide interstate. The radio traffic about the shooting, beyond Theo at the moment, came thick and fast.

"This look like 900 Elm?" Hermondo asked in a conversational tone, as he turned the volume down on the radio.

"No sir," a subdued Theo answered.

"I don't think so either. Do you know where we are?"

"Not exactly."

"Why don't you find a street sign?"

Theo put the unit in gear and drove over to an exit, signaling to make a right onto the major road.

"Partner, if you drive on up to the corner, you can shine the spotlight right on up at that sign over there," Hermondo said patiently.

Theo put the car in reverse and backed further into the gas station. He then put the car in drive and turned the front toward the corner Hermondo had referred to. Aggressive turning and backing had put them in an awkward position relative to the sign.

Theo felt his old lack-of-confidence feeling again, a tightness in his gut that had plagued him all of his life. He never liked the tightness feeling and that started to make him mad.

Theo shifted into reverse again and pulled out, turning the wheel in the wrong direction. He caught the mistake. Before the car stopped rolling, he forced the shift lever into drive and leaned a little too heavy on the accelerator. The transmission made a loud clunking sound and the police car jumped forward, chirping its tires. Theo tried several ineffective measures to move the situation in a more positive direction, but ended up with the car hurtling toward a brick retaining wall.

"Partner, stop the damn car!" Hermondo yelled.

Theo slammed on the brakes and stopped the unit inches from the gray bricks.

Theo heard Hermondo take in a deep breath and let it out slowly.

"Partner," Hermondo said calmly, "put it in park. Good. Now get out of the car and walk up to the sign."

"Okay," Theo said.

Theo opened the door and he felt his face redden with shame. At least it was the middle of the night, he thought. He did not get far before Hermondo called out to him like a mother might to a little boy.

"Don't forget to take your flashlight," he said.

Bill and Roy had joined in the chase to find the shooter, driving northeast through the diminishing rain. Bill drove carefully on the wet pavement, his sense of caution competing with his desire to really step on it. Every time he got a little ahead of himself and sped up, the rear end of the car would start to fishtail, introducing a spot of panic into the night's mix. He despaired of ever catching up to where ever the action was taking place. Then he turned left onto Ross and ended up behind a parade of white police cars, all lit up. They were following a 1988 or 9 blue over white Ford Bronco.

Bill was reaching for the radio when Roy stopped him. "No need to say anything. Watch and listen for instructions," Roy said.

The shooter led the growing procession of police cars onto southbound Central Expressway. He was not driving very fast, slower than normal in fact. Merging with light but fast highway traffic proved trickier than Bill would have thought. Eventually, everyone made it into the right or center lanes of the elevated freeway.

"One-Dog-Zero," Bill heard Costas, the sergeant, come up on the radio.

"Dog-Zero," the dispatcher said.

"Dog-Zero, okay listen up, the following units drop back and block traffic," Costas conversationally called off the rearmost units in the procession, one of which was Bill and Roy.

"We're going to form a rolling roadblock for the takedown team," Roy said. "Stay right here, in the center lane, but slow down. We need to keep the traffic off of the guys who are going to be working," Roy said, rubbing his left arm again.

A unit driven by officers Bill did not recognize swerved suddenly in front of Bill and Roy and neatly ended up next to them in the left lane, matching their speed. Bill watched other units deploy without any further instructions from the sergeant. Soon a line two police cars deep stretched across the three lanes of traffic, keeping the civilians out of harm's way.

"Great. Partner, start slowing down," Roy said.

Robert's heart hammered away under his ballistic vest. He had a hard time catching his breath. He and Tom were the second police car behind the Bronco. Certain that at any minute the rear window of the truck was going to erupt with submachine gun fire, he had scrunched down in the front seat as much as the vest and seatbelt would allow. He wanted to curl up on the floorboards with the engine and firewall between him and the lunatic with the machine gun.

Robert had yet to act constructively during this emergency. So far, Tom had done all the police work. Some small part of Robert's brain was not too happy about this, but fear kept the rest of him paralyzed. Foremost on his mind was his not wanting to get shot on southbound Central Expressway and never mind protecting and serving.

The Bronco slowed to a crawl and then stopped. Tom's door opened and he was gone. The open door and empty seat highlighted Robert's own inaction. He wanted to move, but the flashing lights, sirens and shouted instructions scared the living hell out of him.

Then his door opened. "Let's go," he heard. A grim faced David Lane, the same officer that had backed him up on the freeway materialized next to him. Robert was damned glad to see him.

"Bob, we have to go," David said.

Robert wanted to comply. As he leaned forward, the seat belt strap pinned him in. He looked up at David and shrugged, very sorry he could not get out. Now David would leave him alone. Robert did not especially like the idea of being alone.

"Release the seatbelt, Bob," David said.

"Huh?"

David holstered his pistol, a Beretta M-9, Robert idly thought. Then the experienced officer leaned across Robert's chest and released the catch of the seatbelt. Robert felt himself pulled from the car by the back of his collar. He stumbled for a moment before finding his feet.

"Don't stand up, crouch," David said. "Pull out your pistol."

Robert felt himself pushed down and forward at the same time. David still had him by the collar and was the prime source of Robert's movement, but Robert did not mind. It meant he was nearby. Robert pulled his pistol and remembered to hold it out in front of him.

David pushed him up to the open door on the passenger side of the first police car. At David's insistence, Robert knelt, taking cover at the end of the open door. A young Hispanic officer with a large amount of dark black hair, parted in the middle, sat in the passenger seat. He leaned out slightly, his pistol held with both hands, covering the passenger side of the Bronco. Robert thought that looked pretty cool, like an action shot in a movie, until he realized he ought to do the same. He looked over his left shoulder at David, who had his pistol out again. David knelt behind and slightly to the left of Robert, with much less cover. He held his pistol in his right arm, locked straight, pointing down, trigger finger along the receiver. David still had a powerful grip on Robert's collar, and Robert appreciated the close contact with the experienced officer. Suddenly rapid commands were shouted over a loudspeaker somewhere to Robert's right.

"Stay here," David said. "Don't move."

Robert watched David leave the relative safety of the shadow of the car door and run up to the Bronco. Now his pistol was out in front of him. He moved with a competence and economy that bordered on grace. With a second officer covering him, David checked the interior of the Bronco, working his way to the front.

"Clear!" David yelled, loud enough to pierce the controlled chaos.

David opened the door and said something to the officer he had cleared the Bronco with. That officer leapt into the Bronco and pulled out an Intratec TEC-9, holding it up for all the officers to see.

"Got it!" he yelled.

David walked back toward Robert with a slight grin. "Let's go," he said, as he waved Robert to his feet.

Robert complied, but almost fell flat on his face. His thighs had cramped up. Eventually, he made it to David's side and the two of them walked between the police car and the Bronco, over to the driver's side.

A large white good ole' boy lay in the middle of the center lane, hands cuffed behind his back. Two officers Robert did not know stood over him, one conducting a thorough search, the other covering. The handcuffed man followed all instructions, submitting quietly to the search of his person.

"Okay, open the left lane. You guys, get out of the left lane, we're going to open it!" Sergeant Costas Karangekis stood just to the rear of the Bronco, surrounded by a small group of officers. He brought his radio up to his mouth and keyed the microphone. "Dog-Zero, let's get that left lane open."

"10/4." Robert heard the response over the dozen or so hand held radios clipped to the Sam Browne's of the officers in the area.

"Okay," Costas said, as calmly as if they were all in the detail room, "You guys go ahead and transport."

"10/4," said one of the two officers standing by the handcuffed man.

"Tom, can you wait for the wrecker?" Costas asked.

"Sure, Sarge."

Costas brought his radio up to his lips and, by unit, assigned them new duties ("block the center lane") or cleared them from the scene. After only a few minutes, Robert and Tom were the only officers left, their car and some flares blocking the right lane, preventing the Bronco from being hit by the late night traffic. They both sat in the car with their seatbelts on. Tom had finished settling in when he slapped Robert on the chest, thumping the ballistic vest through his shirt.

"So! I saw you managed to get in the game. How'd you like it?" Tom asked, smiling.

Robert's mouth was dry and he had a hard time answering at first. "I did not like it at all," he managed to say.

Tom laughed. He left the car to deal with the wrecker that had pulled into the right lane ahead of the Bronco. The paperwork was done and the Bronco hooked up in no time. Tom, back in his seat, shifted the police car into drive. The wrecker with the Bronco started to accelerate and Tom followed suit.

"What about the flares?" Robert asked.

"What about them?"

"On days we put them out."

"Haven't you figured out you're not on days any more?" Tom asked quietly and with more sensitivity than Robert would have thought possible. "Look, Bobby, it's turning into quite a night, and it's not even the weekend. It's about surviving out here, not putting out flares. If we make it through the night, that's a touchdown. If we do some law enforcement on top of that, well, that's a conversion."

"I see," Robert said.

Tom changed his tone and said with animation and humor, "I saw you get in it, Bobby. That David is one hell of a cop. Stick by him and you won't go wrong. I was glad to see you out of the car." Tom slapped him again, the way one football player might another after a play. "Relax, you'll get it."

Robert was not sure he wanted to 'get it.' The whole incident was so suddenly frightening and moved so fast he still wasn't sure what happened. He felt very uneasy. He did not say any of this to his training officer. Instead, he muttered underneath the radio traffic.

"It's Robert," he said, looking down at his feet.

Theo had managed to get them turned around and headed south when the whole shooting thing peaked on the radio. He felt the adrenaline hit and the police car seemed to pick up speed of its own volition. He was terribly disappointed when Hermondo slowed him down.

"Partner, that deal will be long over before we can get there," he said, by way of explanation.

They drove south on Preston with Theo listening to the radio traffic intently.

"Partner, you might want to stop for those red lights, seeing as some day—"

Theo slammed on the brakes and brought them to a squealing stop in the middle of an intersection, thankfully free of traffic at the late hour.

"As I was saying, seeing as some day you will be writing tickets to folks who don't," Hermondo said. "Back up out of the intersection, please."

Theo did as directed. They drove the rest of the way downtown in silence. Theo grew disappointed as the radio traffic told of the successful, safe arrest, and then returned to normal. He wanted to at least drive by the location. He drove down Preston hoping he would find a way to get up onto Central Expressway. He persisted in that project until he became hopelessly lost after the curves of Turtle Creek Drive.

"Partner, where are you going?" Hermondo asked conversationally.

"To where they were on Central Expressway."

"Why? They're all gone. Didn't you hear them clear on the radio?"

Embarrassment closed Theo's throat and he could not answer.

"We on a call?" Hermondo asked, calm as ever.

Now that Hermondo brought it up, Theo remembered that they were, although the immediate details escaped him.

"Um, I don't know," Theo said.

"Let's save the suspense. We needed to be at 900 Elm a long time ago. Let's say we head on over there now, okay?"

Theo nodded and stepped on the accelerator again. He passed four blocks before he realized he had no idea where he was going.

Bill and Roy had followed a small caravan of Dallas police cars to the Joker's for a beverage of their choice and access to the bathroom. As they rotated through the back area, they drank their caffeine-loaded brews and recounted their contributions to the arrest up on Central. Bill loved it. He felt accepted as he sipped his Diet Coke and listened.

"Partner, let's go find us a Lyzel," Roy said. "I'm tired of listening to all this revisionist history."

It was now the deepest of the night and traffic had lightened to the point of scarcity. The clouds had rolled in again and both Roy and Bill put on their regular issue, two piece rain suits. Bill settled himself behind the wheel and cleared them on the radio.

They drove down Ross Avenue toward the central business district and then south on the Central Expressway service road. Without having to check the map once, Bill was able to put them back in the neighborhood of the earlier call. They drove down the empty and deserted alley without incident. The rain started about then.

"Let's swing by her home address," Roy said.

Bill stopped the police car and started reaching for his notes. Roy gave him the address from memory, as well as the instructions for finding her block in the warren north of their current location.

Bill started driving as the rain came down in a steady stream of large drops. They covered the several blocks in just a few moments.

"Pull into the parking lot," Roy said.

A short driveway led around the side of a dilapidated two story apartment building. There may have been 10 units, total. The doors to each individual apartment faced out onto a sidewalk on the ground floor or a walkway on the second. Even in the darkness, Bill could see the unrepaired effects of time on the structure. He had the impression that several of the units were vacant, but he could not be sure. Bill swung the car around. As he turned, the glare of the headlights fell upon a tall, thin black male, wearing a white t-shirt and warm-up pants pulled low. The he top part of pink boxers showed over the top of the warm-up pants. He looked at the officers with an anguished expression, rainwater streaming down his face.

"That's Lyzel, get him!" Roy yelled.

Bill reacted. He opened the door and stepped out of the car, grabbing his PR-24 baton and his four cell flashlight as he went. Lyzel was having nothing of waiting to be got. He pivoted and started sprinting for the back of the parking lot.

Bill's first foot chase had an energizing effect on him. He felt elation at doing some real police work. He saw Lyzel easily vault the fence at the rear of the lot and thought he might do the same. His elation fled him, as did his breath, when he crashed into the fence instead of vaulting over it. He hit it so hard that he flipped over the top, landing almost head first in a pile of wet leaves and rubbish.

Like a majority of male Texans, Bill had taken many hard shots on the football field. Out of habit, before his head cleared, he popped back up and resumed his sprint. He caught a glimpse of Lyzel across the street, passing between two buildings into an overgrown lot. He heard the radio squawking, but he could not make out the traffic. With his baton in one hand and flashlight in the other, he could not slide the radio out of its metal clip and bring it up to his ear.

Bill ran through the two buildings, into the lot. He ducked under a low branch and ran up a small rise, gulping air. He saw another street just ahead and prepared himself mentally to be running on pavement again. His lungs burned. He planned to lightly leap off the rise and land in the street and continue running, but he had not counted on Lyzel.

Lyzel was standing with his back towards Bill, bent over at the waist, with hands on his hips. By the time Bill saw him, there was no time to stop or change direction or anything. Bill plowed into Lyzel at full speed.

The impact sent the two men tumbling and when they stopped, Lyzel was on all fours over a prostrate Bill. Lyzel's eyes were wide and he looked fearful, Bill thought. He realized he was quite scared himself. The two men looked at each other for just a moment, frozen in position.

"You're under arrest!" Bill yelled, his mouth on automatic pilot.

That caught Lyzel's attention. He evidently did not want to be under arrest, because he tried to get up and get on his way. Bill grabbed at Lyzel, his fingers catching a purchase on the waistband of Lyzel's pants. Bill pulled him back down. Perhaps out of surprise or perhaps clearly intended, no one will ever know for sure, Lyzel responded by punching Bill in the face.

Bill took it well. The shock and humiliation that hit him shortly after the punch itself did not cause him to loosen his grip on Lyzel. Lyzel must have been disappointed at that. His next course of action gravely escalated the conflict playing out at the edge of the abandoned lot in the middle of a rainy, late spring night.

Lyzel grabbed the handle of Bill's service weapon.

Bill instantly followed the training he received in Defensive Tactics at the academy. He let go of Lyzel and grabbed his holster, trying to wrap one hand around the thumb break on the holster and shoving the pistol deep into its holster with the other. He tried to roll to the side at the same time.

Lyzel tugged several more times on the pistol. When he could not pull it out, shifted its grip to another inviting target. Lyzel, out of rage or fear or frustration, grabbed Bill's throat and started squeezing. For real.

It dawned on Bill that he was in serious trouble. He tried to push Lyzel off, without success. He tried hitting Lyzel and a reverse wrestler's bridge. Nothing worked. Bill started to fade. He looked into Lyzel's eyes and saw fear and anger and confusion. Bill realized he needed to shoot Lyzel.

The lack of air after so much exertion accelerated the strangulation processes, and Bill became light headed. He tried to pull his pistol, but found it blocked by Lyzel's thigh. He thought his pistol being blocked by Lyzel's thigh was very unfortunate. He pushed against the thigh, mostly because he could not think of anything else to do, as the streetlights dimmed and his lungs burned. He started to panic. Rational thought let go. He rebelled against the idea that he was going to die here, in the rain and South Dallas mud. Bill rocked from side to side and struck out at the thigh blocking his pistol, without effect.

Then Bill looked up. He saw a giant bat. Orange flame shot out from under its wings. Maybe from rocket engines. With that, he knew it was over.

His resignation lasted only a moment because the bat knocked Lyzel right off of him and the two of them tumbled away. Bill sucked in large, lung bursting amounts of the cool evening air, unable to think of anything other than the joy of breath. When he regained his bearings, he rolled over and up onto his hands and knees. With his chest heaving, he looked toward the street and saw an officer in a blue rain slicker kneeling on a prone, face-down Lyzel. The officer held Lyzel's arm in an awkward manner and then snapped his silver handcuffs on his wrists, first one, then the other. The officer conducted a rapid but thorough field search of Lyzel's pockets and waist line before turning to face Bill.

"How you doing?" David asked.

Bill's first attempt at speech came out as a croak. He swallowed and tried again. "I'm okay," he said. He thought he ought to help with the prisoner, but as he moved to get up, David waved him back down.

"Sit for a while, you've had a rough go," David said. Then he pulled his radio from the clip on his Sam Browne. He waited for a gap in the radio traffic and said, "Dog-Five."

"Dog-Five," responded the calm male dispatcher.

"Five, suspect in custody and rookie found on Four's deal. Start an amb-lance to Clarence at King. The rookie needs some looking at."

"10/4. Do you need cover?"

"10/4. We'll need a two-man for transport. I'm away from my car."

"10/4."

"Hey," Bill said, starting to get up again. "I'm okay. I just need—"

"Sit down," David said sharply.

Bill complied.

David rolled Lyzel on his back and then sat him up. He had Lyzel bend his knee and move a foot close to his crotch. On command, he helped Lyzel stand up and walk over to Bill. Then he pushed Lyzel down onto the wet leaves.

"Lay still, my man. Won't be long now," David said to the prisoner.

Lyzel started crying.

"What's wrong with you?" David asked. David's slicker hung open and Bill noted the reversible orange liner.

"Man, I can't believe I was chokin' the Man. I'm fucked now," Lyzel said. Then he started sobbing.

That Lyzel could have been choking him to death one moment and crying, handcuffed, the next seemed unreal to Bill, who shook his head in disbelief.

"Bill, listen. You've been choked pretty good. We need to get you checked out. People who've been choked out may suffer a stress reaction that stops their breathing later, so we need DFD here and then we'll transport you or take you back to the station," David said kindly.

"Oh, I see."

"There's more. Roy's down. They're working on him now."

What was left of the bottom of Bill's world fell out. Several conflicting emotions clamored inside his chest. One on top of the other, shame that Lyzel had beaten him on the street, then fear, then shame at needing looking after. Roy's condition scared him and he hoped Roy would be okay. Then shame reared up and stayed as he realized he had not been around to help his partner.

"What happened to him?" Bill asked.

"They think he had a heart attack as he got out of the car back at the apartments."

With that, a bright red DFD pumper truck pulled up the street and turned the corner. David stood up, pointed his flashlight at it and shook it several times. The firefighters hit their air horn twice in recognition.

Firemen poured off the pumper and filled the street. A tall, lanky white man dressed in DFD blue, with his DFD baseball style cap on the back of his head opened a compartment on the truck, not far from the pump's control panel, and pulled out a large plastic tool box. Then he and a smaller man walked over to the two police officers.

"How y'all doin'? Quite a night for po-lice needin' care, ain't it?" the tall firefighter said. "What have we got here?"

"Rookie got choked out," David said, motioning toward Bill.

The firefighter knelt in front of him and smiled. "You go all the way out, partner?" he asked.

"No, just got lightheaded."

He nodded. "What about him?" he asked David, pointing at Lyzel.

"No, he's all right. Ain't that right, Coach?" David said.

"I can't believe I choked the Man. I am fucked for sure," Lyzel said.

"I guess you are," the shorter firefighter said. "It's a wonder you ain't dead."

They went on to examine Bill's throat with glove-clad fingertips, probing and feeling. He asked Bill if he had hit his head, and how the struggle had gone. After taking Bill's pulse rate and blood pressure and checking his pupils with a pen light, he rendered his diagnosis.

"He's okay. Someone ought to stay with him for another hour or so, but after that, he's good to go. Sorry y'all got a pumper, but the amb-lances are running tonight, I can tell you," he said. With that, the firefighters packed up and drove off, giving the police officers two blasts of the air horn as they left.

Mike and Randy arrived just as the fire truck pulled away. David leaned close to Bill and said quietly, "It would be really great if you could drive your unit back to the station."

Bill nodded in the affirmative.

"Hey Dave. How's the rookie?" Randy asked.

"Pretty good. What do you hear about Roy?" David asked.

"He was alive when they transported him. We haven't heard anything from the hospital," Mike said.

"Well, no news is good news, I guess. Say, can you guys transport Lyzel here and book him in?"

"We can do the reports, too, if you need us to."

"Nope. Rookie's going to do his own arrest report from the station," David said.

"What about Roy's unit?"

"Rookie's driving it back," David said.

"That true rookie? We hear you got choked damn near to death."

"Not so bad," Bill said.

"Need a ride to your car?"

"No thanks. Its just a block over. Me and rookie will walk it. Thanks, guys," David said.

As the rain slowed to a stop, the officers searched Lyzel again. After switching handcuffs, they packed him up and drove him away. Then Bill and David had a quiet walk back to David's patrol car. Bill had noticed the positive reaction of the covering officers to the news that he would do his own driving and paperwork. As he walked, he thought about the magnitude of the favor that David had done him.

The only solace Robert had was time. Time had allowed him to calm down from the shooting incident. Now his time was up. unfortunately, they were ready to clear again. Robert had dragged his feet, but Tom wanted to go back out there. That was how Robert found himself in the front passenger seat of One-Dog-Six's car in the wee hours of the morning when he would have much rather been changing in the locker room.

"One-Dog-Six, clear," Robert said into the radio.

"One-Dog-Six," was the dispatcher's response.

They drove away from the station, down empty roads, in silence. The radio broadcast a slower stream of traffic than earlier in the evening. Even after several blocks, Tom had nothing to say. Robert started to relax, thinking that maybe the rest of the night would be quiet, both inside and outside the car.

"One-Dog-Six?" called the dispatcher.

Shit, Robert thought, ignoring the call.

"That's us, partner," Tom said helpfully.

"Oh yeah," Robert said. He picked up the radio. "One-Dog-Six," he said.

"Six, it's the Six X. Domestic in nature. No comments but crying in background," the dispatcher said evenly, giving an East Dallas address.

"10/4," Robert said.

Tom leaned on the accelerator and pushed the police car. They would come up on an intersection where they had a red light and stop. Tom looked both ways, making sure there was no oncoming traffic before running the light and speeding off to the call. They arrived at an apartment complex typical for the area; two rundown floors of apartments arranged around an overgrown courtyard. Each home had an individual entrance facing the center. They walked up an open stairway and stopped by the call location, standing on either side of the doorway. Robert reached up to knock, but Tom stopped him.

"Let's listen for a minute, rookie," Tom said.

Robert did not hear anything.

"Pretty quiet for a Six X, don't you think?" Tom asked.

Robert nodded even though he did not have a clue as to what Tom meant. He was impatient to knock. The sooner they got in, the sooner they would get out and that would be that, he thought.

"Okay, go for it," Tom said.

Robert knocked on the door, several civilized raps. "Dallas Police," he said.

No answer.

Tom banged on the door loudly and rapidly. "Dallas Police, open up!"

"What—the hell—do—you—want?" a man yelled from inside.

"We would like to talk to you. Please open the door," Robert said.

"Open the door? It's the middle of the night!" the man inside asked.

"Yes sir," Robert answered.

"Okay, I guess I'll open the goddamned door."

A dead bolt turned and a chain slipped. Robert stepped up to the door way.

"Rookie, get back—" Tom started to say.

The door opened and the man inside was already committed to swinging the full sized axe. Tom shouldered Robert out of the way as the axe head struck, biting deeply into the framing for the doorway.

"Fuck you! Tonight you die, fuckfaces!" the man yelled.

Tom ended up directly in front of a white male, about thirty five or so and clean shaven. He had a manic, wild-eyed look to him, even without the blood that dripped down from his mouth and covered his chin, neck and most of his chest and stomach. He was bald on the top of his head and the hair that grew on the sides had been manipulated up into tiny bloody cones. He yanked mightily to free the axe from the doorjamb, but it remained embedded in the old wood.

Robert watched the man's head rock back on his neck. Tom had hit him so fast that Robert missed the first punch. Not the rest, though. Tom rapidly pummeled the center of the man's face with very competent, alternating straight punches, left right, left right, smashing his nose and adding more blood to the mix.

The man lost his grip on the axe and fell back into the apartment under Tom's onslaught. The bloody suspect and his training officer passed out of Robert's sight. All Robert could see was the wall with the axe sticking in it. The scuffling and grunts of effort coming from inside scared him. It scared him more than the action up on the freeway had. It rooted him in place and paralyzed him, and he knew enough to hate himself for it.

"Rookie," Tom called out, strain evident in the guttural outburst.

Robert said nothing.

"Rookie!"

Robert could not move.

"ROOKIE!"

Robert heard a loud crash and felt the vibrations of something heavy falling to the floor through his shiny black dress shoes. The loud grunts culminated in an unearthly scream, as high up the register as a young girl's. Robert's heart was in his mouth, and he could not move at all. Not to help Tom, who Robert now thought was dead, or to run and save himself.

"Will you get the hell in here?" Tom ordered conversationally from inside the apartment.

Robert's surprise and relief at hearing Tom's voice got him moving.

"Watch what you're doing—" Tom shouted, pointing at Robert.

As Robert entered from the hall, he brushed up against the axe, which loosened in the wood and fell to the floor.

"Dammit rookie, this is a crime scene!" Tom yelled. "No, don't touch it, for god's sake, don't touch the damn thing," he said, in response to Robert's bending over to retrieve it. "Get over here."

Tom had the man handcuffed. The prisoner lay face down in the living room, hands behind his back. He rolled from side to side, muttering and screaming. Robert was afraid he would get up and get away, but then he noticed Tom had his neck pinned to the ground with his left hand. Tom's left arm was locked out as he used his weight to put downward pressure on the man.

"Did you call for help?" Tom asked, glaring at Robert.

"No."

"Put out a signal 15."

Robert could not remember what that was. He knew a signal meant talking to someone, and right there was a wall mounted telephone. He thought he could remember what a signal 15 was if he had a second or two, and the walk over to the telephone would do him good. He was sure he could put it together in the walk over.

"Can I use the telephone?" he asked Tom.

"What the hell . . . Robert, you okay?"

"Yeah, um, yeah, I guess," Robert said. Tom was squinting up at him as he pushed down on the prisoner.

"Robert, look, this is going to get worse before it gets better. We need help and then we need to search the apartment. See the toys?" Tom said. He gestured to the left with his chin.

A press-board coffee table with pine laminate had been chopped nearly in two.

"That table is a mess," Robert said.

"Never mind the table. See the toys?"

Robert saw a cardboard box overflowing with old, dirty toys of different kinds. Several action figures, three ratty stuffed animals and a soccer ball were on the floor, against the far wall.

"Yes."

"You don't see any kids running around screaming, do you?"

"No."

"Robert, we need help and then you and I are going to search the apartment and it is going to be bad. You need to be with me here. Are you with me?"

Something about what Tom was saying, some conclusion that Tom was getting at, flitted around in Robert's brain, but Robert refused to pin it down and examine it. Tom looked at him with intent concern. In spite of hating him, Robert did not want to disappoint his training officer.

"Yes, I'm with you."

"Good. See that radio on your belt . . . that's it. Take it out."

Robert slipped the hand held radio out of its metal clip.

"Good. Wait for a pause and then say 'Dog Six, signal 15, our location.' Go ahead, do it."

Robert nodded and followed Tom's instructions. After his call, he heard the dispatcher put out their current address and the signal 15. Then the dispatcher tried to raise them again.

"Let it go for now," Tom said. "Get ready, Robert, because it is not going to be pretty."

"Why don't we let someone else do it, if it is going to be so bad?" Robert asked.

"We're the police, Robert," Tom said, with the emphasis on the first syllable, so it came out like 'PO-leece.' "We are the 'someone else.'"

Robert heard running boots on the walkway. He looked at the doorway, waiting with anticipation to see other blue sheathed people and feel the safety they would bring with them. He saw a young, black head appear and then disappear, rocking into and out of sight from the side. Then that officer stepped into the apartment, pistol out and in both hands, wary eyes in a young, handsome face.

Jimmy John slid in right behind him, scanning the room. He held his pistol in one hand, pointing down, trigger finger extended straight along the receiver.

"How you doing, Tom?" Jimmy John asked.

"Middling, Jimmy John. Mind the axe."

Jimmy John moved to the right and stood over it. "Evidence?"

"10/4. Could you guys take control of the prisoner? Me and Robert are going to search the apartment."

Without being given instructions, Jimmy John's partner holstered up and reached into his shirt. From the pocket of his ballistic vest that held the shock plate over his heart, he pulled out a pair of rubber gloves. He snapped them on and knelt near Tom. They silently switched out and he put his hand on the man's neck, where Tom's had been, and gathered up the fingers of the prisoner's 'cuffed hands and held them, as well.

"Partner," Tom said to Robert, "go take a look in that kitchen."

Robert looked to his right, at the kitchenette and breakfast bar arrangement.

"Go on, take a look between that bar and the refrigerator. We are looking for any little kids that may be hiding. Go on, now."

Robert started walking over when Tom stopped him. Tom made an exaggerated show of drawing his pistol and holding it in two hands, in front of him, but low and pointed straight down.

Robert understood and pulled his own pistol, a large frame double action automatic. The Sig Saur P226 carried fifteen rounds in the magazine and one in the chamber. Robert slowly stepped around the bar and looked down at the tiled floor.

"Nothing," he said. He almost laughed with relief.

"Okay," Tom replied, "come on back over here."

Robert did so, instantly feeling more stress than before he looked into the kitchen.

"We're going to the check down that hall, and the rooms down there. You follow me."

"Tommy, you going to need many more units?" Jimmy John asked.

Robert looked over his shoulder at the doorway and saw that a crowd of blue had gathered. All those officers knocked back his stress a little.

"Jimmy John, go ahead and slow them down. Can you send some folks to the neighbors? See what happened and maybe get a count of how many live here?"

"10/4." Jimmy John started talking on his radio and passing out instructions.

"Rookie, Tom said, "follow me."

Robert nodded and adjusted his grip on his pistol. With Tom instructing him, they leap-frogged down the hallway. Robert checked a linen closet without feeling too much stress. All the officers in the front rooms made him feel much better. While Robert thought about how much better the other officers made him feel, he and Tom stopped at a bathroom located off the hall. Tom stood in a combat crouch, pistol pointed down.

"Take a look in the bathroom," Tom ordered.

Robert immediately stopped feeling better. He wanted to ask Tom to look, or bring someone up from the front. Robert felt the urge to cry, and beat it back. He knew that would be a serious, serious mistake.

"Partner, you need to look in there," Tom said.

Robert decided there was nothing to do but go. He steeled himself and walked into the small room. The dirty pale yellow wallpaper was covered with blood splatter. Not just drops here and there, but whole sections of the wall were covered with sheets of drying blood. Blood pooled on the floor, centered around the toilet. Two gouges scored the lid. Enough blood had hit the tank, walls and shower curtain so that it had run in thick streaks. A sharp metallic smell left a coppery taste in his mouth.

"Partner, pull back that curtain and take a look in the tub," Tom said.

Robert thought Tom had to be kidding. He could not possibly look behind the curtain. Certainty regarding the unspeakable horror that waited in the tub froze him. He could not even turn away from the curtain to face Tom.

"You have to do it, Robert," Tom said.

Robert took a deep breath and shuffled up to the curtain. He forced his left arm out. He forced his hand to open, and then grab the edge of the curtain. Then he forced himself to slide the curtain open.

The tub was empty. This time Robert did laugh with relief.

"Okay, two more rooms and it's over. Follow me," Tom said.

Robert's relief faded. He followed Tom out into the short hall and then into the first of two bedrooms. A mattress with one sheet lay on the floor. Clothes suitable for a toddler were strewn about. Several brightly colored toys were in the middle of the room. A broken pressboard dresser sat deteriorating along one wall. Robert again felt sweet relief when Tom quick marched to the closet and looked inside.

"Okay, next room," Tom said, quickly passing Robert on his way out.

The master bedroom door was closed. Tom positioned himself and Robert on either side. Then he shouted a warning to the officers in the front that they were going in. Two officers that Robert did not know came up, automatically falling in behind Tom and Robert, one on either side of the doorway.

"Three live here, Mom, Dad and a little boy!" someone shouted from the front room.

"10/4!" Tom shouted back. "I'm going to call them out," he said to the little team. Then, to the door, "You in the bedroom, come out!"

"Fuck you, fuck you, fu-" Robert heard from the front; the handcuffed man shouting a stream of vitriol, quickly cut off by several loud thumps.

"All right partner, open it up," Tom said.

Once again, Robert felt fear and stress build to a suddenly unbearable level. He told himself the quickest way out was to go ahead and open the door. With his pistol in his right hand, he reached over with his left, turned the knob and pushed in.

Tom started moving and then suddenly stopped in the doorway. The two other officers plowed into him and each other (the one next to Robert had moved around him when he did not step off fast enough). Robert felt quite content out in the hallway.

"Partner, cover me, I'm going in," Tom said, without moving his eyes from whatever spectacle the room held.

The two other officers shuffled back to make room for Robert. They looked from the room to him with grim expressions set in pasty white faces.

"Come on Robert, it's our call, we have to handle it," Tom said.

Robert slid around so he could see. Two bodies were resting on linens that had been pulled off the queen sized bed. At first Robert thought the sheets were reddish-brown, until he noticed that the edges were a washed out beige. The amount of blood had overwhelmed the absorption ability of the sheets and had puddled on the worn out carpeting.

Of the boy, Robert could see only the small, blond head and shoulders. The woman had covered him with her own body while kneeling on the floor. His head was tilted back, but not excessively so, and his mouth was open slightly. His sightless eyes stared at a point somewhere above Robert. His mother's body must be covering up whatever damage had been done to him.

The damage done to her, on the other hand, was clearly visible. Several long, deep but narrow wounds were easily seen in her upper back. Her head had been almost completely severed from her body at the neck. The angle was wrong for Robert to see the severed bone and windpipe; but he could see the open space where her neck should have been and the flap of skin that only just held her head to her body. Luckily, she was face down. Robert would never have to deal with the memory of her lifeless expression.

"What do you think," Tom asked nobody in particular, "you think she sat here and took it?"

None of the officers answered.

"Cover me, I'm going to check the closet," Tom said again, and he moved into the room.

Tom stepped carefully, being sure to avoid the drying blood. He looked in a wall closet with sliding doors and then under the bed before retreating. Once out in the hall, still looking in, he slid his radio out of his belt clip.

"Dog-Six."

"Go ahead Six," the ever-calm male dispatcher replied.

"Six, call Homicide. We've got two 27s."

"Just because Homicide will want to know, if they're not all the way 27, how close are they?" the dispatcher asked.

"Also call the coroner. We don't need an ambulance."

"10/4."

As Robert listened to the radio exchange, he began to feel light headed. The floor started to undulate. He holstered his pistol and leaned against the wall. Tom had walked over to say something, but Robert could not make it out. His stomach flipped over once. Then its contents started churning. As he was about to open his mouth, his stomach flipped over again and a rising tide of bile reached the back of his throat. Robert clamped his right hand over his mouth.

"Not in here, partner!" Tom shouted.

Robert pushed himself off the wall with the idea he might strike for the doorway. Before he could take a step, he felt himself propelled forward at a run. Officers scattered every which way. He managed to step over the suspect, still cuffed and on the floor. He was pushed right to the railing of the second story walkway until it hit him in the stomach.

"Look out below!" Robert heard Tom shout.

Robert threw up, his first heave made up of some wet solids, then two that were just liquid and finally several that were dry. Tom, who had his collar and Sam Browne gripped firmly the whole time, yanked him back onto the walkway.

"Take a seat. I've got to finish up, then we'll give it to Homicide and get out of here," Tom said.

Robert sat on the walkway with his back to the wall. He wiped his mouth and hung his head down in embarrassment. Then with his hands on either side of his head, he gave in to the urge to cry.

Theo and Hermondo pulled up to the skyscraper trimmed in bright green neon. Theo felt the power of his office when he parked the police car in a no-parking zone convenient to the first entrance he saw. Theo knew the street was empty at this hour, just before dawn, but that did not stop him from puffing up considerably. In that they had finally arrived, Theo reached for the radio.

"Don't do it, partner," Hermondo said.

"But I have to mark out," Theo said.

"I marked out three hours ago when it became apparent that not only didn't you know where you were going, but wouldn't look in your Mapsco or ask directions. Now what are you going to do?"

"That's not fair, it's my first night!"

"Now what are you going to do?"

Theo fumed for a moment. "Get out of the car?" he finally asked.

Hermondo shrugged.

Theo opened the door and stood up. It felt good. It had been over an hour since they left the gas station. He bent at the waist and gathered his flashlight and his baton. Theo noticed Hermondo was not moving. He sat still, gazing forward. That annoyed Theo, who thought the old man could at least get out of the car. They were a two man element, after all. Theo interpreted Hermondo's lack of action as laziness, and decided to carry on alone, in the best tradition of young police officers confronting the old, entrenched mentality of careerist apathy.

Theo walked across the broad sidewalk to a line of glass doors. He tried each one in turn and found them all locked. He put his nose on the glass and looked into the deserted lobby. Theo was trying to figure out what to do next when the air horn from the police car went off right behind him.

Theo jumped about three feet. Upon landing, with both hands over his heart, he spun around to see that Hermondo had switched seats and driven onto the sidewalk, right behind him.

"Partner, get in the car," Hermondo said through an open window.

"But we have to—"

"Partner, get in the car."

Theo slid into the passenger seat, stung by the disrespect his training officer showed him. He even considered reporting Hermondo's conduct to the sergeant. Theo could recommend to the sergeant that he be assigned a new training officer, not that he would want to see Hermondo fired. Perhaps Hermondo could be saved as a trainer. Maybe the department had a re-certification process for training officers that had become complacent.

Hermondo drove slowly to the curb and gingerly dropped the car back onto the street. They turned left onto Houston and left again onto Commerce.

"Partner, what is the status of our call?" Hermondo asked.

Theo put aside his thoughts of Hermondo's termination in disgrace from the department to consider this new challenge.

"I don't know," Theo finally said.

"Look it up."

Theo considered the mobile display terminal, a black plastic box with a small screen, keyboard and several function buttons. It sat on a pedestal between the front seats. He pivoted it around and looked at the screen. The call sheet for their current assignment was showing and to buy time before answering, he read it carefully.

"Hey, this shows it was cleared on an n-code hours ago," Theo said indignantly.

"When I thought you wouldn't turn around until we got to the Canadian border, I had another unit swing by and handle the call. Now check our status."

Theo punched in the code to pull up his unit's current condition and found that they were off the call roster, on a specific assignment. "We're on a special," Theo reported.

"Yes," Hermondo said, "our special was driving around all night with me listening to you talk about everything except how to get to our call and what we were going to do when we got there." They stopped at a red light controlling an intersection empty of traffic. "Tonight was the last night of that, one way or another. Tomorrow night you will not have the luxury of taking all night to get to a call. I suggest you study up on your Mapsco. In the mean time, when we get to the station, fill out the rookie paperwork and mark yourself a five for tonight. In the comments section write 'trainee officer has incomplete grasp of city geography.' Then bring it to me to sign."

For the first time that night, the only sound in the car was the police radio traffic. Theo remained silent for the rest of the ride back to Metro, burning at the gross unfairness of it all.

Bill sat in the lounge area in front of the detail room watching the pre-morning network news. His eyes were on the screen, but he did not have the concentration necessary to focus on the news reader. Her voice buzzed in his ears. He felt drained to the point of exhaustion.

"Bill? Roy's out of immediate danger and admitted to the cardiac ICU. I've got to run out to the double 27, so I'm going to leave you with David here," Sergeant Karangekis said.

Bill could only nod. David and the Sergeant exchanged comments. Bill paid no attention. Then the Sergeant left.

"You did a good job tonight, especially for a second phase rookie," David said, sliding one of the chrome chairs with the blue molded plastic seats out from under the table and sitting down.

"Good job getting choked out," Bill finally replied.

"Not that part. What came after. You got back here under your own steam, took care of the equipment and finished up the paperwork. That's about all anyone can ask."

Bill shrugged and looked away.

"Anyway, shift's over for you. Shut down the unit and get out of here," David said, slapping Bill on the shoulder. "See you tomorrow."

"Will I get another trainer?" Bill was disgusted with himself as soon as he asked. Of course he would get another training officer. What the hell was he thinking?

David looked at him for a moment, without answering the question. Then he looked around the empty lounge area. "Want to get some breakfast?"

Bill felt awkward. He did not think it was his place to detain the senior officer. He thought he should have what it takes to get choked out and go home like it was the most routine of things, but he still felt afraid. He did not really want to go home to his place just yet. It made him feel weak.

"Sure," Bill said. "That would be fine."

"Then let's shut down our units and get the hell out of here before the days supervisors show up."

Long after Tom had failed to make good on his promise of giving it to Homicide and getting out of there, Costas had come and gone. The rest of the deep nights officers had switched out with days weenies. Robert and Tom were still at the scene. Robert had regained his composure and spent the balance of the morning following Tom around in a manner reminiscent of a chastised child.

The press had arrived and established their assault lines around the apartment complex. Television media deployed their cameras like crew-served weapons. Newspaper reporters, lonely displaced infantry, walked the lines in the shadows of their more glamorous compatriots.

"All right, Lieutenant," Tom said to a days supervisor, a female in her early thirties with a broad backside, a nickel plated revolver and mustache. "That will do it for us. We're gonna call it a night, if that is all right with you?"

She eyed the television cameras with a wary lust. "Go on then, have a good day," she said, without looking away from the people that could put her on television.

Tom nodded at Robert and indicated they should get going. In no time they were in their marked unit heading downtown. At this hour, with the sun fully up and the start of the workday not far off, they traveled down Gaston Avenue in a pack of commuter traffic.

"Will you look at this," Tom said. "We can't speed off because someone in this group would report us. They can't go there usual speed because they're afraid we'll ticket them. I mean this is crazy. All of us are actually going thirty-five. Can you believe it?"

Robert sat still and silent. Tom tried again.

"Well, I have to say that was a busy night," he said cheerfully.

Robert did not answer. The events of the night ran through his mind again and again. He felt disgust at his conduct, the residual fear from his confrontations and horror at the double murder. The clear, bright morning did not register with him at all. He was still in a strange bedroom with a dead family in the dark of night.

"They don't all go like that," Tom said, dialing up the good time radio to a country and western station.

A thought bubbled up to the surface of Roberts consciousness. Tonight would not 'go like that' if he was not out there.

"One-Dog-Six first from One-Dog-Six second?" a well rested male voice called.

"One-Dog-Six," Tom said, not waiting for Robert to pick it up.

That was okay with Robert. He was done with policing for the day.

"Six, you on your way in?"

"10/4," Tom said, "you need the car?"

"Negative, just the call sign."

"10/4. Dispatch?" Tom called.

"Six?"

"Show us out for the night."

"10/4."

"One-Dog-Six days, clear two." the other party said.

Tom had Robert log off the mobile display terminal.

"When we are like this, logged off, you can use the radio with your badge number as your call sign," Tom said.

Robert thought this idiot must be kidding. Robert could care less about how to use the damn radio. Who really cared how to use the radio when they just spent the morning cleaning up after a wack-o who chopped his family to bits? Robert remained motionless and silent, but incredulousness built in him to dangerous levels.

Tom must have picked up some of Robert's tension. "Don't worry kid, tonight will probably be a whole lot slower," he said, as they pulled into the Metro parking lot.

"Tonight!," Robert shouted, "Tonight? Stop the car." Robert yanked on the handle of the passenger door.

Tom swung the car around and parked in a spot. Robert had figured out that the door was locked by then. He slapped the power door lock switch and pulled violently on the handle. The door opened and he scrambled out.

"There won't be any tonight! I quit!" Robert yelled. He turned on his heel and stomped off towards the building.

"Hey! Bobby! Hey, wait up!" Tom yelled.

Robert stomped off for the sergeant's offices. Tom caught up with him at the door by the tall conference table.

Robert saw a days sergeant sitting behind the nearest desk, his head down, filling out a form of some kind.

"I quit," Robert said.

The sergeant looked up. Older than Costas, thin to the point of noticing, with a long neck, the sergeant wasted no more than a moment on Robert.

"Costas," he said, before hunching back over his paperwork.

A tired and harried Costas stepped out from one of the interior doorways.

"Tom. Robert. Hell of a night, huh?" Costas asked.

"I quit," Robert said. He felt frantic at this point. His heart beat as fast as a runaway train. He felt sweat bead on his forehead.

"Hey now, this type of thing happens from time to time. It's nothing to base a career decision on. I mean, you can't quit a job after a tough day every time one comes along, right Tom?" Costas said with a soothing voice.

"Uh, yeah." Tom tried as well for a reassuring tone, with somewhat less success. "Stuff like this doesn't happen every night. Just sometimes."

Robert saw Costas shoot Tom a look of annoyance.

"I don't care!" Robert shouted. "I never spent a night like that before and I don't plan to ever do it again. I quit!" He went to take his badge off his shirt with the idea that he would give it to Costas. His hands shook so badly he could not operate the clasp. He started to hyperventilate. Frustration grew and turned to rage.

"I quit! I'm not going out again!" Robert yelled. He realized neither Costas nor Tom were saying anything. He looked around. The days sergeant flipped his form over and started on the back. Costas looked sympathetic. Tom tried to suppress a smile, without complete success.

"Fuck you!" Robert yelled. He grabbed his badge and yanked as hard as he could, literally ripping it off his shirt. He held it in his right hand and considered the back of it. The front shiny part faced his palm and all he could see was the rough, unfinished metal and the heavy duty clasp. He slammed it down on the desk, shiny side up.

"Robert, go home and get some sleep," Costas said. "Consider what you're doing. A little rest and a meal, you'll feel better. Why don't you wait until you come in tonight to do this?" Costas said.

Robert asked himself why they were so dumb. In an effort to make them understand, he leaned forward and shouted to the point of spraying spit, "I quit! I'm not coming back!"

Robert saw Costas's expression firm up. His eyes turned hard and his mouth became a tight line. "Okay Robert, I hear you. I'm sure you understand I'm going to need your pistol, too." Costas spoke in a tone no longer friendly, but not unfriendly either. Robert got the idea he was not getting to his car with the weapon strapped to his hip.

"Okay. Okay. You want it?" Robert reached for his pistol.

"No!" Costas yelled. It was not a high pitched, out of control yell, but an authoritative bellow that stopped Robert cold.

"I'll need the whole belt," Costas said conversationally.

Chapter 4

Andree woke later that day, in the early afternoon. He had slept in his Oak Cliff house; a small neat two bedroom home in a middle class, black and Mexican neighborhood. Andree didn't know or care anything about some white guy named Oswald shooting another white guy named Tippet long ago, right around the corner.

Andree slid along the silk sheets of his king sized bed until he was able to swing his bare feet onto the floor. He stood up and stretched his compact body. He was very strong, and possessed impressive muscular definition, if not bulk.

Andree surveyed the room. The tan of the walls complimented the expensive pine bed, dresser and matching hardwood floor. It pleased him. He liked rest of the house, too. He felt pretty proud of himself that he owned this property and that he had the foresight to live this way.

'This way' meant the apartment at Akard and Belleview, for business, this house, for getting away, and the place he bought his Mama in Garland. Andree padded along the cold wood to the bathroom, where he took a long hot shower, easing the knots and kinks the trip south of the border had left in his muscles.

Andree finished up and dried himself off on a soft thick cotton towel. Then he threw it in the basket with the dirty laundry from his trip. He liked having a Mexican woman come in to straighten up and do his laundry. He insisted on a clean place and clean clothes. Andree liked things spotless and organized in general. He slipped on a pair of shorts from the dresser and walked out of the bedroom to the kitchen. The walls of the hall and kitchen were painted eggshell and like the bedroom, were bereft of wall decorations.

Andree opened the refrigerator to find the juice had turned and the milk curdled. He poured the remainder of both down the drain and sat, frustrated, with a glass of water. Andree considered his day. The H was safe for now, so that was not a problem. He wanted to see his mother, and the kid that sold for him over on Hall. Shuka, his chief lieutenant, would be pissed he didn't run right over, but what the hell. Shuka was getting a little too big for himself, especially considering what the kid over on Hall had to say.

Andree returned to his bedroom and dressed in a collarless, white short-sleeved pullover and baggy black cotton trousers. He put on two gold necklaces, a thin gold wristwatch with a gold band on one wrist and a thick gold bracelet that looked like nuggets strung together on the other. He slipped his money clip loaded with cash, his driver's license and nothing else into his pocket. After he clipped a beeper to his waistband, he grabbed the keys to his "off-duty" car and made for the garage.

When shopping for the house, the detached, two car garage had been a big seller for Andree. He had room to keep both cars off the street. He pulled the full-width door up and there sat his old, knocked about Grand Fury and his newer, perfectly detailed, brown over tan Cutless. He unlocked the Cutless and slipped into the leather seat. The meticulously detailed coupe, with its acres-long waxed hood, started right up; the air conditioner already in the 'on' position. Soon he was styling down the freeway, radio blasting R&B, the manufactured cool breeze blowing on his face. He ruled out eating on the way to Mama's, because if she was breathing, she'd whip him up something good and see to it he cleaned his plate.

He drove into another working class neighborhood, this one off of Centerville Road, outside the LBJ Freeway loop. Not all of the homes on the block were neat and organized, but the small three bedroom his Mama lived in was. Andree made sure of it. He even paid for the landscaping, done by a white college dropout and his crew of wetbacks. Andree pulled into the driveway behind the purple Chevy Nova he had bought his Mama two years ago.

He smelled it as soon as he walked in. Andree's mood changed dramatically, from even-keeled to raging angry. He found his Mama and Auntie Lita in the kitchen. Mama, a small stout church lady with glasses and short black and gray hair, wore a bright house dress. Auntie Lita, a long time friend of his mother's, as opposed to her sister, wore bright yellow stretch slacks and a loose white v-neck t-shirt. Both women were in a state. With the tangy, sweet odor of marijuana hanging in the air, Andree could figure out why.

Andree knew his mother had no tolerance for drugs at all. He took great pains to hide his own involvement in the trade from her. Long ago he told her he had gotten out of it and had used the money he had made to start an import-export business. Auntie Lita had moved into his Mama's house with a niece a while back. Andree could guess who was doing the smoking that had the church ladies all wound up.

Andree tip-toed deeper into the house. When the ladies saw him, he put a single vertical finger to his lips to keep them quiet. He stalked his way down to the bedrooms. Two doors were open and one closed. He tried the knob of the closed door and found it locked. Andree stepped back, raised his right leg and kicked the door. The cheap nob sprang open.

Andree sauntered into the room as two teenage girls scrambled about. Both wore tank tops and panties. Lita's niece, holding a joint pinched between a thumb and index finger, and her friend waved their hands frantically, trying to move the smoke out the open window. Andree grabbed Lita's niece by the wrist and picked the joint out her fingers.

The girl, a trim pretty thing, made a try to snatch it back. "Gimme that, it's ours!"

Andree reared back and slapped her hard enough to knock her to the bed. She landed with a yelp.

Her friend, rounder with amazing breasts bobbing under her tank top also tried, only to suffer the same fate. The two of them nursed smarting cheeks and nasty expressions.

"You don't go smoking shit in my Mama's house," Andree said quietly. He squelched the joint's glowing tip with fingers and sniffed the smoldering, home-rolled cigarette. "This is about some sorry shit. Where did you get it?"

The girls glared at him.

"I asked you a question," Andree said, with menace and quiet authority. "Where did you get it? Don't make me ask you again."

"At school," Lita's niece said.

"That no-good school. I should go down and talk to that principal again," Lita said. She and his Mama had come down the hall to supervise the goings-on.

"You ladies go on back to the kitchen now . . . Mama, go on," Andree said.

His Mama turned to go, but Lita had more to say. "Why I ought—"

"Get your fat ass back to the goddamned kitchen!" Andree roared.

Both of the old ladies scampered away.

"You little bitch," Andree continued, only a little less forcefully, grabbing Lita's arm and yanking her to her feet, "this sorry shit can cost Mama her house! The Man will take every damn thing! Where is the rest of it?"

The girls looked scared now. "Esse has it in her book bag," Lita's niece said.

"Give it to me."

Esse jumped up and dug through a blue book bag full of everything except books. In short order, she produced a plastic sandwich bag with two more joints in it. Andree grabbed the bag away and pointed to the bed. Esse sat as ordered, all her sass gone.

"Only losers use," Andree said, reducing the three joints to paper and leaf in the sandwich bag. "It fucks up your head. And then the Man comes and takes everything. If I ever find shit in this house again, I'll put you and Auntie out on the street. You see what I'm saying?"

The girls sat mute, watching him work the joints into litter.

"You see what I'm saying!" Andree yelled, taking one step toward the girls while raising his hand as if to slap one of them backhanded.

Esse recoiled and the niece winced.

"You ain't shit to me, either of you. I'll put you slut asses out, understand?"

He had their attention now. They nodded in unison.

"Bitches," Andree muttered, as he walked over to the bathroom. He dumped the contents of the bag into the commode and flushed. Then he threw the bag in the waste basket.

In the kitchen, he kissed his Mama. "Hey you, Mama?" he asked.

"Them girls gave me such a fright, Andree, I don't know what to do," She said. "Can I fix you something?"

"Got anything made already?" he asked, sitting down.

"Got some ham and cornbread and yellow rice I can heat up," Mama said, placing a pitcher of iced tea and a glass on the spotless kitchen table.

"Mama, that would be real good," Andree said, pouring for himself. "Auntie Lita, that girl brings any more shit into this house and I'll put you both out," he continued, before taking a long pull at his drink.

"Now you wait just one—"

"Out. O-u-t."

They locked eyes, until she looked away. "Go on and find something to do. I want to visit with Mama in peace. Go on now."

The woman slowly shuffled out of the kitchen.

"Andree, I don't know what to do," his Mama said, as she puttered around the kitchen. "Auntie Lita is a good Christian woman, but that no good Towanda brought the Devil into this house. Heaven knows about your struggles with the Devil, but what am I supposed to do?"

"Pray on it Mama," Andree said, rubbing his hands together over the meal Mama had heated in the microwave oven he had bought her. He dug into it with appetite.

"Andree, they still saying bad things about you." His Mama sat down herself with her own glass of tea. "They say you are still in with the Devil. That you deal with them drugs. They afraid of you. I know you had your struggles. Andree, tell me they is wrong."

Andree put down his fork and knife. "Mama, on my word, I ain't down with that no more. They is just jealous. I do the import thing. Right now I got 15 washing machines in a warehouse. They up from Mexico. It be small, but that's how it be, a little at a time. For now."

The old woman incompletely held back some tears as she stood up and walked over to him. She hugged his head to her chest from the side. "Praise Jesus. Don't give in to no temptation, son. Praise Jesus."

The rest of his meal, and the visit itself, went well. Lita and the girls stayed out of sight. As the sun began to set, Andree extracted himself from his mother's kitchen. Behind the wheel of his car, he did not think at all of the lying he had done. He thought instead about coming back in a few days. Coming back and running Lita and the girl off. They ought not be talking all that trash to his Mama. Then he decided to let his Mama handle things a little longer. Andree found it important to see to it that his Mama be as comfortable as possible. He knew she liked Auntie Lita's company.

After a quick drive down I-30, the last of the evening rush hour traffic slowed him down as he crossed the Trinity. Once back at his house, he opened the garage and pulled the Cutlass in. He left the garage door up and went inside.

Andree put a sea green shirt on over the one he wore. Then he slipped into a short-sleeve button-down shirt in a green and white plaid. He wore it open. He switched the baggy pants for jeans several sizes too large. He pushed them low on his hips, exposing his boxer shorts. After adding more gold to his neck and wrists, he put on an expensive pair of basketball shoes. Andree headed back out to the garage.

This time he sat behind the wheel of his battered Plymouth. He turned the key and the large engine caught instantly. It settled into a low rumble. Andree drove back the way he had come.

The going and coming, the back and forth annoyed Andree keenly. Then he reminded himself about his plan for success. He kept his professional life sharply separated from his personal life. He forced the self-discipline necessary to spend time on such things. Switching cars and the like were a way to beat the Man. He knew intuitively that when he got weak, the Man would win. The Man would swoop in out of nowhere and take everything, the money, the property, his life. Then he would be locked up or dead, a bad thing either way. So he switched cars and retraced his steps, forcing himself to stick to the plan.

This time, however, he stayed off of the freeway. On the streets, he drove north through the busy central business district and picked up Ross Avenue. He drove out of downtown with the business commuters. The whites that left this area for their subdivisions of fenced-in single family homes rarely came back after work. When they did, they were usually looking to score product. Andree and his colleagues charged them retail, special inflated prices for whites with cash. He made a left onto Hall Street. Several blocks later, by the Thompson's Chicken place, he turned right into the projects.

The Hall Street projects were several acres of red brick town homes with peeked roofs and faded brown doors. Dantwan had spent his life confined to this area, a world of single parent families, where the police were ubiquitous and hope was not. Where the children that had grown up and out never visited after dark. Where business competition for the most valuable retail space, the corners of the project streets and Hall, expressed itself as bullets from the barrels of .25 and .32 automatics carried in the underpants of the local entrepreneurs.

Andree parked on the southern edge of the neighborhood to facilitate a quick getaway, although it was still too early for his enemies to be about. He threaded his way around small groups of residents. There were the young women with young children, the lethargic young men, and the teenagers, all visiting in the late afternoon heat. No one paid him much attention. He found the home he wanted, climbed the concrete steps and knocked softly through the screen-less screen door.

"Yeah?" a woman's voice called out from within.

"Dantwan around?" Andree answered.

There was a scramble and a scuffle from inside, the sounds of a sliding chair and moving feet. Andree hoped they wouldn't dump any inventory down the john.

"It be Andree," he said, tapping the door again, in an effort to be helpful.

Finally, a head appeared in the front window. A young woman took a quick look at him and disappeared into the town home. A moment later, the door opened.

"Yo, man, come on in, come in," Dantwan ushered him inside.

Dantwan was taller than Andree by quite a bit. His well muscled body, long and lean-limbed, moved with a natural grace. The nineteen year old had freshly shaved his round head, which matched his features. Andree looked up into round brown eyes, round cheekbones, a round chin and a handsome nose with wide, round nostrils.

"Man, you back? Good to see you, man," Dantwan said, guiding Andree through the living room.

A couch missing legs on one side lined the far wall. A television set stood on several plastic beverage crates close to Andree, blaring a movie no one watched. Two mismatched armchairs were positioned haphazardly. Dingy paint and ratty carpet set the tone for the place. Two girls in their late teens, possibly related, stood in the opening between the kitchen and the living room, waiting with watchful eyes for whatever might happen next.

Dantwan raised a large hand and motioned toward the two girls. "Ladies, this here be Andree. My man, this be Annabel and this here is Mikalia. They be sisters."

Both girls wore their hair moderately short. Annabel had dyed hers blond, a look that annoyed Andree. Blond hair on a sister, like she be from Norway, he thought. Both were thin-limbed and had generous breasts, which strained against t-shirts. They wore stained shorts and flip-flops. Annabel's legs were dynamite, and Mikalia's were thin, but not overly so. Annabel seemed older. She was the taller of the two, about as tall as Andree, and her waiting included a dose of attitude. She must have been a little older than Dantwan. The younger sister, younger even than Dantwan, smiled a little at Andree, then looked down at her feet, then at her sister.

"Hey," Andree said, sporting his best come-to-sell-you smile.

The girls murmured a greeting, still unsure of what was expected of them and where the meeting would go.

"Andree be the man, so let's get him something. Andree—"

Annabel cut Dantwan off. "You done ate and drank everything in this house," she said in mock anger, crossing her arms underneath her breasts and shifting her weight to one side, canting her hips. "Just what you think we got left to give him?"

Andree pulled out his cash. "What say we get some Thompson's and some malts from the store over there on Hall?" he asked, counting out several twenties, more than enough for dinner for four, although he himself was not yet hungry again. The taste of Mama's ham was still in his mouth. "Maybe y'all could run and get it?"

Annabel appraised him with a flat stare, which he met with a smile, before taking the money and sauntering off. Mikalia followed her sister out, shyly smiling at Andree as the door closed behind her.

"Anyone know you're here?" Andree asked, all business.

"Um, no, like you said."

"Okay. Did you give him numbers?"

"Yeah. I told him the right numbers. I'm, like, I'm sorry Andree, but they's lower than I expected." Dantwan walked over to the couch and sat down, looking sheepish.

Now Andree wondered if they were in it together, but then had second thoughts. If that were true, he would probably be dead by now. He sat down in one of the armchairs.

"How much lower?" he asked Dantwan.

"Yo, not lower, I mean not as high as I thought. Like, the new corner only brought it up to $7,463.00. I thought it may be more, you see what I'm sayin'?" Dantwan shrugged, looking worried.

Andree noticed the sweat on Dantwan's brow. He liked it when they sweat. He hoped this kid would always sweat at coming in lower than projections. Shuka used to sweat, although he doesn't any more.

"That's it? Total? Like, for the week?"

"No my man," Dantwan laughed and reclined in the couch. "Like, that's what I gave up to Shuka, after the payments."

Andree did the math. With what the street sellers earned, and his payments to Z-ho', the gang leader that controlled the corners, and Dantwan's take, they brought in almost $14,000.00 for the week. Andree was pleased with the figure. First off, Dantwan was not smart enough to skim only a little (his kind would take a lot). At that amount, they were only a little off. Also, it meant some $5,200.00 to him (he rounded Shuka's take up, for old times sake), out of which he would be responsible for providing the wholesale cocaine for the crack that they were selling.

He laughed to himself at this, because while he did not know the exact proportion of raw cocaine that went into the crack that became the $5,200.00, he did know he was rich and getting richer. The Hall operation was the smallest of four that he owned. He bought the powder they cooked into crack directly from a source out of the country. By not having to pay the man who brought it in, he was making a killing. The heroin thing was going to really put him on the map. Too bad about Shuka, though.

"You gave Shuka the money?" Andree asked.

"Yo, Andree, you know it, man." Earnest expression on Dantwan's face.

"You been out of sight since?"

"Right here with the sisters, bro'."

"Who saw you pay up?"

"Yo, Andree, you sayin'—"

"I'm sayin', 'who saw you pay up?' mother fucker."

"Yo, yo, okay. Me an' Shuka did it at the McDonald's on Commerce. No one from us, but you know, someone may have seen."

"At the McDonald's? You crazy? What the hell you do it there for?"

"Shuka said. He say he can't make the time at Splendid, man. We did it at lunchtime, too. It be crazy. All them people." Dantwan scoffed and looked disgusted.

The girls came in carrying bags and jabbering about their purchases. There was the chicken and fries, chitlins and malts and cokes. As the others prepared the spread in the kitchen, Andree evaluated Dantwan's veracity. He considered the situation and thought it unlikely that Dantwan was either lying to him or deviating from the plan. He trusted the kid. Of course, he had trusted Shuka for years and now look at what was going on.

Mikalia came out with a plate of Thompson's chicken and fries and a can of malt liquor. She knelt at his feet and rested the food on his knee. Smiling shyly, she opened the can and handed it up to him. He smiled back and accepted it. He kept his eyes on her as he sipped at the cold golden liquid.

The others came in with their food and sat down. A little party broke out, with Annabel and Dantwan making enough noise for the four of them while Andree and Mikalia sat next to one another in comfortable silence.

"Yo, Andree, what you gonna do tonight, man?" Dantwan asked.

"Later I need to visit Z-ho'. Pay my respects, you know what I'm sayin'?"

"I know it, man. He be coming around later, like way after dark. Stay here, man. Let's hang."

Hang indeed. Dantwan and Annabel obviously had something going and Mikalia appeared ready to get something going with him. He needed to lay low. He wanted Shuka to stew for another day, anyway. For now, he needed to kill some time in private before he could see Z-ho'. After that, he could crash back in his Oak Cliff house. He liked that house. It was a lot cleaner than this dump.

Still and all, some young stuff to pass the time in the early evening would be nice. Andree looked over at Dantwan. He and Annabel were deep in a private conversation. Dantwan was a smart young up-and-comer, but he still had a lot to learn. One of the things he needed to learn was how to live in a clean place. Andree did not think he would have any trouble teaching him that.

Chapter 5

At the same time Andree was visiting his Mama, David was dreaming about running across the hard packed Iraqi soil with the pistol in his hand. He wore the old olive drab sateen fatigues from the first part of the Vietnam war. A gunmetal sky met the low horizon ahead of him. He pumped his legs like pistons, but never came any closer. He felt fear as something disquieting more than disrupting. Even as he knew he ran toward something unpleasant, he kept at it. His paratrooper boots slammed into the hard, hard ground. His running with the pistol in his hand bothered him because that was something he would never do. Everyone knows you run holstered, drawing only when you need to have the heat out. The bell rang and rang.

David tried to concentrate on his running, but the bell kept ringing. There was nothing on the horizon but he knew about ground contour. Wasn't the team behind him in a fold by the main supply route? No telling what waited for him up ahead. David tried to turn, to look behind him, but in the context of the dream, he was unable to even look over his shoulder. The bell kept ringing and pulling at him until the desert faded into his Dallas apartment. He sat up, sweat covering his neck and chest. He had accidentally left the telephone ringer on. Rookie shit. He looked at the digital clock with the blood red numbers. It was a wonder his first call hadn't come in before 2:00 PM.

"Yeah?" he said into the receiver, as he wiped the sweat from his neck with the edge of a sheet.

"David?" a lovely female voice asked. Charlene calling during the school day, now that was something.

"Yes, how are you?"

"Its Carrie. I didn't wake you, did I? Tom's been gone for a while."

Carrie. Tom's wife. David could see her clearly. Blond pony tail, thick glasses and cheekbones like apples. The body of a tall thin teenager with absolutely no indication she pushed out kids like clockwork.

"Carrie, how are you?"

"I'm doing good. How are you? David Lane, you need to come on out here. Tom is going to smoke some bar-b-que soon. Can we count on you?"

"You sure can Carrie. I can't wait."

"That's great David. Hey, I'm calling because Tom told me about the thing with the news people at the airport and what Charlene done, you know, about what she told them and all. I just wanted you to know, that is not the way things are done in Texas. Engagement is an important thing, and it could be handled better than that. In fact, a friend of mine will be visiting soon, up from the hill country, and, maybe, if you wanted, I could introduce you, and you could maybe see that things are done differently out of the big city."

"Carrie, I might take you up on that."

"I can't believe I'm doin' this. I don't mean nothing bad about her, but David, that woman just does things different, is all. If you could see me, I'm all red in the face. When Tom finds out about this. He's goin' to kill me."

"I'll never tell," David said.

"No, but I'll snitch myself off just as soon as he walks in the door. Oh, I need to go. Pammy is pouring milk all over the floor. I'm sorry for meddling, please forgive me?"

"All is forgiven."

"David, you come on out any time and don't wait for an invitation. I have got to go. One of the dogs is in the milk. Buster!"

David hung up the dead telephone. He thought the world of Carrie and Tom. Carrie had adopted him as soon as she knew for sure that David was one of those Yankees that could be trained.

He had gone to his first rodeo with them and had his first home-smoked brisket, actually his only home-smoked brisket, at their place. Carrie, with Tom right there, had taught him enough of how to two-step to venture out and find a partner by himself.

Carrie was not known for her outspokenness. David guessed Charlene's large scale fibbing about the engagement was something Carrie could not take lying down. Not when it involved someone she cared about. In small and subtle ways, she had let him know before that she thought he could do better than Charlene. She had never stated the case so bluntly before.

David dragged himself to the bathroom where he shaved and showered. He wanted to get to the station before a certain days sergeant went home. Then, already downtown and with time to kill, he thought he might use the station weight room for a workout and afterward, get something to eat. Maybe if he called Charlene, they could get together. They had not even talked since David arrived back in town two nights ago. Calling her now would not help. She was in school and would not be home until four.

David slipped on some blue jeans, a button-down khaki shirt with a button-down collar and a pair of black ropers. After grabbing his badge and wallet, he slid his small holstered Beretta inside his jeans and put the spare magazine on his belt in a holder. At the hall closet he put on a faded denim jacket. As he scanned the room before he left, his eyes fell on the kitchen table. He had sifted through the mail and made two piles, stuff to deal with and junk to get rid of. One letter sat off by itself. He had not decided about it yet.

David drove down to Metro, struck by the normalcy of the afternoon traffic and people going about their business with only their personal cares on their mind. He seemed to be stuck in a loop contrasting busy, normal America with the devastation he left behind in Iraq. Not that he had a problem with the results. The war in the gulf had probably been one of the least wasteful wars in history. Whatever the real reason behind the American intervention to save Kuwait, kicking ass on Saddam Hussain bothered David not at all.

It did, like a rough shift on deep nights, make him tired. Tired and surprised that life went on, errands run, dinner made and the small emergencies of American life dealt with. Like, for instance, it always surprised him when the buildings of the central business district were still standing after a particularly bad shift. He always expected bombed out ruin, wisps of smoke rising from the rubble. Damn, if he wasn't tired.

David parked in the back. He skirted the patrol hangouts on his way to the offices of the Special Operations Division. The Mounted Unit, the Aviation Unit, the Bomb Squad and all the other really fun, non-detective assignments in the department were part of Special Ops. So was the Tactical Unit, the DPD's high risk response and riot control element. If he were lucky, Sergeant Foster would be in. If not, David would have to keep coming back. Some things had to be handled face-to-face.

"Lane, how in the hell are you, boy?" David had lucked out. The sergeant was at his desk, paperwork strewn all over the top.

The sergeant, a white male in his early forties with a bushy red mustache and a full head of red hair turning toward gray, looked the part of a tactical unit leader. Even sitting he appeared tall and radiated command presence. His arms and neck were corded with thick muscle and large purple veins.

The sergeant came to his feet, standing taller than David, and they shook hands before he waved David down into a nearby chair.

"You was off to the wars, weren't you?" he asked.

"Yeah, nothing like sand in your food. How are things at Tactical?"

A troubled look passed over Foster's face. "See here, Lane," he said, "I know why you've done come around. I remember what we were talking about before you left. On account of this here budget project," Foster waved his hand over the mess on his desk, "I ain't got the time to dance you up and down. I got no slots left. You hear about what's been goin' on lately?"

What could David say? He looked at the Tac sergeant with his poker face, the one he favored while out on patrol, and remained silent.

"Well, I had to use all my slots up. Now what I got is a platoon with thirty per cent ineffectives. Take you for instance. Your learning curve would be real short. I could use that military training and experience. You would be effective almost immediately but son, that kind of thing doesn't matter anymore. There's a color of the day today, and you ain't it."

David sat there meeting Foster's stare, trying to think of something to say. Disappointment at the unfairness of it and embarrassment, like he had been caught doing something wrong, danced around inside his chest. The silence became heavy and David decided not to plead his case or object, but to get the hell out of there instead.

"Okay Sarge, what can I tell you?" David asked rhetorically. "Maybe some other time."

"Sorry son. It really is our loss."

"Thanks. I won't hold you up."

David left the Special Ops area quickly. Back in the Metro patrol area, David stood in the hallway sorting out the situation. He stood in front of a communication that had been framed and posted on the wall, but did not read it. Instead, he worked over what he had just heard in his mind.

David was used to excelling. In the Army, he had worked hard and gotten a shot at Special Forces school. He worked hard again and qualified as a team member. After his enlistment, he had taken the college money and worked hard at school. He had carried a full course load, held a job and drilled regularly with the Ready Reserve. After college, he had worked hard to find a department that was hiring. After getting on with Dallas, he worked hard to be a good patrol officer, exercising common sense and fairness on the street. And now that he had paid his dues and would have already been in the Tactical Unit if he hadn't gone to Iraq, his luck had tapped out, qualifications notwithstanding. David's embarrassment gave way to anger.

"You suddenly take an interest in the Black Officer's Association, David?" Calbert said, appearing next to him from out of nowhere.

David had stopped in front of a posted copy of that association's most recent newsletter. He looked at the newsletter and then back at his black friend. Anger flared up like a hot spot left over at a structural fire. He was about to say something he would regret when his brains got a stranglehold on his emotions. After a brief but elongated pause, David noted Cal was wearing his uniform.

"Been to court?" David asked, as casually as possible.

Calbert's expression switched from open and friendly to wary. David thought that he may have shone some anger on his face.

"No, David. I'm on days now," Cal said.

"Days! You switched to days? Cal!"

"I know, I know," Cal said in a muted voice. He leaned in to talk with David as privately as possible. "But honest to God David, working with guys that knew me before I got the senior corporal thing was too much. People is choosing sides all over the department. You know, you the only white officer to congratulate me on my stripes."

Anger drained out of David. He sighed before he spoke. "Cal, you were one of the old-heads that taught me this job. Truth is, you should have been a senior corporal years ago."

"I can't take them tests, is all."

"I know it," David said. Then the men stood in comfortable silence for a moment. "Anyway, sorry to see you go. You've been on deep nights longer than I have. You've been there always. It won't be the same."

"Eleven years," Cal shrugged. "Anything on this here embarrassment interest you?"

David scanned the first paragraph of the newsletter, which started off with a purported summary of recent events around the department. It referred to the different patrol divisions as "plantations" and the deputy assistant chiefs that ran them as "Masters." The lead sentence read as follows: "Master Reed of Pleasant Grove plantation is keeping the community down by...."

"No, nothing," David said.

"Me neither. Hey, did one of the new rookies throw his badge on the sergeant's desk last night?"

"News to me. What happened?"

"Nobody really knows, just that y'all had a hard night and one of the rookies couldn't take it. He came back and threw it down on the sergeant's desk."

"Hadn't heard. Went out with style, anyway. You hear about Roy?"

"Oh yeah. Old ticker. Word there is he's doing okay, but won't be back for a while."

They walked slowly down the hall in the direction of the exits.

"Hey, you're still on deep nights. Why are you here this early?" Cal asked.

David really did not want to tell Cal. He thought that they had discussed enough of the race stuff. He wanted to come up with something else to say, but disappointment locked his brain on the one subject he did not want to talk to Cal about.

"David?" Cal asked, reaching up and lightly touching David's shoulder.

David allowed Cal to turn him so they faced one another again. David looked him in the eye and maintained his silence. Cal leaned forward and raised his eyebrows, emphasizing his question with body language.

"Before I was activated for the gulf, I was trying to get into Tactical. I just saw Sergeant Foster," David said.

"And there ain't no way you're going to get on now," Cal said.

"That's right."

"Even though you was in the green berets," Cal said.

"Right."

"Even though some of my people got on recently with no military at all and only two to three years with the department," Cal said.

David shrugged. "I don't know anything about who got on recently. I just got back."

"Well," Cal said thoughtfully, "that don't seem right. All your experience, plus your reputation in the department. That just ain't right."

Suddenly the situation, and even the department in general, made David even more tired than he had been earlier. He did not want to discuss it anymore, and did not want to be here until his shift started. And he was hungry.

"Cal, I got to run. I'll see you in the morning, I guess. Stay safe," David said, as he turned on his heel for the exit.

"Yeah, I'll see you later," he heard Cal say.

David decided on Mexican food at the Blue Goose up on Greenville. Then he thought Charlene might like to meet him there. He stopped at the nearest pay telephone and called her. Even though school was out, he knew he could leave her a message. Her machine answered and David told it where he would be before hanging up and heading on over.

At the restaurant, the pretty Hispanic hostess seated David right off. He ordered a plate of chile rellenos, rice and beans, and a dark Mexican beer. As he ate, he tried not to think about the department or Charlene. A cute, petite waitress with long blond hair hovered around, even though she was not waiting on him. He liked her bangs. The feelings that came up at the station had settled themselves into a tight little knot in his gut that ruined his dinner. He paid and headed back to his apartment.

Once there he found his running shoes and some shorts. After a stretch, he hit the pavement. By then, it was early evening and traffic approached its rush hour peek. He ran on the sidewalk until he reached a local park, where he ran the concrete paths that followed the course of a creek. After a short run of several miles, he showered, ignored his mail and watched television until he had to leave for work. Charlene never called. He ended up back at Metro, reading the latest Dallas Police Association newsletter at a table in the lounge area.

"A little early tonight, David?" Costas asked when he saw David at the table.

Costas smiled a salesman's smile. The sergeant also wore his uniform, his brown hair neatly parted. Even considering that sergeants started their day before their respective shifts, Costas was early.

"Costas, how are you?" David asked.

"Pretty good, I guess. May I sit down?"

"Sure, sure. What's up?"

"David, I've been out to Parkland. Roy is doing okay, but he's out for a while. I don't know if we'll ever see him on deep nights again, either."

"At least he's okay."

"Yup, at least that. But his rookie needs a trainer."

David saw what was coming, but had a sudden thought. "Hey, did some rookie quit last night?"

"Tom's rookie came in and threw it down on my desk. Can you believe it?" Costas leaned back in his seat and shrugged.

"Did he just throw it down with a 'this sucks,' or what?" David asked, curious now.

"No. He and Tom came in when they were done at the double homicide. I was still here. He stumbled into my office white as a ghost fighting back tears. Couldn't get the badge off fast enough. Me and Tom tried to talk to him, but he would not have anything of it. Threw it down and stumbled out."

"Wow. Did you get his gun?" David asked.

"Yeah. Gave it right up, belt and all."

"What if he want's to come back tonight?"

"Too late. I wouldn't have made a big issue of it if he had agreed to think on it some overnight and came in today, saying it was all a mistake. But he was adamant. I ran the paperwork through this morning. He's gone."

"Costas, that's not like you," David said, his surprise showing.

"He came to us shaky off days and with a questionable reputation from the academy. I thought his quitting might be best. Could you believe all that 'Robert' stuff?"

They shared a laugh at that.

"Anyway," Costas continued, "I need a trainer. I know what I told you yesterday, but I'm down senior corporals. What do you say?"

David did not particularly want a rookie. He wanted to relax and do the job without having to worry about a junior officer every minute.

"Wait, the rookie quit, so what's the problem?" David asked.

"Roy's guy needs a trainer."

"Um, I'll do it Sarge," David said, clearly meaning he would rather not, "but what about Tom? His guy quit, so now he's free."

"Ah, Tom." Costas lowered his voice, hunched his shoulders over the table and looked around. "He was already over at Vice when the recent personnel policy change came down, you know, the one about . . ." and here Costas hesitated.

"Yeah, I know."

"So they sent him back, even though his cousin runs Vice."

"Caroline is his cousin?" David asked. "I never knew that."

"Yeah. Second or third, I think. They officially told him it was because we were so down senior corporals that he had to go back to train. Once his guy threw it down, Tom went to see Caroline. She burned up some markers and he starts over there in the morning. Last white transfer for quite a while, I bet."

"I see."

"Roy's guy needs a trainer. Leslie isn't back yet and everyone else has rookies." Costas smiled at him. "Hell of a welcome back, especially since you don't have a cousin over at Tactical, but there it is."

"How'd you know about the Tactical thing?"

Costas shrugged. "Heard you took it well, too. There's been a lot of whining and crying around here lately. What do you say?"

David laughed. "Do I have a choice?"

"The rookie is a good guy. Did well on days and at the academy. He keeps his mouth shut. Not really, about the choice thing. I'll throw in Roy's days off, Sunday Monday."

"Well, weekends off. How can I refuse? I'd love to," David said, with a mild touch of friendly sarcasm.

"Sure. Thanks, Dave. I wanted a better homecoming for you, but it is what it is."

"It is what it is," David agreed.

Something down the hall caught Costas's attention. "I've got to go. See you in detail." Costas stood up. "Hey, Willie," he called out, taking off after another officer.

Well, it was just turning into a banner day, David thought. David knew from experience that when it's just you and the public, everything could go down the toilet in an instant. With the added responsibility of a new officer, that complicated matters. There was no telling what a rookie would do at any given time. The training officer had to watch them all the time. The rookie may or may not protect himself, never mind do the job. He did not want that responsibility until he had been on the street again, for a while.

"Whatever," David muttered to himself.

Eventually, theme music from HILL STREET BLUES played over the televisions and the officers filed into the detail room, taking their seats as they always had. The rookies, one body light, sat in front. He saw Bill sitting next to the tall goofy rookie that drove Hermondo to Denton last night. Everyone else ringed the room, backs against the wall, sitting by sector. David was not sure, but his rookie appeared a bit nervous.

"Okay, let's get started!" Costas shouted down the din. "Roy is doing okay, but is still in the hospital. We don't expect him back right away. Visits ought to be okay soon, I'll let you know what I know as soon as I know it.

"Tom's rookie quit last night. Kid threw it down on the desk after they got back from the axe murders. I have not heard from him, so I guess that's it. Tom himself was so broken up over it, he transferred to Vice."

Officers murmured to one another about Tom's transfer. David overheard several exchanges. None of them were favorable about management or the department itself.

"What that means is," Costas continued, "Roy's rookie goes with David."

Costas pointed at David. Bill turned around and David waved. The look of relief and the small smile that played briefly across Bill's face, visible in the instant it took for him to turn back, tickled David. Costas continued the announcements, reading off the rest of the administrative items.

"That's it. Stay safe out there," Costas finished.

Detail broke up and the officers filed out of the room. David dealt with the condolences of his fellows, until Bill made his way up close. David spoke before Bill could say anything.

"Why don't you start up the car," David said. "Log on the MDT, but don't clear until I get out there."

"Okay. What car is it?"

David gave him the number and the keys. He watched Bill quickly gather his and David's gear in two arms and half run out to the parking lot.

"Looks like that old boy was happy to get you," Jimmy John said, after sliding up next to David.

"No accounting for the judgement of young people today," David replied. "How are you doing tonight?"

"Getting by. You know how it is. Heard you struck out over at Tactical."

"Oh yeah. The new Dallas Police Department, I guess."

The two training officers strolled outside. Jimmy John's more advanced rookie waited in the idling car, transmission already in reverse. Jimmy John waved casually at David and sat in the car. Before he had the passenger-side door closed, the rookie powered out of the parking area. On the other hand, Bill stood in front of his unit, fidgeting.

"I'll drive tonight, but don't worry, you'll be behind the wheel soon enough," David said, opening the driver's side door.

Bill sprang for the passenger side of the car like a track star at the sound of the gun.

"Let's go to Joker's and then find a hole to talk in, okay?" David asked.

"Okay."

Once they were on the street, David picked up the radio. "One-Dog-Four, clear two. Show us on a special, please."

"10/4," replied the even male voice of the dispatcher.

They made miscellaneous conversation as they filled their white courtesy cups and then drove to a deserted elementary school. Since it was after midnight, they had the dark grounds to themselves. David backed the car into the loading dock and they were covered from the passenger side and the rear. They only had to watch the driver's side and the front.

"Watch for what?" Bill asked, sipping his soft drink.

"They take pot shots at us out here all the time."

"Who does?" Bill asked.

"Jicks. Sometimes you can hear a popping sound and if you look in time, you'll see the bright blue muzzle flashes blocks away. It's not really very effective fire, but every now and then they get lucky. Just before I left for the gulf, a deep nights cop in Oak Cliff took one in the leg."

"I remember that. That was someone shooting for no reason?"

"They had a reason. We were cops. But yes, that's it. Even a spent .25 can put you out for a few days."

Bill sipped his drink. David could tell Bill contemplated this new bit of information by the thoughtful expression on his face, illuminated by the security lights that half-lit the schoolyard.

"Anybody arrested?" Bill finally asked.

"Not that time. They were too far away. Kind of dangerous out here, huh?"

"You could say that," Bill said.

"Take last night. You got the shit choked out of you."

David was not sure, but it looked like Bill blushed a little. The kid kept quiet.

"You came back," David said.

Bill did not answer right away. "Well, yeah," he finally said.

"Robert didn't, and nobody choked the shit out of him."

David watched Bill smile. "No, I guess not."

Neither man said anything. The radio spit out a stream of traffic, filling the car with the sound track of real life.

"So this is second phase," David finally said. "You're assigned to three officers, one from each of the watches, not to learn how to be a cop. You do it to see how those three officers handle the job. I don't care how you did it on days. You are out here to learn how I do it. I don't care what you do when you get past me, but while you are out here, you'll do it my way, understand?"

"I understand."

"First rule is this: go home at the end of the night. Not to the hospital or the morgue, but home. This is something to remember every night for your whole career. Go home at end-of-watch. No arrest and very few situations require you to get killed. No law says you have to get killed. First thing is to stay alive. Everything else can be dealt with. Got it?"

"Yeah."

"Next, handle each call as they come up and that means finish the paperwork before clearing. Other officers might not do this. If you clear before the paperwork is done, you will end up doing it on your own time. Supervisors do not authorize overtime for paperwork.

"While we are on the topic, our paper is the only evidence of our work. When a cabinet maker is done, there are cabinets all over the place. When we are done, there is nothing except the paperwork. Good, thorough, brief paperwork is important. Our badge numbers at the bottom of the page is like the carpenter's signature on the inside part of some well-made cabinet. It's what we do and we need to do it well. Speaking of paperwork, have you got a notebook?"

"Um, yeah, right here," Bill said, as he checked his pockets.

"Domestic violence cards? Mental health rights cards? Police report number cards? Business cards for yourself? Complaint contact cards? Let me see them."

Bill frantically slapped his pockets, finding his notebook. "Um, David, I've got that other stuff around . . ." Bill said uncertainly, able to produce only one battered blue domestic violence card.

"Okay, our betters have decided we will carry and give out all these public information cards. It does not matter that they are completely ineffective, half the people we deal with can't read and the other half lose the cards before we pull away, but it is what it is. Can't give them out if you don't have any with you. When is your next court date?"

"Um, I . . . ."

"Next day off? Holiday?"

"I don't know."

David handed him a pocket calendar. "It fits in the shirt pocket. Like the one hundred percent genuine fake leather cover? Lovely shade of blue. Note the stamped departmental and association logos. Write down every subpoena and day off you get in here as soon as you get it. Guys blow court or come in on days off all the time. Deep nights has a way of confusing the hell out of you. Slide the number notification cards into this flap and slip it into your right shirt pocket, with the notebook in front."

Bill did as he was told.

"I carry my template for accident reports in there, too. Have you got one?"

"Yes, the little one."

"That's the only one you need. Arrange the other cards by size and put them in your right shirt pocket. After a while, you'll be able to tell which ones are which by feel. You'll be able to pick the right one in the dark."

Bill arranged the cards and slipped them into his shirt pocket, as directed.

"Where is your ticket book?"

Bill reached around his seat and brought up an aluminum clipboard that had about an inch of depth to it. Bill opened the hinged writing surface. He handed David a blue leather book, about as long and wide as a common business envelope and some two inches thick.

"You've got parking tickets in here, too," David said.

"Yes," Bill said.

David could hear the hesitation in Bill's voice, and wondered if he thought he was in trouble for carrying parking tickets.

"Good job. Like everything else out here, parking tickets are a tool. Not to carry them is foolish, because they can help, on occasion. Rest assured, however, we won't be riding around writing parking tickets."

Bill looked relieved.

"I'd like you to consider keeping this handy. When you step out of the car, slide it into your right rear pocket. This way you always have it. Nothing like directing traffic at a wreck, being disrespected by a driver and having to rummage around for your ticket book. Jam it up here, where the windshield meets the dashboard. By the way, that's a good place for a hamburger if you can't finish it due to an emergency call. Throw it out the window like on TV and you may just have thrown out your last chance for a meal that entire shift. What else is in the clipboard?"

"Um, ah, let's see, I've got . . . no . . . ." Bill said, sifting through the contents of the clipboard's main compartment.

David, looking over Bill's shoulder, saw mostly scrap paper and departmental memos of a general nature.

"Okay, those aluminum deals are nifty, but you need to carry something in it." David reached around behind him and pulled out his own old fashioned clipboard. David had stored a thick stack of different forms on it, secured with a thick rubber band. "I've got Detox forms, property forms, arrest forms, accident reports and a bunch of other junk on here. Good to keep in the car. We can get started on the paperwork on the way to wherever we need to go after a call. Take a look." David passed his clipboard over to Bill.

While Bill examined the clipboard, David thought about Charlene. He had to admit to himself that the situation did not look good. Truth was, he and Charlene had started off as a summer romance. From the beginning, David felt the relationship had a terminal date on it, based on comments she had made about the start of the school year. The war had lent a dramatic air to things. It occurred to David just now that the war may have been why she had stayed with him. Certainly his homecoming had been less than he had hoped, with that deal at the airport and her disappearing act.

Realizing Bill was done, David said "Make up something like that for yourself." He took back his clipboard. "Can I see your flashlight?"

Bill handed David the department issue four cell Maglight.

"Okay," David said, "this is what they gave you at the academy, right? Now here's the thing, you have to carry a decent light out here. One powerful enough to punch through the darkest aftermarket automotive tint. It could save your life, or more importantly, mine. This won't do it. Also, your light needs to be rechargeable or you'll go bankrupt buying batteries. You need to buy a proper light. Maglight makes one, I use a Streamlight and there are others. I don't care which one you buy, but you need to have it by next week. I can't make you get one. I can, however, fail you in the equipment category every night you are out here without one."

Bill nodded solemnly.

David felt like a pinhead for saying that, but he knew just how important a quality flashlight was on deep nights. The thought that he was right quickly overwhelmed his discomfort at spending $100.00 of his rookie's money, just like that. Suddenly, David became tired of listening to himself. He grew annoyed at his posture of omnipotence. He felt he had nothing more of value to say.

"What do you say we clear and answer some calls?" David asked.

"Sounds good to me," Bill replied, looking in the half light like he would much rather stay right there, where nobody was choking the shit out him.

"Dog-Four," David said into the microphone.

"Four," the dispatcher replied.

"Clear us from our special and show us two man."

"10/4. Dog-Four, it's a 6X, man blocking traffic, Ross at Greenville."

"Code 5," David said, heading east. To Bill he said, "lucky for us. That's way out of our sector, but not far from here at all."

David drove down some dark side streets before emerging at the intersection in question. A crowd had gathered. Cars trickled through the junction, most trying to turn from Greenville to Ross, in a very confused traffic pattern. David parked the unit.

"What do we do, Rookie?" he asked.

Bill looked back and forth between the intersection and David. "Direct traffic?" he finally asked.

"Hmm. Where does the dispatcher think we are?"

"Oh yeah." Bill marked out over the radio and then sat still.

"What's going on?" David asked.

"I don't know," Bill said.

David raised his eyebrows, but said nothing.

"Should I get out?" Bill asked.

"Why don't we?"

The two men exited the car and walked closer. David saw a black man wearing sweat pants and a white t-shirt rolling around in the middle of the intersection.

"Stay away! Stay away from me! I got the smilin' mighty Jesus! The smilin' mighty Jesus be on me! If you come close, it be on you! Stay away!" the man yelled.

"Any ideas?" David asked Bill.

"Should I arrest him and drag him out of the street?"

"While rolling around in the street is a traffic offense, I don't think we could get that arrest past the jail sergeant. Besides, I don't think this guy needs to be arrested. Let's call an amb-lance and see what DFD has got to say. And maybe some units to help control the traffic?"

"I got me the smilin' mighty Jesus! Y'all stay away!"

"Now would be a good time," David said.

"Sorry," Bill pulled the radio from his belt and started calling for the ambulance and some cover. David heard him put out it out as a signal 15.

"Negative, negative. We just need two one-man's to help with some traffic, probably be for a few minutes. Negative on the 15." In an instant, David had pulled his own radio and corrected the rookie's mistake. As units marked out over the radio that they were coming to help, David spoke to Bill.

"Be careful how you ask for help out here. A signal 15 means you are up shit's creek and you need all the help you can get right now, lights and sirens. For this," David pointed to the man rolling around in the street, "we ask for a one man. It doesn't matter how many people show up. It's just a way of letting the others know the situation isn't critical."

"Should we direct traffic around him?" Bill asked.

"I got me the smilin' mighty Jesus! The smilin' mighty Jesus!" the man yelled.

"The cars are going around him on their own. Listen, you don't direct traffic if you don't have to; it just causes wrecks. One lesson at a time, and right now we're on calling for help. At the middle level, when the situation could go down the crapper but hasn't yet, put it out as a 'two man, no hurry.' That's when you're doing the right thing and calling for cover before it all goes to hell, but not waiting for the shit storm to hit. Got it?"

"Got it."

"Good. This way no one wrecks out on the way over for no reason and you get a reputation as a level headed-officer who can be trusted. Right?"

Just then the Dallas Fire Department mobile intensive care unit arrived, with two more police units following. David had all the officers force the traffic into right turns only while the firemen approached the rolling man in the street.

"I got me the smiling' mighty Jesus, I do! I'm gonna die! Stay away or you die too! It's the smiling' mighty Jesus!"

With practiced efficiency, the firemen had the rolling man strapped into a stretcher and in the back of their vehicle in moments. The officers opened the intersection and congregated at the back of the ambulance. David was the last to walk over.

"One of the paramedics noticed a patient bracelet on him. He's calling the hospital now," Bill said.

"I got me the smiling' mighty Jesus!" the rolling man yelled.

The paramedic hung up the telephone. "Shut up, you idiot. You have spinal meningitis." Then to everyone else, "He walked out of Parkland this afternoon. What do you say we run him back?"

David liked that idea, since the paperwork for the rookie would be minimal. "Sounds good to us," he said.

Doors slammed shut all around. Officers and firefighters piled into their respective vehicles and took off in independent directions. David drove north at first, and then west. When Bill reached for the radio, David told him to leave it alone.

"The call ain't over until the paperwork is done," David said.

David parked them in another hole, this one in a freight yard north of Deep Ellum. He backed into a quiet corner and killed the headlights, leaving only the parking lights on. David pivoted the mobile display terminal so that it faced Bill.

"This is the MDT. We can check subjects and vehicles, run wants and warrants and write most paperwork on it. I like to use it as much as possible. The only offenses we can't write up on this thing are murder, rape and—"

"Actually, those pages were added over the winter. The only thing we can't write up on here are wrecks. Would you like an MIR?" Bill asked.

"Yeah, an MIR would do it. Have you got the subject information?"

Bill smiled slightly. "Right here," he said, waving his notebook. Then he pulled out a thick stack of photocopied papers, stapled together, out of his aluminum clipboard. "Would you like to see the newest MDT manual?"

David took the manual and started thumbing through it. Bill had impressed him. He had not seen the rookie get the information on the rolling man. While Bill typed, David thumbed the manual. It was all here. The requisite pages for offenses like murder and sexual assault were available. That meant that officers could use the MDTs for almost everything. Finally, a change in the right direction.

"Done," Bill said. "Would you like to see it?"

"Sure." David swung the MDT around on its pivot and read Bill's report. It was accurate, complete and brief. "Okay, send it and we can get going."

Bill did so. "Should we clear?" he asked, reaching for the microphone.

"Let's hold off on that for a minute. You know, not everyone can come back from being choked and start working like nothing happened; not even guys who have been out here for years. I think a reward is in order. You a religious man?" David asked.

"Well, I go to church most Sundays. I don't know."

"If duty called, could you go into a strip joint?"

"I guess so."

"Duty is calling. The Texas Alcohol Beverage Commission mandates that liquor selling establishments display the proper licenses prominently. We need to do our duty and ensure that the club is in compliance with the applicable regulations. What do you say?"

Bill smiled shyly and shrugged.

"The club is right up here. The thing is, these girls, they have their issues. Some guys get all caught up in how they look. Remember, these aren't the girls you bring home to Mama. Also, don't ever give one any money. They have no respect for any man that slips bills into their underwear," David said.

"They don't?"

"Well, think about it. They parade around without their clothes on and men trip over themselves to give them cash. From the dancer's point of view, what does that say about the man? Best you don't bother getting their real name. They all dance under aliases. And don't give them your full name. Here it is, the Silver and Gold club. Seriously, we'll duck in and out and get back to answering calls. A quick peek. TABC walk-through, right? Let's go."

David made sure there were no other police cars around before parking on the street, near the valet stand. They exchanged greetings with the valets and the bouncers. David walked by the cashier taking the cover charge from the well-dressed patrons with a wave and a smile.

"Fifteen dollars!" Bill exclaimed in surprise.

"Keeps out the riff-raff."

David led the way into the cavernous club. The ornate, gaudy decor, silver and gold accents around red velvet everything, struck David as way over the top. A leggy woman with gravity defying breasts spun horizontally on the pole that pierced the main stage. Tables and booths filled with men in suits and ties covered the main floor. Secondary stages were positioned strategically around the perimeter, lit by spotlights. Exceptionally attractive women danced on each one.

"Let's go upstairs," David said to Bill, whose concentration was elsewhere.

"Rookie, upstairs," David said again, as he guided Bill toward a staircase that was wide enough for their police car.

On the darker, more secluded mezzanine level, tables were positioned against the railing, affording views of all the stages. To David's left, a lovely brunette whose long hair swayed with the music straddled a patron's lap. The city fathers, or perhaps mothers, had forbidden that kind of dirty dancing. David stood directly behind the patron and coughed discreetly, or rather as discreetly as the loud rock music would allow. The dancer looked up and frowned. Slowly, she disengaged herself and sat on the table.

"What the hell you stop for?" her customer asked.

"Hello officers," she said, folding her arms across her abdomen, underneath round breasts with large round areola.

Her customer, a paunchy white man, about 35, wearing a golf shirt, spun his head around.

"Oh, hello officers. I didn't see you there," he said.

"Have a good night," David said, continuing down the aisle.

"I didn't know that wasn't allowed. I asked for it, please don't get her in trouble," he shouted after them.

David stopped and turned around. "No problem," he said.

"Can I buy you guys a drink?"

"No thank you, sir."

"Even Cokes?"

"It would be the appearance, you know?"

"Oh. I guess so."

"Have a good night."

"Okay. Hey, where are you going?"

His dancer had jumped up from the table and run over to a nearby drink station. She leaned over the bar and spoke to the bartender briefly, before walking back. She smiled and waved before stepping between David and Bill and her customer, with her back to the officers, allowing them to get away. David and Bill walked further down the mezzanine. Bill took in the sights, while David thought about what that dancer could have said to the bartender. A few steps later, a shout brought David up short by another table.

"Lois! Hey, Lois, I didn't know you were back," a white man with balding brown hair, hard little eyes, a brown mustache and a double chin called out.

"Don't call me Lois, Ralph. Hello Andy," David said to the second man at the table, a thin stick with a bobbing Adam's apple, prominent cheekbones and thick black hair. "Hanging around with this guy, people could get the wrong idea about you, you know."

Ralph and Andy were somewhat underdressed in white t-shirts and jeans. They must have badged their way in, David thought. They were attended by two dancers, one with long red hair and smallish, upturned breasts and the other a blond with a pair of enhanced, conical breasts and brown eyebrows. The girls appeared to be lounging rather than hustling for a table dance or drinks.

"David, glad to see you back," Andy said hesitantly. He started to reach out to shake David's hand and then thought better of it when David made no move to respond.

"Hey Davie, you know I'm funnin' with you. You get a rookie already?" Ralph asked.

"Yup."

"Showing him the sights?" Ralph asked, eyes narrowing.

"Got flagged down by a bouncer as we drove by. How about you? Badge your way in?"

"Hey now, we just came to catch up with our friends here, Rain and Tiffany," Ralph said, waving at the girls.

"I see," David said.

David looked away from Ralph, mostly because he did not like Ralph. He looked to the left, for no other reason than he had to look somewhere, and saw her walking toward him.

She was something else again, like a first among equals. White, with a peaches and cream complexion. In her early to middle twenties, as best as he could tell. Green eyes and blond hair with matching eyebrows. Her thick full-bodied hair curved around her face and fell in a wave to her collar bones. Her face was oblong rather than round, with prominent cheekbones, an aristocratic nose and a cute chin. David assumed her red, red lips were courtesy of Este Lauder or something.

She was slender by body type, and athletically built. Her well defined muscles were not especially large. Her obviously low body fat did not affect her breasts, though. They were moderately sized beauties whose areola pointed straight out, with a linear rise to prominence from the top and healthful roundness from below. Her mid-section was vertically lined, toned without the severity of a six pack. She walked up to him on long, lithe legs as gracefully as a finishing school graduate. She managed a smile, even though all that stood between her and the world was some butt floss.

"Hello, Senior Corporal Lane," she said.

"Misty," he replied, with a cool nod. David never gave his first name out in a place like this, an idea probably motivated by the aliases the girls used. Not that it mattered with Ralph blabbing it all over, anyway.

"How long have you been back?"

"Almost a week."

"I see. Do you have a minute?" She gestured for them to move off to the side.

"Sure."

"No private parties on duty, Lois!" Ralph shouted over the music.

"I'm real glad you came by." She opened a hard, hinged eyeglass case David had not previously noticed and pulled out a pair of glasses. "They cost me over $300.00, but listen to this. I'm reading now. Really reading, like books and all." She snapped the eyeglass case closed.

"Which books have you read?" David asked.

"Listen to this." Misty looked out over the sea of clothed patrons and nearly naked women and began to recite. "A—single—man—in—possession—of—a—good—fortune,—must—be—in—want—of—a—wife." She recited, finishing with a broad smile. "I don't get headaches at all now," Misty said. "Thank you very much for telling me about Doctor Tomforty."

Misty and David locked eyes. She looked at him with an affection and attention so obvious that David felt bashful for a moment. They drifted back to the group.

"All she does is read and read," the redhead said, sounding more like a proud parent than a friend.

"How did you find Austen?" David asked.

"You recommended it when you came by with the doctor's name," Misty said. "I've read everything so far. It's great!"

"Hey, did this place turn into a library or what? How about a beer?" Ralph interjected, indignantly.

"Ralph, I just wanted to thank Senior Corporal Lane for a kindness, is all," Misty said in the gentlest mien and with a generous smile. "And maybe talk books with him for a minute."

"Oh yeah, I bet. Books!" Ralph snorted. "How about some beer over here, sweet cheeks?" Ralph called out to a passing waitress.

"We better be going," David said, "I'm glad your glasses worked out."

"Maybe you could come by a little more often than before," Misty said.

"Yeah, you both can sit around and read!" Ralph shouted before he burst out laughing. No one else laughed.

"Maybe. Good night." Without waiting for good-byes, he walked away, expecting Bill to follow. Soon they were in the unit, heading downtown.

David thought about Misty as he drove in silence, unintentionally ignoring the rookie. The radio traffic squawked in the background.

"I'm sorry," Bill said after a while, "but I can't keep from asking. What was that about a doctor? You know, back there?"

"I was between rookies last summer and paired up with an officer that liked to do these walk-throughs. He only did it when it was slow. Anyway, one night we were in there. I overheard Misty talking about why she never did well in school. She said the words on the page moved around and jumped and so forth. She never could get what was going on and complained of headaches when she read.

"My brother had something real similar. Over the years my parents tried everything, tutors, innovative programs, everything. Nothing worked until they found this eye doctor. He discovered Ben had really bad astigmatism. The doc ground up some expensive lenses and gave Ben some eye exercises and next thing we knew, Ben was college bound."

"That's something," Bill said.

"It sure was. A big change. I was away in the Army then, but I read about it in the family mail. That first letter from Ben was a hell of a surprise. Anyway, I called the developmental optometrist that fixed up Ben and got a referral here in Dallas. Then I stopped at the club and gave Misty the name and number. We talked about books for a moment. I guess I said something about Jane Austen. I was activated for the war about a month later. Break's over, let's clear."

The dispatcher assigned them to a domestic disturbance in a neighborhood north of downtown. David turned onto Pearl Street and followed that to McKinney Avenue. They continued north until they entered a quiet neighborhood that bordered Highland Park. Mostly single family brick homes lined the quiet streets. New Accords, Camrys and Sables were in the driveways. Pickups and Suburbans were parked along the curbs. As they closed in on the address, a small white Nissan sedan motored past them.

"Here it is," David said, parking in front of a large brick structure.

Once a larger single family home, it had since been cut up into apartments. Bill marked out.

"Feels like rain," David said.

"Sure got humid real fast," Bill said.

Two apartment doors faced front. Neither was the right one. They followed a gravel driveway that led to the rear and found the apartment about half way back.

"Rookie, this will be your call, beginning to end," David said, as he took up a position to one side of the door.

"Okay," Bill said seriously and he stepped in front of the door, raising his hand to knock.

"Partner," David said.

Bill froze and looked over at him. David reached out and used his finger tips to gently push Bill to the side. Bill smiled sheepishly. With both of them arranged on either side of the door, Bill knocked hard, three times.

"Dallas Police Department!" Bill shouted.

A thin white male, about as tall as David, answered the door. He had long blond hair and a wide smile.

"Yo, dudes, come on in," he said, stepping out of the way.

David followed Bill into a kitchenette without room for a table and chairs. Several handfuls of macaroni and cheese with ground beef had been thrown against the walls. David looked for the empty pot and saw a stainless steel sauce pan on the floor. Remnants of the same orange mixture were inside.

"So dudes, what gives?" the young man asked.

He could not have been older than 20. David read the clues in the man's skin over bone build, like a rock star's, and his wet eyes. David thought he was on crystal, and remained watchful.

"Could you step back please? Thank you. Good evening, sir," Bill began, "we got a call here, is all. Anyone else around?"

"No, just me."

"Then you wouldn't mind if my partner had a look in those rooms there?"

"All yours, dudes," the man said.

David decided to grade Bill high tonight, based on his presence of mind to get consent. Backing the young man out of the kitchen, away from the knives, was elegant police work. David briefly looked inside a small living room and tiny bedroom. In the background, he heard Bill get all the necessary information from the young man, who's first name was Allen. David returned to the hall where Bill interviewed Allen and waited until Bill ran out of investigative steam.

"Would you excuse us?" David asked.

The two officers stepped back into the kitchenette.

"What have you got?" David muttered to Bill, as the two men stood close together.

"I got macaroni and cheese and hamburger on the wall, that's what I got. And that isn't illegal, best I can tell," Bill said.

"That's right. What are we going to do?"

"Say good night?"

"Sounds like a plan."

They walked back over to Allen.

"Thank you for your cooperation," Bill said. "We'll be going now."

"Good night officers. And thank you for protecting our fair city," Allen said, as he escorted David and Bill to the door.

David looked at Allen and saw it. The expression on Allen's face, as plain as day, contained equal parts of contempt and superiority and arrogance. Allen had beaten the police. David knew it, and Allen knew David knew it. David wondered how Allen had gotten the woman he lived with to leave.

"Next time," David said conversationally.

The comment startled Allen. Before Allen could say anything, Bill, oblivious to the exchange, opened the front door. In the center of the doorway stood a slim young woman, about the same age as Allen. She had curly black hair, dark eyes and a smashed nose. Blood fanned out over her mouth and down her chin. It dripped onto her creme blouse.

"Who are you?" Bill asked.

"Christie."

"Christie, did Allen do this to you?"

"Yes."

Bill spun around and lunged for Allen. This time, Bill's face displayed the interesting emotions. Or, rather, emotion. Only one: anger. It amazed David that easygoing Bill could generate that much hostility that quickly. Allen saw it, too. His mouth opened in a large O as he retreated so fast that he tripped over his own feet. Allen landed hard, no longer looking so cocky. David stepped out of the way and Bill pounced. Bill spun Allen over and ratchetted on the handcuffs.

"No!" Christie yelled over the commotion, "I just wanted you to talk to him!"

Christie refused an ambulance. David gave her a domestic violence victim card. Bill dragged Allen out of the apartment, onto the gravel driveway.

"You see what you're doing to me!" Allen yelled, loud enough for a neighbor to turn on a light and come to the door to watch.

Christie followed them down to the police car, wailing mournfully.

"See what you're doing to me, you goddamn bitch!" Allen yelled as Bill searched him thoroughly.

Bill buckled Allen in the back and jumped in next to him. David pulled the driver's door shut, put the car in gear and drove away to the sound of Christie's screams. They did not say much on the ride to the Lew Sterrett Detention Facility or on the trip from the sally port to the intake area.

While Bill and the prisoner were waiting on the book-in line, David wandered around looking for someone to talk to. All the other officers were strangers to him. Eventually, he found a piece of the Dallas Morning News. As he scanned the paper, he kept a weather eye on Bill.

After Bill booked Allen in, he walked over to a bank of tables with telephones on them. Bill dictated his arrest report to a typist over the phone. When he was done, he printed out a copy and brought it to David. David read it, and with a nod, sent Bill to the supervisor. Bill hand-carried the hard copy to the jail sergeant, who sat high up behind his counter, for approval. Bill handled the process fairly efficiently, and soon they were back in the car.

"Okay, your report was not too bad. Good enough for now. Next time, be sure to document that the victim was given a domestic violence card," David said.

"Okay."

Using the MDT, David checked and saw that there were no calls holding. "Hungry?"

If Bill noticed that they did not clear with the dispatcher after leaving the jail, he kept his own counsel. Soon they were seated in a Jo-Jos off of Industrial, tall glasses of iced tea on the table and sandwiches ordered.

David had scanned the restaurant as they entered. Three middle aged white couples took up the far corner, a group of fashionably dressed college-age people, conversing in sign language, occupied another corner and two obviously drunk young men sat at a table not far from Bill and David. Everyone had food in front of them and seemed to be behaving themselves, so David took the a seat facing the front door. Bill sat facing the other customers.

Their food came, and as they ate, they discussed the call.

"I can't believe that girl wanted to stay with him," Bill said.

"Was that your first domestic?"

"Yes."

"That was a good one, because of the blood. She was okay. Before you are off training we will go to a domestic where the victim will be barely conscious from her beating. All she will want to talk about is her snookums. She'll tell us we shouldn't drag him away in 'cuffs even though he beat her to a pulp and tried to shoot us full of holes."

Before Bill could respond, one of the drunk men yelled "and the fucking pie, try it, it's great!"

David turned immediately. The drunk with his back to the deaf people had leaned over and turned his head as far around as possible so he could look at them. He waved a fork-full of pie around in his left hand. The deaf patrons continued signing, their attention completely directed within their group. David suspected that if one or more of them could hear, they were choosing to ignore the slight in a display of good Texas diplomacy.

Not so the others. As David turned back around himself, he caught sight of the party at the far corner table. Every one of the people there were eyeballing David and Bill hard. David did not linger on them, but continued to turn, catching sight of the Hispanic night manager and the short black cook. They also looked to see what the two members of Dallas's Finest were going to do. Even Bill failed to provide a safe haven for David's eyes. His questioning gaze asked what they were going to do next. David sighed with fatigue.

"You'd think we could eat a couple of sandwiches, for crying out loud," David said, as he stood up. "Wait here. After one of those little shits gut shoots me, you may return fire. Try not to hit anyone else."

"Okay," Bill said, all serious.

David walked over to the drunks, in their busy western shirts and pressed jeans, and pulled a chair up to the table. The man that had yelled, the drunker of the two, saw David coming and decided to concentrate on his food, a worried expression on his face. His friend, also worried, tracked a little better.

"You," David said to the less drunk man, "have a lot to lose. Any more acting out by your buddy, and I'll arrest the two of you. That means neither of you will get out of Detox until," David looked at his Casio G-Shock, "about lunch tomorrow. That your car? Yeah? Then, because you can't leave your car here overnight, I'll impound it. It will cost you over $100.00 in fines and fees to get it back. So are you going to behave for the rest of the night?"

They both heartily agreed to behave the rest of the night.

"Nobody really cares if you liked the fucking pie or not, right coach?" David asked the major drunk.

He answered with a vigorous nodding of his head. David got up and walked back over to his dinner, or lunch, or whatever it was called at 2:00 AM. The restaurant returned to normal.

David's club sandwich, cut into four triangles, with its side of fries, waited for him at the table. He sat down and started eating fast, biting off large chunks and washing them down with tea. Bill did not get the hint. He ate his roast beef sandwich politely. David was reaching for the last triangle when the drunk he had just warned staggered over. David leaned back, reached for his tea with his left hand and dropped his right below the tabletop, where he rested it on his pistol.

"I want your badge number," the drunk stuttered.

"Yes, sir. It's . . . hey, do you know the manager?" David asked the drunk.

"No," he scoffed.

"Well, he's waving at you," David pointed at the deserted cash register.

The drunk was too drunk to turn only his head. Instead, he turned his entire body 180 degrees to look in the direction David had gestured. David, using hand motions and mouthing the phrase 'handcuffs' communicated to Bill that he wanted the drunk arrested. Bill looked stupid for a moment and then jumped out of his seat. He 'cuffed up the drunk before there was time to fight.

"You want my badge number?" David asked. "It'll be on the bottom of your arrest report." David looked for the other man, who continued to sit at the table. He had not even turned around to see what his friend would get himself into. David took this as a good sign.

"You at the table, put up your hands!" David shouted.

The free drunk complied and lifted his hands over his head.

"Open your hands! Extend your fingers, that's it. Get up and come over here. Do not touch any tables on your way." David was concerned about the cutlery at the place settings. It would be hell to get stabbed to death with a dull chain restaurant knife.

"All right, put your hands down," David said after he arrived. "What is your story?"

"Hum, I, er—"

"Empty your pockets on the table."

The drunk threw a wallet, some change and car keys on the table.

"Want to go to jail?"

"No, sir."

David motioned for the manager to come over with the check.

"Pay your bill."

The drunk and the manager settled up, with the drunk taking bills out of his wallet.

"My grandmother said to always—" Bill's prisoner said.

"Take him out to the car," David told Bill.

Bill jerked Grandma's favorite toward the door.

"You have an extra set of keys for your car?" David asked the remaining drunk.

"Yes, I think so."

"On you?"

"No, at home, sir."

"You have two choices," David said. "You can come with us, under arrest, or you can lock your keys in your car and call a taxi. The taxi can take you home, if you have enough money. What will it be?"

"A taxi. May I call a taxi?" the drunk asked as he swayed.

"You sure can." David picked up the drunk's keys. "Pick up your stuff." He pointed the drunk to the telephone. "Call."

The drunk staggered off. David waved over the manager. He made sure the there would not be a problem with the remaining drunk waiting for his taxi, or with the car left in the parking lot overnight. Then David paid for his and the rookie's meal.

"Wrap that to go, please," David said, pointing to the three quarters of Bill's roast beef sandwich that was left on his plate.

"And yours?"

David took up the final quarter of his club and jammed it in his mouth, tucking the corners all the way in with his fingertips. He could barely chew it. Talking was out of the question, so he just waved at the manager. The deaf people signed on, seemingly oblivious to everything that had happened. After watching the entertainment, the couples in the far corner had gone back to their own conversation. The non-arrested drunk sat quietly at the counter. David took Bill's food outside, stopping to lock the drunk's keys in the passenger compartment of his coupe.

He caught up with Bill at the car. Bill had already begun the Detox paperwork. He would have to remember to rate him highly regarding motivation for the day, too. David got in and before he closed the door the prisoner started talking.

"My grandmother always said to get the badge number," he said, and then started to cry.

"Shuh ah fuh uh," David said around the food in his mouth.

He pointed the police car north again on Industrial, heading for the Salvation Army's Detoxification Center. They pulled up to a lot filled with police cars in front of a large white building. Bill escorted the prisoner in. David followed behind. Once inside, he saw that he did not know any of the other officers there, either. David asked himself where the hell everyone gone. After all, he had not been off fighting for years, like in World War II. He left the drunk with Bill and went back out to the car.

In the parking lot, he turned the good-time radio to a country and western station and reclined the driver's seat. A wave of tiredness washed over him. He closed his eyes and listened to Alabama sing about the glories of down home. He was back only a matter of days and he was tired of it, of not making Tactical, of the games Charlene played. And of drunks and domestics and all the other calls they went on. Call after call, night after night. This was just the way he had felt before the war. Of course, the race thing was new. For him, anyway.

Bill came back to the car and thanked David profusely for bringing along the rest of his dinner. David turned off the good time radio and drove away. The dispatcher filled the rest of the night with residual overnight calls. The complaints about loud music, racing cars, the homeless downtown and a broken-down vehicle blocking traffic had been held while more serious calls were attended to. All had long ago gone stale. The neighborhoods were quiet and they could not find the stalled car. David looked over at Bill and saw the rookie nodding off.

"Hey rook, why'd you become a cop?" David asked, as the police radio finally went silent.

Bill jerked awake. "I wanted to—"

"Help people, yes," David said, finishing Bill's sentence. "Never mind. What did you do before?"

"Carpenter."

"No kidding. Where did you pick that up?"

"At college."

"You majored in carpentry at college?"

"Sort of. I got an advanced certificate in building science technology."

"Where was that?"

"Midland College."

"Midland? You go to college out there?"

"I'm from there."

"From Midland?"

"Well, from out in Midland County. My parents got some land out there. They work in town, run some cattle and stuff on the side, you know."

"I'm from Westchester County, New York. Believe me when I tell you I don't know. Why didn't you join up out there, like the sheriffs or Midland PD?"

"Um, maybe I shouldn't say, but I hope to eventually. My Dad is friends with a Texas Ranger, and he suggested a few years in the big city before coming home. He suggested Houston, but I didn't think there was any reason to go crazy."

"No, I guess not."

"Anyway, how did you get here from Westchester, New York. Is that near New York City?"

"Oh yeah, a border county. I was looking to get into police work after college, but nobody up there was hiring. I was on the list for everybody, New York, New Rochelle, New York State Police, when I saw an ad for Dallas in the New York Times and—"

Bill snored loudly. He had passed out, head resting on the pillar between the doors. David pushed him. His head shifted, ending the snoring. David decided to wait for end of watch up on the Trinity River levy. He loved to watch the sun come up over downtown. They sat there, David watching the lightening sky, and almost made it to the end of watch without another call. At the last moment, they were dispatched to a rush hour wreck. It made them late, but even so, before the office workers were through with their first cups of coffee, David was home and asleep, running across the hard Iraqi dirt in his dreams.

Chapter 6

David heard the ringing and tried to ignore it. Instead, it pulled him all the way back to consciousness. His forgetfulness regarding the telephone annoyed him. He wondered how he had survived on deep nights before the war.

"What?" he answered, testy at himself but taking it out on the caller.

"Well you're just a little too brusque, mister."

"Charlene?"

"Yes sir. Couldn't you sleep?"

"I forgot to turn off the ringer. I was sleeping just now."

"I can't talk long. I wasn't planning on you picking up the phone. Mom and Dad would like you to come to the house on Saturday, say, around one? They're planning a little get together, kind of a welcome back thing."

"I guess so. Does this include something involving just us two afterward?"

"I'm so sorry, but I can't make that," she said abruptly. "Can you come on Saturday?"

David wanted to slam the telephone down. Instead, he said, "Sure. Hey, Charlene, do you feel—"

"Gotta go, the little guys are done with phys. ed. See you at the house on Saturday. At one," she said, immediately hanging up.

David muttered curses and slammed down the receiver. He wanted this situation with Charlene resolved. But not right now. Still tired, he decided to go back to sleep. He stretched out on the bed. He could hear the faint sounds of rollicking children in the apartment complex playground. The afternoon sunlight snuck around the heavy-duty shade he had installed over the large window.

He looked around the beige room, his home for the last five years. It just then struck him that he had never decorated the walls. The room held a bed, night table and desk with a matching chair. He had bought the assemble-yourself pieces at Target when he took the place. His one personal touch was the pile of Army issue equipment in the corner. That and the police uniform hanging off the back of his desk chair. No family pictures or big boy toys, just gear. He put his head back down on the pillow and closed his eyes.

He had started to drift off when the telephone rang again. Why the hell had he not remembered to turn off the ringer?

"What?" he answered, as testy as before.

"Dave, it's Andy. Did I wake you?" Andy asked, with a nervous tremor in his voice.

"Why the hell would anybody think that? Just because I work all night long and sleep during the day?"

"Um, how have things been going?"

"Andy, What's up?"

"Oh. Yeah. Um, there has been a discharge."

David caught on to that right away. "Anybody hurt?"

"No. The sh—"

"Shut up Andy. Just answer the questions. Was 911 called?"

"No. I couldn't think who to call, so I called you."

"Any witnesses?"

"Yes, the homeowners."

"They in a panic?"

"No, they seem to be all right with it. It's Ralph. He's really mad. Could you get down here?"

"Did he do it?" David asked, because Ralph could really go to hell as far as David was concerned. He'd back up Ralph on duty, but off duty? He'd rather go back to bed.

"No, I did it."

"Okay. Where are you?"

Andy gave David an address in Pleasant Grove division. David took his time, shaving and everything before dressing in Levis, a black Army t-shirt and an old pair of running shoes. He killed some more time looking for his ankle holster for the smaller Beretta. Once he could not stall any longer, he headed for the Grove.

David had learned from his years in law enforcement that if you took long enough to get to a call, the worst of it would be over before you got there. Someone may even beat you there and handle it for you. He rarely put this policy into practice on duty, but this situation, an accidental discharge of a firearm by an off-duty officer, could get very sticky for everyone involved. The further David drove, the more he thought about that, and the more he thought that not showing up would be the best course of action. What stopped him from ignoring the situation was his commitment to Andy. David had already agreed to help. Even though it now seemed like a bad idea, David kept going.

David pulled up to the house in question. It sat on a quiet, narrow street, rough asphalt joining uneven grass without the benefit of a curb. In front of the house were several cars, including a newer Honda Civic in lime green, a Ford Ranger and two General Motors sedans of a certain age. David parked in the driveway, behind the Honda. There was no sidewalk to block.

David knocked on the door. Rain opened it. It took him a moment to place her. He had to look past her puffy eyes, disorderly hair and garment of choice. "Glad you're here. The fat one is ready to kill Andy."

"Everyone okay?" David asked, stepping past Rain, into the living room.

"Yeah. You'd think we went to their house and shot it, as upset as they are."

Rain led him through the carpeted but unfurnished living room. The usual suspects had congregated in a bedroom at the rear. Ralph saw him first.

"Lois, this loser tried to shoot me. What are you going to do about it?" he yelled.

David thought that Ralph had quite a temper, for a native Texan. "Don't call me Lois, Ralph. Come from court?"

Ralph was in a rumpled uniform, swaying on his feet, eyes half closed. Andy sat on the bed in the civilian clothes David had seen him in last night, looking doleful. Mike Michaelson, also in uniform, stood in a corner. The normally spiky black hair of the tall, young officer drooped and his eyes were downcast. Ralph didn't answer.

"Mike, how are you doing?" David asked.

"Not so good. For the report, I didn't want to come by. It was all Ralph," Mike said.

"Y'all coming from court?" David asked him.

Rain laughed. "Sounds funny with your accent," she said to David.

David smiled at her.

"Stick with that at IAD," Ralph snapped at Mike.

"All right, none of that." Then David saw the ugly, irregular hole. It was three quarters down from the top of the window frame, on the right side of the only window in the room. The panes were complete and there were no other holes nearby, so he allowed himself a little hope. "Just the one?"

"10/4," Andy said.

"We had city court," Mike answered.

"Take off," David said.

"What about my window frame?" Rain asked.

"I'll take care of it, Rain. You two, take off."

"You're going to call a supervisor as soon as we leave," Ralph challenged.

"About what?" David asked.

"The gunshot," Ralph said.

"What gunshot?" David asked.

"Well, I—" Andy started to say. David slapped Andy in the back of the head, lightly, interrupting him.

"I'm talking to Ralph. Ralph, what shot?"

Ralph did not answer. He scowled at David instead.

"Mike, isn't it true you were in the neighborhood and you heard what could have been a shot, but could also have been fireworks or something? Maybe you were walking around, investigating?"

"I guess"

"And when you saw Andy, Andy reassured you everything was okay, didn't he?"

"I guess he did."

"Having no reason to doubt him, you took off."

"We did," Mike said, with the first stirring of confidence. "Let's go, Ralph."

"The hell you say," Ralph yelled. "That bastard tried to—"

"Ralph, you need to take off," David said. What patience he had left drained away like water after a West Texas rain. Anger replaced it, which he held in check, just under the surface.

Ralph glared at him now.

"Ralph, you only heard something loud, that's it. Nothing happened that you know about for sure. Now get going," David said quietly.

"If that's the way you want to play it."

"That's the way it will be played."

For a moment, David thought Ralph was going to take a swing at him, but reason held. Mike was able to lead him out of the house.

"You know what really happened, don't you?" Rain asked him. She sat on the bed next to Andy, appraising David shrewdly.

"If something happened, let's say Andy and Ralph separated sometime last night. Andy ended up here and Ralph ended up in court. After Ralph got out of court this afternoon, he figured out or knew where Andy would be. Let's say he came around to give him a hard time," David's tongue felt like it wanted to stick to the inside of his mouth. "You wouldn't have something to drink, would you?"

"Beer?" Rain asked.

"Iced tea?"

"Sure. Come on."

David and Andy followed Rain into a dated but neat, clean kitchen. She poured him a tall plastic glass of tea and David drained about half of it. Then the door opened.

"Senior Corporal Lane!" Misty and another woman, a wraith-like girl, really, in her late teens or early twenties, with straight light brown hair and striking, ice blue eyes walked in. Each carried two bags of groceries.

Misty wore her hair pulled back in a ponytail. She had not put on any makeup before going out, and David thought she looked prettier for it, in a girl-next-door kind of way. Two crescent shaped trails of faint acne scarring curved around her prominent cheekbones, not much on either side, but less on the left that the right. The "v" of a high quality white t-shirt emphasized her graceful neck. Her washed out Wranglers followed her curves and covered up shined brown cowboy boots.

"Misty," David said, by way of greeting.

"I'm glad you have something to drink," Misty said. "Do you know Kylie?" Misty asked, indicating the young woman with her chin. The two of them put their bags on the table.

"Kylie? No fake name?" David said.

"I don't dance, not enough assets," Kylie said, arching her back to give her juvenile bust line its greatest effect. "I tend bar."

"It's always a pleasure to see you, Senior Corporal Lane, but what are you doing here?" Misty asked, going through the plastic bags.

"Andy shot and killed the window," Rain said, opening a bottle of light beer for herself.

"Let's see!" Misty put down a gallon of milk and ran for the bedroom.

Andy slumped in his chair and covered his eyes with his right hand. Kylie looked at him with sympathy and then smiled at Rain. She followed Misty to the bedroom.

"Might as well go, too," Rain said, trailing after her friends.

David tagged along with Rain, carrying his tea.

"It's just this little hole," Misty said. "What's the big deal?"

"No big deal," David said.

"The landlord may not think so," Rain said ironically.

"Ah, I forgot. I'll take care of that. Can I use your telephone?"

David called police headquarters at 2014 Main. A helpful clerk gave him Bill's home telephone number, which David dialed right away.

"Hello?" a male voice answered.

"Is Bill there, please?" David asked.

"Yes, but he's asleep. Would you like to leave a message?"

"Could you wake him up?"

"He would not like that too much. Do you have a message?"

"I'm sure he wouldn't. I need to talk to him."

"Who is this, please?"

Gambling that Bill was living with another rookie, David said, "his FTO."

"Sorry, I didn't know who you were. I'll get him. Sorry."

David heard a series of bangs and crashes.

"Sorry," the male voice said, "I dropped the phone."

"Of course you did. Bill around?"

"I'll . . . I'll, okay," the man said, before putting the receiver down on a hard surface.

David waited and eventually a groggy Bill answered.

"How would you like to do some carpentry work?" David asked.

"I don't know," Bill answered.

David wondered how many times Bill had gotten into unprofitable, time consuming projects by a candid answer to that question.

"It's a small job. A window frame was damaged at the home of the girls we met last night. Could I get you to come over and take a look at it?"

"The dancer girls? I'll be right there," a re-invigorated Bill answered.

"Bring something to fill holes up with." David gave him directions and then hung up.

"You're bringing a rookie into this?" Andy asked.

"Into what?" David replied innocently.

Andy didn't answer, but instead sat down and dropped his head into his hands.

"You never finished your version of what happened," Rain said.

"Right. So Ralph shows up, goes in the back and starts playing around. Maybe he knocks on the window of the bedroom where Andy is sleeping. Andy wakes up startled, grabs his pistol off the night table. Then he shoots at the window, killing the frame. Hypothetically speaking." David drank some more tea.

"Like, that's pretty good, but maybe he wasn't sleeping." Rain smiled seductively at David.

"I'll give him the benefit of the doubt."

"So now you have to do something about it, like officially? Something that gets all of us in trouble with the department?" Rain asked, suddenly cool.

"Something about what? Andy pointed out to me your frame needed fixing and I know someone who can do it. Big deal."

"And that's it?" Rain asked, relaxing a bit.

"That's it for me. Was Andy with you last night?" David asked, looking for firm confirmation.

Rain's eyes narrowed. "So what if he was?" she asked.

"If he was, it would be great if you and he could be somewhere else when the guy gets here."

"Where else?"

"Who cares? Go shopping. Andy has money, don't you, Andy?"

Andy groaned.

"Were you in the room with Andy?" David asked Rain again.

She nodded in the affirmative.

"Then the two of you ought to be going."

They finally agreed. Rain changed into sweat pants and a t-shirt and the two of them left. On the way out, Andy started to say something about a spent shell, but David shut him up.

David considered the two remaining women. He realized that Kylie wore the same outfit as Misty, a quality white t-shirt, jeans and boots. The only difference was the painful newness of Kylie's outfit. The shirt was bright, the jeans blue and the boots un-scuffed. Both of the women looked back at him, waiting. Misty smiled slightly, a very cute Cheshire Cat grin. David decided not to inquire about what she thought was funny, and addressed Kylie instead.

"Been tending bar long?" he asked.

"Just this semester. I came back from break and found out I was laid off from my office job."

"You go to college?"

"Yes. You sound surprised."

"I'm not surprised. Where do you go?"

"Texas Woman's University."

"What's your major?"

"Education."

David noticed that Misty sat back and watched this exchange carefully, not seeking to join the conversation at all, but paying close attention to it.

"Can I ask you a question?" Kylie asked him.

"Okay."

"Ho—, um, Misty said you were in the war. Were you?"

"Yes."

"Were you in the Army?"

"Yes, the Special Forces."

"What was it like?"

"Sandy."

"Sandy?"

"Yup. Sand in the food, sand in your hair, under your clothes, in all the equipment. Sandy. That's what it was like."

"What did you do?"

"Mostly waited around, until the whole Scud thing. Then I went on Scud hunts."

"Scud hunts?"

"We'd get dropped behind enemy lines and run around looking for the Scud launchers. Until the ground war started. Then we were flown far into Iraq, to see if we could find the Republican Guard."

"Did you?"

"Not that time." Talking about it made David thirsty, and he drained the last of his tea. He did not want to talk about it, not that he was in the throes of some dramatic emotional response. He simply did not feel like talking about it.

"David, do you need more tea?" Misty asked, as she leaned forward to look in his cup.

"Yes, please."

"Kylie, could you get some tea for David please?" Misty asked the younger woman.

"Sure," Kylie responded, taking David's cup and leaving the room.

In the resulting silence, David looked over at Misty. She smiled at him easily, comfortably, and waited for him to take the lead in the conversation.

"Been reading much?" he said.

"Everything! All the authors you recommended and some Kylie has told me about, and magazines and everything. The glasses have made such a difference."

Someone knocked on the front door and they went to answer it. Kylie came from the kitchen as well. The three of them faced a disheveled Bill Cobb, obviously fresh out of bed. Misty waved him in. Kylie gave David his tea and walked back into the kitchen.

"Officer Cobb! Thank you so much for coming!" Misty said, shaking his hand. "We are in such a jam. It's so great you came over."

Bill smiled shyly through his puffy eyes. Kylie returned with a large plastic cup of iced tea, like David's, which she held out for Bill.

"Thank you," Bill said, taking the tea with his right hand.

"Officer Cobb, this is Kylie, a friend of mine. Kylie, Officer Cobb the policeman."

"Do you have a first name?" Kylie asked, while extending her right hand in greeting.

"Bill," he said. He switched the tea from his right to his left and took her hand. Bill stood there, tea in one hand and Kylie in the other, for a long moment. Other than his mouth sagging open, he did not move. Eventually, Kylie became nervous, and glanced at David and then Misty.

"So much for the full name rule. Um, Bill?" David asked.

"Don't blame him," Misty said, "I heard you ask for Bill on the telephone."

Damn, David thought to himself. He tried to hide his embarrassment.

"Woe," Bill said, without taking his eyes of Kylie.

Then Kylie blushed furiously and lowered her head. Her bangs fell over her eyes and she shifted her weight from leg to leg, but she left her hand in Bill's.

"Come, Doctor Eloquence, you've got a patient in room three." David slapped him on the back and pointed to the bedroom in question. Bill disengaged with another shy smile and a muttered, "sorry."

At the window, Bill conducted his examination. "This is it?" he asked.

"Can you fix it?" Misty asked. "We rent."

"Yeah. Just a hole," Bill said. He took a small knife out of his front pocket. "This paint is a common white semi-gloss. Easy to sand it and paint it. Owner will never notice." Bill opened the knife and reached up toward the hole. "Looks like there's something in it. I'll—"

"Leave it, partner," David ordered.

"I can dig it—"

"Leave it, partner. Not that you know for sure anything is in there, do you?"

Bill was no idiot. "No, not for sure." He drank some tea. "A little wood filler and such, and good as new."

"Okay. How long until it's done?" David asked.

"About ten minutes today and, what, an hour tomorrow? You wouldn't happen to have the paint, would you?" Bill asked Misty.

"No, sorry."

"No problem. I'll go to the store and get some paint and wood filler and stuff. Y'all going to be around?"

"Actually, I think I need to get going," David said, without anywhere special in mind.

"I'll be around," Kylie said quietly.

Kylie stood next to Misty with her hands slid into her back pockets. The three others looked at her, and she blushed again, behind her bangs.

"Kylie, you could go with Bill to the store," Misty said.

"That would be great. Let's go," Bill said, with a decisiveness that surprised David.

Soon the two of them were in Bill's truck, motoring away.

"I guess you have to go now, too?" Misty asked, after they were gone.

"Yeah, to dinner, or breakfast or whatever it will be," David said. "Want to get something to eat?" he then asked, without thinking.

Misty smiled radiantly. "I'd love to, Senior Corporal no-first-name Lane."

Misty locked up, assuring him Kylie had a key. At his truck, he held the door open for her and wondered if she and Kylie had a thing going, what with the same clothes and all. He slid into the driver's seat and slammed the door, dwelling on whether Kylie liked girls.

"Do you think Kylie likes girls?" Misty asked.

"Why are you asking me? She's your roommate."

"I don't know. Besides, she just moved in. What do you think?"

"Based on her reaction to Bill, I'd guess she swings both ways, at least."

Misty had a good laugh over that one. They took his truck to Deep Ellum and found a booth in California Joe's Tropical Tex Mex restaurant. Misty had never been there before. At David's recommendation they ordered beers and chicken burritos, large tortillas overstuffed with chicken, cheeses, vegetables and a fresh salsa that possessed hints of pineapple.

"So by now, Kylie knows your first name," Misty said, after the waitress left. "How about sharing it with me?"

"At least you know my real last name! That's more than I can say about you."

"I would tell you my name, but a big city, New Yorker type like you would laugh."

"I won't."

"You're already smiling!"

"With a lead-in like that, what do you expect? Okay, here we go." David put on his street face.

"Okay." Misty took a deep breath. "Holly Dawn Snyder."

David smiled only slightly. "I think that's a lovely name. I'm David."

Holly made a big show of sticking out her right hand. David took it and they shook. Their food came. David waited for the results of Holly's first bite, only starting on his own food after she gave him the rounded forefinger to thumb signal that all was well.

"Are you from Dallas, Holly Dawn Snyder?" David asked.

"Buffalo Gap. With your accent, I don't have to ask where you're from."

"Oh? Where do you think I'm from?" David asked, already knowing she was going to say Brooklyn.

"Brooklyn."

David laughed.

"No?" Holly asked, surprised.

"Nope. I'm what the city guys call a suburban cupcake. I grew up in Westchester County."

"Then you went in the Army?"

"Right after high school."

"Wow. Did you go to a lot of places?"

"Central America and Europe. Germany, mostly."

"Did you like it?"

"It had it's moments. But after a while, I thought I might want to be an officer, so I decided to go to college."

"Did you go, then? To college?" Holly asked.

"Yes, I got out and went home. That was when I went back to school. Never did become an officer, though."

"Up in Westchester? Which college did you go to?"

"Yes, Pace University."

"Never heard of it. What did you study?"

"English Literature."

"So that's how you know about those books."

"Yup."

Holly stopped talking and seemed to be deep in thought. David finished off his food first and watched Holly eat as he nursed his beer. She had impeccable table manners, right down to sitting up straight and chewing thoroughly.

She swallowed and looked up at him. "I'm going to go to college," she said. She said it with resolve, looking at him out of steady green eyes, watching him closely.

"What do you want to major in?" David asked.

She looked away, smiling that sly, shy smile David noticed earlier.

"You're the only one who asked me that. Men either laugh or talk to me like I'm a dreamy child," she said. "Thank you."

David nodded. "So what do you want to major in?"

"I don't really know. I like the sound of that literature, you know, sitting around reading and stuff."

"Reading and then writing papers about it. Eventually, reading about what other people said and writing papers about that."

"Writing, huh?"

"Lots of writing."

"Maybe something educational, like Kylie."

"Sure. Have you applied anywhere yet?"

Now Holly squirmed a little. "Actually, Kylie is helping me get my GED. We've been studying since I got the glasses. She is so nice. I met her when I went to the TWU campus to find some help. Originally, I was supposed to pay her, but she won't take no money. I'm going to take the test soon."

The waitress cleared their plates and David ordered a coffee. Holly asked for some ice water.

"Was the war hard for you, David?" she asked out of the blue, and with some concern.

"What makes you ask?"

"You always seem so confident, so in charge. When you were talking to Kylie about it, I thought maybe there was something there."

"Nah, nothing there. It was a jolly little war," David said, shooting for a light-hearted tone. "They activated me in the autumn. They surprised the hell out of me when they sent me over there."

"Why? That's what the Army does, right?"

"Yes, but the Army is a great big large beast. I thought I'd be in a training capacity, or serving at a garrison or something like that. I figured the glory stuff would go to the regular guys." David idly spun his cup in a circle on the table. "I'd been off of active duty for so long. Next thing I knew, it was 'next stop, the gulf' to do my best Lawrence of Arabia."

Holly laughed. Despite himself, David felt stoked.

"Anyway, when the Scud situation broke, every stud and snake eater in theater that didn't object got put on the project. So I got assigned to a team of six and off we went." He broke eye contact with her and stared into the black liquid in his cup.

"David?" Holly asked.

"Sorry. You were saying?"

"You were, about the war."

"Oh yeah. So they organized us extra guys into teams and sent us looking for Scud missiles and their launchers. I made four trips into the desert in Iraq. It was the flattest terrain I had ever seen, made Dallas look like the Catskills. Sometimes we could find little folds in the ground to hide in. Sometimes, if we got really lucky, there would be a wadi or hills where we really needed them."

"What happened?" Holly asked, wide-eyed and leaning forward, almost over the table.

"They sent the new teams to the places least likely to contain the launchers. The first trip went off without a hitch, in and out without seeing any military at all. We found an empty mobile launcher on the second trip. The next trip was a dud. Then we had a contact with an Iraqi unit, but did not find any launchers or anything. Then we inserted in direct support of the war, and then it was over." David shrugged and sipped some more coffee.

"David, I don't think I understand a word of what you just said. What does all that mean?"

David looked at Holly dead-on. "Take the incident with the missile launcher. They had stopped for the night, in a roll in the ground that they probably thought gave them sufficient cover. We topped the one side in a skirmish line and readied our weapons. I had an M-16 with a grenade launcher attached to it. They did not even have sentries out. They sat around a little fire, brewing tea.

"When we got to the launch vehicle, we placed small crippling charges all around and detonated them. That turned the thing into so many tons of useless junk. We blew out all the sensitive systems, launch control, communications, the engines, transmissions and stuff. Then we left."

David did not tell her how his team had shot the shit out of the crew. How his first grenade went wide, but every one after that was on target. Or how, after they blew the launcher, they left the dead and wounded right where they were. He did not tell her how the wounded guys rolled around and moaned and how the whole camp smelled like burnt plastic and electrical insulation. Or how they melted into the night afterward.

"Oh my."

"Then we went out and tried again. This time, we ended up in the middle of some kind of Iraqi Army unit. We tried to hide out, but a civilian came up on us. We managed a fighting withdrawal and hid until they could pull us out." Fighting withdrawal my ass, David thought. But he did not want to tell her about that, either.

"David," Holly said, sliding her hand over the distressed tabletop and covering one of his.

Her gentle grasp felt good.

"The fortunes of war, I guess." David lifted his empty cup to his lips. He put it down and looked at the beautiful woman sitting across the table.

"Then the offensive started," he continued. "They flew us so far north, I thought we'd be living with Eskimos. Holly, I'm not so much of a man that I won't tell you I was scared shitless. We covered a possible egress route out of the kill zone for Iraqi units. I had visions of being a speed bump for a Republican Guard division. Just six of us in a hole in the ground."

"What happened?"

David laughed. "We spent the four days, and two days after that, sitting in that hole, crapping in plastic bags. We didn't see so much as a jet flying overhead. Great way to fight a war, if you have to fight a war." David noticed the dinner crowd had somehow snuck in, and customers were even waiting for tables. "Maybe we should think about going?" David motioned to the waitress they were ready for the check.

"I'm glad you're paying, because now I can offer to buy you dinner another time, as a way of thanking you for your help with my eyes," Holly said.

David counted out his money in preparation for handing it over to the waitress. He looked up at Holly and noted her hopeful expression, eyebrows raised, lips open in a fragile smile. Even though he knew better, he started to think about it. She was so damn hot.

He knew far too much about her already. His personal standard operational procedure regarding women who took their clothes off professionally was to give them wide latitude. But he was having a good time. Charlene was nowhere to be seen. Even still, he knew better than to get involved with Holly Dawn. He fully intended to tell her that he would not be available for another dinner.

"You know you don't have to do any such thing, right?" he asked.

"I know. That's what makes it better, that you weren't hitting on me or anything. So how about it?"

"All right, sounds like fun." He winced inside. He had planned to beg off with an excuse.

Holly chirped with glee, clapped and bounced in her seat. "When?"

To salvage his own position, he deliberately chose a stripper's busiest night. "How about Saturday?" he asked, knowing she would never give up her biggest haul of the week.

Holly's face fell. "Saturday? Can't it be some other time? "David told himself he was glad that he had found a way out. While good company, Holly was still a stripper and that meant trouble. "Sorry. That's the only night I'm free for some time. Perhaps we can figure something out in a few weeks?"

"No." Holly's expression firmed up. She balled up her right fist and placed it on the table. "The least I can do is sacrifice one Saturday night for someone that did so much for me. I'll just take the night off. I won't get paid, but who cares? There is more to life than money, right?"

A shocked David continued making arrangements for the date while thinking to himself that he could always cancel at the last minute. Hell, he and Charlene might even go out that night. After the party. You never know.

He and Holly agreed on a time when David would pick her up at her place. David settled up with the waitress and they left, with David thinking he had plenty of time to drive her home, catch a workout and make detail.

Chapter 7

Later the same night that David and Holly Dawn ate at California Joe's Tropical Tex-Mex, at about half past midnight, Andree fumed as he waited for Shuka. As far as Andree was concerned, Shuka's job meant that he needed to be available for problems that arose throughout the prime selling time of the night, which was, like, now. The various addicts and whores that Shuka allowed to hang out in his crib were telling Andree that they had no idea where Shuka had gone. Perhaps Andree had stayed too distant, trusting Shuka for too long. Andree depended on Shuka to mind the store. What the hell was he up to now?

Andree looked around the dump Shuka conducted his business from. Shuka had taken no steps to maintain the clapboard, single level, three bedroom house since Andree had put him in it. Andree sat in the livingroom with street jicks that he did not recognize and that did not recognize him. They sat on two couches and a love seat that looked and smelled like someone had pulled them in off the street some long ago trash day. After a rain. Andree felt like he would need a hot soapy soak after he left this hole. And maybe he ought to burn his clothes, too.

Andree heard a car screech to a halt in front of the house. He jumped up off of the couch, ready to run in case it was police. Looking out the window, he saw Shuka's red Nissan 280 ZX parked awkwardly by the curb. A new ugly dent on the front right quarter panel and mismatched tires marred the car's value. A faded Chevrolet Citation that, like the house and the neighborhood, had seen better days, pulled up and parked behind the Nissan. A posse of young black men poured out of the Citation. Shuka and an even larger, more muscular brother stepped out of the Nissan. Everyone brandished pistols.

The crew piled into the house. Everyone was dressed in multiple layers of old athletic pants and t-shirts. There were about six men total, all with weapons in their hands. The weapons ranged from stupid little .25 automatics to the two Glocks Shuka wore conspicuously in his waistband.

Shuka, who was the same age as Andree, stood slightly over six feet tall. He had come back from prison, years before, very muscular. While some of the definition had faded, and a slight gut had formed, impressive bulk still filled out his layers of athletic clothing. Andree recognized that Shuka was still one intimidating brother. From the scar on the left side of his shiny bald head, whose tentacles spread both above and below his left eye, to the eyes themselves, wilder than usual, Shuka was one son of a bitch that meant business. At least, he used to.

Shuka saw Andree and pointed at him with both hands, one arm cocked and the other outstretched. "Yo," he shouted over his shoulder, "my little man in here! Little man come down to the town!" Shuka walked up to Andree and spread his arms wide. He embraced a reluctant Andree in a big gentle bear hug.

Andree felt the handles of the two pistols dig into his middle. The cordite smell on Shuka's clothes stuck in the back of his throat. Shuka held on to him for a while, and then squeezed tighter. So tight that Andree rolled a shoulder and snuck an arm between the two of them; ready to grab and tear at Shuka's balls of if the bigger man tried to crush his ribs.

Shuka pushed Andree away hard enough so that the man he bumped into fell to the floor. By all rights, Andree should have stumbled as well. Andree, however, leapt lightly and landed a short distance away, cat-like, on the balls of his feet.

"Mother fucker! You come down to visit Shuka! What the fuck you doin' here?" Shuka yelled while walking a circuit of the living room, slapping hands and caressing cheeks.

"Come to see you, my man," Andree said.

Shuka turned suddenly and pointed at Andree. "You come to see the man! You come to see me!" he yelled.

Andree looked into his friend's feral eyes, round as saucers with little black dots in the middle, and figured out the problem. He knew that there would be confirmation in a few minutes, if he just waited. Now everything made sense to Andree. But there was still business to discuss.

"That's right, my man. Come on over here and let's talk some bid-ness," Andree said, no longer subservient in tone.

"Bid-ness?" Shuka said, then to the assembled throng, "I brought this mother fucker up, taught him everything he know, protect him on the street, and now he come in here and order me around. What the fuck, mother fucker!"

Andree held his ground and met Shuka's stare. A standoff ensued. Andree felt sure that Shuka was deciding to make a move. Andree concentrated on the man's hands, because truthfully, he had never needed much protecting. Traditionally, he was the someone others needed protecting from. It was a shame Shuka had forgotten that.

"Yo, Shuka, where One-eye and Leroy?" Andree asked.

Shuka became watchful and subdued. "They had to go."

"Go where?"

"Go. Like to the curb, man." Shuka then had a sudden inspiration, visible for all to see on his face. "They be taking the presidents, you know what I'm sayin'?"

"You should have come to me."

"That be my decision! I make the decisions, ah-ight?" Shuka screamed.

Andree stopped pressing Shuka, and stop speaking at all. He wondered if their two old friends were dead, or just gone. If they were gone, they could have gone to the police already. One of these jick mother fuckers that Andree didn't know could easily be an rat or even a cop. Andree wondered exactly when Shuka had taken a turn for the worse. He asked himself what signs he had missed before tonight, before this whole thing with the money.

"Ah-ight, anyway, tonight, them niggahs that be tryin' to take over that corner there, by Fair Park? They's history now mother fucker," Shuka said.

The crowd whooped it up. There was much hand slapping.

"What did you do, man?" Andree asked calmly.

"Tuned them mother fuckers up!"

Andree thought very poorly about that. He had no idea who Shuka had killed, or at least shot up, but it could not be good. First of all, Andree believed that killing was counter-productive and always an action of last recourse. Then there were operational issues. If they were backed by an organization, there might be a war. If they were independents, who knew what would happen. Either way, the police would be on the case and that might result in unwanted attention. Unwanted attention always negatively impacted profit. Andree was all about profit. Andree had not stayed out on the street all this time by generating or tolerating unwanted attention. Shuka knew that and lived by it with Andree. How stupid had Shuka become?

"What mother fuckers, Shuka?" Andree asked as if they were talking about a new rap group.

"The mother fuckers that been sellin' on the corner, man. You know, they's daddy drivin' around in that yellow Cadillac, the one the bitches like so much," Shuka said.

Andree contemplated this new development. Then Shuka answered all of Andree's questions. A skinny, pockmarked woman with matted hair handed Shuka a glass tube and a disposable cigarette lighter. As Andree watched, in front of everyone, Shuka brought the tube to his lips, lit the lighter and moved the orange and yellow flame to the end of the tube. As the crack heated, Shuka inhaled its deadly fumes deeply. As Shuka stood with his eyes closed and head back, an expression of joyful calm on his face, Andree slipped around him and walked out of the house, fading into the night.

Chapter 8

At about the time Shuka arrived home to meet Andree, the police radio came alive.

"One-Dog-Four, shots fired, Matthew at Cullum, possible man down," came the call, spoken in the preternaturally calm voice of the male dispatcher.

Bill still rode shotgun. His heart leapt into his throat as David's driving left his stomach back there on the road. He reached for the radio. "Dog-Four, en-route," he said. He heard other units join their call after his response.

They were north of the freeway, and more importantly, the train tracks. David slammed on the brakes, barely keeping the rear end behind them. A stalled freight train blocked the way. Bill watched him stab the car into reverse and stomp on the accelerator. The front of the car dipped slightly as they accelerated backwards. David steered with one hand, the other resting on the back of Bill's seat as David craned his neck around to see behind them. In moments they were flying down the narrow road. What David did next had not been taught to Bill at the academy.

David looked forward and put both hands on the wheel. "Hold on," he said.

The tires squealed and the car rocked dangerously on its springs. Then they spun to the right, turning 180 degrees in almost their own length, while staying centered in the road. As soon as the front of their unit pointed north, Bill felt pressed into the back of his seat as they powered up the street. David made two quick left turns and Bill saw that he found a street that went under the tracks. The car roared down the underpass, lights and siren screaming.

"I want you to get there before these guys die," David said.

Bill's stomach, still back behind them, flipped over.

The road they were on t-boned at the state fair grounds. David followed the Fair Park fence south. After two more quick turns, they drove up on the crime scene. Jimmy John and his rookie had beat them. Both men were looking into an older but immaculate Cadillac El Dorado, the color of custard. David parked the car and got out, leaving Bill to mark out and pull up the rear.

"Rookie, come on!" David shouted. "Got a blood trail."

Bill ran past the car, where he glimpsed Jimmy John and the rookie talking to a young black man who had pivoted around in the seat, resting his feet on the ground. A sheet of blood ran down the seat between his legs. An ambulance's siren wailed in the distance.

Bill caught up with David and the two of them started following the drops of blood on the sidewalk. The drops became a connected stream. The stream veered off into some shrubbery, large and malevolent in the night. They followed. It seemed cooler to Bill inside the leaves, and smelled sweet.

David pulled his pistol and Bill followed suit. Bill watched David assume a combat crouch and carry his pistol in front of him as they followed the blood further into the shrubs.

"Let me see your hands, coach," David said.

A thin teenage black male with short hair, lying under a bush, gestured weakly, trying to comply with David's order. David slipped his pistol back into the holster.

"The docs can't help you in this bush, so we need to drag you out," David said. Then he told Bill to grab his other hand.

Bill holstered up and stepped around David. He found the boy's other hand. It was covered in blood. Bill did not hesitate, he took hold and they quickly dragged him out to the grass. David called in their location. Bill looked down at the victim, who looked back, young and scared. In the glare of the streetlight, his skin appeared to be chalky-white. It occurred to Bill he might be watching this boy bleed out.

Another mobile intensive care unit pulled up and several tall white paramedics jumped out. One sucked on a lollipop. After a quick examination of the boy, the paramedic with the white stick protruding from his mouth walked over to David with his hands in his pocket.

"This old boy been shot through his femoral artery, so we're goin' to transport right now. Goin' to Baylor." He turned away, toward the ambulance, and said over his shoulder, as an afterthought, "ain't goin' to make it."

The boy was already loaded up on a stretcher and halfway into the wagon.

"Come on, I want you to work your first 27," David said to Bill.

They ran back to their car. David shouted out to Jimmy John that they were going to the hospital with a second victim who was in a bad way. David and Bill were soon in their unit, flying north with lights and siren, trying unsuccessfully to cut down the wagon's lead. The next time they saw it, it was parked under the overhang at the entrance to the Baylor emergency room.

The clean bright facility impressed Bill as orderly and organized. Nurses and staff in different colored scrubs greeted David by name and with obvious delight. Bill missed David turn sharply to the left and enter a large treatment room. Bill made it all the way to the reception desk before he realized David had gotten away from him.

"Partner!" David shouted.

Bill turned on a dime and ran over to the treatment room. The scared boy he had seen in the bushes moments before had a pressure cuff around his thigh. His color had returned and he had adopted a sullen, uncommunicative demeanor. David spoke briefly with a man Bill assumed to be a doctor. Then he made eye contact with Bill and motioned him back out to the hallway and off to the side.

"I had hoped you'd be able to get a statement before the guy died, but it looks like he beat the clock tonight," he said.

"I can still interview him, right?" Bill asked.

A team pushed the victim past them, in the direction of the elevators.

"Not tonight. They have to cut. They want to see if they can repair the artery. I guess it's theoretically possible that he could die on the table, but I doubt it."

"Don't take it so hard," a cute brunette, freckles across her nose and a red barrette in her hair, called out from the reception desk.

"Hey, hey, how are you doing?" David called back, as he walked over, with Bill following him.

"New rookie?" the woman asked.

"You guessed it. Jody, meet Bill, the department's latest addition."

After Jody and Bill exchanged greetings, she asked David where he had been.

"Fighting the war," he said.

"Oh my God, are you okay?" Jody asked, her good humor morphing into solemn concern.

"Sure, just a little sandy."

"Well come on back and tell us all about it. There's coffee in the break room and Mary brought apple pie."

Theo and Hermondo missed the aftermath of Shuka's shooting because Theo had a lot on his mind. First, the hot, humid Dallas night, more reminiscent of summer than spring, had him sweating into his ballistic vest. The vest, in turn, had begun to stink. In fact, tonight, as hot and humid as it was, seemed to especially bring out the stink in Theo's vest. Theo had come to detest the stink. Not do anything about it, just detest it.

Second, it had dawned on Theo that Hermondo did not like him very much. Every night, night after night, Hermondo had Theo fill out the blue rookie evaluation forms with five after five, the lowest mark, in category after category. These downward ratings were making Theo nervous. His nerves, in turn, affected his concentration. Even now, he was having a hard time concentrating on the young black fellow shouting his head off right in front of him.

Then there was the geography thing. Theo kept getting lost. Why even tonight, on this call, they had driven out of the division and around White Rock Lake. Try as he might, at first Theo could not find the apartment complex where this here fellow was bothering his girlfriend, or ex-girlfriend, or something like that.

"Well Partner, what are you going to do?" Hermondo asked.

The young black man appeared fit in his jeans and a neat form-fitting golf shirt. He smelled of beer and swayed in the courtyard between Hermondo and Theo. He yelling at the window of the apartment in which the complainant, the young woman in question, resided. She had neglected to come out, even after Theo and Hermondo had arrived.

"Partner, how about sometime tonight? What are you going to do?" Hermondo insisted.

And that was another thing, Theo thought. Hermondo's sarcastic way with him had begun to vex Theo. There was no call for the old officer to speak to him with the shortness in his voice. The same shortness he had heard from others all of his life, come to think of it. These thoughts swirled around in Theo's head, blocking his ability to come up with a clear, cohesive plan of action.

"Come on, Partner, what are you going to do? He's here yelling up a storm at one in the morning. He threw a brick through his ex-girlfriend's window. Why, he has been tying us up for almost an hour and a half, including travel time. What you going to do?"

"Yeah," the young man said, turning his attention to the officers for the first time. "What you going to do?"

The confusion clouding Theo's brain cleared. He zeroed in on the sass the young man had just handed him. With this sudden, new-found clarity, came a plan. He liked it, so he executed this plan without the benefit of review or consultation with his field training officer.

Theo drew his PR-24, the nightstick with a perpendicular handle sticking out of one end. According to the manufacturer, the PR-24 absolutely, positively was not modeled after the tonfa, an ancient Okinawan karate weapon of the same exact shape. Then he started hacking away at that young fellow's thigh like a lumberjack taking down a redwood.

In the academy, they had wacked on one another's thighs and dropped each other like bad habits. It disconcerted Theo that the young fellow simply stood his ground, looking at Theo with amazement. While getting repeatedly hit had shut him up, he had not yet crumpled to the courtyard concrete as prescribed by police regulations.

"I can't believe this," Hermondo said, loud enough for Theo to hear.

Then Hermondo stuck his arm straight out over the young fellow's shoulder, from behind, in preparation for throwing the old choke hold on him. Hermondo had to stand on tippy toes to get his arm over the young man's shoulder. Theo thought Hermondo moved kind of slow to get that choke hold going. Evidently, the young fellow thought so, too.

The young black man grabbed onto Hermondo's arm and rolled Hermondo's wide girth over his hip. It did not look neat and complete like one of those chop-socky movie moves Theo loved to watch, but by golly it got the job done. Hermondo dropped down hard between Theo and the suspect.

Theo was a lot of things, but coward was not one of them. He shifted position around his field training officer and was about to start wacking away at something other than a leg, perhaps an arm, when the young man they were trying to gain control over surprised him. Instead of standing still, waiting to get whacked in the approved departmental manner, he stepped up to Theo and gave him a mighty push with both hands.

Theo was loath to yield ground, but the push overwhelmed him. He felt himself falling backward. In an effort to stay on his feet, he stepped back. Instead of regaining his footing, he tripped on a piece of broken concrete paving. Theo rocked back on the points of his heels. He continued to grip the PR-24 in the regulation "ready" manner.

Theo's fall abruptly ceased with a metallic clang. It took a moment for him to realize that he had slammed into the wrought iron decorative gate at the courtyard entrance. Theo rested on his heels and hung from his PR-24 at about 45 degrees. Theo risked a quick look behind and saw that the diamond pattern of the gate had grabbed the end of the PR-24 tight.

The young, tall black fellow saw that Theo was stuck. He stepped forward in an effort to either get Theo or run past him and out of the courtyard. Instead of finishing the fight or getting away, he fell forward over the same loose piece of paving. His face fell against the short, forward protruding end of Theo's PR-24, which then arrested his fall abruptly. Theo felt the jarring impact in his arm and across his torso. The young fellow went limp and landed on Theo, mirroring his 45 degree repose, except that he was face forward.

Theo was still stuck, as letting go of the baton had not occurred to him. All he could effectively do was buck his hips. The young fellow slipped to the ground, and sprang up again like a child's toy. He and Theo looked at one another. Theo saw that copious amounts of blood poured out of a bad cut next to the young fellow's nose. For his part, the young fellow looked dazed. He turned his head from side to side, apparently attempting to regain his bearings. He stood there, looking confused, until Hermondo, again on his feet and moving his notable mass across the battlefield with impressive speed, slammed into him. Hermondo took him to the ground and handcuffed him with no further trouble at all. The three of them gasped for breath, the young fellow on his side, handcuffed and bleeding, Hermondo on all fours next to him and Theo resting on his heels and baton.

Finally, Hermondo spoke up. "Anytime you want to quit hanging around, rookie, and get this guy in the car would be fine," he said.

Bill did not know how hungry he was until he had cut himself a slice of Mary's pie. After bolting a piece and shooting a quick cup of coffee while David spoke to several nurses about the war, Bill was once again riding shotgun in the squad car. They had not gotten out of the parking lot when they were dispatched to an apartment complex for a disturbance call. The neighborhood was near Central Expressway. David made quick work of getting to the scene. Bill walked into the courtyard not knowing what to expect, as usual.

A screaming black woman stood on the second floor walkway, outside. She gestured wildly, shiny from sweat. Bill followed David up the stairs at a run. The woman, dressed in a faded tank top and shorts, had backed into a corner. Her bare feet were bloody from shards of glass that were all around her on the walkway. She screamed incomprehensibly at the top of her lungs, bent slightly at the waist, with barely a break for air. In one hand she held a large glass ashtray. She had a white ceramic vase decorated with a delicate blue pattern in the other.

"Watch out for the kids," David said, as he pulled out his radio and called for help.

Bill looked around. Somehow he had missed the two little girls, perhaps seven and four, standing between the woman and the open door of one of the apartments. The girls were in the middle of the broken glass, also in bare feet, crying and trying to move toward the woman. Bill could tell that both girls were hurt. Little red footsteps gleamed on the concrete. Bill assumed that the girls were daughters to the woman. He felt nothing but horror at the abrogation of what he took for the norms of the parental relationship. And that was before the woman threw the vase at the girls.

She missed and the vase shattered against the wall, notching up the general hysteria. Bill, at a complete loss as to what he could do, felt powerless. He looked at David in time to see him sprinting into the glass field, past the girls, directly toward the woman. Bill watched him duck the substantial ashtray the woman swung at his head. She swung it in a wide roundhouse so hard that it smashed upon impact with the wall to her left.

David adopted a combat crouch and brought up both hands like he was going to catch a basketball in front of his face. He held the edges of his hands against the woman's upper right arm, pinning it across her body and against the wall. Then he slid the hand closest to her hand down her arm, grabbing her wrist. Bill saw him twist it clockwise while at the same time continually pushing with his other hand against her upper arm. He spun her around and walked her out of the broken glass. Then he pushed her to the ground and handcuffed her quickly, despite her kicking and screaming.

"Grab up them kids! Get them into the apartment!" David yelled, as she bucked at him and tried to bite him.

Bill did as he was told, scooping up a child under each arm and jumping into the apartment with the open door. Two lamps were on in the living room, which felt very bright to Bill after the half-light of the dark courtyard. It took a moment for Bill's eyes to adjust. He saw a clean shaven, middle-aged black man, wearing blue laborer's trousers and a clean white t-shirt, sitting in an arm chair, watching television. He put down the girls.

"What are you doing?" Bill asked, incredulous that someone could be so close to this mayhem and remain uninvolved.

"Watching TV," the man answered, without looking up.

The girls had calmed down some. They stood still, sniffling by the door. Their feet were in better shape than Bill had first thought. They regarded the man solemnly. Bill heard booted feet running and eventually cracking glass on the walkway. He stuck his head out the door and saw the Mutt and Jeff team of Mike Michaelson and Randy Coffman running up. Randy had leather leg restrains. They joined in with David, fighting with the woman until her legs were bound in heavy tan cowhide. When they were through, the three of them picked her up and carried her to the door.

"Hey," Randy said to Bill at the doorway. "Some night, huh?"

"Oh yeah, some night," Bill replied, distracted by Randy's shiner and split lip.

Randy must have figured out what Bill was looking at, because he cheerfully volunteered, "last call was a doozy, man."

"Can you guys take her down to our car?" David asked.

"Sure, Dave. You want us to start an amb-lance?"

"Negative, we'll take her to the hospital ourselves. I'm thinking psych eval, and we'll run her through the ER. Meet you guys by the cars."

Randy and Mike lifted the woman by her arms and carried her away. Inside the apartment, the man had stood and faced the doorway, waiting to see what would happen next. Bill saw David nod at him in a casual greeting.

"Do you know this man?" David asked the oldest girl from down on his knees, who by now had stopped crying.

She held her sister's hand and swung it back and forth. Tears dripped down the smaller girl's face and chin as she sucked the thumb of her free hand.

The older girl nodded. "He stay with us," she said.

David looked up at the man. "How long have you been with the girls' mama?"

"Since Thanksgiving," he said.

"Can you stay with them tonight?"

"Yeah, I'll stay with them."

"What about tomorrow?"

"I got work, but they got school and day care. I can take care of that."

"You got something for their feet, or should I call an amblance?"

"No, I got something," the man disappeared into the apartment.

Bill wanted to arrest the man for sitting on the couch when he should have been involved. He wanted to ask David about arresting him, but some instinct kept him quiet.

"Well, things are looking up," David said to Bill as he sat first one girl and then the other on the couch.

The man returned with adhesive bandages and peroxide. David pulled out a pad and efficiently took down all the information, names, dates of birth, addresses and telephone numbers. They were about to leave when Bill, watching the man tenderly care for the girls, blurted out a question.

"If you give a shit, why weren't you out there helping?" he asked.

"Partner," David said, low and cautionary.

As the man wiped and bandaged little feet, he did not even look up. "The last time, she put the domestic violence on me. I had to spend the night in jail and pay fines and costs. This time I figured it was best to wait for you."

"Partner, let's go," David said. Then to the man, "have a better night, man."

The man waved them away without looking up.

As they slowly walked down to the car, still breathing heavy, David asked, "That guy get under your skin?"

Bill felt like the dam holding back his words broke. "I have never seen anything like that! He just sat there, not doing a thing!"

"What did you want him to do?"

"Hold his wife down or something. His children were at risk! Something other than sitting in front of the television, anyway."

"Didn't you catch the names? The woman, him, the kids; all the last names were different. They weren't his kids and that isn't his wife," David said.

"But still, he obviously lives there," Bill said.

"Yes. Lives there and cares about the people he lives with and knows the system better than you do, rookie. He did us a big favor," David said.

They had arrived at the parking lot. Mike and Randy had the woman bent over the hood of the car. Handcuffs bound her wrists behind her and leather leg restraints kept her from kicking them. They were concentrating on keeping her from smashing her head against the hood. David touched Bill on the shoulder and stopped him at the edge of the lot, outside the range of hearing of the other two officers.

"Our mandatory arrest rule means someone goes to jail," David explained. "Probably last time, the woman told the officers that the man hit her. Whether it was true or not, he was transported. My guess is that tonight, instead of fighting it out with her and risking arrest, he let her melt down all by herself.

"This was good for him, because he stayed out of jail. It was good for us, because we had somewhere to park the kids. It was good for the kids, because they will be in their own beds tonight, instead of a social services shelter. It may not have looked pretty, but it was the best thing he could have done. Got it?"

With a nod of his head, Bill indicated that he did.

"You strike me as someone with a strong sense of fairness, so I thought you ought to know that taking out your frustration on that guy wasn't the fairest thing. Don't worry though, rookie. You're coming along."

"Hey Dave," Mike shouted, after noticing David and Bill at the edge of the parking lot, "where do you want her?"

"In our car, we're going to run her to Parkland," David said.

They buckled her into the back, and clipped the leg restraints to the eye bolt that protruded from the floor. David drove and Bill sat in the back. The woman, whose name was Lynette, according to her companion, fought against the restraints and refused to answer their questions.

David picked up the cellular telephone and dialed a number from memory. He identified himself by name and soon Bill realized that he was talking to the admissions people at the hospital. That little touch just impressed Bill to no end. His trainer knew just what to do and say. He knew all the ins and outs of the calls they went on. And he knew the telephone number of the emergency room, and when to call it. Bill wanted desperately to be that kind of officer.

When they pulled up at the emergency room entrance, they shagged a stretcher and, preparing for a fight, unhooked Lynette. She bucked twice, but then settled down on the stretcher and allowed herself to be rolled into the ER.

Dave persuaded a nurse he knew to look at Lynette's feet. When he told her that Lynette would be a psych eval, the nurse, who had the same dimensions as an NFL tight end, found a free intern and convinced him no stitches were needed. He passed Lynette through the ER. Before long, Bill and David were presenting Lynette at the entrance to the psych lock-down facility. They had to walk her over because two orderlies had come by and grabbed their stretcher.

"Hopefully," David muttered, "we can drop her off and get the hell out of here without getting bogged down in procedure."

David leaned on the buzzer until the door slid open. The three of them walked into a sterile, white intake area devoid of furniture, fixtures or wall hangings. Lynette shuffled forward from the knees, still in the leather restraints. The camera above the door at the far end caught Bill's eye and made him feel uneasy. After the door to the outside slid shut, the far door opened. A tall, slender, blond nurse with a middle-age face and a body decidedly younger walked into the intake area. The door behind her remained open, and Bill could see the corridor turn to his left.

"What have you boys brought us tonight?" she asked.

"Lynette is having a bad night," David said, handing over the clearance paperwork from the emergency room.

"Okay, what were her symptoms?"

David told the intake nurse about the uncontrollable rage, the broken glass and the children placed at risk.

"Sounds fine," she said, "I just need to get the resident to approve the admission. Y'all want to wait here?"

"That will work," David said.

The nurse disappeared into the unit, leaving the inner door open. The three of them waited. Bill became distracted, forgetting about the camera. David, muttering, walked into the unit and came back rolling an office chair, into which he lowered Lynette, who allowed herself to be maneuvered into the chair without a comment or a fight.

A short, stoop-shouldered, round-bellied white woman in her late twenties showed up. From her fast walk to her pinched, mean face, she broadcast the message that she had no time for involuntary commitments brought in by police officers. The tall blond appeared from somewhere and stood behind the young doctor without indicating she was there.

The doctor walked up to Lynette without acknowledging David or Bill. "What's wrong tonight?" she asked, in an accent Bill found similar to David's, but thicker.

Lynette continued to look down. She muttered something incomprehensible and squirmed around in her seat, trying the bonds that held her.

The doctor grabbed Lynette's chin and forced her face up. She shined a pen light into her eyes and stood up with a snort of disgust. She clicked off the pen light and slipped it back into a pocket.

"Don't you people know anything?" the doctor asked, her words short and hard. "She's not psychotic, she's high on cocaine. What the hell is wrong with you?"

"My medical degree hasn't come in yet, coach, so unlike you, I'm not clairvoyant." David ladled sarcasm over his comments as thick as gravy over morning biscuits.

"No admission. Take her to the ER."

Bill reached out for Lynette's arm to lift her out of the seat but stopped when he saw that David had not moved. David and the doctor had locked eyes. Bill looked back from one motionless professional to the other. Then Bill noticed the nurse standing directly behind the doctor. She nodded "yes" and silently mouthed "I'll take care of it," over and over, to David.

"Oh!" the doctor said, as she stamped her foot in frustration. She dragged out her exclamation and turned it into a growl. She turned to the nurse and said, "take her to the ER," before stamping off down the corridor and making that left turn.

"Don't y'all worry about that, just bring your friend right around here to the office," the nurse said.

David and Bill escorted a now compliant Lynette into the corridor and to the right instead of the left. A small partition hid an office area with a desk and several chairs. Within moments the nurse had filled out the paperwork and had David and Bill remove Lynette's restraints.

"I'll take it from here," she said.

David thanked her and the two officers wearily walked out into the parking area. At the car, Bill flopped into the passenger's seat, exhausted. He leaned his head back and closed his eyes. He heard David start the car and then play with the MDT.

"I'm hoping that there aren't a whole lot of calls holding. We need to get something to eat," David said. "Crap. Three pages holding. Looks like it's a quick stop at a Seven-Eleven and then we'll clear."

David backed the car out of the spot and drove out onto Industrial Boulevard, heading south.

"Only half way through the watch," he said.

"Half way?" Bill lifted his head and turned to face David.

"Half way. How about that Yankee bitch? High on cocaine my ass. She was crazy."

Bill did not know how to take that last comment; after all, David himself was from New York. When David momentarily turned from the road to look at Bill, Bill could see him smiling. Bill relaxed and smiled as well.

"Medical doctor a requirement for the job nowadays?" Bill asked, in the same joking vein.

"I guess so."

David pulled into a nearby Seven-Eleven and parked. It took forever for the two worn out officers to get into the store.

Theo pulled the unit up the ramp, out of the county jail's sally port and pointed it downtown, because he felt secure in his knowledge of where downtown was in relation to the Lew Sterret Justice Center. He took no notice of Hermondo typing away on the MDT. He had finally gotten that young man into jail. He had to run him through the emergency room for stitches, wait on an extra-long book in line and make all those report revisions, first for Hermondo and then for the jail sergeant. Things sure weren't shaping up for Theo the way he had expected, like helping the public and all.

Take this call he just wrapped up, for instance. The young fellow turned out to be a good guy. He must have sobered up at the hospital. While they waited for attention, he and Theo struck up quite an acquaintanceship. He was just upset at the abrupt end to his relationship with the woman whose window he had sailed that brick through. Theo could sympathize with that. After all, when he did date, didn't it often end suddenly? What was it with women anyway?

"Rookie, do you know where you are going?" Hermondo asked, without looking up from the MDT.

"Yes, I know where I'm going," Theo replied testily.

That was another thing, this whole field training experience. Days had been bad enough, but deep nights was impossible.

Hermondo did not have a neighborly bone in his body. Taciturn and judgmental, Theo did not rate him highly as a partner. And all those fives and fours on his rookie sheets. Completely uncalled for.

Theo realized at the last moment that he had mistakenly turned left, off of the city streets and onto northbound I-35. He tried to fix it by moving onto the shoulder, planning to back down the ramp. This only succeeded in motivating Hermondo to yell at him.

"Just get on the freeway, rookie!" Hermondo instructed, "forget about the shoulder!"

"One-Dog-Three, shots fired, man down, the game room at 800 Carroll," the even voiced male dispatcher said.

Theo heard the call and it made him very nervous. He had stayed in the right lane and accelerated to freeway speed, but had not made any decisions about what to do next. In his nervous state, he decided to try backing up on the shoulder again, down the entrance ramp. Theo had forgotten that the ramp was miles behind them at this point, as well as Hermondo's recent objection. His jittery state and the unit's highway speed caused him to over control the unit. It swerved hard up onto the right shoulder. The back end broke free for a moment, fishtailing to each side until Theo got it under control.

"What the hell are you doing!" Hermondo shouted again. "Get back on the freeway and take the next right onto Woodall Rogers, will you?"

"Let's go!" David shouted.

Adrenaline hit Bill like a truck up on the freeway. Although startled, he managed to finish filling his courtesy cup without dropping it. Still hungry, he followed David's example and grabbed a doughnut from the Dunkin' Doughnuts display. He sloshed some Coke onto his trousers as he hurried to catch David.

"I've got yours!" David shouted, dropping some money on the counter as they ran past the startled clerk.

David unlocked the car and they each jumped in. David gulped about half of his drink down. Then he shoved the cup into a secure perch between the equipment brackets and seat, Styrofoam squeaking as it slid into the tight space. He grabbed his chocolate doughnut with his teeth and started the car.

Bill copied every move David made. He gulped down some of his drink a little too quickly. Parallel trails of Coke dribbled out either side of his mouth. He found a place to jam his cup and then took a large bite out of his glazed doughnut, which he swallowed without chewing.

"What's going on?" Bill asked.

David accelerated out of the parking area. He activated the light bar and got the car going straight. Then he bit into his doughnut and took hold of the excess.

From around his food he said, "mark out code five."

In the meantime Bill had taken another bite of his doughnut. With his mouth full, he picked up the microphone.

"Use the button on the MDT," David said.

Bill hit the button marked 'Code 5.'

"10/4, Dog-Four," the dispatcher said.

"What's going on?" Bill asked again.

David took another bite. "You got to start listening to your radio all the time, rook. Your buddy and Hermondo were dispatched to 800 Carroll for a man down call. There's what they call a game room at that address. Nothing more than an after hours place. Several different gangs go there on a regular basis, so there will be a crowd at this shooting. That means Hermondo is going to need a lot of help, like right now," David said. He pushed the rest of the doughnut into his mouth and lit off the siren to push some traffic out of the left lane.

Bill's mouth dried out and a chunk of doughnut became caught in his throat. He found it necessary to wash it down with his sweet, sweet drink.

Theo drove east on Woodall Rogers. He did not know exactly where he was in the scheme of things. Even so, he felt confident he would be able to figure out where to go from here to get to wherever the call location was, which he had forgotten anyway, if he could only get a moment to think. Theo had also forgotten, if he had ever known, that Woodall Rogers Freeway skirted the northern boundary of the central business district, ending at Central Expressway after only several miles.

In fact, he had burned up those several miles thinking about his current location and was now facing the point where he had to decide whether to pick up Central northbound or southbound. The sudden appearance of the end of the freeway, coupled with his need to decide where to go immediately, threw him into a state of indecision. Theo kept driving straight.

"Rookie, get on the exit ramp now! Turn right!" Hermondo yelled.

Theo turned the car hard, almost losing it. He knew enough not to lock up the brakes. He managed to keep it under control all the way down to Central, and from there, at Hermondo's instructions, onto eastbound I-30.

"You better get your head in the game, rookie. This call is going to be hotter than Hades," Hermondo said, once they were safely on eastbound freeway.

As soon as they turned onto the street, Bill saw the crowd and felt fear tighten up his insides. David snaked the car through the smaller knots of people that stood at the edge of the mob proper and came to rest between two units that had already arrived. David was out the door, shouting a greeting at an officer on his right before Bill had his seatbelt unbuckled.

Bill opened the door and stepped out, grabbing his flashlight, which automatically slid into his right rear pocket, his PR-24 and his ticket book. Sweat dripped into his eyes from the heat and humidity and fear. He shrugged and wiped an eye on each shoulder.

A large black man with an impressive waistline lay motionless on his back where the pavement of the parking lot met the concrete sidewalk. A restless crowd of young African-Americans milled about in the parking area, which serviced a five store strip mall. The crowd seemed to emanate from the second storefront from the corner.

"Help him, you mother fuckers!" someone yelled.

Several police units had arrived and none of the officers had begun to render aid. Bill wondered about this, but kept his silence and his distance from the injured man.

A glass bottle sailed through the air in a grand arc, smashing near one of the other police cars. A fan shaped pattern of shattered glass and beer spread across the pavement.

"Wondering why no one does the first aid thing?"

Bill jumped, startled by David, who had sidled up next to him.

"Um, now that you mention it . . . ?" Bill replied.

"You have any first aid qualifications?" David asked.

"Yes, standard and CPR, from the academy."

"They still good?"

"Sure, they're brand new."

"Do you think the department will re-certify you when they expire?"

"I guess so."

"None of us have been re-certified."

"None?"

"None."

A frantic young woman broke free from the crowd, her large breasts swinging, and ran up to the man who had been shot.

"You help him, you bastards, help him!" She screamed, her hoarse yelling adding to the tension. Then she dropped to her knees next to him.

"One of the reasons the department doesn't do the first aid thing is that the paramedics are so good. Amateurs set them far back when they try to help. It's better to do nothing and wait, than to do something ignorant that becomes a fatal mistake," David said.

The young woman raised a balled fist and brought it down hard four or five times on the man's chest. Then she started mouth to mouth resuscitation. In her hurry to save the victim, she failed to check for breathing or tilt his head back. She just started blowing hard onto his closed lips, as far as Bill could tell.

"Well, he had a chance, anyway," David said dryly.

The dispatcher added comments to the call: that the victim had been shot in the chest, the suspect was a black male, five foot seven to five foot eleven, one sixty to one hundred eighty pounds, black hair, possible beard. No age noted. Theo tried to take it in and keep the car moving and listen to Hermondo's instructions all at the same time. He was sweating profusely. His fight-or-flight response kicked in. Hermondo had him take an exit off the freeway.

Theo made the exit, but was quickly feeling overwhelmed. Panic welled up in him, coming up from his insides. He was about to say or do something, he had no idea what, when he saw the suspect walking on the sidewalk, facing traffic. He turned the car sharply to the right, stopped short as the right front tire hit the curb, and bailed out of the car.

Theo used the front door and body of the car as cover. He pulled his pistol out of his holster and pointed it at the pedestrian, shouting "police! Don't move!"

Theo noted that the man he had stopped, that he held the power of life and death over at this very moment, looked to be about sixty years old. He wore a dirty red baseball cap, a white shirt and blue jeans, shirt neatly tucked in. In his right hand he carried a cheap white plastic bag with what appeared to be groceries in it. He froze, but his expression never changed. He looked at Theo with tired eyes that had seen the wrong end of a police officer's pistol before.

The mobile intensive care unit pulled up and into the parking lot at 800 South Carroll, fairly close to the motionless body and the woman practicing her mouth to mouth. A large white paramedic, the approximate size and coloring of a Viking, exited the cab with his hands in his pockets and his cap tilted on the back of his head. He took two steps toward the body and pivoted right around, retreating toward the ambulance.

"Shit, wrong move cowboy," Bill heard David say. "Form up on me!" David shouted, as the first volley of bottles started shattering on the concrete.

Bill had no idea what to do, but saw that without further instructions, the officers moved to either side of David, batons in the ready out position, forming a line. On one side was the crowd, on the other the victim, the woman and the best of the Dallas Fire Department.

"Rookie, get up on my left and stay close!" David yelled at him, gesturing with his left hand, in which he held his walkie talkie. Bill heard him call Theo's unit, telling them to get here as soon as possible.

Bottles, cans and rocks started falling like rain.

"Dog Three, this is Four. This party is about to start. Y'all better hurry up if you want to be in it," was exactly what David said into the radio. Theo heard it plain as day.

"10/4, we'll be there as soon as my partner figures out he stopped the wrong man," Hermondo replied.

"Thank you sir!" the man Theo stopped said to Hermondo, with a small stomp of his foot.

Embarrassment burned Theo's cheeks. He holstered up and looked to Hermondo for instructions.

"Well, get in the fucking car already," the trainer said.

Bill caught sight of the Viking approaching the victim, carrying a backboard, collar and pressure cuff. He knelt down next to the woman and put down the equipment. He touched her on the arm and said something. She lashed out at him wildly, hitting him in the center of his broad chest. Bill thought he might go over and control the woman while the paramedic worked on the victim.

While still trying to decide if he should help, two other officers grabbed the woman by the arms and spun her to the ground.

A sharp pain erupted on the left side of Bill's face. He flinched and stepped back, fear burning bright in his mind, erasing everything for a moment. Then he saw the bottle that had fallen to the ground by his left boot. It had not broken. Bill realized he had just taken a bottle in the face. He shook off the blow to his cheek and held his position. He did, however, shift his attention back to the front of the line. The crowd milled about, ever more restless, moving closer.

A young man broke free of his knot of friends and rushed Bill. The man was unsteady on his feet and moved slower than Bill would have otherwise expected. Bill grasped his baton in the regulation manner, with his right hand on the handle and his left positioned on the long side of the shaft, forward of the handle. He stood in a combat crouch, right side back. When his assailant came within striking distance, he did not hesitate. Bill stepped in and jabbed at his solar plexus with the business end of the baton. At the same time he gave out a short, sharp shout and stepped down hard with his front foot, just like they showed him at the academy. His aim was true, and the assailant doubled over and sank to the ground.

A vehicle door slammed shut behind him and Bill heard the ambulance's engine gun.

"They're leaving!" David shouted. "Fall back on the cars!"

Just as Bill was wondering how they were going to get out of there without getting blitzed by the crowd, Theo and Hermondo arrived.

Theo drove erratically into the parking lot. The unit jerked from side to side. Theo narrowly missed colliding with the ambulance and two of the parked police units. He turned widely around in the parking lot, scattering the crowd. Even Bill did not need to be told to take advantage of the distraction. The line collapsed as officers ran for their own cars, or dodged Theo and Hermondo, whichever act was more important at the moment. A line of police cars formed behind the ambulance, the whole formation speeding up Carroll with lights turning and sirens blaring.

"How the hell was that! Some little light entertainment there, partner?" David asked as they crossed the freeway into East Dallas. His face beamed with glowing energy, his eyes wild. David laughed, downshifted and over-revved the engine.

"A little something to pass the time, sure," Bill said, grinning despite himself.

"Let's clear and—woe, partner, you took a good one," David said. David's demeanor instantly sobered up. He came off the gas and up-shifted. As things calmed down, David grabbed the microphone. He waited briefly for a gap in the traffic before asking the dispatcher where the shooting victim was going.

"Baylor," came the reply.

"Show us out to Parkland. My rookie took a hit in the face and needs some stitches."

"Dog-Four," the dispatcher replied, by way of confirmation.

"I did?" Bill asked.

"Use the rear view," David said.

"Holy shit," Bill said, taking in the blood that flowed from a respectable cut on his left cheek. He brought up a hand.

"Don't touch it. We'll be at the hospital in a minute," David said.

Bill leaned back in the seat. Somehow, Bill had not noticed when, they had gotten onto the freeway. David drove fast, the scenery a blur as they looped around the lower part of downtown, exiting conveniently close to Parkland.

"I didn't think anything of it at the time," Bill said.

"That's a good sign," David said.

Bill thought it was great that David was all smiles and relaxed and everything. He had never had stitches before, and really didn't want to get any now.

"Dog-Zero," came over the radio just then.

"Go ahead, Dog-Zero."

"I'm heading on over to Parkland."

"10/4."

"Well, Karangekis is coming on over to see how badly I broke you up. Must be nice to have friends in high places, kid," David joked.

Bill didn't respond. So the sergeant was coming over to see him. Great. He would rather not have the attention. Of course, he would rather not be the cut guy, either. A low grade headache started behind his forehead.

"You think that victim is dead?" Bill asked as they pulled into the same emergency vehicle parking area they had used earlier.

"No miracles this time. All that chest thumping did him in for sure. No need to worry about him, though. Let's get you in there."

Bill opened the door and stood up. He felt mostly okay. David had run around to his side of the car. They walked next to one another. Bill felt good as David joked and kept it light on their way into the ER. David was just as relaxed as anything. He directed Bill to the closer gurney entrance, and walked him through the automatic doors.

"Looks like Costas called ahead," David said.

Two nurses in dark blue scrubs, one of whom was a short, really cute brunette, were obviously waiting for them. Bill thought it was cool that they took up positions on either side of him. They spoke to him in the same tones David had used. As Bill thought about that, and tried to steal a glance down the front of the short nurse's shirt, they led him to a trauma room, leaving David to trail behind.

"Back by the game room? What in the damn hell was that?" Hermondo asked.

Theo jammed the transmission into park. They had pulled into a spot by the Baylor emergency entrance, arriving shortly after the ambulance.

"I drove up to the location—" Theo stammered, before being cut off.

"Drove up? That was the best example of an out of control plane wreck I ever seen, and I been in the Air Force. You're lucky you didn't hit anybody. I got to tell you, partner, you need to shape up starting yesterday. This ain't no game out here, understand?"

"I understand," Theo said. He knew from experience that when they get like this, the best thing is to just wait them out. Theo bowed his head and squinted against the glare of the flourescent lighting.

"All right. Get inside and find out if we need to wake up a homicide detective," Hermondo said, without much sympathy for anybody.

A young male doctor, thin as a post with a bobbing Adam's apple, finished stitching up Bill's cheek. He clipped the thread, said some cliches and walked off to the next disaster of the evening. A nurse with a compassionate demeanor and a wedding band slapped a bandage on Bill's cheek and left the two officers with their sergeant.

"You remember this from the choking, right?" Costas asked.

"Yes, Sergeant," Bill replied, embarrassed that his sergeant should see him this way twice in less than a week. He wanted to fade into the white tile walls of the trauma room. Bill took the three page form and started filling it in.

"I guess if you get injured one more time, we'll have to get you a new training officer," Costas said.

"What?" David asked.

"Yeah Dave, you know the most precious asset the department has are its rookies. They're the hope of tomorrow and if you can't safeguard the one we have assigned to you, then you ought not be training at all."

"Hell Sarge, if hurting this guy was all it took to get out of training, I'd have shot him in the leg days ago."

"Thanks a lot!" Bill interjected, unable to stop himself.

The two other men laughed.

"Drop that by the station when you get a chance," Costas said. I've got to run. Glad to see it wasn't any worse than what you got."

"Thanks, Sergeant."

"David, see you later."

"Stay safe, Sarge."

Bill filled out the form quickly, familiar with it from earlier in the week. David lounged in a chair, head back and feet up on the bed, ankles crossed, eyes closed. Bill wrote in silence. After a while, he assumed David had fallen asleep. He jumped when David spoke.

"You did good out there. Many veteran officers would have gone right to ground after being hit like that. You held the line. Good job, rookie." David said those things without looking up, or even opening his eyes.

Bill did not respond, other than to smile as wrote.

Chapter 9

By the time David and Bill cleared Parkland, it was just about end of watch. The sun had come up in a bright, cloudless sky. The temperature had shot up to past 85 degrees. Due to the high humidity, David was sweating under his ballistic vest before they even reached the car. Inside, it felt like an oven, and David set the air conditioning as high as it would go. He saw Bill reaching for the radio.

"Never mind, rookie. We're done for the night. You're going home," David said.

"If you insist," Bill said, with evident good humor. He sat back and closed his eyes.

David felt comfortable inside a police car. As he drove, he spun the MDT around and paged through the message screens. Many were work related. Some were stupid. Several were inquiries into Bill's health. With one hand on the wheel and the other on the keyboard, one eye on the road and the other on the display, David typed replies and cleared out the screens. When he was done, as they drove south on I-35 in the thick morning traffic, he took the microphone and changed their mark-out to the station. Immediately, the MDT beeped and the following message, sent from Jimmy John's unit, appeared in the center of the screen: "breakfast?"

David had forgotten. Friday mornings were breakfast beer mornings. "10/4," he messaged back. He thought for a moment about bringing Bill. After all, the kid had done very well at the game room. He decided that Bill was still too new, and besides, the other guys might not be as welcoming. David turned on the good time radio and spun the dial until he heard George Jones singing about something. For the rest of the ride he hummed with the music and watched traffic creep by, as he drove the speed limit in the right lane. At the station, David drove over to Bill's truck. Bill had fallen asleep and David lightly shook him awake.

"Huh?" Bill came back with a jolt.

"Get in your truck, partner, and go home," David said.

"What about the paperwork?"

"On me tonight. You did a good job. Go on home. Leave a message for me if you want to call in sick. If you have a headache or anything. How you doin' now?"

"I'm not going to call in sick or anything like that. I'm all right, just beat. But I need to get my clothes out of my locker."

"Well, maybe you ought to wear the uniform home. You need to wash it in a machine anyway. Wear it home and wear it back if you want to."

"Why do I need to wash it? I'll take it to the dry cleaners."

"Your shirt is full of blood. If you have it dry cleaned, that stain will set and so will the stink. Wash it in a machine first, then take it in."

"Okay."

"You still need to hit the locker room?"

"No, I guess not. I'll just get that stuff tonight."

"Not so fast. I just thought of something. Maybe you ought to get your stuff," David said. "Think about it. If you called in tonight, you'd have a three day weekend."

"Huh?"

"Look, we've worked four days this week. You had one days day, then three deep nights days. My regular days off are Sunday Monday. That means we don't work Saturday night for Sunday or Sunday night for Monday. Today is Friday. When we come in tonight, it's for Saturday, right? We work midnight to eight AM, so relatively speaking, tonight, after it turns into tomorrow, will be Friday for us, even though it's Saturday. Take off tonight and you'll have a three day weekend."

"Now I have a headache," Bill said.

"Seriously, any problems, take a day."

"Okay, but I'm all right. It just hurts around the stitches, is all. I'm pretty sure I'll be in tonight."

"Good. Go on, get outta here."

Bill did. David drove around to the apron and parked. He ran several reviews on the MDT, making sure all his calls were accounted for and that he had nothing pending. Then he logged off the MDT and marked out with the dispatcher, an irate female, upset one of her units bowed out a little early.

He made his way to the conference table in the administrative area. Several officers were already there, working on their statistical accomplishments form, claiming credit for their activity. David took his place and began writing.

"What did you do with the rookie, Dave?" Mike asked.

"Got him stitched up and sent him home," David replied.

"That old boy just doesn't have the luck," Jimmy John said.

"Why's that?" Andy asked, looking over his tickets for accuracy.

"Choked out Tuesday for Wednesday, hit in the head tonight," Jimmy John said. "Of course, he's still on his feet, so it could have been worse. Anyone for breakfast?"

A bunch of affirmative murmurs came from around the table.

"Got anything going for the weekend?" David asked Jimmy John.

"Got tickets to catch Nolan tonight. He's starting against Cleveland. You?"

"Party at Charlene's house," David said.

"How is that situation going?"

"I don't know. I can't get her to talk to me, yet here I am going to a big party at her place. Her parent's place, I mean. She still lives at home. Truth is, I'm pretty disgusted."

"Eight o'clock," someone said.

As one, the officers threw their completed paperwork in the different bins set up in the middle of the table, then moved off in the direction of the locker room. After changing and collecting their personal cars, a much smaller group ended up at an early-opening bar along the west I-30 service road. David had taken his time and was one of the last to arrive.

Inside the plain gray cinder block building, a black wooden bar competed with the two pool tables, two ping pong tables and televisions in every corner blaring country music videos for the customers' attention. It opened at about eight for what David thought of as the alcoholic trade. He never considered his own eight in the morning drinking in that category, however. He had just gotten off work and who would really begrudge him a couple of cold ones before a day of fitful sleep?

"All hail the conquering hero!" Guts shouted when he saw David enter the cool, dark bar.

Guts was a former Metro sergeant, now a headquarters lieutenant, by the name of Patton. The nickname had been Blood and Guts, shortened to Guts. Guts had been miserable ever since his promotion and transfer to 2014 Main. Once there, he quickly abandoned the career track and found himself a niche in an overnight position on the Chief's staff. It worked because he made sure to be out long before the Chief showed up at the office. Guts never missed the Friday breakfast beers.

"How goes it at headquarters, Guts?" David asked, knowing full well that Guts hated it.

"I hate that shit," Guts said, returning to his beer. Guts may or may not have ever been in the Army, but ever since his nickname stuck, he had been cursing like the real Patton.

"I hate that shit," Guts said again, this time to Alice, the barmaid.

Alice, a thickening brunette of a certain age, a contemporary of Guts himself, as it were, had heard it before. "Guts, save it for someone who cares."

David thought that although Alice gave Guts quite a hard time over his flirting, she liked the attention, deep down. Really deep down. Many of the usual suspects were there this morning, sitting in line at the bar. Erliss, Wayne, Jimmy John, Randy, Mike, Chivas and Baker were laughing at the shot Alice took at Guts.

"Don't do me like that, sweetheart. How about a little loving?" Guts replied, arms wide.

"No lovin,' and no more serving you beers, either, after today," Alice said.

"Alice, you wouldn't be moving on to another bar, would you?" Randy asked with mock hurt.

"Where else could we get your stunning beauty, cold ones, and Reba in every corner?" Mike asked.

"In technicolor," Chivas said.

"Chivas crossed the Rio Grand just to get technicolor cold ones in your esteemed presence," Erliss, the spitting image of a young Sam Elliot, said, motioning for another.

"Oh, brother." Alice poured, taking several bills from the pile of money in front of Guts.

"Alice, seriously, you moving on?" Jimmy John asked.

"Jimmy John, I will answer you as you have always been a gentleman with me," Alice said gravely, shooting a withering glance at Guts. "The fact of the matter is that I have a new career."

"New career? What the hell can you do but pour beer?" Guts shouted.

"A lot more than serving you piss!" Alice shouted back.

Alice stepped out from around the bar to pour a telephone company technician and a cable television man their morning courage. When she returned, she spoke to Jimmy John, in more civilized tones.

"In a moment, I'm going to meet with two executives," she said. "Did you hear that Guts? Executives! I'm getting the exclusive Dallas territory for . . . cheese. Cheese from Wisconsin. This company sells it. And that will be the end of serving the likes of you."

"C'mon, Alice," Guts said halfheartedly.

His heart was not in his pleading. The country music television station had started the second of two back-to-back Reba videos, and the opening scene had his attention. By the time the video was over, Alice had disappeared from behind the bar and the cops were getting thirsty. They started reaching around for their own cold ones. Jimmy John separated the money into two piles; money they had already spent and money they would spend. Jimmy John conscientiously kept track, not allowing anyone to reach over the bar until he had moved the money from one mound to the other.

They watched videos and drank beer and heard about the war from David, who told the generic type of stories vets tell when they want to keep things light. David thought that Jimmy John must have read his mind when he threw the conversational ball onto the next field.

"Erliss, when they canceled the funding for the supercollider, did that mess up your deal?" Jimmy John asked.

"Gone to settlement just before the funding dried up. I walked out of the closing with a check in my hand. When I got in my truck, Me and Jill heard it on the radio. I ran to the bank it was drawed on. We made them cash it and give us a bank check. Then I drove code three to the credit union and deposited it. We laughed like Bonny and Clyde all the way."

"The government bought a strip of land from Erliss through his back field for the Superconducting Supercollider," Jimmy John explained to David.

"Just a strip of it, you understand," Randy said.

"But now, his cattle can't get to his back acreage," Mike said.

"Only a sliver of the property, brother," Erliss said, unable to contain his smile.

"But the government paid him rights money for the whole thing," Jimmy John said.

"Wonderful phrase, 'market rate,' don't you think?" Erliss asked no one in particular.

"Won't tell us what they paid him," Chivas said. "Jimmy John, how about another?"

"Those guys Alice is sitting with over there, aren't they from narco?" Guts asked.

The conversation ceased, and everyone concentrated on the bottles in front of them, while the two most senior officers present tried to determine who was sitting with Alice.

"I don't know the other guy, but one is Rapier Navaroux and he's over at narco, last I heard," Jimmy John said, turning toward his beer like the rest of them.

"Yeah, I recognize them both as narcos. Cheese my ass. Okay everybody," Guts said, muttering almost to himself, "peel off in pairs and drift on out of here. Meet you at the place in the river bottoms. I'll arrange a couple of cases and we'll settle up then. First two, go."

They did as they were told. The two undercover detectives studiously paid no attention as the patrol officers left. Once in the parking lot, David quickly looked around. He picked up two unmarked cars and the takedown van. He could not help feeling nervous, like he did in grade school when perpetrating some mischief that would incur parental wrath, if caught. Once in his truck and driving away, he decided he was hungry. He swung by a McDonald's and ate an Egg McMuffin and hash browns in the parking lot. Then he drove to the river bottoms to continue the morning's socializing.

David guided his truck around the levy in Oak Cliff Division territory and into the bottoms themselves. The pre-arranged clearing they were heading for was deep enough into the thick foliage of the bottoms to be private, high enough to be dry even in the spring and large enough for their vehicles. As long as the Chief wasn't flying around in a department chopper looking for them, they ought to be fine.

By the time David drove up, even the beer had arrived. The cast of characters had changed, with Chivas and Erliss dropping out and Ralph and Andy taking their place. Ralph and Andy sat on the hood of Andy's older Camaro, several empties scattered around Ralph's feet. Unlike David, who had locked his small .380 pistol in his glove box, Ralph had jammed his duty Sig Saur into his waistband. David parked and walked over to Jimmy John's ancient Dodge Ram pick up. He reached into the cooler and grabbed himself a cold Budweiser.

"What's the damage?" David asked.

"Don't worry about it. We had enough. Sit," Guts said, motioning to the horizontal gate. "Could you believe that bitch? Selling drugs while we were sitting right there, peace officers commissioned by the governor of Texas? I've never seen such disrespect for the badge."

Fact was, they had all seen such disrespect, and worse, but the expression, a favorite, remained in use. David was about to pipe up with his own commentary when a pale green Ford Explorer sped into the clearing and skidded to a stop. Hermondo, still in uniform, jumped out of the truck and kicked at the ground.

"That stupid kid is going to drive me to drink before he will ever figure out how to drive me to a call!" Hermondo shouted.

"Come to the right place, I guess," Jimmy John said.

Guts threw a cold Budweiser to Hermondo, who smoothly caught it, pulled it open and drained off half in one gulp. He wiped some foam off his upper lip and pointed at David.

"After the game room call, that loser couldn't find Parkland. Then he couldn't find the station. And he couldn't find the call in the first place. If we drive up to Love Field one more time, I'm going to shoot myself," Hermondo said in a disgusted rush.

"Rookies are a pain in the ass," Guts said.

"Lois's rookie stole my whore," Ralph said, slurring the words together.

"Don't call me Lois, Ralph," David said.

"We've been drinking a while," Andy said, shrugging as if that explained everything.

"No rookie could steal a whore from you, Ralph," Guts said.

"Fucking rookies are a pain in the ass. Give me another beer," Hermondo said, throwing his empty into the bed of Jimmy John's pickup.

"She was my whore, Lois," Ralph said.

Anger coursed through David. He never liked that joke in general and it galled him even more coming from a fuck-up like Ralph. And talking about whores, what the fuck about Charlene, anyway? He did not say anything to Ralph in response. Instead, he started a slow, angry burn.

"Calm down Ralph. Have another," Jimmy John said, opening the cooler in invitation.

Ralph stood up. He walked slowly and with great care in the direction of the cooler, and of David.

"Fucking Lois's rookie," Ralph muttered.

"Ralph," Jimmy John said, "you ought not call him that."

"Fuck him and fuck you, too, Cowboy Bob," Ralph said.

"Ralph, don't pick on Jimmy John and don't call me Lois," David said, putting down his beer and standing up.

"Why *Lois*, what you gonna do? Is Superm—"

While Ralph talked, David walked over to him. Fed up with everything, he screwed his heels into the clay, bent his knees and hit Ralph with a short right to the middle so hard it choked off his comment and lifted him a foot in the air. David stepped around Ralph so that they faced the same direction. As Ralph landed, David slid his hand around Ralph's ample soft belly and caught hold of the large automatic pistol, pulling it free. Ralph fell over and hit the clay pretty hard.

David pressed the magazine release. The thick metal box magazine slid out of the handle and dropped to the ground. Then, with his left hand, he sharply pulled back on the slide, ejecting the round from the chamber. Every eye in the clearing watched it fly, spinning on its wide arc. Then David gave it several more sharp pulls to the rear, just to be sure.

As the cartridge hit the ground, Ralph started throwing up.

David flipped the pistol to Andy, who dropped his beer in an almost bungled effort to catch it. "When he gets up, Andy, I'd appreciate it if you told him not to call me Lois," David said calmly.

Andy nodded silently. Ralph was down to some final, weak heaves, his head resting in a puddle of his own vomit.

"Good fucking advice," Hermondo said, dropping his empty and taking a fresh one out of the cooler. "See you all later," he said, getting back into his Explorer and driving out of the clearing.

One by one, the rest of them headed to their vehicles and followed Hermondo. The last thing David saw of the clearing, in his rear-view mirror, was Andy helping Ralph to sit up.

David wasted no more time on Ralph. He drove home the long way around and stopped at a Baskin-Robbins. He was gratified to see the teenager he had taught to make chocolate milkshakes with chocolate ice cream still worked there. Not only that, but he remembered David and his Yankee peculiarity. Sucking the dessert to his breakfast of champions through a straw, he drove the rest of the way home, feeling much better.

Chapter 10

That night found Andree sweating next to a four door junker. He had driven it into the middle of the very same clearing the police had used earlier that morning. The day had remained hot and humid and sundown had not brought any relief.

Andree looked at his thin gold watch. It was now 11:30 PM. Anticipation kept him literally on his toes. Nervous energy had him bouncing up on the balls of his feet. Up and down. Up and down. While the waiting was always the hard part, it could be worse. Dantwan could have been a talker. Instead, the younger man stood off to the side, motionless, tolerant of the waiting. Dantwan had no idea what was coming.

Andree had told him to dress in old work clothes and wait for him at the last minute. Dantwan had complied and after a meal of Thompson's fried chicken and fries, they had driven around, eventually ending up in the clearing. Andree had followed his own advice about clothing and wore a loose, dark blue work shirt and dark blue chinos, like those a custodian might wear. He would have worn a Casio, but the thing acted weird when he put it on, all eights on the numbers, so the gold watch had been it.

Andree bounced up and down on the balls of his feet as sweat ran down his back. It ran down his crotch. It ran down his forehead into his eyes. He was sure Dantwan was near ready to explode from the need to know what was up. They still waited.

Before midnight, the dented red Nissan 280 ZX made its way into the clearing. It stopped about two car lengths from the rear quarter of the junker. The driver turned off the headlights and left the parking lights on, illuminating the area with a dim amber glow. Both doors opened and men stepped out on either side. They walked toward Andree, coming closer together between the cars.

"What the hell you bring him for?" Shuka yelled, louder than usual.

"Who, Dantwan? Just giving him a taste, man. I got your cut from the Mexico trip," Andree said.

Andree chose to ignore the brother Shuka brought with him. It did not really matter. Andree had expected him. Andree also expected the big retard to be wearing the dark, streamlined sunglasses he had on, too. Andree thought they made the man look like an idiot. He hoped that Shuka would fall for the distraction regarding the word 'cut.' After all, he had gone to Mexico to buy, not sell. There ought not be a 'cut' for Shuka.

"I got it here in the car," Andree said.

Moving at a relaxed, unhurried pace, Andree opened the rear door on the passenger side of the junker and took out a black nylon carry-on. He placed it on the trunk lid, turning his back on Shuka and the retard, who smiled broadly under his idiot sunglasses, probably high as a kite.

"Wait 'til you see this, mother fucker," Andree said lightly.

Now was the risky part. If Dantwan was in it with them, if Shuka smelled something, if the retard was not retarded—it could all go to shit. Andree believed in limiting risk as much as possible. He also believed that taking risks was necessary to achieve success. Andree greatly believed in risk management, but sometimes he knew you just had to go for it.

He unzipped the bag and reached inside. "Some big green in here, mothers," Andree said.

Shuka and his bodyguard walked up to Andree as Andree wrapped his fingers around the taped end of a two and a half foot length of pipe. He smartly pulled it out of the bag and spun around, jumping up just a little, for clearance, and swinging hard. In his last snapshot glimpse of the undamaged men, they were smiling. Shuka had a self satisfied told-you-so smirk on his face and his "bodyguard" smiled even wider, showing white, even teeth. The pipe hit its target, smashing into the center of Shuka's friend's throat, nailing his Adam's Apple.

Andree landed in a crouch, ducking underneath Shuka's unaimed haymakers. He swung around backwards as fast as possible, pivoting on his toes while crouched, hitting Shuka's shins before Shuka could backpedal out of range, or pull his pistols, or anything. Andree hit Shuka hard enough to knock his feet out from under him, so that a surprised Shuka fell face first into the clay. Andree stood up and struck like lightning, slamming the pipe into Shuka's head, once, twice, a third time. Stunned, Shuka abandoned all pretext at offensive conduct. Instead he tried to shield his head with his arms. Andree quickly found both Glocks in Shuka's waistband and pulled them free.

Andree surveyed the scene. The retard had tumbled to the ground. His back arched with the struggle to get air into his lungs. He clawed at his throat. His feet worked, lurching him around as his heels dug deeply into the clay. Shuka cowered face down, his head bleeding, both hands up by his ears, shaking. Andree scanned around the clearing, seeing only a shocked, frozen Dantwan. Good. Let him see what doing business with Andree was all about. Shuka had known, but he forgot. Now Dantwan would know.

Andree put Shuka's pistols in the carry-on, along with the pipe. He turned around and saw Shuka trying to crawl away. He was not moving much, but his toes cut shallow parallel trenches in the dirt. The retard bucked horrifically and rasped out his death groans. Andree saw no reason to see the idiot suffer, so he walked over to him, lifted his shirttail, pulled a fine Browning Hi Power from underneath and shot the man twice in the head. He flopped once and was still.

Andree stepped over to Shuka. He grabbed Shuka's shoulder and flipped him over so that he lay on his back. Shuka mistook the gesture and bent at the waist to get up, probably thinking that the worst was over. Andree rang his pistol off of the left side of Shuka's head, dropping him back to the clay.

"Ow, shit, motherfucker!" Shuka yelled.

"Where's my money, you mother fucker," Andree said conversationally.

"What money? You was giving me my cut tonight!"

"What cut, jick? I got take from the Mexico trip. They's no cut. Where's my money?"

"I be givin' up everything, man. Everything!"

Andree bent over Shuka's legs. They were the legs of an athlete. When they were kids, they had carried Shuka and Andree and the rest of them to victory after victory on the courts. They had run him to safety, from the cops, from older boys, from real criminals. Now Andree put the barrel of the automatic against Shuka's left knee and pulled the trigger.

The loud, crisp shot shattered the man's kneecap and caused him to howl in pain.

In no mood for screwing around, Andree, who had just shot his oldest friend in the knee, who knew his oldest friend would need to thrash around a bit before they could talk again, walked over to Dantwan.

"We gonna have to carry these niggers out of here. You up for that?" Andree asked him.

A speechless but attentive Dantwan licked his lips and nodded vertically.

"Come here," Andree said as he grabbed Dantwan's upper right arm and pulled him over to Shuka.

"I been working with Dantwan for weeks, man. Watching you smoke that shit. Watching you steal my money. You went bad, brother. Went bad and tried to leave Dantwan in the air. Where's my money?" Andree asked.

"There ain't no money, man. I'm fucked up, man. Fucked up in the head, fucked up in the knee. Get me amb-lance, man. Hurry the fuck up!"

Andree pointed the pistol at Shuka's good knee, but Shuka, intent on his pain, did not notice.

"Look here, you stealing jick motherfucker," Andree said.

Shuka looked up and saw. He started wailing and kicking out his good leg to get away, moving in a slight arc, going nowhere.

"My brother, where be my money?"

"Ain't no money."

Andree adjusted his aim and pulled the trigger again, loudly shattering Shuka's very last good knee.

"Oh mother fucker! In the car, in the car, in the car!"

"What's left of it, I bet. Go look under the front seat," Andree said to a frozen Dantwan. "Go get it!"

Dantwan shot over to the Nissan and crouched by the front seat. Now was the time when he might come up shooting. Andree was ready. He had plenty of bullets in the fine Browning he had stolen in a burglary years ago. He had been young and stupid then. He felt very confident that if things broke bad, he'd be the only one driving out of this here clearing.

"Got some!" Dantwan shouted.

Andree watched closely now.

Dantwan stood up quick, holding something up in his right hand. Panic grabbed Andree. Andree brought his pistol up and started to pull on the trigger. Just before the weapon went off, Andree thought the object in Dantwan's hand might not be a pistol. He cut off his instinct to shoot Dantwan. He could not make out what Dantwan held up in the low light. Andree forced himself to drop his pistol down until Dantwan came closer.

Dantwan ran over, oblivious to his near-death experience. He handed Andree a roll of bills. Andree slipped the roll in his pocket and breathed a sigh of relief. He willed his panic to subside and loosen its grip on his chest. That had been fucking close, Andree thought.

"There man, there. It's all they is, man. Get me an amb-lance, man," Shuka pleaded.

"That ain't no $17,000, man," Andree said sadly. "You smoked and spent the rest, my brother."

"No! No man, it weren't like that, Andree, my man, it weren't like that!"

"Tell me what it be like, then."

"No, I meant to pay it back, I can pay it back. It be just a thing, I be's a little slow, Andree, man, I can, I can pay you it."

Andree looked down at his old friend, his comrade of the courts, his schoolmate, the man he called his brother. The enormity of the situation saddened him greatly, but what needed to be done, needed to be done.

"Okay, my man. I'll get you the amb-lance. Just close your eyes while I put some first aid on your ass," Andree said, walking closer to Shuka's head. "What you looking at me like that for?" he asked an incredulous Shuka. "I'll send Dantwan to the car to get my first aid."

"Dantwan!" Andree shouted, "go run up to that junker and get my first aid, mother fucker!"

Dantwan, looking confused, scampered over to the junker.

Then he looked down at Shuka again. "Go on, brother. Shut your eyes. Them bandages gonna hurt you a little, when they go on. Close your eyes."

Shuka, who had propped himself up on his elbows, started to cry as he slowly lowered himself to the ground. By the time his head rested on the clay, he was crying quietly, fighting back the sobs.

"Don't be like that, nothing is going to happen," Andree said.

"I know, I know," Shuka said between sobs. "I know it." Then he closed his eyes. "Tell Mama?"

"I'll tell her," Andree said, just before he pointed the Browning at Shuka's forehead and blew a dime sized hole in it, just over his right eye.

The bullet passed though Shuka's skull and brain and out the back, taking a quarter sized chunk of bone with it. His body jerked, lifting his torso an inch or so off the ground, and then dropped. His blood poured out onto the clay that had so accommodated Ralph's bodily fluids earlier that day.

"Oh, man," Dantwan said softly. Somehow he had made his way over to Andree without Andree noticing.

"When they steal from you, you can't let them get away with it," Andree said, hiding the surprise he felt at Dantwan's close proximity. "Even if you know them. First they take a little, then a lot, then they kill your ass. Out here, it's always them or you," Andree said, regarding the dead man who used to be his friend. He turned his head to look at Dantwan. "And it ain't goin' to be me, aight?"

"Yeah, man," Dantwan said.

"You done right by me and I appreciate it. But what I got to know now is, you in this? You with me?"

Dantwan looked back and forth between Shuka and Andree. "Ain't no time to be sayin"no,' my man," he said.

"I guess not."

"Eyes in it. All the way."

"I mean Shuka's job, all the territories."

"Oh yeah, I'm up for that shit."

"Okay. Go through the retard's pockets."

While Dantwan rifled the muscular corpse, Andree did the same with Shuka. The only thing Andree found was another $500.

"Say, Andree, look at this!" Dantwan stage whispered excitedly.

Dantwan ran over and showed Andree another pile of bills, roughly the same amount as the one he collected out of the Nissan.

"Where he be carrying all that shit?"

"All his pockets, man."

"Then you put it in your pockets. We'll count it later. Help me drag him to the trunk."

The two men dragged Shuka and then Shuka's bodyguard to the junker's trunk. Andree opened the lid, and they heaved both men in, one at a time, Andree at their heads, Dantwan at their feet.

"See here, man," Andree said, "drive that Nissan over to Lew Sterret and park it. Then walk over to the bail bondsman across Industrial and wait for me. When I roll up, get in. We goin' to dump these mothers in East Dallas at a place I know."

"Okay," Andree said.

"When you drive away from here, don't turn on your lights until you get to the road. It be shift change for the po-lice, ain't none of them goin' to be around. Don't worry and just drive like normal. I'll be five minutes behind you, aight?"

Dantwan nodded earnestly. Andree knew he would follow directions. He was a good boy, ambitious, smart, ready to work. So was Shuka, once. Damn.

They each slid behind the driver's seats of their respective vehicles and started them up. Dantwan did as he was told and drove away with only the parking lights on. Andree thought about Shuka. Him and Shuka could have gone the distance. Then they could have quit when they had enough for their mamas and everything. If only Shuka had listened to him. Andree continued to think about his friend, in the trunk, dead at his very own hand, as he drove out to the street. He thought of him, and cried a little, before turning on the junker's lights. Then he turned onto the macadam and drove away from his killing ground.

Chapter 11

By now, Bill tried his best to avoid Theo. Bill walked into the station that night, dressed in a clean, pressed uniform, ready to go out. The smallest Band-Aid type square bandage possible covered his stitches. He received a warm welcome from the deep nights officers waiting around for detail. They shouted him over and made room for him at a table, asking after him and slapping his back, while Theo sat alone across the room. At one point, Theo caught his eye and waved. It was like they were in high school and Bill, having finally made it in with the cool guys, could afford to jettison his former associate. Bill, knowing Theo was having problems making it and probably needing a friend at the moment, looked away from Theo's wave.

Bill felt relief at not being linked to Theo in the eyes of the established officers. At the academy, it seemed like anyone who made time for Theo ended up in some kind of trouble either with or because of Theo. Rookies were on a period of probation where they could be fired without cause, and Bill reasoned that he needed to protect himself out here. He did not want to get fired without cause. That cold pragmatism did not help him at all with the shame he felt at abandoning Theo to whatever lonely fate he had coming. While Bill did not know anything about Theo's training progression officially, he had overheard more than one officer say that it did not look like Theo would survive deep nights.

"People, let's get in the room," Sergeant Karangekis called out.

He and a pack of supervisors, including Lieutenant Fortnoy, walked rapidly down the hall. Their grim expressions and spirited movement propelled the deep nights officers forward.

"Don't sit," the Lieutenant called out. "There's a lot going on out there. Please excuse us at rushing you, but you're all going right out. As the cars come in, switch out and take up your assignments. Sergeant Washington has arranged alternate cars for some of you. Basically, there is a barricaded person in Baker Sector and five pages of calls holding. Please hit the street and get on your assignments. We are going to try to keep the lid on without holding over third watch, so please get out there as soon as possible. Costas?"

Costas, who had been leaning on a table, stood up straight. "If your car is not in, get with Sergeant Washington for an alternate. Baker Sector units, get right out to Fitzhugh and Alcott and relieve the perimeter guard. Tactical has been called in and is responding to that location. The rest of you, prepare to answer calls all over the division. Oh, and one more thing, Lew Sterret called. The jail is full, so we are only transporting felonies and "A" misdemeanors wherein you do not have any other choice. Space is limited. Use your judgement. Thanks for your flexibility. Stay safe!"

By the time Costas had finished, officers were heading out, others were trying to get in and there was a general knot of confusion at the door to the detail room.

"He said get in a car and get out there, so go on and git," a short, barrel chested officer said in thick Texan. His brown hair was parted neatly over a weatherbeaten face. He squinted over half glasses and had a wad of chew jammed in his left cheek. Three rows of hero bars capped his left pocket.

"Leslie, what's going on?" someone shouted.

"Ain't nothing you rookies need to know 'cept Baker units get out to Fitz and Alcott, and the rest of us clear for calls, like yesterday." Leslie moved to a blocking position, allowing officers out of the room but not in.

"What is it, Leslie?"

"What part of 'git to your car' didn't you understand?"

Jimmy John and Hermondo herded the crowd that had been inside the detail room out into the hallway. There was still a stubborn knot of police officers waiting for more word before they moved.

"Lieutenant said to git, now go on, git in your cars. Y'all can do without a gabfest one night now," Leslie said.

Bill realized with a jolt Leslie was talking to him. Not to him personally, but that he needed to stop taking up space in the hall and get out to the car. Bill started working on the car problem in his head when he saw David and Leslie shaking hands. Curious, he moved a little closer.

"... Not as bad as it could have been, for sure. A couple of contacts, mostly LRRP work in an empty desert. How have you been?" David asked Leslie.

"Some vacation. Peggy wanted to visit Liz at school, so we drove on over to Tulane. Weren't bad."

David noticed Bill hanging back. "Leslie, this is my rookie. Don't mind his looks, he took a bottle in the face last night."

Bill stepped up to Leslie and they shook hands. Bill couldn't help himself. His eyes drifted over to the hero bars, the small rectangles of color over Leslie's left breast pocket that signified police awards. That was when he noticed the pin with a vertical knife over crossed arrows. The motto 'De Opresso Liber' appeared underneath on a scroll. David wore the same pin in the same position.

"Bottle in the face? What you doin' in here tonight, boy?" Leslie asked.

Bill, brought back to the matter at hand, could not think of a decent reply. "I don't know."

The senior officers smiled at one another.

"We better appropriate a car and get out there," David said.

"Yup. Let's get some coffee later. You can tell me all about the modern Army."

"You got it," David said, before leading Bill away.

They grabbed their gear and walked through a ramp and parking lot covered in a sea of blue confusion. Officers milled about, looking around for units. Others pulled out in anything that ran. Some blocked the smooth flow of traffic by talking to the third watch officers wherever they happened to bump into them. One unit blocked the exit onto Hall Street and four officers gossiped in the middle of the roadway, two doors open on the car like wings. An air horn blast from a unit that wanted to get out, polite in its brevity, brought them to their senses. They all jumped into the car and drove the rest of the way into the bedlam.

"Lane! Hey, Lane!" someone called out.

As luck would have it, the third watch boys had brought their regular car in. In the middle of an access road by the credit union, the four officers swapped out. All four doors opened and gear bags and brief cases flew back and forth. Then all four doors slammed closed at about the same time.

"Let's get the hell out of here," David said.

Getting out to Hall was out of the question. While Bill logged them on the MDT, David drove through the city parking lot, around the offices and garage and passed the line at the city gas pumps. They sped out the back of the complex, under I-30 and into the very northern reaches of South Dallas. Then David pulled over to the side of the road.

"Let's see what we've got," he said, spinning the MDT around so that it faced him. He started typing. "Look at this, almost five pages and they've been holding priority ones for ten, twelve minutes. No Joker's tonight, at least not now. Go ahead and clear us. It's time to rock and roll."

Bill forced a nervous swallow down his dry throat, picked up the microphone and cleared them as a two man.

Theo struggled to get a car. Universally ignored by the other officers, watching the hand-offs of the units occurring between friends and acquaintances, and with Hermondo nowhere in sight, he felt very isolated. His inability to procure a car added to his despair. He did not want to face Hermondo's ever-growing and ever more vocal displeasure. This hot, sweaty night promised all sorts of problems. The least Theo wanted to be able to do was get them a set of wheels without any complications. Before dawn.

Theo planted himself next to Sergeant Washington. When this proved insufficient, he moved to right in front of the supervisor until the Sergeant could no longer ignore him.

"What do you want?" the sergeant finally asked.

"A car?"

"You're Hermondo's rookie, right?"

"Yes, Sergeant."

"Dog-Three, usually?"

"Uh, yes Sergeant."

Sergeant Washington pointed slowly to a car not five parking spots away. It sat idling in its spot. Hermondo occupied the passenger seat. His arm rested on the door, through the open window. He looked at Theo, but said nothing. Theo's heart fell.

"The car didn't go out on third watch tonight," Washington said, before turning his attention elsewhere.

Theo started his lonely processional toward the car, with Hermondo's expressionless stare on him the whole way.

"Sure is hot for spring," Theo said when he finally arrived, opening the driver's door.

"Get in the car, rookie," Hermondo said, not bothering to hide his disgust.

A chastened Theo threw his bag in the back seat and slid behind the steering wheel. He put his PR-24 on the floor between the seat and the door while keeping the heavy-duty flashlight on the seat, underneath his thigh, like Hermondo had taught him. He shifted into gear and followed the line of cars out of the parking lot, onto Jeffries and then north into Deep Ellum.

"Dammit, turn left and pull over!" Hermondo yelled.

Theo instantly complied and found himself pointing the wrong way down Commerce Street. Thankfully, the police car ended up just about parked, so he had no worries about safety at the moment. He wanted to ask Hermondo about what was going on, except just then Hermondo ran around the front of the police car. As Theo watched, Hermondo pushed two men who were grappling with one another to the ground.

Theo wanted to ask someone about that, but the sight he picked up on next diverted his attention. Little knots of men and women were struggling with one another up and down the sidewalk. Some were throwing punches, some wrestling and others just shoving. To Theo, it looked kind of like a riot. And there was Hermondo, out in the middle of it.

A riot! His training officer out there alone! Why, Theo thought to himself, he needed to get out there, too. He opened the door, put one foot on the ground and pulled himself out of the car. As he transferred his weight to his feet, a bald, ill-tempered young man in a dirty khaki shirt with loose threads where the sleeves had been torn off, dived at him. The bald man grabbed him around the waist. In an instant, an off-balance Theo felt the man pulling at his pistol.

It had been drilled into the rookies that an officer who loses his weapon ends up dead, usually shot with his own weapon. Again and again, based on years of research, the rookies were told they had to keep their weapons in their control at all costs. Theo had paid attention. The number of officers that were killed with their own side arms had impressed and frightened him. Now here he was, some bald perpetrator pulling on the butt of his weapon.

It took a moment to sink in. When it did, fear and adrenalin motivated the hell out of Theo. He would never remember picking up his flashlight. He would always remember the sound and feel of swinging it at his assailant's head, the jarring impact of the blow and the blood that shot out everywhere.

The young man dropped to his knees and then slowly stood up. He was about Theo's height, but somewhat heavier. With blood running into his face, he smiled, ducked his head and started punching Theo in the mid section. Theo's vest absorbed most of the punishment. The attack so startled him that he fell back into the car. The man leapt on him like a jungle cat, and the fight, as they say, was on.

Bill cleared them, but with so many elements clearing, dispatch had a time separating out the critical priority one calls and assigning them. While the dispatcher worked his way down the list, Bill and David remained clear. David drove them toward Dog sector, southbound on Oakland. Bill took the time to arrange his equipment. He had begun to pick up a personal style, the particulars of which were based on what he saw David doing. David always knew where everything was and everything was always just so.

That kind of organization appealed to Bill, who ran his carpentry jobs, tools and personal truck the same way. He was concentrating on setting up the carbon paper on his pad of detox forms, preparing them for immediate use, when Hermondo's call came out over the radio.

"Signal 15, Commerce at Walton!"

David spun the car around and turned the lights and siren on before Bill processed the meaning of the call. Soon they were hurtling through the evening down the center of the road, straddling the yellow line. David made minor adjustments to either side as necessary, swinging totally around cars that wouldn't or couldn't get out of the way.

"Show us en route! Use the radio so everyone knows!" David shouted, turning off the siren so Bill could speak. David continued to part traffic with the air horn. They made a skidding right turn onto Commerce and David wound the large v—eight up as tight as it would go. They shot down the street like a bullet. In the blink of an eye, they were stopped at the side of the road and David's door was open. Bill saw the fighting and several officers in the middle of it, including Hermondo.

"Get on those two!" David yelled, pointing to Bill's right, to two men standing on the sidewalk close to the unit.

Bill attacked his assignment. He bounded out of his door, taking his flashlight but leaving his PR-24. He stepped up close to the two white men, both of whom had full heads of hair and were dressed in work clothes. They were no older than himself. The one on the left wore a swastika tattooed on a cheekbone. Bill assumed a good defensive stance, his right foot back and knees bent, expecting a fight.

"Get on the ground, do it now!" he shouted.

Bill did not expect at all what happened next. The two young men dropped like stones, ending up spread eagle on the concrete. They looked at him with big puppy eyes, waiting for their next instructions.

It tickled Bill that he had his situation under control. He looked around and saw that about five officers were in similar positions.

They were standing calmly over two to four young men who had been proned out on the side walk or in the street at the curb. The others were wrestling and shouting and fighting, failing to gain compliance.

Bill saw David duck a punch and come up blocking his bald white assailant's arm so that he could not recover from his swing. David slid behind Baldy and grabbed both his shoulders while stepping back with his right leg and twisting to the right. David threw the man so he landed face down on the sidewalk. David quickly pounced and had him in handcuffs in an instant.

A little further down the street, Bill saw Leslie lean into a police car and pull out another bald white male. Leslie had him by the scruff of his neck and the waistline of his ratty work pants. While keeping him bent over, Leslie spun the man around 180 degrees and ran him into the brick wall of the corner building. Leslie then let him fall in a pile of akimbo limbs. Bill saw Theo struggle out of the car and stand there, disoriented. Leslie pointed at the assailant and said something. Theo staggered over, reaching for his handcuffs. Bill suddenly had an idea that he needed to confirm. He went down on one knee near the faces of the two hairy-headed guys on the ground at his feet.

"What exactly is going on here?" he asked.

Both men started speaking at once. Bill shut them up and indicated the closer of the two should speak.

"We're from Gamma Gamma Delta? And we're having a skinhead party? And then these bald guys came and wanted to come in? And like, one of them hit a girl? From school? Like, right at the door—"

"I got the picture," Bill said. "You're not from around here, are you?"

"No, I'm from Colorado, well, really California, and I came here to go to Southern Christian, you know, and—"

"Okay, I got it."

Bill felt the need to share this information with someone. He looked out over the scene and saw all the hairy-heads complying while the last of the skinheads were put down and handcuffed.

Similar conversations were going on all over the sidewalk. Those officers who did not have their hands full were getting up and rolling their eyes at one another in vague disbelief.

Once the core fighters had been identified and transportation arranged, the officers started pairing up and heading out. David and Bill slid into their unit and drove away.

"Since when is a swing and a miss at an officer a crime?" David said, in answer to Bill's question about the prisoner David had let go. "Never gets prosecuted in Dallas County, or anywhere else I know of. Besides, this is the best part of the night. Don't want to waste it on line at Lew Sterret, even if there was room for the little turd."

Theo could not release his prisoner even if he wanted to, and he didn't want to. Instead, he came up with a plan all by himself. They had figured out their skinhead had been one of the original suspects, and that meant that he faced several assault charges, including the one against Theo. Smacked up as good as he was, he needed to go to Lew Sterret via the Parkland emergency room. Without asking Hermondo what to do or how to get there, Theo drove through downtown and then north on Harry Hines. He felt pretty pleased with himself when the large white hospital came into view.

As Theo unpacked the prisoner, Hermondo rifled through his gear bag. He came out with a thick paperback, which he placed under his arm. He clasped his hands behind his back and started walking toward the sliding glass doors of the emergency room. Theo wondered what the book was for, but didn't ask. Inside, Theo moved to the head of the line of walking wounded and slightly sick at the administration desk.

"Hey rookie," Hermondo said from the end of the line, "over here."

Theo walked over to his training officer.

"Something bothering you?" Hermondo asked.

"We shouldn't have to wait," Theo hissed, "we're on police business."

"Paperwork is paperwork, rookie. Besides, waiting is going to be the dominant theme for the rest of the evening."

David and Bill drove two blocks before the next signal 15 came out. "Hall at Croom, we can't control the crowd!" someone put out over the radio.

David must have stomped the gas pedal straight to the floor because the cruiser fishtailed just a bit before accelerating down Commerce. They had the green at Hall, so David took the turn without letup, sliding around to the left, the back end trying to lead the front. Whatever David did with the wheel, the tires bit at just the right time and they continued accelerating north. Tearing by Baylor, they would turn out to be the first supporting officers to arrive.

"See it?" Bill asked, as he noticed the flickering flashlight held up over someone's head, a bit further down the block. The glare of Thompson's Chicken Palace almost washed it out.

"Yeah, I got it."

David slowed down considerably, as the crowd of young and old, male and female African Americans milled about, mostly on the project side of the street. David pulled up next to the officer, who turned out to be Randy.

"Hey, y'all. Kid from Southern Christian had to come down for some fried chicken. Witnesses say the suspects shot for really no reason. Right in the chest," Randy said.

Behind him a small group of white males and females, college age, cowered in the glare.

"He doesn't look so good, Randy," David said.

From inside the car, at their angle, Bill could not see the victim, only the boy and two girls that huddled together, crying. One of them, a small blond in a red sweater with mascara running down her cheeks, made eye contact with him. He could think of nothing else to do, so he smiled and waved. She looked away.

"Where's Mike?" David asked.

"Inside, taking statements." Randy looked over his shoulder as he spoke, checking on his partner.

They could see Mike behind the counter, talking to a fry cook, pad out, gesturing with his writing hand, pointing with his pen.

"What have you got for suspect information?" David asked.

"Black male, seventeen to twenty five, dirty white shirt, small silver automatic," Randy replied in a businesslike monotone.

Randy and David kept talking. The blond looked over again, making Bill feel stupid because he had no idea how to handle it. He looked to his right, just to look away, and could not believe what he saw. Leslie walked through the crowd as calmly as could be, holding his PR-24 in an arm lock around a young black male's right arm with his own left. Leslie's prisoner wore a dirty white shirt. A sea of angry black faces followed the police officer and his prisoner. Here we go again, Bill thought, getting good and scared.

As Leslie made his way toward the police near the chicken stand, the crowd that already filled the intersection noticed him. Then an ambulance followed by several more police cars pushed through from the south. The ambulance pulled around David and Bill's unit, and the paramedic firemen filed out of the vehicle. All Randy needed to do was point, and they went to work.

"Hey, boys," Leslie said.

"Leslie," Randy replied.

A lone bottle smashed on the ground near the ambulance.

"Ask the victim if this is the shooter," Leslie said.

Randy didn't have to. The remaining male in the little group of the victim's friends started shouting and pointing and making a general ruckus. Randy walked over to the small group and tried to simultaneously calm them and get information out of them. After a moment, he turned around and nodded affirmatively.

"Throw him in and let's go," David said.

"What the hell you doin' with my baby! What you doin' with my baby!" shouted the largest woman Bill had ever seen.

She came at them from between a row of residential units and the small strip mall that bordered either side of Croom Street, the way Leslie had come. A huge group of men and women followed her, echoing her indignation. The present crowd picked up on it. Anger swelled across its face like a storm surge at high tide during a gulf coast hurricane.

"Too late," Leslie said calmly. "Got any chew?"

"Get out," David ordered Bill.

Bill pushed the door open and stepped out into the madness, slipping his flashlight into his back pocket and keeping his PR-24 in his left hand.

The woman closed in on Leslie at high speed, her hair pulled back, a round nose protruding out of features scrunched up with anger. She cruised by a motionless Bill, frozen by indecision, and closed in on Leslie. David had moved around the front of the police car and taken charge of Leslie's prisoner. That left Leslie free to turn and face the irate mother.

"You white son of a bitch!" she yelled, arms spread wide in what Bill thought would be an attempt to grab Leslie in a bear hug.

Leslie disappeared from view, blocked by the woman's girth as she closed in on him. Bill thought that maybe he needed to help somehow. Before he could even think of anything, the woman stumbled back and fell into the street, revealing Leslie in a stable, bent knee stance, his arms positioned out in front of him, hands open. Leslie must have shoved her hard enough that she fell backwards. Bill grabbed the handle of his baton with his right hand, lining up the long end against his forearm.

"You son of a bitch!" she yelled.

"Look sharp, rookie!" someone yelled.

Bill spun around and crouched himself just in time to see a young man lunging at him. He brought his right forearm up reflexively, the arm that held his PR-24 by the handle. The man slammed into the long part of the baton. Bill pushed him away. As Bill's assailant gathered himself up for another rush, Bill swung the baton out, long end spinning, and hit his assailant along the side of the thigh. The strike caused his assailant's leg to buckle, just like at the academy. The man fell to the ground, surprise on his face.

"Good shot!" David yelled, on his right.

"On your left!" a Hispanic officer Bill had only seen around the station but did not know, shouted, appearing out of nowhere.

Bill took his eyes off the mass of people for a moment to see that he was now part of a line of uniforms separating the mob from an angry mother, the suspect and the victims. The elements of the situation—the anger of the crowd, the sight of the large woman, pinned now to the street by Leslie while he called for another set of handcuffs, her shirt hiked up, exposing rolls of fat that oscillated with the ebb and flow of their struggle—all this combined in a surreal moment. Bill felt like an observer as opposed to a participant. Then a bottle smashed on the pavement, making him flinch visibly.

"Steady Bill, we'll make it," David said, low enough for the others to miss.

Bill smiled weakly.

"Hey!" Randy yelled, "they need to transport. Push the crowd back so they can get out!"

"Okay, on me!" David yelled.

The line of officers shifted as one. They adjusted their individual stances so that they held their batons by the perpendicular handle, long part out. Each officer held his weapon side back and kept his knees bent, looking like they were ready for anything.

"Ready! Step!" David yelled. His voice was deep and loud.

Bill suddenly remembered this from the academy. He stepped down hard with his forward foot, as did the others. They called out a vigorous "Huh!" when their forward feet hit the pavement. They jabbed forward with the business end of their batons, whether someone was in front of them or not. Then they slid their rear feet up so they stood in a balanced combat crouch again.

"Ready! Step!"

They repeated the process several times, pushing the crowd across the street and opening up Hall. The ambulance roared out, followed closely by a unit filled with the three witnesses. Another unit, with two officers in front, and Leslie and the suspect in the back, immediately followed. Randy and Mike were shoving the suspect's mother into the back seat of their unit, pushing against her ample backside and cursing a blue streak. When they were ready, they pulled out in a cloud of dust and burnt rubber.

"Let's go!" someone yelled.

The police line collapsed and officer pairs ran for their cars. The crowd surged forward. As soon as Bill's backside hit the seat, they were off in a confusion of white cars, billowing refuse and angry pedestrians. Cars flew north or south on Hall, squeaking out before the road closed again. Bill saw at least two cars cut across a field to the service road for Central Expressway.

"How the hell much fun was that!" David said, grinning like a kid at Fair Park. "That was about the biggest woman I have ever seen. I thought for sure Leslie was gonna take a beating."

Bill found himself grinning like an idiot as well. When he considered the shooting, arrest, riot and the dishonorable retreat of the entire division, he had no idea why.

"Uh, yeah. You know it. I love this job," Bill said, unsure if he really did or if he was being sarcastic.

Theo, his training officer and their arrestee waited on the intake line. Then they waited in the waiting area. Eventually, they made it into a treatment room, where they waited some more. After a while, hurried medical types with no time to talk came by and wrapped a gauze turban around the suspect's head. Handcuffs secured his ankle to the gurney. He did not mind them. He was fast asleep.

That gave Theo some concerns, the skinhead sleeping so soon after sustaining a head injury. Nobody else seemed bothered by it. When he asked, Hermondo ignored him. Members of the scrubs-clad emergency room staff merely shrugged and continued on their way. Theo resumed his waiting.

Hermondo had taken up position in the only chair in the room and buried himself in his paperback. The room itself barely had space for the patient, Hermondo's perch and the counter that ran along one wall. As far as his personal comfort went, Theo was out of luck. The floor and walls were tiled, the first time Theo had ever seen that. It made him think of a large shower stall. He had grown tired of standing and had sat on the floor at the foot of the gurney with his back against the wall.

"How long we got to stay here?" Theo asked.

"Until the sheriff's department takes over," Hermondo muttered, without looking up from his book.

"When will that be?"

"When they admit this guy."

"When will that be?"

"Sometime tomorrow, probably."

"What! We got to stay here 'til then?"

"Yup. Now be quiet or get out of here. You'll wake the dirtbag."

"You never said we had to be here all night."

"Son, get out of here before you really try my patience."

"I can't go nowhere. This is a hospital."

"Go find the McDonald's. Bring me a Big Mac and a Coke."

"Where is it?"

Hermondo stood up so that he could see Theo over the dirtbag. By the tightly featured expression on his face, Theo saw that he had pushed his training officer too far. Theo hopped up to his feet and left the room running.

"I'll find it. Big Mac and a Coke, you got it," Theo said, scampering away.

"Let's ride this one and get something to drink," David said.

Bill's mind immediately seized on the thought of a cold drink. His dry tongue rubbed against the top of his mouth like sandpaper. Before he could indicate his agreement, the MDT beeped. A new electronic message had arrived in the buffer.

"See what it is," David said.

Bill swung the machine around on its pedestal and pulled up the message. "It says 'can u clear for a OMS death?' signed 'ch1.'"

"Send back '10/4, good for the rookie,'" David said.

Bill felt funny writing about himself like that.

Their number came over the radio. "Dog-Four, 10/4, thanks. Call sheet coming over now, it'll be up on Buckingham at Lemon."

David grabbed the microphone. "10/4." Then to Bill he said, "pull up the call sheet."

Bill did so and read off the address before moving on to the details. "'Death occurred OMS, coroner notified,' is all it says," Bill related. "What's OMS?"

"Outside medical supervision. Okay. Basically, we go to these things and make sure the dead guy wasn't murdered. You can handle that, right?"

"Um, yeah."

"Remember all your training?"

Bill racked his brain, trying to remember if they ever covered this stuff in the academy.

"Rookie, got your portable lab to check for poisoning?"

"Um, no."

"Me neither. No training, no lab, no nothing. Not only are we medical doctors, but I guess we're fucking clairvoyant now, too. Don't sweat it, we can handle it. But the moral of the story here is, unlike TV, don't get caught up in the details. Here we are," David said, pulling in front of an attractive row of townhouses framed by large trees and neat landscaped beds, thick with bushes.

"Got some rubber gloves?"

"Yeah, rubber gloves."

They found the right number and knocked on the door. A thin white male opened it. He had been crying. Dark stubble incompletely covered his jaw. His hair fell listlessly over his forehead. He wore a white shirt, half untucked and stained, and brown slacks.

"You got here fast," he said sarcastically in a nasal, effeminate voice.

Bill thought that the comment was unfair. After all, they had been pretty busy, but he followed David's lead and kept his mouth shut.

"He's upstairs." The man led them to a dark staircase and pointed up. "Make a left, first room on the left. If you don't mind, I'll be in the kitchen. Drinking my fifteenth cup of tea." Without waiting for a response, he walked down the dimly lit hallway.

Bill noticed a black and white photograph on the wall, mounted lengthwise. Sky, ocean and land divided the image in thirds. A figure ran down a twisting path through the sand. A trick of perspective showed the trail abruptly terminating at a sharp line between the sand and water. A boat sailed in profile where the sea met the sky. The sun, a big ball meeting the wet horizon, anchored the top right of the image. The sun, sail and running trail were bright white. The ocean and running figure were black, the sand gray.

"Bill?"

"Coming."

They followed the directions, turning left at the top of the stairs. At the next left, they found an open door leading to a dark room.

"Let's go," David said, all business and motioning to Bill that he should step into the room.

"Um," Bill said, "it's dark."

"Yeah, gets that way at night. Use your flashlight."

"It's in the car."

"What? Speak up, rook."

"It's in the car."

David reached around and pulled his own battered Streamlight out of his back pocket. "You're a deep nights officer, Bill. You need to always have your flashlight." David clicked his light on, illuminating the room.

A hospital bed sat in the middle of a spacious bedroom, facing a window. The front of the bed had been raised to the 30 degree position, blocking the decedent from view. A round wooden table with a small lamp in the middle stood off to the right.

"Well, let's do it," David said.

He walked into the room and turned on the lamp with his right hand while he clicked off the Streamlight and slipped it back, bottom first, into his left rear pocket. The small lamp gave off minimal light, creating shadows rather than brightening the chamber. They stood in a neat, orderly space, closets closed, furniture tops bare. Everything appeared sterile except for the top of the wooden table. Pill bottles, a pitcher, a cup with a chewed straw resting on an edge and loose papers were strewn about.

They walked around to the right. Bill watched David put on his rubber gloves. He thought he ought to do the same. He reached up behind his shirtfront and pulled a pair out of the pocket on his ballistic vest that held the shock plate in the center of his chest. He took his time snapping them on.

By then, he could see the decedent. A bald man who had withered away to nothing, looking lost in the spacious mattress. Some hair ringed his head, appearing as tufts above each ear. His skin, mottled with brown spots, was tight as a drum. His eyes were closed, nose pointy and mouth opened slightly. A receding chin led down to a throat whose working parts were visibly outlined by the tight skin. A white sheet covered him until the upper chest. The framework of his shoulders, upper arms and chest were as visible as if he had been constructed for a medical school display of the human skeleton.

David reached out and gently touched the receding chin with his fingertips. He pushed, and then pushed a little harder. The head did not turn at all.

"Rigor has set in. They must have been waiting a while. What's this guy's name?" David asked.

The question took Bill by surprise. "I, ah, I don't know."

Without looking up, David pointed to the pill bottles on the wooden table. A flash of embarrassment coursed through Bill. He would have liked to have figured that one out for himself. He leaned in to the table, pulling a pad and pen out of his shirt pocket. He spent a moment reading the labels of the different sized bottles. They were all for Jordan Leet. Bill wrote down Leet's name and the doctor's name and the pharmacy's name. He had started on the medicine names, squinting in the low light, when David interrupted him.

"Ready to help me with this?" David asked.

"Oh, yeah." Bill tried to slip his pad into his pocket, missing on the first attempt. He ran around to the other side of the bed.

David pulled the sheet all the way down. "First, I like to look for serious bruises. Serious, because these AIDS guys are all banged up by this point. I guess they become so fragile that everything bruises them. See anything?"

"No, but it's dark," Bill said.

David flipped out his flashlight and shined it slowly over Leet's trunk and limbs, up and down each side of his body. "Looks okay to me," David said, more question than statement.

"Me, too."

"Next, I like to check hairline and extremities," David said.

He passed the flashlight to Bill. Bill held it on Jordan Leet as if he were a dead car engine the two of them were trying to repair, at night, on the side of the road. David ran his fingertips along the border of the dead man's skin and what was left of his head hair. Then he tried to pick up his hands, but couldn't.

"Rigor has hit pretty hard," David muttered. "You know what? Ask the dispatcher what time the call came in. Then again, never mind. We don't need to advertise on the radio that we were five hours late. Some reporter will hear it and splash it all over the front page of the Dallas Morning News. 'Cops Ignore Fags.' Something constructive like that."

Bill knew from hunting that rigor mortis did not occur right away. "When does rigor mortis hit?"

David had moved to the feet and toes. As he scrutinized them, he said, "onset in two to seven hours, depending. It can last up to twelve. Want to bet the guy downstairs called this in at suppertime last night?"

Bill thought about having to spend seven hours in a house with a dead guy upstairs. He found the idea unappealing.

"Partner, check his hand over there. I look for angry track marks between his finger and in the skin folds. Also look for matter under his fingernails, like maybe he fought or something."

Bill reached for the dead man's hand. The skin felt waxy and fake through the rubber gloves. The wrist and shoulder held tight, leaving Bill unable to rotate the arm and view the hand at eye level. He bent down to look, and found the shadow thrown by the torso impenetrable.

Bill clamped the handle of the flashlight between his upper left arm and his own torso. He pried the stiff fingers apart enough to see down in there and shined the bright light on yellowed, cracked fingernails. Sickness smells wafted up to him. Under the odors of disinfectant, soap and feces, he picked up the coppery smell of death. Bill abruptly let go of the hand and stepped back, standing up straight. He swayed for a moment, lightheaded, before he got a grip on himself. Then he made eye contact with his training officer.

"If anyone killed the gentleman, he did him a favor," Bill said.

David laughed without humor, his eyes hard. "Ain't that the truth."

They heard someone walking up the stairs.

"Hey boys, thought I might drop by," Sergeant Karangekis said, stepping into the light.

"Hey, Sarge. Just in time for the turning," David said.

Costas already had gloves on. "Let's get to it, then."

The three of them turned the dead man over and tried to place him on his stomach, only to be defeated when the rigor would not let them bend him at the waist.

"Let's put him on his side," Costas said.

The man was no bigger than a twelve year old. His boney back was nothing more than a rack for stretched skin, which was worn white where the jutting pelvis threatened to punch through. Bill thought no one ought to die like this. David and the Sergeant continued looking for indications of foul play, be they bruises, fractures or evidence of illegal drug use. When the Sergeant and Senior Corporal decided they were done, they gathered by the head of the bed and whispered, as if they did not want to wake the decedent.

"When I heard the call I had a feeling it had been holding for a while. I looked. It came in at about 7:30. I decided to come on over. This way we can all get jammed up with Internal Affairs together," Costas said, pulling his gloves off, holding the first one he had removed with his remaining gloved hand, and then pulling that one inside out, over the empty, creating a neat ball, ready for disposal.

Bill found that very impressive, and copied the maneuver down to the sergeant's physical attitude of weary competence. He looked over at David and saw him execute the same glove removal method. Bill felt like he had entered the big time.

"Sarge, you are a gentleman and a scholar. I did a few of these AIDS deals before I left, but that seems like a while ago. Appreciate your coming by," David said. "Shall we?"

"Oh, I hate this part. I hate the death notifications, too," Costas said, as they trooped down the stairs.

They found the man who had let them in sitting in a dark kitchen with his arms around his stomach. The truth was, Bill thought to himself, he looked only a little better than the dead man. He had an expression on his withered face of sadness and misery and loss that couldn't help but pull on Bill's heart.

"We're done upstairs, sir," David said. "We just need to ask you a few questions before we go." David nodded at Bill.

Bill had not expected that. Relying on the long honored rookie trick of buying time by taking down pedigree information while concurrently figuring out what he was supposed to be doing, Bill flipped open his pad and asked the man his name.

"Randall Frayn," he said. He tiredly supplied his date of birth, work and home addresses and telephone numbers.

Bill ran out of questions, and then ran out of things to write. David, who had moved slightly so that Randall could not see him without turning his head, coughed slightly. Randall, other things on his mind at the moment, ignored David, but Bill glanced over. David jabbed an extended index finger at the ceiling several times.

"Sir," Bill said to Frayn, "can I have the name of the man upstairs?"

"Jordan Leet," Randall said, looking pained.

They ran through the same information, date of birth, address and telephone number, which was the same for the two men. Frayn did not provide work information for Leet. When they were done, Bill could not contain himself.

"He was only forty one!"

Randall could not hold back either, and let out an explosive sob followed by a burst of frenzied tears. Bill looked to Costas and David, who stood by, immobile, saying nothing. He followed suit.

Randall fought for control and finished soon enough, for the moment at least. He wiped the last of the tears from his cheek with the back of his hand.

"What the hell do you care, anyway?" Randall said spitefully.

"We—" began Costas.

"We were together twelve years. Twelve years! He was the most gentle man," Randall said. "Twelve years. He was my world, the only person who ever really cared for me. Now he is just a, a bureaucratic problem for you." Randall sighed, his burst of energy fading as quickly as it had come. "Get out."

"Sir, on behalf of myself and the Dallas Police Department, we apologize for your loss," David said.

Randall nodded without comment. He turned his back on the uniformed men. Bill felt someone tap his shoulder, and saw that the other two officers were heading for the front door. He fell in behind Costas. Bill closed the door behind them after they had stepped out into the hot, humid night.

Bill felt decidedly uncomfortable. He felt like he had just presided at Jordan's death, maybe even causing it somehow. He found the redundant sex of the couple disorientating. He had never spoken to a homosexual before in his life. He felt kind of sad for Randall, too. Clearly, that man was woeful.

"That was great!" Costas said.

Now that was a statement that shocked the hell out of Bill. Bill could not think of anything great about that call.

"I came up here to give you a hand," Costas continued, addressing David, "but oh boy, what you just said! I don't ever know how to end these things," Costas continued to gush. Then he whipped out a pad and pen. "You don't mind if I steal it, do you? What was it you said?"

Theo had wandered the halls of Parkland until he had found the McDonald's, which was about to close. Hermondo was getting his Big Mac and a Coke, but also some french fries he had not asked for. Theo was pretty proud of that, thinking of the fries. For himself, he had ordered a nine piece Chicken McNuggets, a fish sandwich and a Coke, with french fries, which was what made him think of fries for Hermondo. Well, not exactly, because the clerk had also asked him about it. He said, 'fries with that?' and Theo said, 'sure.' He was a nice enough young kid, that clerk. Now Theo was on his way back to the ER, carrying a large white bag of food and a pressed paper tray holding two drinks.

He did not know the way, of course, but confidently continued moving down the endless white corridors. He knew deep in his heart that he would eventually make the right combinations of turns that would get him to the emergency room. As the food cooled, he would stop and read signs, often finding the multiple arrows confusing. Then he would start off in a new direction, whistling. Each time he went his way with a calm certainty that this time he would end up by the right reception area. The one where blood marked the floor.

At one such sign he stopped next to a matronly woman wearing her blond hair in a complicated, off-the-neck style and a white cardigan over a formal gown. He paid her no mind as he tried once again to figure out the arrow scheme. Did the arrows that point up mean straight ahead, or upstairs? He figured out left and right, those were easy enough, but what about the ones that were at some kind of 45 degree angle? What did those mean? At first he thought—

The stifled sobs of the woman standing next to him broke into his reverie. He chanced a look and saw that her head was bent forward and she held a ball of tissues to her nose and mouth. Her shoulders bounced up and down as she labored mightily to maintain her composure. Theo faced quite a quandary. His desire to get back to Hermondo with the food conflicted with his neighborly instinct to see if he could help. After a long moment of deliberation, he decided to ask. After all, that was why he became a police officer. To help people.

"Excuse me, is there something I can help you with?" he asked.

"I can't, I can't find the emergency room," she said so low that Theo almost asked her to speak up.

"Well ma'am, neither can I, but you don't see me crying about it," Theo said.

He laughed after he said it. Sometimes, people did not get his jokes. He thought by laughing he could help them along. It did not work too well this time, as a fresh round of great racking sobs poured forth from the woman.

"Um, really, it was a joke," he said. The woman fought for control. Theo waited next to her.

"Where is the emergency room?" she finally asked. "My son was married today. When he and his Stacy left the church in the limousine, a man came very fast and hit the limousine right where they were sitting. He was a drunk, the police said. They came with a helicopter and took Brian and Stacy away. Now I can't find them. Do you think they will be all right? I hope they'll be all right. I don't know. I don't know." When the woman finished speaking, she started to cry quietly into her tissues.

Theo had no idea what to do now. Her tragic story shocked him. The food was getting cold. Coke trickled out of the overfilled cups, onto his hand and down his forearm. He had no idea where the emergency room was himself. He felt awkward, to say the least. He was just about to confess that he was lost when he heard a girl call out.

"Mom?" A slender teenager with straight blond hair, braces and red-rimmed hazel eyes came running up. "Mom, where have you been? We've been looking all over for you."

The girl put her arm around her mother and turned her in the direction she had come from. They started crying and walking together.

A large black Arlington police officer stood back somewhat. He was as tall as Theo, and only a little older. He sported an impressive spread of chest and shoulder muscle, even after accounting for the ballistic vest. Theo absorbed the man's regular features, narrow waist and massive Colt Delta Elite pistol. Now that was the way a police officer was supposed to look, Theo thought.

"Hey," the Arlington officer rumbled, "how you doin'? That lady, she won't leave. They told her her boy was dead hours ago.

Man, what a mess. Drunk done killed them newlyweds. Their limo was making a left out of the church parking lot when a drag racing drunk hit 'em hard. What are you here on?"

The officer turned and started walking in the direction the two woman had gone. Theo walked beside him, hoping they were all going to the emergency room.

"This old boy got his head split open," Theo said.

"Drunk?"

"No. He was punchin' on me, is all."

"You don't say," the officer said, admiringly, as they strolled together down the hall.

Costas had to run over to a shooting in East Dallas, so David and Bill were free for a moment.

"Let's run down to the Joker's before we clear. I need a drink."

They crossed Central Expressway, avoiding main roads and a convenience store or two on their way.

"Hispanic gang-bangers, most likely," David said.

"Hum?" Bill had been thinking of the unfeeling dead man and the miserable live one they had dealt with at their last call.

"The Sergeant's shooting. I think it's time the gang-bangers got started. I bet that's the shooting."

"I guess so," Bill replied.

"Thinking about the gays?" David asked.

"Yeah. That guy was pretty messed up."

"They were together for some time, although with them, you never can tell. It's easy to step out, I guess. Not just Riverside Park, but restrooms, too. Seems like they can get together anywhere."

Bill did not understand the restroom reference, but chose not to ask about it.

"I never gave much thought to gays. It never came up in the Army. Even at college, when it seemed that they wouldn't be happy until we were all gay, I never really thought about it. But then I handled my first one of these calls.

"It was at the Stoneleigh; two old guys who had been together forever. The private nurse had the day off. During the course of the day the guy got worse and worse. He died in the afternoon and we went over there and did what we just did here. The survivor was so distraught, not like screaming or anything, just quietly falling apart, that I had to think of them as a real couple. Such genuine emotion, you know?"

"Yeah," Bill said. He really did not know. He wanted to talk about something else. The dead guy freaked him out.

They ended up popping out onto Ross at Henderson, and after several more turns, into the parking lot of the Joker's. Crowded with civilian cars, David pulled into the last open spot on the end. They both opened their doors and stood up. Bill looking forward to a trip to the restroom. Then a petite white female in her mid-twenties approached David.

"Where have you been?" she demanded.

"Something we can help you with, Miss?" David asked, deadpan.

"There are always police here. Where have you been?"

"Miss, if you don't have a problem, you need to move on."

She was cute, Bill thought, and dressed well in a silk type blouse and slacks, looking up at David with her brown eyes from under little girl curls. Bill thought that she probably had not been talked to like that by police officers in the past. He hoped David knew what he was doing.

"I, I'm sorry. I'm just scared. I live several blocks over. When I came home tonight, I found my front door open," she said.

"Did you go in?" David asked.

"No. I came right here, because I always see cops, I mean police, parked here."

"Why didn't you call 911?"

Here she looked away. "I didn't want to be a bother. I thought maybe one of you could come with me and go in, but that was 45 minutes ago."

"That's a good call, Miss," David said, his tone softening. "It would have been fine to call on an open door like that. Any one of us would have been happy to help. Partner, what do you say we drive on over and check it out?"

"Fine with me," Bill said, both surprised and happy to have been consulted.

"I just didn't want to be a bother, is all."

"No problem," David said. "Which car is yours?"

They followed her small Japanese sedan for a short distance, parking in front of a vinyl-sided ranch in a neat neighborhood. Bill could see that the front door was barely open.

"We're up on channel two. Hopefully, this won't turn to crap," David muttered, as he shifted the cruiser to park.

They exited their respective cars and stood in the street. The neighborhood did not have sidewalks.

"You sure you did not go in?" David asked.

"No, I went right over to the Seven-Eleven," the young woman said.

"Anyone else living in the house?"

"Well, my parents, but they're in Lubbock right now."

"Any boyfriend or girlfriend problems, or problems with an ex-boyfriend?"

"No," she said, with a show of annoyance that even Bill saw was meant to cover her embarrassment at the questions.

"Everyone at work know you're alone at the moment?"

"I go to school."

"At school, then. They know you're alone?"

"You know, I could have a boyfriend. How do you know I don't? Maybe I do, I didn't say and you didn't ask specifically about a current boyfriend."

"Right. I'm asking you about being alone in the house. Everyone at school know? Like the weird guy in class?"

"Oh. I'm sorry. No, just two of my girlfriends."

"Last question. Any police activity at the house in the last couple of days?"

"No," she said, elongating the 'no' to emphasize the stupidity of the question.

"Okay, we'll be out in few minutes. Why don't you wait here?" Then he said to Bill, "Partner?" as he pivoted sharply and strode off for the house.

David concurrently drew his pistol from its holster and his flashlight from his back pocket. Bill did the same, trying to imitate the casual flip of the light into its proper tactical position. As he thought about how cool this would look in front of the young woman, he dropped the flashlight onto the manicured lawn. He managed to scoop it up without tripping. By the time he had settled down, he and David were arranged on either side of the front door.

"Dallas Police, come on out!" David shouted, after pushing open the door.

Bill listened intently for an answer, or any other interesting noise, like the sound of a bullet being chambered in a firearm or someone rushing the door or breaking glass or whatever. What he heard was a whole lot of nothing. The tension began to drain out of him. They waited long enough for Bill to grow a little bored. When David finally said something, he interrupted Bill's evaluation of the state of the shine of his boots.

"Partner," David muttered, "we'll do a nice, calm walk-through, not like a tactical room clearing or anything. You follow me around and we'll take it nice and easy, right?"

"Right," Bill said.

They entered the house and David led to the right. They walked down a hall and checked out three orderly bedrooms. David shined the light on the attic hatch and made Bill guess what was important about it until he hit it on the head: a fine network of unobtrusive spider webbing on two sides of the square hatch. They moved back down the hall to the central entrance way, and then into the eat-in kitchen. Bill thought his mother would like the china tea service that decorated the table, with its delicate—

A noise from his left startled him. He went from completely calm (well, maybe a little on edge) to scared stupid in an instant. Without thinking, he spun toward the sound. He raised his flashlight and pistol. His finger went inside the trigger guard. He shouted out the warning the academy had drilled into his head until it had become automatic.

"Police, Don't move!" he shouted.

"Don't shoot!" David yelled simultaneously.

Bill had moved instantaneously to the point where he was, in fact, about to shoot. He was steadying his right hand, his shooting hand, with his left in a manner that allowed him to hang on to the flashlight as well. He had taken up the slack on the trigger of his Sig Saur P226. He did manage, however, to freeze at David's shouted instruction. Then he saw what had made the noise. They had come close enough to a gray and white striped cat to cause it to flee its hiding place. It had jumped off the counter, knocking over a pine spice shaker. Bill caught the last glimpse of the cat's tail as it sprinted into the living room.

"You okay?" David asked.

Bill nodded in the affirmative. He took a deep breath and relaxed his arms. He and David resumed their walk-through. They followed the cat into the livingroom. Everything was fine, except that the cat, which Bill expected to see, had disappeared. Bill noticed the open door and wondered if he should voice the idea that someone could have come in behind them. He decided against it. He followed David through the living room and out the door onto the front steps.

"Where the hell is she?" David asked.

Bill looked around, seeing only a quiet suburban street late at night.

"We don't have time for this," David said, slamming the door shut behind him. "I hope she held onto the keys."

Back in the police car, driving away, an idea popped into Bill's mind. "Do you think the cat ran out the front door?" he asked.

"And that she took off after it?" David asked in return.

"Could be, I guess," Bill said. "Do we go back?"

"Are you kidding? I don't think so." David thought for a moment. "Our luck, the damn cat was a house cat, declawed and everything. Probably the next time she sees it, it'll be all chewed up, the other cats having kicked its ass and all. How about that for another satisfied customer?"

Theo sat in the room with the skinhead and Hermondo. The skinhead still slept on the bed. Hermondo still sat on the chair, the one piece of furniture designed for sitting in the room. With his back against the wall and his feet up on a counter top, he looked pretty comfortable to Theo, who had returned to his place on the floor. Theo licked the last of the dipping sauce off of his fingers. Thumb, forefinger, middle finger, ring finger, pinky, each slurped clean in turn. Theo sure did like dipping sauce. He started on his left hand, thumb—

"Knock it the fuck off," Hermondo growled, without looking up from his paperback.

Hermondo's half eaten Big Mac lay on its wrapper by his elbow. He had taken several bites before complaining that it had cooled past suitability for human consumption. The muttering that followed had concerned itself mostly with Theo's competence, or lack thereof, regarding a future position in the fast food industry.

Theo had no empathy for Hermondo. Cold McDonald's had never stopped Theo before. In fact, when the dead woman came into the emergency room, Theo was wracking his brain for a way to get his hands on Hermondo's leftovers. The ruckus distracted him. With a guilty glance at Hermondo, because lately Hermondo made him feel guilty all the time, he got up and left the room.

He stepped into a maelstrom. People wearing green and blue scrubs worked in every trauma room. Some teams worked almost silently. Others shouted at one another or at no one at all, as far as Theo could tell.

The latest fracas concerned two gurneys that had been rolled into the area in front of the administration desk. One trauma team was working on a white female bleeding profusely from the head. On the other gurney, two petite women were struggling against a white man who was almost completely covered with blood. He gave out a mighty yell and bucked the white nurse to the floor. The second woman was a black Dallas police officer, who looked like she weighed about 90 pounds with her gear on. She had her arms around his throat while he rose to an upright sitting position. Theo noticed her feet dangled in the air.

It dawned slowly on Theo, as everyone shouted and the man screamed, that as a police officer he needed to get involved in this.

By their own volition, his feet carried him forward to where the officer dangled in mid air.

"Help me get him down!" she yelled. "He's been shot a couple of times!"

"Now, you get on down there. You been hurt," Theo offered.

This only stoked the man's rage.

"Thank God you're here," the petite officer yelled, as the victim swung her from side to side.

Theo felt a little embarrassed at that. He froze up in his embarrassment.

The nurse that had been knocked to the floor had regained her footing. Without a word to Theo, she pushed past him and tried to grab both of the victim's shoulders. Theo could see that she meant to strong arm him down onto the gurney. The victim had other ideas though. With one of his great big hands, he slapped her back down to the floor.

"Hey there," Theo said. "Hey there now."

Watching the nurse get slapped to the floor made Theo feel uncomfortable. The gender thing bothered him, but so did the size difference. He thought that a great big boy ought not be slapping around a little woman that is trying to be of help to him. Theo drew his baton, ignoring the perpendicular handle and holding it in a conventional manner. He raised it over his head and brought it down hard on the thick muscle that ran from neck to shoulder of the man who had been shot. It made a meaty, solid 'thunk,'

"What did you do that for?" the man asked, focusing his attention on Theo. Theo saw tears forming in the man's eyes, but could not be sure if they were from the baton blow or his being shot up.

The two women did not hesitate at all. As the men looked at each other, the nurse hopped back up yet again. She and the officer then jumped him from either side. They took the stunned man down until he lay prostrate on the blood soaked mattress.

"Restraints!" the nurse yelled.

Several orderlies that had been waiting for an opening rushed in. They used thick leather fetters to bind the man to the metal frame, wrist and ankle.

"Trauma Six!" someone yelled.

The hospital staff rolled the man away at a run, leaving the two police officers standing alone and a fair amount of blood on the floor. During the struggle, the gurney with the woman on it had been rolled away.

"Thanks," the officer said, wiping some sweat off of her brow. "They pulled off the freeway to score some crystal in Bachman Lake Division. The suspects ringed the car and started shooting. He's been hit about five times, but the woman got it much worse. Come on, let's go find her."

By the time they found her, lying still on a gurney placed up against the wall in the hallway, the team that had been attending to her had moved on to a motorcycle rider who had wrecked out. His helmet-less head had slammed into a curb at 45 miles an hour.

"Look at that," the female officer said.

The female victim lay on her back, eyes closed. Someone had cleaned up her face. Her features were angular in repose. In fact, Theo thought, except for the quarter-sized hole in her forehead, she looked as if she could be sleeping. Pretty attractive too, he thought. Checking out her body, he observed two pert breasts swelling under the sheets. In fact, she was a darn good package overall.

"We recovered a .45 Colt at the scene. One of those could have caused that," Theo's colleague said quietly.

The hole in her head was so large that Theo had enough perspective to check out the details of the damage. The skin, turning gray in death, seemed no more than a coat of paint over the layer of thick white bone. The stout slow bullet had cleaned out all the brain behind the hole as it passed through, creating a great empty cavity.

"Oh my God, will you look at that," the female officer said reverently.

"Yup," Theo replied in the same tone, "I can't believe how much that bone looks like coconut meat on the inside of a shell."

Bill felt exhaustion wrap around him like a thick blanket. He looked out at the dark night through half closed eyes, squinting against the haloed street lights and head lights whose glare hurt his dry eyes. Radio traffic came out of the speaker in a steady stream. Bill could not figure out what was being said or pump himself up enough to care. They had reached the part of the night where he had to fight to stay awake, where he felt tired beyond all measure.

Bill and David were not far from the Joker's, which was good for Bill, because he really needed to relieve himself. And he was thirsty. He told himself repeatedly that nothing bad had happened to the woman whose house they had searched while she looked for her inside cat. He needed to repeat it because he was having a hard time selling himself on the idea. David, however, did not seem put out at all. Bill turned his head to look over at David. Just then the police car leapt forward yet again, engine revving up, transmission slamming itself into a lower gear.

"You going to get that?" David asked.

"Huh?"

David snatched the radio and brought it close to his mouth. "Dog-Four, we're in that. We're about three blocks out."

"Dog-Four," the dispatcher replied, his voice calm and even.

"Charlie-Seven is behind a stolen in the drive through line at Jack-in-the-Crack," David said. "It's right up here."

Bill watched David work the brakes, gas, steering wheel, lights and siren. It looked to Bill like some kind of sitting down dance. David's hands whisked around over the different controls while his legs worked the pedals and braced him in the seat. David whipped the car around several turns and then toward an overpass that would take them across Central Expressway.

"Seven, we're southbound on southbound Central service road. He's picking up speed," the chasing unit put out over the radio.

David accelerated over the expressway and turned left so aggressively that the rear end of the big car broke free. They skidded around the turn until all four tires stuck again. Then they were barreling south, that sliding feeling a memory.

"Up yet?" David asked calmly.

"Oh yeah," Bill said, wide awake now.

"We're southbound on Central," Charlie-Seven put out.

"Gotta be in it to win it," David said.

Bill only nodded as they swung around an old pick up truck and cut in front of a Mercedes sedan to get on the expressway.

Sergeant Karangekis came on the radio. "Dog-One, is that a confirmed stolen?"

"10/4. Armed and dangerous out of Houston," the dispatcher replied.

"10/4."

"And the chase is on!" David shouted over the siren.

"Seven, westbound Woodall Rogers."

"10/4," the dispatcher calmly repeated, "westbound Woodall Rogers Freeway."

They had the left lane to themselves and David did not waste the opportunity. Bill sneaked a look at the speedometer and saw they were flying at an honest 125 miles an hour. He started to feel giddy and tried hard to keep a smile off of his face.

"There he is," David said.

Bill saw Charlie-Seven's lights exit to the right.

"Cut the siren, will you?" David asked.

Bill turned off the siren as David shot through traffic to the right.

"Now pick up the mike and call the chase. Tell dispatch we're second car."

Bill removed the bulbous microphone from its clip, feeling the snick of the spring steel through the plastic case. He felt nervous holding it in front of his mouth. Other vehicles were blurs. His nerves at having to call it ousted the sensation of speed from his body. Finally, after an apparent eternity, he felt ready to get on the radio. They were coming up on the end of Woodall Rogers, and the bad guys had three choices. They could lead their pursuers straight onto Industrial, or pick from north or southbound I-35. Once he saw them commit, Bill keyed the mike.

"Dog-Four, we're second car. Southbound I-35 at Woodall Rogers," Bill said.

David piloted them into the exit viaduct still several car lengths behind Charlie-Seven. The viaduct took them up and around. Bill felt the car lean heavily to the right, until it seemed to be riding on his door. They blasted into traffic and David deftly moved them through the pattern, gaining on Charlie-Seven, until the three vehicles were in line in the left lane.

"Dog-Four, what's your location?" Dispatch asked.

"Coming up on the I-30 split, wait, he's taking it, we're heading east on I-30."

"10/4, eastbound I-30 from southbound I-35. Units, be advised, the helicopter is down for fuel."

First the stolen vehicle, a BMW, entered the four lane banked turn that would take them to eastbound I-30. The stolen car disappeared behind a retaining wall for the overhead viaducts, followed shortly by Charlie-Seven. He and David entered the turn and quickly regained sight of the stolen vehicle and police cars. Bill noticed the stolen sedan had started to wobble back and forth, slightly at first and then with greater and greater violence. The wobbling knocked speed off the fleeing car, and the marked units quickly closed.

While the suspects had slowed, they were still running faster than the flow of legal traffic. They came up on a civilian Chevy traveling much closer to legal speeds. Everyone was now driving in the second most left lane. The far left was clear. Bill watched with growing alarm as the sliding suspect vehicle ran up to the rear of the civilian car, so close Bill thought for a moment they had touched. It changed lanes at the last minute.

They all came out from under the end of a series of overpasses as the suspect vehicle turned to the left. The abrupt lane change had caused the car to finally loose complete control and yield to the laws of physics. Bill watched the front end dip and the car slow further. It orientated itself toward the left lane, but also slid further left, onto the shoulder.

The car continued to slide obliquely to the left, through the shoulder and into the grass of the wide but narrowing median. The median dipped inward to a drainage ditch that ran down its center. The car, continuing its half sideways, half forward motion, slid down the incline and slowly tipped up onto two tires, then onto its side and then all the way over onto the roof. As the wide median narrowed, the origin of a metal barrier presented itself. The robust concrete and metal assembly anchoring that barrier did what the police could not. It stopped the chase cold when the upside-down suspect vehicle hit it dead on.

Charlie-Seven slid to a halt, and David slowed the car and then put it in the grass, turning slightly for cover. Yet again, David's door was open and he was out before Bill realized he was gone. Bill himself almost jumped out, until he remembered he was calling the chase.

"Dog-Four, suspect wrecked out, eastbound I-30, three miles east of the I-35/I-30 junction."

"10/4. Do you need an—"

Bill did not hear the rest of the question because he jumped out and ran up to where David was yanking a scruffy, dazed white male out of the car by the collar of his denim jacket. Both the driver and the passenger were quickly handcuffed and left lying by their respective sides of the wrecked car. Neither was ready to talk. As a rookie, Bill was responsible for the post-arrest search.

Bill ran his hands over and around old, soiled clothes that stank. Their lack of washing gagged Bill. He had not yet gotten used to pawing through the dirty pockets of filthy criminals. No matter how necessary, it struck Bill as something degrading. He was no more used to searching than he was riding around at 125 miles an hour.

Bill checked the pockets of blue jeans so dirty they were black, the prisoner's waistband and crotch for hidden firearms and everywhere else for any other weapon or contraband imaginable. The search of the prisoner's matted, brown hair triggered dry heaves. Bill kept them hidden by the narrowest of margins.

"Nothing," Bill said aloud, but no one was paying attention.

The other officers were surveying the damage to the stolen vehicle. Resting on its roof, it had come to a halt after sliding along the grass. First the front end and then the windshield and the leading edge of the roof had come into destructive contact with the barrier. The front end took a good hit before sliding over the top. The hood had scraped its way along the barrier and was now as creased, folded and torn as a letter brought home from school by a third grader. The final impact had shattered the windshield and bent the metal of the roof at its leading edge, right in the center.

Just then Jimmy John and his rookie came sliding up on the shoulder.

"Hey," he said, "y'all need some help?"

Details were quickly attended to. Other units were cut loose, a wrecker was ordered and the prisoners, the consensus being they were probable crystal salesmen out of Houston, were transported by Charlie-Seven. Soon Jimmy John, his rookie, David and Bill were standing in a semi-circle on a wider part of the median, facing their police cars and oncoming traffic, their backs to the wreck. Jimmy John and David discussed the reputation of a lieutenant rumored to be coming to deep nights while the rookies listened without comment.

Bill enjoyed listening to the conversation of the veterans with one ear while basking in the aftermath of the action. It had been exhilarating and terrifying. The result, the capture of dangerous criminals without anyone getting hurt, had been satisfying. Bill felt like he had accomplished a complicated task in a worthy manner. He felt pretty damn good, actually.

As Bill savored the moment, he noticed a small red economy car in the southbound I-35 to eastbound I-30 banked turn. It had come into view around the retaining wall. Originally in the left lane, instead of straightening out as it came out of the turn, it kept traveling its arc, as if to complete a full circle.

"Hey, look at that," Bill said, as the red car crossed four lanes of traffic and spun one complete rotation before leaving the roadway.

It crossed a grassy area and smashed head-on into the tan brick retaining wall.

Conversation stopped. The officers avoided looking at one another. Bill was not so rookie that he needed to be told the last car to move would be honor bound to deal with what obviously was an uncontrollable drunk. As if some unseen authority indicated that it was time to start, all four officers commenced walking casually towards their respective cars.

The edges of Bill's mouth started to creep up. To prevent the others from seeing him smile, he bowed his head. He heard footsteps become more urgent, probably as Jimmy John and his rookie realized distance would defeat them unless they ran for it.

"Move it, rookie!" David shouted, as the other two officers broke into an outright sprint.

Bill reached his door, grabbed the handle and yanked it open. He looked over the top of the car at David, excited at being first in and about to laugh out loud. He saw that his trainer had come to point like a hunting dog, facing that huge highway turn. Bill, interested in what had gotten David's attention, looked that way and saw a late model yellow Corvette leave the roadway back end first, cross the grass and also crash into the wall, a little further on than the red car.

"Something must be on the road!" Jimmy John shouted.

"Yeah. Let's go! You rookies put out flares. We need to close it down! Bill, put it out on the radio, ask for cover, code three!" David's shouting sounded like rapid gunfire to Bill.

Before Bill could even formulate a question to ask, the three officers were in motion. Jimmy John and David were loping down the left side of the freeway towards the wrecks. Jimmy John's rookie, the sharp black guy, had their trunk open, probably going for flares. Bill ducked inside the cabin and reached for the radio.

"Dog-Four, we have two wrecks at our location. Be advised we are closing the ramp from southbound I-35 to eastbound I-30 due to something being on the ground. We'll need some help, code three."

"10/4, Four. Do you need the fire department?"

Bill panicked at the question. He had no idea if he needed the fire department. He definitely did not want to be responsible for calling a bunch of them out for nothing. Bill stared at the microphone and started to sweat.

David broke in over his hand-held. "Dog-Four, 10/4 on Dallas Fire. There is something on the roadway. We need a Haz-Mat unit and one am-blance," Bill heard David say.

"10/4, units be advised . . . ."

The dispatcher went on to repeat everything. With something on the roadway, Bill figured they would need more flares. He slipped his new $100 flashlight into his left rear pocket, as was the fashion on deep nights. He grabbed an armful of the red tubes out of the trunk and started for the turn where he could help the others keep traffic from exiting onto eastbound I-30. As he walked, he watched a mid-sized sedan come out of the turn, spin 360 degrees three times and straighten out. Bill saw that fear had widened the driver's eyes and pinched his mouth when he drove by in the left lane. Bill started to run when yet another vehicle, a mini-van with plastic wood panels on the side, spun out and wrecked next to the Corvette, sending Jimmy John diving for cover.

Bill stepped onto the freeway opposite the wrecks and started walking across the four lanes of traffic. He could feel the slippery substance under his boots. He carefully put one foot down, obtained his balance, shifted his weight and repeated the process, slowly making his way across. He hugged the flares to his chest like a life preserver. Bill concentrated on what he was doing, looking down at each footfall before moving.

"Bill! Move it!" someone yelled.

Bill looked to his left and saw an eighteen-wheeler come into view. He could see the driver, a white man with a beard, wildly spinning the steering wheel. Bill picked up the pace. No sooner had he started to run than his feet flew out from under him. He landed hard on his left forearm and hip, dropping the flares everywhere. He watched his flashlight roll away, changing direction so that it lined up nicely with a sewer grate. Then he heard the horn.

The truck, a black Kenworth, was almost on him. In an amazing feat of skill, the driver had kept the tractor-trailer combination upright, sailing it through the turn. The last thing Bill noticed about the truck was that he could make out the tread pattern on its left front tire. That meant that the wheels were not turning. That meant the truck was sliding down the freeway at some 50 miles an hour.

Bill knew he had to do something right now to avoid getting squashed like a spider in the kitchen. He realized that getting up would take too long and instead started rolling after the flashlight. He managed to get all his precious parts out of the way just in time. He tucked up his legs as he felt the wake of air from the passing truck wash over him. His luck held. As he rolled up over the sewer grate he managed to grab onto his flashlight as it began to drop into the sewer. He did not stop rolling until he was on the grass, where he sprawled out on his back, spread eagle, breathing hard.

David appeared in his field of vision. "You all right?" he asked.

"Yeah, I think so."

"Can you believe that guy kept his rig upright?" David asked, pointing down the interstate at the retreating truck.

Bill looked up and saw the rear of the dirty white trailer as the truck made its way into the night.

"Thank God that man knew what he was doing," Bill said.

"Amen to that. Come on, can you stand?"

Bill took David's outstretched hand and stood up. He catalogued the damage. The worst of it appeared to be his left forearm, split and abraded along its length. Also, his hip ached.

"Do you think I'll ever come to work and not get hurt?" Bill asked.

"I don't know, will you?" David answered, smiling. "Why don't you sit down and wait until the fire department gets here. They'll have a look at you."

"No, I'm okay. I'll run those flares up around the turn, they probably need them up there."

"Okay. I'll get back to the cars."

Most of the flares had rolled of their own accord to the shoulder. Bill picked up the ones he could reach without stepping into traffic and started walking, in the grass, in the direction of I-35. After a few steps, he started limping against the pain in his hip.

The two rookies laid a quarter mile flare line. They maintained it while the accidents were worked and the fire department conducted its investigation. Bill got a good look at the Haz-Mat truck as it drove up. Men poured out of the muscular red and white vehicle. Eventually, David called him down. They walked over to a regular pumper, where a crew member dressed his wound, wrapping his forearm in clean, bright gauze. Before long, an accident investigator from the traffic division came to take a look at the carnage. Then the fire department washed down the freeway and tow trucks came for the cars.

As they walked backwards down the left side of the freeway, watching the oncoming traffic speed down the newly open interstate, David asked after Bill's welfare.

"I'm alright. Did Haz-Mat say anything about what the stuff on the road was?" Bill asked.

"Let us know in a couple of days. I put you on the contact list because of your arm. Oh, by the way, they said they'll have to amputate if the cut starts to burn."

"Don't sweat it," Bill replied, "I'll do it myself at the rate I'm going."

"No, really," David said, all seriousness, "How are you doing?"

"Since you're asking, I really got to pee."

Both Hermondo and the skinhead were sawing logs and it annoyed the hell out of Theo. Their braying kept him from falling asleep. He sat on the floor in the treatment room with his back against the wall. The cheeks of his backside had long since fallen asleep. The tingling had started to hurt. He decided to get up and walk around.

Since the shot-up drug purchasers, there had been two victims of motorcycle wrecks. One of them, due to the lack of a helmet, made several patients across the region waiting for organ transplants very happy. The ER had also hosted numerous stabbing victims, assorted poor folks suffering from various acute illnesses and a heart attack or two. With nothing better to do, Theo had watched them all. The fragility of the human condition left him worried. What if he should need medical care one day? Theo now saw the ER as a place where mayhem congregated, not where people were made well.

"At least the worst of it seems to be over," Theo muttered to himself, just before the latest drunk driver was propelled through the double doors by the emergency services workers. Theo decided to check out the latest guest.

The picture had become familiar to Theo. The backboard and neck brace and the studied nonchalance of the ambulance crews were commonplace. The staff efficiently moved to provide the required care. The shouting. All routine. Even when the next victim shot through the doors, the rhythm of emergency care carried on.

Then a third body came in strapped to a gurney. And one after that. And a next one. And another. And a few more still. The ER was full of motion and sound. Finally, after the last victim, an accident investigator strolled in, a shiny aluminum clipboard under his arm. When they made eye contact, he nodded at Theo.

"What happened here?" Theo asked.

"Hey, this ole boy, drunk off his ass, smashed into a retaining wall down by Highway 182. A family traveling through from," and here the AI checked his clipboard, "Levelland stopped to help and a second drunk smashed into them. Two fatalities so far. See you," he said, walking off, literally whistling Dixie.

Theo stood in the middle of everyone's coming and going, mouth agape.

"Rookie!" Hermondo shouted from behind him, making him jump, "deputies are here. Let's get going."

David and Bill drove through the lessening gloom, heading for the Joker's, with an eye on some drinks and the restroom. They drove north, the false dawn beating back the night to Bill's right. Bill's morale had fallen pretty far by this time. He had not had anything to eat or drink since they started and he felt sluggish. He fought both to stay awake and against a growing headache. His mind drifted and he was taken completely by surprise when David slammed on the brakes. They skidded to a stop several car lengths from the intersection of a side street and North Peek, even though they had the green.

David put the car in park, unhooked his seatbelt, opened the door, stood up and drew his pistol, all in an instant. Bill fumbled to catch up. Outside the car, Bill noticed a short, fat Hispanic man with heavy indio features standing in the right lane of traffic. He held up one hand. The other hung down at his side, looped through a leash leading to a small brown dog. The dog sat in the street, leaning against the man's leg. Bill stepped out of the car and stood between the open door and the body of the vehicle. Luckily, there was very little traffic that early in the morning.

"They's two bodies in there, officer," the man with the dog shouted, pointing to a service ally to Bill's right. "I think they're dead."

The man appeared shook up. It did not surprise Bill when David adopted a conciliatory tone.

"Okay sir. Why don't you step up on the sidewalk and talk to my partner here while I move the car?"

The man nodded and walked up onto the curb.

"Get his info before he takes off, okay?" David asked quietly. "Be ready for anything."

"You got it," Bill replied.

Bill slammed his door shut and walked over to the man that had flagged them down. He heard David putting their location out over the radio. Bill slid his pad out of his shirt pocket and flipped it open, all the while watching the man closely. At least he would not have to worry about the dog. No bigger than a woodchuck, Bill felt that even if it did bite him, and seeing how things were going for him on deep nights it surely would, it probably would not be fatal.

"Good evening sir," Bill said, sounding to himself acutely like the rookie he was, "what can we do for you tonight?"

"They's two men and I think they're dead. They're in the ally, in the middle of the ground," he said, pointing again. "I think they been there a while."

"Okay, can I get your name?"

By the time David walked over, Bill had finished his interview of the witness. He brought David up to speed.

"Mr. Verdugo, a repairman of the different machines used in dentists' offices," Bill said, pointing, "was walking the family dog down the alley when he stumbled over the bodies of two black men. He immediately ran out to the street to get help, and waved us down."

"I was half asleep. I really wasn't watching," Mr. Verdugo said apologetically.

"Pretty early to be walking the dog," David said.

"Yes, I work early and late, before and after the patients. I have a service call this morning on upper Greenville."

"Okay. Why don't you show us where the bodies are, and we'll try not to keep you too long."

David had parked the police car at the mouth of the alley. The three men and the dog had to squeeze through a gap between the car and a chain link fence. They walked down the uneven concrete paving, behind homes whose rear borders were heavily wooded and the parking areas of apartment complexes. Bill noticed what appeared to be two sacks spilled on the side of the alley, half into some shrubbery. They walked up on them quickly enough. The closer they got, the more apparent it became that they did indeed get flagged down for a double murder.

"One-Dog-Four, confirm on our double 27 and call out homicide," David had pulled his radio and put out the message while Bill's eyeballs were still glued to the bodies in front of him.

Bill heard the dispatcher's "10/4." Several units advised they were on their way.

The three of them and the little dog considered the bodies. They had been tumbled to the ground next to one another, without regard for placement. Not hidden or arranged in any way. Both were black males. The one on the right was on his side, legs scissored and muscular arms stretched out in front of him. The one on the left had fallen on his back.

"Look at this one," David said, kneeling. He pointed to the man on the far right. "Two in the head and a smashed throat. Somebody sure was mad at him."

Both Bill and the civilian laughed nervously.

"This guy, too," David continued, moving over. "Both kneecaps and a bashed up skull before the kill shot to the forehead. I think these guys royally pissed someone off."

"Why do they do these things?" Verdugo asked.

"I don't know," David replied sadly, "and I feel like I've been to a million of them."

"You think they from around here?" Verdugo asked.

"I don't know where they were from, but this is Mexican gang territory. I think these guys were trucked in," David replied. Then he pointed around at the ground. "Not much of a crime scene. No blood, confused tire tracks. Someone was careful last night."

The little dog became agitated. He started jumping around and whining.

"You don't mind if I take Simon home, do you?" Mr. Verdugo asked.

David's face became hard. "Not as long as you come right back. The detectives will have some questions for you."

"Yessir, I'll come right back."

"Mr. Verdugo, please don't make us have to come looking for you. It's pretty important that you be around," David said.

"Yes, I'll come right back."

"Okay then."

The man and the dog walked away. David and Bill stood still, regarding the bodies. Finally David spoke up.

"Ever think about the waste of it all?" he asked, as if Bill had seen hundreds of these scenes.

"Not really. What I'm thinking about is that I really got to pee," Bill said, embarrassed at his own truthfulness.

David motioned toward some thick green bushes nearby.

"You sure it's okay?" Bill asked.

"You gotta go, you gotta go," David said, his New York accent suddenly thick.

Bill walked the short distance to the vegetation David had indicated. He decided to work his way into the middle of it, conscious of the lightening eastern sky. As a probationary officer, he did not want to get caught urinating in public. Bill looked back before plunging in. He saw David kneeling by the dead men, regarding them without expression. He struck Bill as a little melancholy. Bill did not dwell on it. He had some important personal business to attend to.

Chapter 12

David woke with a start and bolted upright in his bed. He looked around his bedroom. The heavy duty window shade kept out most of the light, but there was still enough to see by. Last night's uniform lay draped over the back of a chair, his boots and belt on the floor. The alarm clock said two thirty-five in the afternoon.

"Shit," David said.

He had finally gotten free of the double homicide crime scene at about ten this morning. David and the rookie had gone off duty and onto their weekend without changing. The rookie had done pretty good for his first week of second phase, other than getting smashed up on a regular basis. Well, David thought, for the next two days he'll be able to lay low and recuperate.

David had come straight home after the unscheduled overtime dog tired. He remembered carefully setting the alarm for his big social day: a party at Charlene's and his date later with Holly Dawn, stage name Misty. David wondered to himself about what the hell he was going to do with that stripper. He thought he might cancel. Better yet, he could stand her up and never do a walk-through of the Silver and Gold Club again.

He swung his feet to the floor and rested his head in his hands, elbows on his knees. Thoughts of backing out on Holly dueled in him with thoughts of those fantastic breasts. Well, the whole damn body when you came right down to it. That, and lastly, there was something in her eyes the last time, some intelligence mixed with fun and a little—

"Oh shut up," he said out loud.

He turned his attention to the alarm clock. The party had started at two, sharp. He picked up the small box with its red digital readout. He saw that he had set the alarm and turned it on. Then he discovered that he had set it for 1:00 AM instead of PM. He sighed and turned it off, putting it back on his night stand next to his duty Beretta.

The party had started at two. Even before his morning crap he was a half an hour late. Add that to the 45 minutes it would take him to get ready and drive over, and you had a recipe for Flaming Charlene. At least he had remembered to turn the ringer off on the telephone. That showed some improvement.

He walked into the kitchen and checked the answering machine. The envelope from New York, the one he had set to the side by itself on the kitchen table, caught his eye. He noted the return address that started with the line "New York School of Law." Beyond that, he successfully ignored it. After all, he knew what the letter said.

There were 13 messages on the answering machine. There had been none before he had gone to sleep. Charlene dialing fast and doing a lot of screaming, no doubt. Certainly no need to check 13 hits of that. David poured himself a glass of orange juice and decided that since he was already late, no one could possibly mind another hour. He drained his glass and, back in the bedroom, changed into shorts and running shoes.

David ran in the heat of a beautiful, clear afternoon. He wound his way through residential neighborhoods up to Oak Lawn and along Turtle Creek before turning around and heading home, about four miles in a little over 30 minutes. Back in his apartment, he cooled off while drinking a beer and watching NASCAR before showering. He nursed his beer while he dressed in a pair of newer jeans, a golf shirt with an Army airborne flash on his left breast and a pair of ropers. He figured this would be good enough for grilling and getting grilled on a Saturday afternoon.

In the pickup, David locked his off-duty Beretta and an extra magazine in the glove box. He wound his way up to Preston Road, staying on until he turned left onto Park Lane. He drove over the Tollway and into the neighborhood built around a wooded creek. The size of the homes still wowed him, large estate properties set back from the road in shaded glens. Whenever he went to Charlene's, he liked to tell himself that only the most misdirected and lost Yankee dog-face patrol cop could ever end up keeping company with a native born North Dallas princess.

The Honeyman property came up on David's left. He pulled onto a washed pebble driveway that arched across the front of a sprawling log ranch. Washed pebble offshoots led to outbuildings on either side: a three car garage with an apartment to the left and a three bedroom "cottage" on the right. The Honeymans used a kitchen entrance most of the time, around the house on the garage side, but today there were vehicles everywhere. Today struck David as a front door day.

David parked amongst the pickup trucks, Suburbans and Lincoln Town Cars. The pickups, work trucks purchased by moneyed men to remind them of their roots, were option-laden behemoths that David appreciated with the fervor of a convert. He only spared a moment to look at a custom-painted, full sized GMC with a leather interior and a neatly applied, spray-on bed liner.

He climbed onto the porch and clunked his way to the front doors, a pair of massive, darkly stained wooden slabs, boot heels ringing against hardwood. Having attended social occasions here before, David knew the drill. Without knocking, he reached out and took hold of the brass knob on the right door and pulled it open.

The entryway ceiling soared over a stone floor. Guests congregated in lose groups deeper inside. Upon seeing the crowd, David grew acutely annoyed with himself. After five years of living in Texas, he ought to be able to figure out when the hell people dress up. He had come out on many weekends and jeans were never scarce. Today, as David looked into a large room that could have been called a living room but wasn't, because there were several of those further in, he saw nothing but well dressed middle-aged folks. The men wore suits or jackets and ties. Their women were all in summer dresses with floral prints or skirt and blouse combinations that looked expensive even to David. At least he had gotten the boots right.

"Hey, Davie, how are you?" one of Charlene's male relatives asked, walking over with his right arm extended, hand out.

"Fine, how about yourself?"

"Not too bad, boy. So, first the war and then you got caught, huh?"

"I don't follow you."

"Why, I mean your engagement, boy. She done caught you good!"

"I'm not engaged." He said in a tone of voice that allowed for no disagreement.

David could not believe that Charlene had not put the engagement fantasy to bed. Then he realized that he was late for his own engagement party. While he wanted to retreat, somehow he knew that the only way to handle this situation was to hunker down and wait for the next barrage.

A small knot of party guests had gathered around. He stood still and remained silent. Finally, a matronly lady spoke up.

"Well, you know we saw it on the TV."

"I'm not engaged."

"Well," she said, puzzling over the problem, "did y'all break up since then?"

"No ma'am."

"Were you ever engaged?"

"No."

"Why would Loreen say they were engaged?" the woman asked her husband, or the man David assumed was her husband, standing next to her.

"Because they are, Betty." A rather severe, older version of Charlene said, nudging her way through the gauntlet.

Loreen, Charlene's mother, was a well-kept fifty year old who looked ten years younger. She wore a sleeveless beige mock turtleneck sweater and matching slacks. A tortoise shell headband held her shoulder length brown hair off of her face. Medium-sized diamond earrings and a look of displeasure made all the harsher by deep brackets around her mouth filled out her suite of accessories.

Betty, and all the others, looked everywhere except at Loreen.

Loreen had made her displeasure over David's presence in her daughter's life as clear as the Stubens decorating one of her mantels. David believed that if she had her way, no police officer would ever marry into the Honeyman clan, despite periodic overt declarations of respect and admiration.

"Loreen," David said, by way of greeting.

"You would not dare break your engagement at the very time it is being announced," Loreen hissed firmly.

"I am not now, nor have I ever been, engaged to anyone."

"Of course you are. Why are you saying this?"

At that, a tall, stoop-shouldered man, mostly lean except for a small but noticeable pot belly, with thick gray hair parted on the right and a neatly trimmed gray mustache, stepped forward.

"Now y'all come on and get yourselves something to eat. Chicken and beef are just about done on the deck and there are cold drinks out there, too. Come on now, y'all," the group slowly osmosed to the back of the house and Hank Honeyman guided David away from it to the left, into a book-lined study.

"Where is Charlene? I've got to find Charlene," David heard Loreen say, somewhere behind him.

Hank Honeyman's clear gray eyes and firm-featured face fit the room perfectly. Dark paneling covered the walls. A large desk and two leather couches framed a blood red area rug. A rock and mortar fireplace with the largest hearth David had ever seen made up the rear wall. Windows allowed for a view of the deck area to the right and the driveway and garage to the left. David idly noticed a small tan Toyota Tercel hatchback parked out there between a Cadillac sedan and a long bed Dodge Power Ram 2500.

"Welcome back, David. How was it over there?" Hank asked.

A small wet bar that included a refrigerator had been wedged into a corner. Hank opened the refrigerator, bent over and brought out two bottles of Shiner Bock, handing one to David. The men twisted off the caps and took a pull from their respective bottles with almost identical gestures.

"Hank, it wasn't the jungles of Vietnam," David said.

"Thank God for that. I'm a little curious, and I don't mean to meddle in your affairs, but where do things stand between you and Charlene?"

"I don't really know. She didn't write much while I was away, but then I came back to that dog and pony show a week ago. After that, things cooled down real quick. She wouldn't even talk to me on the telephone." David drew on his bottle again. "What's going on here?"

"This is a warm up party for your engagement party, Dave."

"I don't fucking think so," David spat out in a sudden rush of anger.

"Steady there, soldier. We can get through this. I guess the next step is to find Charlene."

The door to the study opened and Loreen came in practically dragging Charlene behind her. The door was left open, and David saw a young man hanging back, outside the study.

"I think it is a scandal that this person would come into our home and treat Charlene like this. Hank?"

"Hello Charlene," David said, making eye contact with Charlene for the first time in almost a week.

Charlene looked pretty good. She wore a pink blouse with a flourish around a v-shaped neckline and a pink floral print skirt. Her hair, a little blonder than usual, was pulled straight back from her forehead and had been straightened. It fell to her shoulders and then curled up in a uniform flip. She did not answer him. Her blue eyes looked away.

A slim twelve-year-old with brown hair and eyes and a family resemblance to Charlene gracefully slipped around Loreen and lightly stepped up to David. Barrettes held her straight hair behind her ears and bangs fell in an even line across her forehead. She wore a prim, short-sleeved dress, covering her from knees to throat, tight at the waist, a spray of lace at her neck. Smiling broadly, she hugged him quickly and stepped back.

"Hi David," she said, and then blushed furiously.

"Hello, Ginny."

Behind her came a teenage boy, a younger version of Hank. Doug fell between Ginny and Charlene in age. He wore a button down sport shirt and a pair of khaki trousers. He shook a shock of brown hair out of his eyes with a jerk of his head and, smiling, waved.

David nodded back.

The man he did not know moved his holding pattern from the hall to just inside the door. In his mid-twenties, David tried to place him but finally gave up. He wore blond highlights in his spiked hair, which had been shaved close on the sides. His face came to a point at his chin, exaggerated by a bushy brown goatee. While he was dressed in a manner similar to Doug, the two earrings in his left ear and one in his right indicated he might be more comfortable in even less formal clothes.

David decided to wait Charlene out. In the resulting silence they could hear car doors slamming, engines starting and vehicles pulling away.

Loreen's head whipped around from side to side. "Hank, they're leaving. Do something!"

"Charlene," Hank said conversationally, "Dave tells me he never asked you to marry him. Is that true?"

"Daddy," Charlene cooed, shifting her weight to one leg and looking down.

"Charlene?"

Charlene looked around like a trapped animal. She looked from face to face, receiving sympathy only from her mother. Then, as an afterthought, she looked over her shoulder at the man standing alone by the door. He nodded at her, urging her to some unspoken but mutually known course of action. With a whimper, Charlene whipped her head back around and faced her father.

"It's not my fault! You and Doug and Ginny were always telling me to write him! Always asking me questions about him. I don't know. I don't know who I want to marry!" she yelled.

"Tyler, I think we need some family time," Loreen said, smiling sweetly at the young man in the back.

"Tyler can stay!" Charlene yelled out, stamping her foot a little.

"He's a stage hand," Hank calmly said to David. "Been hanging around a bit lately."

"Stage manager. At the National," Tyler said, in his own defense.

"Some of the time! You've got a part time job!" Loreen said.

David suppressed a smile. He admired the way fate had trapped Loreen between a fully employed cop and an under-employed, well, something.

"Hey Tyler," David interjected, "that your Toyota out there?"

Tyler screwed up his face with an expression of confusion and incredulity. "Yes. Why?"

"No reason."

"Stop it!" Charlene yelled. "I know what you're doing and stop it, stop it, stop it!" She looked around wildly again. Then she put her hands up in front of her with her palms out. "I can't stay here, I just can't." Charlene pivoted around and made for the door. Once in the doorway, she pivoted around again. "I'm sorry," she said to David. "I just wanted . . . I thought . . . Oh, I'm sorry, David. Please call me," she said before she turned again and ran off.

Tyler opened his mouth as if to say something, and then shut it. He looked from Loreen to Hank and back again, and finally waved absentmindedly before running out after Charlene, shouting her name.

Hank and Loreen concentrated on one another, communicating silently. Ginny and Doug regarded them closely and said nothing, waiting for the parental reaction.

While David watched everyone, he thought all he had been doing lately was calling that high-maintenance bitch. Then he decided the hell with all of them. He finished his beer and put down the empty bottle, ready to leave. He was about to say his farewells when Hank spoke.

"David, have you eaten yet?" Hank finally asked.

"No sir, I haven't."

"I'd appreciate it if you came on outside and had a little something," Hank replied.

"Well thank you, I think I will." He had planned to refuse but changed his mind at the last instant. The post workout beers, on an empty stomach, had David feeling lightheaded, and the last thing he needed was a wreck or a DWI.

Ginny took his hand. "Tell us all about the war," she said, leading him out of the room, onto the deck.

David soon found himself at a picnic table, eating a grilled steak sandwich with a side of home-made french fries. He discussed the war with the last of the guests and the members of the Honeyman family that were curious. Loreen could not be found on the acres of deck at all. David sanitized his experiences and maneuvered the conversation to the point where everyone else had something to say, leaving him free to eat. Before long, the conversation had turned to the police department.

"So you must really like action, police and the Army and all," Leonard said.

Leonard and his wife, Magpie, were particularly friendly with the Honeymans and always seemed to be around, in spite of the fact Leonard appeared to be 15 years older than Hank.

"Never thought about it," David said, popping the last of the sandwich into his mouth. The steak had been basted in a slightly sweet and tomato-y sauce that highlighted, rather than overpowered, the beef.

"And those drug dealers, I mean, they are pretty violent, right David?" Leonard asked.

"I guess so," David said, wiping his fingers on a napkin and taking a drink from a glass of iced tea. A black domestic, handsome in her mid-forties, wearing a white blouse and black slacks, leaned over and removed David's plate. "Thank you," he said.

She smiled slightly, saying nothing.

"It's the profitability. That stuff is so profitable, it motivates all the violence."

"Well," David said, overriding his basic instinct not to discuss the subject, because nobody ever believes cops anyway, "I think it's about a lack of opportunity."

"There's plenty of opportunity, David," Hank said, comfortable on his deck, reclining in an Adirondack chair, "public schools, public universities."

"The public schools on my beat suck, Hank. There isn't enough funding. But it's not just that. Those people in South Dallas, they don't see the possibility of opportunity."

"That's why the drug dealing, if the only other visible opportunity is McDonald's," Leonard said.

David felt frustrated. Then he hit on an idea. "Leonard, I never had the opportunity to ask, what do you do?"

"I'm a lawyer," he replied.

"Any black partners in your firm?"

Leonard did not answer.

"The sad thing is," David continued after a moment, "these guys have talent. Talent and smarts. We don't fund the schools and we don't see to it that real opportunities are available. These guys know they don't have a shot at partner in your firm, and that's why the dealing and using. It's got nothing to do with fast food."

"David, you'll just have to excuse me, but I'm no racist. If the right kind of candidate came along, well, we'd hire him and promote him. I don't think it's up to you to pass these judgements about my firm like that."

"No, of course not. And I don't mean what I said that way. The hurdles are huge, starting with access to the fundamentals of education. Realistically, how many kids from low-income type neighborhoods are going to ever be able to grow into the right kind of candidate?" David asked, refusing a strawberry shortcake dessert.

"We would not hold it against him," Leonard said.

The cake continued to hover in front of his face. He looked up at the domestic. David noticed her Mona Lisa smile as she stood there just a moment longer than necessary, before retreating.

"That's not what I mean," David continued. "You take anyone from any old law school?"

"Not really, no."

"So how do you get from South Dallas to Southern Christian University and their law school, and please don't say north on Julius Schepps Freeway."

That brought a laugh that cleared the somewhat tense air on the deck. Before long, the teenagers had drifted off and Leonard and Magpie had driven away. David chose that opportunity to take his farewell, too. Hank walked him to his truck.

"I always wondered about you and this truck," Hank said.

"How did a New York boy like you decide on a nice truck like this?" Hank slapped the hood affectionately.

"When in Rome . . ." David replied, shrugging.

Hank wiped his mouth and became serious. "Guess we won't be seeing it much around here, from now on," he said.

"Not unless you can think of a way for me to wait around for Ginny without raising Loreen's suspicions," David said seriously.

Hank laughed and then his smile faded. "You listen here boy, take care of yourself out there. I can't really say I see how you can do it day in and day out, but I sure am grateful you do. Take care now." Hank shook his hand and without waiting for a reply, went back into the house.

David slid behind the wheel. Out of habit and without thinking about it, he pulled his shirt out of his jeans. Then he unlocked the glove box and pulled out his smaller Beretta, still in its holster, and the extra magazine. He clipped the holster inside waistband on his right hip and slipped the magazine in his left front pocket. David smoothed his shirt over his weapon, adjusted himself in his seat and started his truck. The radio came on and David drove away to the strains of electric guitars, thumping bass and a wailing steel something.

Hank's comments touched him. The recognition felt nice, all the more so because David knew Hank had flown God knows how many missions as an F-4 Phantom back-seater in Vietnam. Hank had more Air Medals than David had soft tissue injuries. It would be Hank, Ginny and Doug he would miss most, not Charlene or her mother. Unless, of course, he called Charlene and patched things up.

David drove through a beautiful spring afternoon, cooling off from the day's high. The sky was large, clear and blue with no visible threat of a thunderstorm anywhere. David still had about an hour and a half before he had to pick up Holly, so he bought a cup of coffee and the last copy of that day's *Dallas Morning News* before driving down to Oak Lawn. He stayed with Preston Road as it merged into Turtle Creek Boulevard and followed the tree-lined street as it wound around, parallel to Turtle Creek and its lush banks. He passed The Mansion and eventually pulled into Riverside Park, backing into a shaded spot amidst families with small children and the much scarcer, at this time of day, strolling same-sex couples.

David opened the plastic cover of his medium coffee. He had prepared it with some milk and sugar and taking a sip, found it okay. After separating the front section from the rest of the newspaper, he folded the broadsheet lengthwise. David enjoyed the feel of newsprint and the sound of the rustling sheaves. He settled down to read about current events: a pregnant woman had been shot in the head in Oak Cliff, everyone was bumping into Kevin Costner, and the Supercross was in town. David made a mental note to run the rookie by the movie set behind Dealey Plaza. Jimmy John had mentioned movie people had turned West End parking back into a rail yard. He did not get far before Charlene pushed her way to the front of his thoughts.

He folded the paper width-wise, sliding his fingertips over the rough stock. He sipped at his coffee and looked out over the park, contemplating the turn of events. He could not sustain any sense of anger at Charlene. Who knew what kind of pressure the situation had placed on her? How much energy did she have to expend defending him against her mother's obvious disapproval, even before he left? In hindsight, he wondered if that in itself may have been what had kept them together.

Although even now David felt affection for Charlene, he did not recall ever thinking about her in terms of forever before the Army came calling. Who knows how it would have played out had those unexpected orders to war not come, or come with plenty of lead time. If the orders had been to a base in the US or Germany instead of the combat theater, he was sure now that they would have politely separated. That's not to say that they had not cared for one another, just that the relationship appeared to lack the strength to stand the stress of separation.

Of course, had they talked more or wrote more, maybe things could have been different. That whole engagement thing was off-putting, but David thought that it did not have to be fatal. Tyler, now he was something else again. David felt vaguely uncomfortable, like there was yet some unfinished business with Charlene. Maybe he should not have treated their relationship so lightly. Maybe he should call her. Maybe he should call her tomorrow. The way it ended today made him feel a little sad.

David let the melancholia wash over him while he nursed his coffee. He moved his eyes all around the park, letting them rest on something questionable until instinct told him nothing was wrong, nothing to see, move along. It was what he did. He watched the park and daydreamed, listening to music as if it were the duty radio. The park thinned out and the sun fell low in the sky behind him.

The DJ announced the time. If David wanted to arrive on his date as expected, he needed to leave. He made no move to start the truck. He did not feel like going out tonight. He felt like going home, finding a game or a movie on TV and drinking a few beers, alone. David thought about the dancer. Holly Dawn was a good looking kid for sure, but did he really need to get involved with that? With the drinking and the drugs and all the other crap dancing in a strip club came with?

"Oh, the hell with it," David said out loud, after a moment's reflection.

Going out once does not mean they would be involved. And all the kid wants to do is give him some payback about the glasses. What would it hurt to be nice to her one more time? David decided to go and cranked up his truck. He would see her this one last time and then never go back to the Silver and Gold. What could that hurt?

David drove through the central business district, deserted on the weekend afternoon, making his way onto the freeways, first south and then east. He pulled up in front of the little house about ten minutes late. The front door opened as he walked around the truck. Holly Dawn stood patiently behind the screen door waiting for him to walk up. She opened the door for him as he came up the steps.

"Hey you," she said, turning to the side to let him walk in. He caught a subtle floral scent as he passed by.

"Hey," he said.

David had expected Holly Dawn to be packaged differently than she was. Her face was the same, same creamy skin and the same fall of thick blond hair down to her shoulders. Her shapely form, however, had been wrapped differently. Instead of the exposed skin and expensive rags David anticipated, Holly Dawn wore a serviceable light brown blouse with slash pockets and plenty of snaps. A dark brown string tie chastely cinched the collar of the blouse shut with a large bow. The shiny pointed toes of brown boots poked out of the bottom of a pair of blue jeans.

"How *are* you?" she asked with a twang, flatter and less pronounced than that of the hill country but pleasant nonetheless. She smiled broadly, showing brilliant even gleaming teeth.

"I'm all right. How about yourself?"

"Oh, you know I took the day off? I hate to say it, but all I did was sleep. I didn't get anything done that I planned to. Do you want to see the window?"

Holly led David back to the bedroom and showed him the rookie's work.

"Can't see a thing," David said, running his fingers over where he thought the hole had been.

"I know it. Did you know he stripped the whole thing down and sanded for hours? He's very nice."

"Good deal."

"You know, he thinks the world of you."

"I doubt it."

"He talked an awful lot about you."

"Don't believe a word of it," David said lightly, with a dismissive wave. Inside though, he felt flattered.

"Oh I believe it. He said you can really handle your business. I believe that, too."

David looked down into a broader and more genuine smile than he had seen in a long, long time. She met his gaze and leaned forward and touched his arm.

"Could we go? I'm starved," Holly said.

"Sure. You don't have anything too expensive in mind, do you? Because that wouldn't be necessary, really," David said.

"Don't you worry about it, Officer. I've got everything planned," she said, smiling mysteriously.

In the truck, with Holly Dawn comfortably seated on the passenger side of the cab and the country music turned up, she refused to tell David where they were going. Instead, she gave him street directions, one turn at a time. In short order, she had him driving up Greenville Avenue, and then into a parking lot on the right.

"Snuffers?" he asked incredulously.

"I said I was buying. Dancing is hard work for the money. Did you think we were going to the Mansion?" Holly asked.

Soon they were sitting in a comfortable booth on either side of a heavy wooden table. They shared heaping baskets of fried chicken strips and french fries slathered in melted cheddar cheese, dipping both into small plastic containers of ranch dressing. They drank from quart cups of soft drinks that a harried waitress kept filling. Holly was obviously enjoying herself. She kept up both ends of the conversation. She gossiped about the Silver and Gold club, talked about Buffalo Gap, her hometown, and told humorous anecdotes regarding her experiences with police officers. She was funny and smart and she kept things light. Her eyes sparkled in the low light as she sat among young parents trying to control small children and dating high school kids oblivious to everything except each other.

"I'm not surprised you get out of tickets," David said, "but there is another point of view out there. I have a friend that writes everyone except, um, shall we say, less-than-beautiful chicks," David said.

"Why is that?"

"Because he says good looking women always catch the breaks. He wants to balance things out a little bit."

"Get's lots of dates that way?"

"Nope. Happily married."

"Figures."

The conversation paused. Holly traced patterns in the condensate that had pooled on the table with her fingertip. She had slipped into some private reminiscence and her expression turned serious. All the animation dissipated from her face. She was even more beautiful in repose than when she was ebullient. She pulled herself back to the here-and-now, looked up at him and smiled with wry humor.

"I guess you are going to want to know how I started dancing," she stated.

A curious David merely shrugged.

Holly Dawn looked away. "Where I grew up, I was getting a lot of attention from boys. One of my friends, an ex-friend, started telling me I could be a model. Over in town, in Abilene, there was this model search company. I went down there to speak with them. Well, to make a long story short, they just knew I had what it might take. They said I'd be making thousands an hour in New York and LA and we could get started any time."

"Let me guess. You had to pay them up front. Them, and a photographer, too," David said.

"You know about this kind of thing? The photographer came later. Yeah, I had to pay them. First it was Benny, a tall thin guy, and his wife, Amy Ann. She was a large woman, in all the directions. She always wore these bright tent things. Both of them could make you feel just this puny. First they needed money. Then the photographer needed money. Then they needed some more money. I've worked since I was twelve and had most of that money saved up. There was my gift money, too. Like an idiot I kept handing it over. It was always just one more bill. And everyone I paid had been a famous model or photographer or had coached Cheryl or Christy or something," Holly sat back on her bench and regarded David closely.

"I should have known better, I guess," she continued, "seeing as I'm a little too short and I've got these horrible scars," Holly said, indicating the acne remains on both cheeks.

David could not see them in the restaurant light at all. Even in daylight they were faint as bird tracks on baked mid-summer North Texas clay.

"You are an extraordinarily beautiful woman by anyone's measure, Holly," David said conversationally, hoping it would not sound like he wanted to get into her pants. Of course he did want to get into her pants, as a general proposition, but he wanted his comment to at least sound like it came with no ulterior motives.

"Thank you," she said, with a little girl's solemnity. "Anyway, I was having trouble in school and my home life wasn't real fun. I fell for the whole thing. They sent me here, to Dallas, for bookings. When I got here, there were more bills to pay."

"Was that when you figured it out?"

"'Fraid not. After paying on an apartment and for more pictures—"

"—from the guy who took Lauren Hutton's first pictures, right?"

"You got it, cowboy. Anyway, and agency fees, I had nothing left. Every cent I had was gone. I went to them to explain why I had no more money and to beg for a booking. They told me to call home and get them to send money. They told me my big break was around the corner. Like my family would send money.

"I went back to my apartment, changed into a bathing suit and went down to the pool. I thought that pool was just the most luxurious thing ever. Since I was going to get thrown out of the apartment soon, I might as well enjoy it now. Down there I started crying like anything. It was the middle of the week and the only other people there were these two really beautiful women, a little older than me. Smart boy like you could figure out the rest."

"They were dancers and once they heard your sad tale, they encouraged you to try out at the club. The next thing you knew, here you were," David summed up.

"That's about it. Hey, we better get moving if we want to get to the movie."

So they argued about the bill, which came to some ten dollars or so. David finally yielded to Holly Dawn's impressive stubborn streak. She had not been kidding, she really wanted to pay for dinner. Back in his truck, she directed him to a neighborhood north of LBJ Freeway that he was not familiar with.

She had him pull into the parking lot for a strip mall anchored by a movie theater that had somehow survived the coming of the multiplex. It's one bow to modernity was the splitting of the screen into two viewing rooms. The marquee advertised two features, both of which he recognized as releases from the year before.

"It's a dollar movie!" Holly said, clapping. "Too bad we didn't come on Tuesday, it's half price then."

"Great," David said as he parked. "Why is it I don't think we'll be watching *Goodfellas*?"

"*Ghost* is like one of the greatest movies of all time," Holly Dawn said, visibly disappointed at David's comment. "Do you really want to see *Goodfellas*?"

"I can wait. *Ghost* will be fine."

"You haven't seen *Goodfellas*?"

"Haven't seen either one. I can't remember if they came out before I went overseas and I didn't get a chance to see them, or if they came out while I was over there."

"Oh. We can see what you want."

David exited and walked around the front of the truck. Out of habit and without thought, he scanned the parking lot for anything out of the ordinary. The bricks of the old theater looked as if exposure to the hot Texas sun had baked the color out of them. The cars and trucks in the lot were older and equally scorched. The casually dressed diverse crowd appeared to be made up of high school and college students and working class families. All was well. David opened the passenger door for Holly.

"*Ghost* will be fine," David said, extending his hand.

She regarded it with raised eyebrows and a smile. "Thank you, sir," she said, before taking it. She slipped off the seat and landed lightly on the cracked, bleached concrete.

They walked into the lobby holding hands. The inside looked as genteelly decayed as the outside, with frayed rugs, stained walls and posters in display boxes whose lights had burnt out. But these injuries were spaced far apart. The children who raced around the nervous teenage couples gave the place a homey, rather than run-down, atmosphere.

The Saturday night crowd felt fairly relaxed to David, probably because it was so early. The Saturday Night Fights and Follies would not really get started until later, he knew. They stood on the fast moving line and for a dollar each, Holly purchased two tickets to *Ghost*. They skipped the snack stand. On their way into the theater, David saw a rest room.

"If you don't mind," he said to Holly, "I've got to return some of that Diet Coke I drank."

"I'll meet you here," she said.

David pushed open the door to the restroom. He stepped into an open area. Three black teenagers, about 15, as close as David could tell, stood in a small half circle. The one on the right held a large, blue steel semi-automatic pistol pointed at the floor in his right hand. With his left, he held the slide back. The other two boys appeared unarmed. The restroom spread out to the right. Empty urinals were lined up on the far wall. Pinkish-beige tiles covered the floor. David could not see the stalls at all.

Instantly, David became hyper-sensitive. He could hear and feel the pounding of his heart. His muscles seemed to swell. He involuntarily bent his knees slightly and leaned forward, as if to ready himself for blows. He could hear the noise from the lobby in the silent restroom. Time seemed to slow down. David looked for a position of cover.

The boy with the pistol sneered at him like a tough guy. His eyes were as black as death. The boy let go of the slide, which then rammed itself forward. David knew it had stripped a fresh cartridge out of the magazine and shoved it into the chamber, cocking the weapon at the same time. David realized that in less than a second, this boy could rotate his wrist and shoot him dead, if he so desired.

There was nothing but space between the boy with the pistol and David. He knew he could be shot several times by a determined assailant before he could escape out the way he had come in. David could see no other alternative. He pulled up his shirt with his left hand and reached for his own pistol with his right. He knew he could not retreat anyway. His clear duty was to get this situation under control, for the sake of the unarmed boys at least.

He wrapped his hand around the grip of his Beretta, so keyed up that he felt the difference between the walnut grips and the metal frame. His plan was to draw and fire, putting a deadly double tap of hollow point .380 ammunition in the sneering boy's forehead while he still had the initiative. Action beat non-action every time.

"POLICE! DROP YOUR WEAPON! DO IT NOW!" David thundered in the small echoing space.

He moved to the modified Weaver shooting position: strong side back, shooting arm locked out, pushing against his non-shooting hand, knees aggressively bent. He focused on the front sight and put it between his eye and the front of the boy's face. He pulled up the slack in the double action trigger. David was about to continue with a steady squeeze when he stopped dead, as it were. Superimposed on his target, in his mind's eye, appeared a future *Dallas Morning News* headline: "White Cop Shoots Black Teen." David froze.

The imaginary headline disappeared. David made eye contact with his target. David had given up his one advantage by not shooting. Unless David was willing to fire unilaterally, the boy was in the tactically superior position. All he had to do was flip his wrist and he could snap off a shot before David had any chance at all to react.

The boy and the man glared at each other, fear fueling the moment. David had not received compliance, but he still did not shoot. No one moved. David felt three icy spots on his torso where he imagined the boy's bullets would strike, tearing his internal organs to shreds, killing him. The moment felt to David as if it could be measured in days, not seconds. Then he saw the boy's eyes flick to the left, checking out the others.

"DROP YOUR WEAPON, DO IT NOW!" David bellowed.

The boy bent further forward, lowering the pistol to the floor. It hit the ceramic tile with a loud metallic "snick" and a relieved David watched the juvenile hand let go of the pistol.

Now David started thinking about safety. First, he removed his finger from his own trigger to eliminate the chance of an accidental discharge. Along the same line, he slid his rear foot back into the arc of the door. This way, someone coming in would not push the door into him and startle him, with potentially fatal consequences.

David turned to the problem of gaining control over the weapon on the floor and then maintaining control of both his own and the boy's pistol. David held no illusions regarding the situation. He knew three teenagers could wrestle him to the ground and wrest control of the weapons from him. To move things along, he decided to put the boys on the walls. David reached into a back pocket and pulled out his shield wallet. He snapped it open and displayed the tin.

"Dallas Police, get on the wall!" He merely yelled, attempting to lower the tension level now that the big pistol was on the floor.

The boys slowly complied. David was thinking about how best to step into the middle of three potential assailants when the door opened and hit his foot.

"What the fuck?" someone yelled.

A black man in his mid twenties, wearing dreadlocks and a goatee, stuck his head into the restroom.

"Say man, go call the police for me. Tell them officer needs assistance, will you?" David asked, as conversationally as possible.

"I got to piss, man," the head said. His light colored eyes peered hard at David.

"You're not the only one. Could you call the police for me?" David asked.

"Motherfucker, let me in," he growled.

David felt him push the door against his foot, not hard enough to get in, but hard enough to test David's resolve.

"Shitter's closed, asshole. Police business," David said, dropping all efforts at collegiality. He ached to spin his Beretta around and point it at this idiot.

"Rodney King!" the face replied, before disappearing.

"So much for the cavalry," David muttered, turning his attention back to the matter at hand.

Before he could make much headway, or even come up with a plan, the door opened again. It came to gentle rest against the back of his right foot. David looked over his shoulder. A young boy's brown eyes made large with surprise and a mouth opened in a silent circle met David's gaze. David noted the young black boy's neatly cut short hair, apropos of nothing.

"Hey," David said, trying to smile through the tension, "go on to that pay 'phone in the lobby and call 911. You don't have to say a thing, just let the receiver hang there. Go on and do that for me, will you?"

The boy's eyes took in the scene again and again. They jumped between each of the teenagers with their hands on the wall, the pistol on the floor and the pistol in David's hand. Ultimately, they rested on David's face.

"Go on now, son, call 911," David said, his hope fading.

The boy backed out. The door whooshed shut.

David considered the problem of obtaining the pistol that rested on the floor anew. He decided there was nothing else to do but to grab it up as fast as possible and hope that he did not get jumped. He was sure now that no back-up would come. He mentally prepared himself to move, and was about to, when the door opened yet again.

"What the hell is going on here?" A not unattractive, middle aged African-American woman demanded.

David moved his foot to allow her further entry into the restroom, grateful that another adult was now in the game. Before David could answer, the door was thrust open further, displaying a white man of similar vintage. He had blond hair, a blond mustache and silver wire rimmed glasses.

"I'm the assistant manager here. What's going on?" he asked.

"Dallas police," David said, flashing the badge again with one hand. "Come on in."

As the bathroom filled with adults and on-lookers, David holstered up. He bent to scoop the pistol up off the floor. As he reached for it, he received a shock that sent shivers up his spine and gave him the shakes. David read the name of a common BB gun manufacturer stamped on the slide. David had come right to the edge of killing a child over a toy. He picked up the pistol and pivoted around. He roughly grabbed the boy who had been holding the gun by his neck.

"That is my boy!" the woman said indignantly.

David's fear embarrassed him. He let anger take control. He stepped close to the woman, dragging the boy with him. The boy yelped and David brought the BB gun up between the woman's face and his own.

"You let your son walk around with a toy that looks like a Colt .45? I almost blew his goddamn brains out." David said through clenched teeth. He did not wait for a reply, turning instead to the assistant manager. "We need someplace private. Now."

"Sure. My office." He led the way out of the bathroom.

David followed with the boy and the gun. The woman brought the other two boys with her. A crowd fell in behind them. Once in the lobby, the little group immediately attracted attention. One of the interested parties was Holly Dawn Snyder.

"Go on in," David said, waving the BB gun, "I've got a little work to do. I'll find you in a bit."

Holly nodded, a concerned expression on her face. The group passed her by as the manager directed them to a staircase on the left of the lobby.

"I'm Lewis Lewison," the assistant manager said as they mounted the stairs. "I'm sure glad you were here to get on top of this."

David did not answer. He struggled to deal with the aftermath of the adrenalin his body had produced, his anger and his fear. He especially wanted to twist the kid's head off at the neck he still held in his hand. He had no patience for Texan pleasantries.

After a climb that left Lewis panting, the group reached his office and filed in. Lewis directed David over to a desk. He indicated David should sit behind it. David did so, placing the BB gun in the middle of the blotter. A young, curvy Hispanic woman sat at another desk off to the side, writing figures in a ledger. She looked up in surprise at the gun and the crowd, unasked questions playing out across her pretty face.

David took a moment to reflect on the situation he found himself in. Children, guns and an off-duty police officer. The press would have a field day. Internal affairs would trip over themselves to find something with which to nail him to a wall. He knew he had to avoid taking the boys into custody. That would attract all sorts of official attention. Then he would have to handle things so that no one involved would slander him to internal affairs, accusing him of using the "n" word, for instance. A headache started right behind his eyes. Might as well get started, he thought. He made eye contact with the woman from the men's room.

"You did not have to grab my son that hard," she said, hands balled into fists and resting on her hips. She had leaned forward for emphasis. She glared mightily at him.

"You taking responsibility for all the boys?" David asked, as dispassionately as a bureaucrat at the federal General Services Administration.

"Oh. They have mothers. I'll call them," the woman said, less sure of herself.

"Who are you?" David asked.

"I'm Channella Hudson. This is my boy Tonell Mohammed," she said, resting her hand on his shoulder.

"Go ahead, give them a call," David said.

Channella Hudson reached for the telephone, but David had second thoughts.

"One second," he said, grabbing the telephone first.

He needed witnesses that would at least be objective, if not outright on his side. He called 911.

"Dallas police, how can I help you?" a young woman trying to hide her natural sweetness asked.

"I'm an off-duty officer and I need an element to respond to . . ." and here David looked around from something with the address of the theater written on it. He found some letterhead and read the address to the police telephone operator. "It's a 6. Ask them to bring up some blank MIRs. I'll need the number," he finished.

The PTO asked David for his badge number and then his name. Then she gave him the number the system automatically assigned his call. David wrote it down. "Thanks," he said, "assign the number to me."

David hung up and turned the telephone around so that Channella could make her calls.

David started collecting the required information. He asked each of the boys their full names, dates of birth and home addresses. At first, the boys were surly and sarcastic. David's demeanor of professional detachment worked at the boys, weakening, for some reason, their posture of insolence. By the time Channella had finished her calls, they were sitting still with innocent expressions on their faces. They only had a few minutes wait before the police element arrived.

A veteran training officer and young rookie made up the pair. The old-head scowled powerfully. He was a forty year old white man who closely resembled a prairie dog. The rookie was a corn fed, pink-skinned, earnest young man that could have been Lewison's younger brother. He looked around with an expression of perpetual astonishment. The rookie held the MIRs rolled up in his hand. David stood and walked them over to a far wall in the large office.

"Hey, thanks for coming," David said softly. "I've got a problem here."

"No sweat," the rookie whispered. "What happened?"

"Give him the reports," the training officer said flatly.

David took the reports from the young officer. "I walked into the bathroom and the kid against the far wall had that BB gun in his hand, slide back."

"Why, that thing looks just like a Colt .45," the younger officer said. "I'd have gone in my pants." The younger officer looked rapidly to his trainer, expecting some comment.

The training officer said nothing. He continued to scowl at David.

"I'm going to get the parents to take these kids out of the theater and go away. I don't think there will be any arrests," David said.

David asked the younger officer for the element number and his badge number. David read the older officer's number off the badge on his chest as he turned back toward the desk, a deliberate insult in their profession.

As the officers were talking, three more women and a man had found the office. David sat back down, identified himself and took everyone's information. He ended up with two pages of notes. When he finished writing, he told the assembled adults what had happened. He commented that he did not know if a robbery had been taking place or not.

"Are you sayin' that my boy is a hijacker? He ain't no hijacker," the lone man said, anger propelling him to his feet. He rested fists on his hips and struck a dominant, dramatic pose reminiscent of photographs of Mussolini.

The man had David at a disadvantage, as David had no idea who he was in the scheme of things. As best David could tell, this man had no biological relationship to any of the boys. He appeared to come with the mother of one of the unarmed teenagers.

"I'm saying children should not be playing with pistols in movie theaters," David replied. "Right now there is no need for anything more than y'all being notified and taking the boys home. If you would like, I can arrest the three of them and we can sort this out down at Juvey."

The man who looked like Mussolini dropped back into his seat like a stone tossed from a sixth floor window of the Texas State Book Depository. The scowl on the senior responding officer deepened. The rookie had a look of delight on his face. The women clucked and the teens themselves had completely lost their earlier gangster affectation, realizing that they were just boys in trouble.

David finished explaining the situation. He felt relief at the attitude of the adults, who were pleased that there were no contemplated trips downtown. David told everyone they were free to go. They started to file out of the office. At the last minute, David noticed no one had taken the BB gun. He recoiled at the thought of having to put the damn thing into evidence.

"Ms. Hudson, your property," David said with as much gravity and authority he could muster, while gesturing at the weapon.

"Oh, no. I don't want that thing in the house," she said, waving casually over her right shoulder with her right hand, fingers up and splayed.

David wanted no part of that thing. He did not want anything to come back to this incident other than the report he was going to write. He wanted this woman to take the damn thing with her on her way out but he had no idea how he was going to make that happen. Then sudden inspiration hit.

"Ms. Hudson," David said calmly, "If these officers have to drive the weapon downtown," and here David noticed the older uniformed officer scowl so deeply that his eyes appeared to touch his chin, "they might as well take the boys to the Juvenile Bureau."

With that, Channella took two quick steps across the room. She whisked the BB gun away. David assured the officers that he would take the number and soon they, too, left. David made himself comfortable behind the desk and looked from his notes to the blank police report forms, organizing his thoughts and getting ready to write.

"Sure glad people like you come here to the movies," Lewiston, the assistant manager, said.

"Don't be watching for my return engagement," David said, picking up a pen and sliding the MIR report form toward himself, at an angle.

Lewison made a gagging noise. David looked up at him. His eyes bulged behind his glasses.

"Lupe, get the officer some of the free passes, hurry up," Lewison said.

David started to write. He filled in all the informational boxes, even the box requiring the exact weather conditions outside at the moment he thought he was going to get his brains blown out by a teenager inside. David documented all the facts his experience taught him were pertinent. He discussed the lack of protective cover and his conclusion that deadly force was authorized. Then he documented his use of an alternative, the shouting, to successfully conclude the confrontation without shooting anyone. He noted how little time he had been alone with the boys. He included the responding officers in the narrative the way a shipwreck victim grabs at a life preserver. All in all, the whole deal, from going into the restroom to finishing the report, took about an hour.

When David looked up from his report, only he and Lupe occupied the office. She smiled at him and then pointed with her chin. While he wrote, someone had placed six free passes on the desk. He gathered up his reports and notes and put them together, bouncing them on the desk top, lining up their edges.

"That's it for me, Lupe," David said.

"Aren't you going to take your free passes?" she asked.

David looked down at the stupid things. He decided not to argue. He scooped them up and jammed them into his right front pocket.

"Gotta go," he said, making for the exit.

It looked to him that Lupe had something else to say, but David did not wait around to find out what it was. He left, taking the stairs two at a time. He ran out to his truck and locked his report in the cab before turning around and going back in.

David found Holly Dawn in the theater and slipped into the aisle seat she had saved for him. He did not say a word. He felt Holly worm her hand into his own. He looked over at her and in the half light, saw her questioning expression.

"It's okay," he said, and leaned back in the seat, turning his eyes to the screen.

David could not concentrate on the movie. His mind swirled around the restroom incident. The movie seemed interminable as he replayed the recent bathroom scene from real life in his head. When the credits finally rolled, David yanked a teary Holly out of her seat and down the aisle.

Holly did not complain, but as soon asked, "what happened in there?"

David gave a brief summary, ending with a question, "do you mind if we swing by the station? I have to file the report."

At the station, David pulled around to the back and parked in the empty change over area, leaving Holly alone in the idling pickup. He photocopied the report, tossed the original into the sergeant's in basket and ran back out to his truck. He threw it in reverse and sped out of the parking lot. Without consulting Holly, he drove straight to his apartment, snagging a parking space mere feet from his front door. He marshaled her inside, turned on one lamp and had her sit on the couch.

"Want a drink?" he offered.

"Have you got a diet Dr. Pepper?" she asked.

"I think so."

David stepped behind the kitchen island and pulled a can out of the refrigerator. He also found a glass tumbler and filled it with a generous knock of Jack Daniels and two ice cubes. He walked over to Holly and handed her the soft drink can. She received it without saying anything and did not make a move to open it. He dropped down next to her, and the leather upholstery ballooned up for a moment. The displaced air drained loudly. David sipped his whiskey leaning forward, his elbows on his knees.

"David, what happened in there?" Holly asked.

This time he explained it to her in depth. He told her he thought the BB gun had been real. Then he mentioned the feral look on the face of the boy holding it, how the other adults involved had acted and what he could expect from the department if the situation broke bad.

"And look, the movie guy gave me these," David said, fishing the free passes out of his pocket. He threw them down on the press board coffee table he had purchased at Target.

"Wow," Holly said, picking them up. "There's six of them here."

"You want them?"

"Why? Aren't you going to use them?"

"Not in this life."

"Why not?"

"For a couple of reasons." David swallowed a mouthful of his drink. "Police can't afford to be where the trouble is when they're off duty. Hell, in this day and age, we can't afford to be where the trouble is when we're on duty. I can't go to the movies at a place where I need to blow away kids in the bathroom."

Holly shuddered. "It was scary to see you come out of there with that black gun in your hand. But you didn't have to shoot someone. You got the gun and everything ended up okay, didn't it?"

"No. I only lucked out. He had me if he wanted me. There was nothing I could do about it. There was no cover. I had no options. He would have shot me cleanly had his gun been real and he wanted too. It was only by the grace of God it ended the way it did."

"But it was a BB gun," Holly said.

"I didn't know that until it was over. And what about next time? Should I just assume any time someone points a gun at me, it's a toy?"

"I just don't get it, what are you so afraid of?" Holly asked.

David regarded her severely for a moment, looking hard at her sweet face. In the silence, he decided her question was honest, that she did not mean anything by it. He finished the last of his drink before responding.

"Action beats non-action every time," he said.

"I don't get it. What's up with that?"

"The person that is going to act will beat the person that is reacting every time. If I'm holding a gun on you, and you have a gun in a holster or whatever, you can draw your gun and shoot me before I can shoot you," David explained.

"No way. Really?"

"I'll show you," David said.

David went to his bedroom and retrieved his M9. Back in the livingroom, he sat down next to Holly again. He dropped the magazine out of the large pistol and locked the slide back, clearing the chamber.

"This is how we render a pistol safe. We take out the magazine, eject a round from the chamber if one is in there and then check and make sure the chamber is empty, both visually and by touch," David said, shoving his finger in the chamber after he looked inside. "Do you wan to try it?"

Holly nodded in the affirmative.

"Okay, here, try it with this one."

David pulled the smaller Beretta out from under his shirt and flicked the small lever on the slide to safe. Then, keeping the barrel pointed in a safe direction, he handed the weapon to Holly, expecting her to need all sorts of help handling it.

Holly grasped the pistol in her right hand and looked at David. Her facial expression immediately changed to one of smugness. Without taking her eyes off of him, she manipulated the magazine release, dropping the magazine to the floor. Then she pushed the slide back with her left hand, catching the ejected round with several curled fingers. She easily locked the slide back and checked the chamber as David had illustrated. Then she put the pistol down on the table, ejection port up.

"Hollow points," she commented, placing the bullet on its base, next to the pistol.

David coughed and rubbed the top of his thighs.

"All right," he said, "let's do the drill. Stand up. Right, here take the .380." David handed her the smaller pistol, after checking it for empty again. "You hold this one on me."

She accepted the pistol and checked it again herself. Her serious expression and complete attention impressed David. No protestations or squeamishness at all. He picked up the M9 and checked it again for empty. Then he showed the chamber to Holly, who tilted her head, looked into the chamber and nodded up and down. David hit the slide release and the slide slammed home, the metal on metal crash loud in the quiet apartment.

"I'm going to put this in my back pocket," David said as he did so. "Then you are going to play the role of the arresting officer. You hold that pistol on me and give me orders. As soon as you see anything funny, pull the trigger. Got it?"

"You want me to point it at you and pull the trigger?" Holly asked skeptically.

"Well, hold it off to the side a little and I'll do the same."

"Okay."

Holly spread her legs and held the pistol out in both hands. She locked both her knees and elbows. Her stance emphasized her breasts, outlining their seductive shape through her clothes. She pointed the weapon off to the side slightly. David could tell she was in the moment, serious about the drill. Charlene would have been an emotional wreck by now. He could not believe how sexy he found Holly, standing in his living room, all seriousness and concentration. That tiny waist, he thought.

"Police officer, put up your hands!" Holly said forcefully.

David drew his weapon and fired four times. The clicking sounds of the empty pistol echoed throughout the apartment. He stopped when Holly let her right hand drop down, still holding the pistol.

"That's not fair," she said.

"What's not fair?"

"Shooting like that."

"That's the way it is."

"Okay, let's do it again."

So they repeated the scenario. This time, David engaged her in conversation. Then he shot at her three times before she got off her first responding shot. They went through it again, and David pulled the trigger another three times before she fired once.

"You know," she finally said, "you're this big ol' Army guy, with a police job and everything. Of course you would beat me."

"Ah. Let's try this. You stand like the boy in the bathroom, that's right, pistol pointing down. I'll be me." David adopted the modified Weaver again. "Dallas Police, don't mo-"

With a flick of her wrist, she had the pistol pointed at his chest and clicked it once before he could respond. Her second shot and his first struck together.

"Wow," Holly said.

"Wow, indeed."

David collected both pistols, the magazines and the loose bullets and locked them up in the bedroom safe. He came back out and freshened his drink. Holly had sat down on the couch.

"By not shooting that boy, I gave him an excellent chance to shoot me down. I acted like a fool. If I keep doing it like that, I'll end up dead out there." David swallowed another mouthful of Jacks.

Holly sat still, quiet and small.

"Do you get it, or is it just me?" David asked honestly.

"I understand about the quick shooting thing, I really do. I don't understand about what's bothering you," Holly said.

She sat with a rigid back, hands clasped in her lap, focusing all her attention on David.

"I mean," she continued, "you always struck me as someone who knew what to do. I know we haven't spent a lot of time together, but every time I've ever seen you, you been on top of things. I remember when the guy was shot in the parking lot. From before you went to the war. The other officer you were with was more concerned that y'all would get in trouble for bein' there in the first place. Not you. You smiled at him and walked right out there to see what was going on. No show or anything. You walked right on out there. I'm thinking 'why is this bothering him so much?' You could have been killed that night, too."

David breathed in deeply. "I guess the difference is that this time, I gave in to a fear. I saw in my mind the headline 'White Cop Kills Black Teen,' and I froze. I was afraid of the repercussions."

"I understand that. Heaven forbid you think I'm calling you a coward, but I'm wondering if there isn't something more goin' on here?"

David loved listening to her accent. He looked down at his left hand for a moment. He picked at a callus. Then he stood with his back to her.

"I don't want to kill any more kids," he said.

David turned around and looked down at Holly. Her position had not changed, except that now she looked up at him. The one burning lamp threw her beautiful face into half shadow. The illuminated part paid keen attention, waiting to hear the rest of it. David felt her silently urging him on.

"I spent the first part of the war doing logistics crap, counting boxes and making sure supplies got to where they were supposed to be going," David said. "Eventually, when the Iraqis started dropping missiles on the Israelis, they grabbed every special ops type in theater to go out and hunt for the launchers. I was ordered to a base by the border, and assigned to one of the hunter/killer teams. They were a pretty good group of guys. Three were on active duty and the others were reservists like me. Of the reservists, I was the only cop. We trained up a bit, got to know one another, and then waited to go out.

"In the end, we only went out twice. The first time was a dud, nothing around. As we were getting ready to extract, a shepherd led some goats into the area. Normally, that would not have been a problem in and of itself. This time the kid minding the goats was about sixteen, seventeen. He carried an AK-47. No other gear, just the rifle with the magazine stuck in it. A lucky shot from one of those could bring down a helicopter. Considering his age, we all knew he'd shoot. Teenagers never think about ramifications. That, and as we had been dodging Iraqi Army elements all patrol, we thought shots might attract some attention before we could make a clean getaway.

"The TL, team leader, I mean, decided we would try to delay the flight, so the communications guy started setting up the radio. We were in a wadi, a kind of deep, dry creek bed, which was good cover. Except that it interested the goats because they started inching on over. It was the only feature in the middle of a whole lot of flat. That place made Dallas look positively contoured.

"Anyway, we all got nervous because sure enough, the kid came our way, too. The TL called for us to hump it down the ravine and the comm guy had to reverse himself and pack up; that was pretty funny. Before he could get packed up, one of the nearby goats got spooked, causing several others to hop around as well."

David felt a current of adrenalin start flowing through him. To fight it, he adopted an official demeanor, and he continued with the narrative.

"We had a team item, a silly little thing, really. A sound suppressed .22 pistol. The team leader had assigned it to me. I was more familiar with pistols than the others due to the police job. The kid had the rifle. He started coming our way. He crouched down like a soldier; it was almost as if he was playing. The TL motioned for me to get the pistol out. I did. I screwed on the suppressor.

"I could tell the kid didn't know what he was doing. He held the weapon like an actor in one of those straight-to-video movies. He looked from side to side. He whispered to himself as he came closer. Using hand signals, the TL indicated he wanted this kid dead. I thought about arresting him, like I was on the beat. 'Course, I didn't have any handcuffs.

"The kid must have seen something. He suddenly stood up straight and started yelling. Then he started running toward the road. I was up out of that hole and moving so fast. I ran like hell after him. I came out of the ravine and saw that there were three green vehicles on the road. It was the only road in the neighborhood but it was still a distance away. One of the trucks was a troop carrier. I ran right up that kid's ass and put a round in the back of his head. It turned him right off. He fell like a rag doll. I dragged his body into a slight depression. We waited until the trucks pulled away. I guess nobody had seen us. We had no more problems. That night a helicopter came and got us."

David felt bad about that kid. In his mind's eye, he could see the two of them in the hollow right after the shooting. The kid's body already looked like it was made out of wax. The dry ground soaked up his life's blood.

"I just don't want to kill any more kids. That's all," David said, as if he were speaking of a distasteful chore.

Holly patted the space next to her. David sat down. He leaned forward, elbows on his knees, holding his drink in both hands. After a long but not uncomfortable silence, he turned and looked at Holly. She appeared drained, making David feel tired, too. Her expression conveyed a weary empathy.

"I know what it's like to feel the walls closing in," she said.

David nodded half-heartedly.

"Are you thinking about leaving the police?"

David nodded again, the same way.

"What would you do."

"I can do this." David, enjoying a sudden rush of desperate energy, jumped up and dashed over to the kitchen table. He picked up the envelope he had set off to the side. He felt its heavy bond, running his fingers over it on his way back to Holly.

"This is from New York Law School," David said, holding the envelope for Holly to see. "They want to know if I'll be going in the fall. If so, they'll want a $500.00 check. All I have to do is cut the check. I can quit the cops with honor. The department and the

Army, too. Who will question it? I'll look like I'm trying to better myself instead of bailing out."

"How do you know what it says? It's not opened."

"Go ahead and read it if you want to."

Holly tore the envelope as David continued talking.

"I applied last year," David said, sitting back down. "For my Mom. She's been nagging me for years to go to law school. Hell, if I go now, I can get out of this shit and make her happy. They accepted me and I asked them to hold the spot for a year. I claimed some big case, testifying at trial, whatever. Really though, I didn't want to go. Between the LSATs and the application process, I was able to stall my Mom for years. It was just one more stall, until the war, which was a great stall. What do you think?"

"I think it says five hundred and fifty dollars, but I can't tell without my glasses," Holly said. "I think you would make a great lawyer, David. I think you would be great at anything you tried."

"You do?"

Holly leaned toward him slowly. David watched her eyes shift from his eyes, to his lips and back again. She kept coming. David tilted his head and accommodated a gentle kiss.

"Yes, I do."

They kissed again, this time with open lips. As the their passion increased, David moved his left hand up to caress Holly's face. He misjudged and his fingertips slid along the outside of her breast. David froze his hand, slightly startled at his forward, unintended course of action.

Holly moved slightly so that her breast ended up fully in his palm. Without breaking their kiss, David hefted it and lightly slid his hand over it. Soon he felt an erect nipple through her blouse. David slid his hand upward. They kissed and repositioned themselves front to front. David cupped Holly's cheek as he held her against him with an arm around the small of her back.

"Can we go somewhere more comfortable?" Holly asked.

David first had to kneel before he could stand up, due to the awkwardness of their embrace. He took both of her hands in his and pulled her up to her feet. He walked backwards, leading her to the bedroom. When they reached bedside, David ran his hands up her arms and touched each side of her face with his fingertips, enjoying the feel of her smooth, smooth skin and kissing her again.

Eventually, he stroked her neck and turned his attention to the string tie. After he untied it, and while they still kissed, he started unbuttoning her blouse. While nuzzling Holly's neck and luxuriating in the honey and spice scent of her hair, he eased the blouse off her shoulders.

David had seen her naked several times but it seemed new and fresh to him now. It took him several moments to figure out that the clasp for her sheer, unadorned bra rested between her breasts. Before he could open it, Holly started pulling on his shirt. In a confused instant, they managed to get it over his head. Holly did some exploring of her own regarding the muscles of his chest and back.

David kissed his way down her neck and between her breasts. Her blouse had gathered around her upper arms. His attentions continued downward until he knelt at her feet. He unsnapped her jeans, pulled down the zipper and slid them over her narrow hips. The extent of her arousal surprised and delighted him. Soon boots and jeans were everywhere.

Holly fell back on the bed laughing. David paid attention to her toned and finely muscled legs. An intimate caress over panties that matched her bra brought an audible catch in her breath and the realization on David's part that Holly was completely ready. David moved up and Holly pulled him onto her concurrently. In moments, they discarded the last of the clothing. David ran his hands over Holly's shoulders, torso and breasts. It became apparent to him that she was interested in a more traditional coupling than he would have guessed and that she wanted it now. He wasted no time complying.

A wonderful experience followed for David. While they moved compatibly, they kissed, caressed and occasionally laughed out loud. For far longer than David would have anticipated, they kept at it. Sensitive to the unspoken cues she gave him, they continued on, enjoying themselves. Holly's breath caught a final time. Her back arched. He caught up quickly.

They finished together, their breathing labored in the aftermath. When he was finally able to move, she would not loosen her hold on him. She forced him to rest his full weight on her. He held her, feeling the warm smooth skin of her back in his hands, her breasts against his chest, her hips against his.

Epilogue

Light knocking on the door to David's law office brought him back to the present. The feel of Holly in his arms, her breasts against his chest, their mated hips, faded slowly. Irritation at the interruption of his reminiscence almost made him reckless with a rude comment, but he remembered where he was and held his tongue.

"Hey," Anti-Crime Officer Brian Donovan said quietly. "Can I come in?"

Irritation drained away and David felt at a loss. He had nothing constructive to say to this man. The only thing that came to his mind was that he had gotten out in time, before what had happened to Brian had happened to him. David did not feel that particular point was worth sharing at the moment. While struggling to come up with something to say, David waved him into one of the two client chairs in front of the small table.

"What have you got there?" Brian asked, making small talk.

David turned the wood framed, glass covered display case around so that Brian could look at it.

"Wow, Army and the cops. Special Forces, too."

"Were you in?"

"No, I'm just kind of a buff, I guess. I know all the emblems and all. Why Dallas?" Brian asked while reaching for the box.

"Because they were hiring."

Maybe David could tell him that youth can end in an evening, be it an evening of love or violence, and that what comes next is survivable. Or that the job is not everything. There is something after that, too. Or that there is no going back, or erasing what you are, after you have chosen what to become. Maybe something as simple as what he had heard many times in locker rooms and bars: that it is better to be judged by twelve than carried by six.

"Will you do it?" Brian asked, without looking up.

David remembered keenly what it was like to shoot that boy in Iraq. And his memory of the incident in the movie house bathroom was equally intense. Only blind luck had kept him out of the shoes Brian now wore. Mostly, David realized that he was, in his heart, a cop and that he could not let this assist officer call go unanswered.

"We're lucky," David said. "My trial that settled today was supposed to go all next week, so I'm free first thing. I'll see you Monday morning. Come prepared to stay all day. You'll have to tell me everything. At the first sign you're lying, I'll throw you out of here myself, your grandfather be damned."

Brian looked up, smiling slightly. Probably his first smile since the incident.

"I'll be here at seven thirty," he said.

"Good for you. I'll be here at nine. Oh, and leave the knuckle-dragger at the station, will you?"

"Okay."

"Brian, the real trick in this case is going to be keeping you employed. Nobody at this firm has any experience with City employment law, and believe me, for that we need experts. My recommendation to you is to get a PBA lawyer to handle the Puzzle Palace."

"Okay."

"As soon as you know who he is, I need to meet with him. He'll need to know everything we are doing, within reason, so he can prepare a complementary case. Lots of people are going to want you out."

"Okay," Brian handed David back his display. "I know you don't want to do this, so thanks a lot."

"Don't thank me now. See how you feel after you get the bill."

"Grandpa's paying," Brian said, smiling broadly now.

"Won't he ever," David replied, smiling back.

Brian left and David killed the afternoon with dictation. Late in the business day, Freddie stuck her head in his office.

"Samuel is on the phone. He wants to know if you still need him tonight," she said.

"Yes, please. Tell him I'll see him at the diner downstairs at about eight. And make sure he still has the thing in the trunk." David had been craving breakfast for supper all day.

"Got it. Then I'm gone." Freddie ducked out again.

"Have a good weekend!" he shouted.

He would tell her about the new case Monday, but he was sure she already knew about it. He hoped it would not be a problem for her.

He had bacon and eggs and the New York Law Journal for supper, and an extra cup of decaf coffee while waiting for Samuel to arrive in his long black Town Car. When David saw him pull into the space reserved for the bus stop, he wasted no time jumping in the back.

"Newark, right sir?" Samuel asked.

"Right. Terminal A."

They flowed with the thick but moving tunnel traffic and made good time to the airport. David had Samuel put the car in short-term parking while he stepped out for the arrivals section. He checked the screens and saw that the flight from Dallas was on time. He walked down to the baggage claim area and stood off to the side. It seemed like forever. When he saw them, his heart soared.

She had cut her blond hair short. It covered her ears but only fell to the bottom of her neck. He liked the part on the side, though. She looked great in her jeans, western blouse and denim jacket, but David knew about the changes. Her breasts were rounder and perhaps more cooperative with the laws of physics now. Her hips were wider.

She saw him and gave him a tired smile. He reached out, meaning to take the folded up umbrella stroller and carry on, but the blond eighteen month old resting his head on her shoulder looked up and faced forward. He focused his large green eyes on David. David's chest filled with a raw and powerful father's love that almost brought him to tears.

"Da-DEE, Da-DEE, Da-DEE," the boy called, reaching out for David from his perch.

Holly Dawn Lane readily handed him over, keeping the other items for herself.

"How's my boy Christopher?" David asked, hugging the child as hard as he dared.

"Airplane, airplane," Christopher said, before dropping his head to David's shoulder.

"He didn't sleep at all on the flight," she said.

"You look exhausted. Beautiful, but exhausted," David said to her, kissing her quickly on her lips.

"It's so good to be home," Holly said.

They reclaimed the one large suitcase from the airline. By the time they met up with Samuel, night had fallen. Samuel had installed the child safety seat, left in the trunk a week and half ago, and Chris was asleep as soon as David had buckled him in.

"How did it go?" David asked.

"He met me. I had to drive in to Abilene. He came down from Lubbock. We met for lunch at Luby's. His hair and mustache were stringy and needed a trim. He wore his shirt buttoned up to the top."

"What did he say about Chris?"

"I left him with Mom. But he said he was a 'good looking partner' when I showed him pictures. He said he's been sober for seven years. He's working at Wal-Mart installing tires. What a change."

David reached around the baby seat and stroked Holly's neck.

"Dave, I haven't seen Dad since I was fourteen. Then I was nothing. There I was, talking about living in New York City with my big shot lawyer husband and our beautiful son."

Holly turned away, fighting back tears. After a moment, she continued.

"I guess things change, huh?"

"Sometimes for the better. You've always been something, you know."

She kissed his hand. "How's work been?" she asked, changing the subject.

"Did you tell him about grad school?" David asked, not letting her.

"No, and not about graduating from college, either. Just about where we lived, the boy and you."

"Time for the rest later?" David asked.

"I think so. We exchanged telephone numbers. Was that okay?"

"Of course," David said. "Work was fine. Settled the trial this morning." He would tell her the details later, when she was rested. She liked hearing about them, about trial strategy and negotiating tactics. The new case was a different story. He wanted to get that one off of his chest right now, even as they drove back to Manhattan. "May I tell you about another matter I was assigned today?"

"Please do," she said.